Killing the President

Teresa Bergen

Baby Lovecat Designs
Portland, Oregon
2007

Cover Design: Ron Mason Gassaway
midtownriot@comcast.net

Copyright © Teresa Bergen 2007

ISBN: 978-0-6151-5156-4

Published by Baby Lovecat Designs
3552 SE Washington Street
Portland, OR 97214
www.babylovecat.com

Killing the President

Thanks to those who read and commented on drafts of this novel, including Maxine Beach, Margo Bergen, Kimberly Dark, Michael Detlef, Thomas Dietzel, Vivien Lyon, Casey Seyb and Jonathan Shapiro. Thanks to my parents for always supporting the arts.

CHAPTER ONE

Before he went underground, Justin lived like all his peers. Everybody rode bikes and brought their own bags to the health food store. They were vegetarian or vegan or at least cutting back on red meat. Fashion was out of style. They read books, drank organic coffee, compared microbrews. They ranted to each other about their jingoistic, imperialist government and its evil actions around the globe. And everybody wished the president were dead.

Back then, Justin lived with three guys in a decrepit house in Southeast Portland. They were strictly creative types, uninspired by brooms, mops or cleaning solution. One might find an exacto blade or a roach in their carpet, or dog hair, pizza toppings, a paint brush, guitar pick, even a condom, though likely unused. They weren't the luckiest guys but they managed some optimism despite the sorry state of the world.

Sam was twenty-nine and working on his ninth year of an undergraduate degree in political science. Publishing a string of small literary magazines had slowed his progress. Pete was twenty-seven, worked full time in a group home for the developmentally disabled, and played guitar. Gillis, thirty, tried to make the small yard yield heirloom tomatoes, peppers and herbs while collecting unemployment checks. And Justin, who was thirty-one and had never accomplished anything in life, had finally fallen in love.

Sure, Justin had dabbled in painting, karate, drums, college, activism, employment, temperance, celibacy, volunteer work and door to door solicitation, but nothing had really panned out. Surprisingly, love seemed to be his life's work.

It had happened to him as soon as he first saw Zoe. She was a skinny girl even back then when she could still pass for healthy. Straight blond hair, big, soulful brown eyes. She looked younger than her twenty-three years. Justin had discovered her two blocks from his house, behind the counter at Jojo's Fair Trade World Coffee Café.

"I'll have the Sumatran," was the first thing Justin said to her. "With room for soy milk," was the second. She smiled vacuously. She had a lot on her mind, but she was a girl who remembered to smile at the customers. She was already having her first symptoms, but hadn't told anybody. "Is that muffin vegan?" he asked, though he wasn't. But it prolonged the conversation, and he figured surely a girl who worked at Jojo's Fair Trade World Coffee Café must, herself, be vegan. She shrugged, the smile still in place. "Uh," he said, thrown off. "I'll take it."

The muffin was blueberry. He picked a table from which he could watch her work. She moved with an expert languor. He told himself her smile looked less sincere when she directed it at other people. Luckily, the muffin didn't taste vegan.

Justin became a regular from his first visit. It turned out his housemates were, also. Pete shared Justin's fondness for Zoe. Sam was too busy to hang out much, but he preferred Brenda, Zoe's loud, dark-haired, busty coworker, a girl who scared Justin. Gillis frequented the place because he truly cared that the coffee was fairly traded.

Life would have been easy. Rent was cheap, everybody he knew was an artist, dreamer or idealist, and Justin still passed for under thirty. But some planes had flown into some major buildings and Justin's government was using that as a reason to turn the country into a police state. Congress passed something called the Patriot Act. Whereas once patriots had fought to win personal freedoms, latter day patriots were expected to quietly surrender them.

Justin and his friends were smart and better informed than many of their country people. While they might not have read Noam Chomsky's books, they'd at least seen his films. They listened to the community radio station because they knew the mainstream media was corporate bullshit. They were hooked on truth, which can easily lead to depression. "How's it going?" Gillis might ask Sam at the end of the day, and instead of the usual benign, careless answer, Sam would say, "There's a reason someone coined the term 'ignorance is bliss,'" and turn back to indymedia.org on his computer screen.

At different times that fall, the medicine cabinet included Prozac, Zoloft, St. John's wort, valerian and Paxil. "Is this your Prozac or my Prozac?" one of the guys would yell to another, then help himself without bothering to wait for an answer. What did it really matter?

Love was the only thing that saved Justin, at least for a few more months. Zoe gave him a reason to get out of bed before noon. She only worked from 6:30 AM to 12:30 PM, so Justin had to readjust his schedule. Don't ask what he did for a living. He doesn't want to talk about it.

He wasn't in the habit of going to sleep before three or four in the morning, but he found that if he got up by eight, he could spend an hour or two in the café, then come home and try to nap before work. He usually drank so much coffee during that hour or two that sleeping was difficult. Justin learned that one can live on love. It certainly wasn't good nutrition or rest keeping him alive.

Justin always brought books and a notebook to the café. He cultivated the look of a writer or scholar or maybe just a student. This would account for why he spent up to two hours there daily. He pondered the complicated political books he'd long meant to read, hoping to impress Zoe. It was easy to maintain his air of mystery, because she never asked him what he was reading or why.

Once he saw her reading something in the *Oregonian* when the rush of customers slowed. He slinked up to add more cream to his coffee and see what had caught her eye. Horoscopes. Justin was so in love, he wasn't even disappointed. Instead, he found himself uttering that dread, outdated pick up line.

"So, Zoe, what sign are you?" he asked her. He had by then managed to learn her name, but not much more. He had never asked a girl her sign, and felt himself blushing for sounding so inane.

"Cancer," she said, wiping the counter with a damp rag. She didn't look up at him. Justin thought she was awfully thin. Her hipbones jutted out above her low-waisted pants. An inch of pale skin showed all the way around her middle. She suddenly looked up, catching him staring at her body. He raised his eyes guiltily to meet hers. "Do you need something else?" she asked. If she had been a flirtatious girl, she could have made this sound like a come on. But her face was blank. Justin had never felt more like a customer.

"Uh, never mind," he said, and went back to his table to mope. A Cancer. That meant nothing to him, as far as sun signs. It sure didn't sound nice. He wished she had said Virgo or Aquarius.

Two of Zoe's friends came in, a skinny boy and a skinny girl. Both wore hooded sweatshirts. Beneath her hood, the girl wore a pink wool hat. The boy's hat was brown. They leaned close to the counter to talk to Zoe. She smiled. Justin couldn't hear what they were talking about. He watched Zoe make mochas for her friends. She didn't charge them. Her friends looked so young! They couldn't have been much more than twenty. Justin began to worry about his looks. Would he appear younger if he shaved his goatee? Several girls had said his blue eyes were beautiful, but had his light brown hair grown too shaggy? He was about to go examine himself in the restroom mirror, but saw Gillis and another guy heading for his table.

"Hey, man," Gillis said, helping himself to a chair. His friend sat down, too. "This is Dale. Hey, did you start going to school or something?" Gillis said, nodding toward the books.

"Hey," said Dale.

Justin shrugged. Just in case Zoe could hear, he didn't want to talk about the books. "How's it going?" Justin asked Dale.

Dale wore a long-sleeved maroon pullover. He shoved his right sleeve back and revealed welts on his wrist and bruises on his forearm. Justin hoped Zoe wasn't watching. Dale's dark eyes darted around, and his legs jiggled.

"Uh, what's that about?" Justin asked, hoping if he acknowledged the irritated flesh that Dale would roll his sleeve back down.

"Fucking pigs," Dale said.

"Huh?"

"Cops," Gillis said, sighing. "Dale's always having trouble with the cops."

"You mean the cops have some trouble with me!" Dale shot back. Zoe's friends glanced over.

"Yeah," Gillis said. "That's what I meant to say, man."

Dale settled back in his seat and rolled his sleeve most of the way down. Justin could still see the wrist welts.

"Handcuffs?" Justin asked, intrigued despite his aversion. Aside from a couple of long ago run-ins related to underage drinking, and a speeding ticket a few years back, the police had never come down on Justin for anything. But he had received hateful looks from them at the few demonstrations he'd attended. What had they been for? Causes to impress one girl or another, he couldn't even remember now. Tibet, maybe? East Timor? Definitely a T country. Taiwan? No, definitely not Taiwan.

"Yeah," Dale snorted. "Their fucking plastic cuffs."

"What did you do?" Justin asked.

"It's not like you have to do anything these days. Pigs got all the power." Dale had the kind of intense, light blue eyes that straddled the line between charismatic and crazy.

"Was it billboards again?" Gillis asked. Dale shot him a look. "Don't worry about Justin, man. He's cool."

"Yeah," Dale said. "Pigs were pissed cause none of them wanted to come up after me. Pigs are land animals, you know. Fucking donut eaters."

Justin looked to Gillis for an explanation. "Dale and his crew deface billboards," Gillis said.

"Improve, motherfucker! Not deface."

"Put up political messages," Gillis said, ignoring Dale. "It's cool."

Dale was as wiry and hyper as a monkey. Justin could imagine him climbing up on billboards. "What did you make it say?" Justin asked.

Dale looked around furtively, even though he'd already been caught for the offense. "'America is the Terrorist.' It was up for about one lousy minute. Someone tipped them off. I bet it was a fucking SUV driver calling from their cell phone."

Gillis nodded. "Yeah, man." Gillis always seemed stoned, whether he was or not. Justin wondered if he'd ever get a job.

"So did they have to climb up there and bring you down?" Justin asked.

Dale smiled for the first time. "Those stupid pigs didn't know what to do. They should have waited till I came down, then nabbed us at the bottom of the billboard. Cause if they climbed up and cuffed me, how were they gonna get me down? I was about thirty feet high. It was a standoff for two, three hours."

"But you finally came down?"

"Fucking pigs started pushing my girlfriend around. She was down below with two of my buddies. So I came down to help her and they threw me to the ground and put the cuffs on."

"Wow," Justin said. He didn't like Dale so far, and imagined how the cops would enjoy roughing him up. But aggravating as Dale was, who was Justin to judge? What did he do? His government was made up of tyrants who bombed and exploited people all over the globe, while Justin sat in Jojo's Fair Trade World Coffee Café, pretending to read difficult books to impress a girl who barely acknowledged him. He had to sort of admire Dale.

CHAPTER TWO

Zoe's friends Rex and T-Bone wanted to borrow money out of her tip jar again. "No," she said, nervously running a hand through her straight blond hair. "You never pay me back."

T-Bone pouted. She was a pretty girl for whom the world provided. "Oh, come on, Zoe. We'll pay you tomorrow."

"Yeah, pay me with what?" Hardly any of Zoe's friends were working. Every Sunday, when her friends looked through the classified ads, that section of the paper had shrunk since the week before. Most of those who had been laid off hadn't worked steadily enough to collect unemployment.

"We have our ways of getting money," T-Bone said, smiling mysteriously beneath her fuzzy pink hat.

"Come on, Zoe. Please," Rex said.

"Please," T-Bone echoed, stretching out the word. "Please, please." They both joined in as though they were her five year-old children. Zoe could feel her armpits moisten.

"What do you want it for?"

T-Bone and Rex looked at each other, transparent as five year-olds trying to decide if they should tell the truth. They waited too long.

"No," Zoe snapped. She grabbed her tip jar and tucked it under the counter, on a low shelf at knee level. They wanted to get high with her money while she worked. Some fucking friends!

"Eric has the best E!" T-Bone said.

"And he's leaving! He's going to Europe. He's selling it cheap to finance his trip."

"I'm not financing your trip," Zoe said. They laughed. She was a detached sort of girl who hardly ever said anything witty.

A customer came in and asked for a double mocha. Zoe turned her back on Rex and T-Bone as she pulled shots of espresso and frothed the hot milk. Once she glanced over and saw T-Bone's incredulous face. The girl was eighteen years old. Zoe couldn't possibly be the first person to ever say no to her.

When she first started working at Jojo's, Zoe had thought the coolest part was that her friends could hang out. As long as she got her work done, the owner didn't mind if she socialized a little. But now her friends only seemed to come by to borrow money or to try to scam free coffee and muffins. Or for really bizarre, annoying things, like the time Rex was trying to get a job as receptionist at a realtor's office, and he put down the café's number and Zoe's name as a reference. He wanted Zoe to answer the phone, "Frankenmorgen Realty, may I help you?" Of course she had refused, and he had pouted. But they finally compromised. "You can just answer the phone, 'This is Zoe.' Like it's your direct line." And she had done this for three days, confusing countless customers until her boss called and reminded her to answer with the business name.

"Just ten dollars," Rex was mouthing at her now as she rang up a mocha. She felt anxious all the time these days. The knot in her stomach ruined her appetite, and sometimes her head pounded so she couldn't think. It was hard to get out of bed in the morning, hard to sleep at night.

She could see Justin stealing glances at her from where he sat with his friends. They were probably debating something political now, because the crazy little guy's arms were flying around and she heard "the fucking fascist government" and "the fucking pigs" now and then. It was kind of funny how worked up they got about stuff. Like it mattered. Like they mattered enough to change anything. Justin was nice, but it was irritating the way he constantly stared at her while she tried to work. And that Guatemalan hat had to go. Shave off the goatee and get a fashion clue, he'd be handsome.

Now Rex had his hands pressed together in prayer position and was batting his eyelashes at her. T-Bone still pouted. "Can I have that cookie?" she asked. Most of Zoe's friends were skinny, but T-Bone looked especially hungry. Zoe might be able to refuse her friend money for drugs, but she couldn't withhold food. Zoe opened the case and picked up an oatmeal cookie with the tongs. "No, the chocolate chip," T-Bone said.

Justin's friend Pete came in and joined the other radicals or hippies or whatever they were. Pete was a good looking guy with dark hair and a nose like a Greek statue's. He wasn't as obvious as Justin, staring at her maybe only half as frequently as his friend. Zoe had always been pretty, always received attention from men, but so what? At twenty-three, this had been going on for years. She was over any excitement caused by her own exterior. No one ever really saw *her* anyway; she was a brooding girl with deep feelings, which she hid behind social distractions and recreational drugs.

As a teenager, Zoe had thought too much, and it had depressed her. She had spent many hours in her bedroom, reading poetry and writing in a journal. A cutting phase had followed a hair pulling phase, both accompanied by the typical eating disorders of American girls. But that was over now. In her adult life, she had found that the key to normality was not to have her own bedroom. Sharing space had ended her most intense introspection and ritualistic abnormalities. She wasn't going to cut herself or pull out her hair for an audience; that would look pathetic, like she craved attention. People would notice if she ate nothing, or only consumed canned stewed tomatoes and unbuttered popcorn, savoring each bite so that sad little meal lasted an hour. No, instead she lived with too many people and ceased her endless self-contemplation. She let herself be less differentiated now. Sometimes, after a late night, she would wake up in the living room amongst her sleeping friends, four or five sets of limbs sprawled out on the floor. And in the first minute or two of wakefulness, she could feel like she was part of one creature with ten legs, not just Zoe, alone in the world and powerless with her own skinny pale arms, a low paying job and no future on the horizon.

CHAPTER THREE

Some evenings, Justin was glad his job was mindless so he could daydream about Zoe. Other nights, he worried what she would think of him if she found out that he did public opinion surveys from a call center. He fantasized about reaching her on the phone, some miracle of wiring, and surveying her about things that really mattered. What made her happy? How did she like to be touched? What did she think of him? But that was stupid. Even if by some magic he did reach her, he would have to ask her the same awful questions he asked everybody else: What concerns you more, Americans having jobs to feed their families, or saving endangered insect habitats? Do you support tough sentences for rapists and child molesters, or do you think they should have a second chance in your neighborhood? Always some faceless, sinister political candidate waiting in the wings to twist the numbers. The call center kept their clients' identity secret, even from the workers, but everyone knew only the worst right wing assholes had money for stupid surveys like these.

Justin sat in a room with twenty desks. Half the people looked as bored as Justin. The dumber half seemed cheerful and enthusiastic. There were no windows. It could be any time of day in this fluorescent tomb, but it always seemed to be nearer to the beginning of Justin's shift than to the end. There were a lot of bad things about the place: the lighting, the just-out-of-college supervisor who wore a tie to work, coffee so cheap you could taste the pesticides, the board with all the workers' names on it and their number of finished surveys that week, the creepy way the phone system automatically dialed numbers for you, making Justin feel even more like a disembodied voice.

But the worst part was the inspirational posters. Footprints on a beach with the words: Every journey begins with a single step. A woman climbing the face of a huge mountain: Only you decide how high you will go.

And, incredibly, an AA poster: One Day at a Time. Justin knew it was an AA poster because he'd put up with years of his father's drinking, then recovery, as a child in San Diego. He honestly didn't know which was worse. His dad had hit him a few times when he was drunk, but mostly he had holed up in the bedroom looking at books on weaponry, a bottle of gin at his side. Lots of times he was gone, which suited Justin fine. But Jesus Christ, as soon as he joined AA, suddenly Justin and his brother and mom were expected to spend every minute with the old boozehound. Dad seemed to become self-righteous overnight, spluttering rules and platitudes. Soon he was sponsoring people, lecturing to shaky men who stank up the sofa, or letting yet another addict sleep over, only to find the VCR and all of Justin's favorite movies missing the next morning. Justin's mom seemed happy about all this, at least most of the time, and insisted that Justin and his brother attend speaker meetings where their dad talked in clichés and bragged about being a real father to his children, and a man to his wife. Justin only had to look at the One Day at a Time poster for it to all come churning back.

"Good evening, ma'am," he said automatically as the next call rang through. "This is Justin of Proactive Solutions. We want to hear your opinion on matters of vital importance to our country. This will only take a couple of minutes of your time. The first of our three questions is, do you feel that your security and peace of mind are worth an extra five minutes, half hour, or one hour of delay at transportation hubs such as airports or ferry terminals?"

"Well," she said slowly, "it's definitely worth the extra hour at the airport. I've been scared silly ever since those awful terrorists attacked us. But if I commuted by ferry every day, like some folks do, I couldn't see an hour on each side. So I'd say one hour for the airport, but only thirty minutes for the ferry terminal."

Justin could feel his blood pressure rise. This kind of thing hadn't been so bad before he turned thirty, but now it was pathetic. He couldn't believe the way people were dying to waste their time supplying opinions to strangers. And worse, people who took the questions as seriously as this lady really fucked up his surveys. He could only check one box, and you never knew when a supervisor was listening in, ensuring you weren't just making up results.

"I appreciate what you're saying, ma'am, but if you could only pick one answer, would it be thirty minutes or sixty minutes?"

"Well, I don't know. I wonder how long the ferry commute would be…"

"Ma'am, you have to pick one or the other."

"Oh, dear. Well, I guess I'll have to go with sixty minutes. Because it's better safe than sorry these days, right?" She sounded sad.

Occasionally somebody rebelled and said, "No, I don't have to choose. You have no right to my opinions or my time." Justin preferred these people, although they cost him surveys. He hated how he could tell people they had to choose, and they chose. How had the population been so brainwashed into obedience? Who gave him the authority? They did. Every shift.

The cute sarcastic girl winked at him as she passed his desk. She had dark hair and wore big glasses and short skirts. Before he met Zoe, Justin had been a bit interested in this girl. Sometimes he drank the awful coffee just because she was in the kitchen area and he needed an excuse to join her. She headed that way now, but tonight he didn't follow her.

He got lucky. Three flawless surveys in a row. Then a lull. "Good evening, this is Justin with Proactive Solutions. We want to hear your opinion tonight on…" Click. "Good evening, this is Justin with Proactive Solutions…" Click. "Good evening, this is…" Click. It could get creepy, the rhythm of automatic dial, then a hello, then part of his spiel, then the phone hanging up, over and over.

Justin had worked many jobs in his thirty-one years. He had seen many versions of hell.

The thing about Zoe, it wasn't as lustful as most of Justin's attractions. Sure, he wanted to have sex with her, but even that felt different. He imagined it slow and tender. She was so thin, so young looking, so hard to read. He wanted to caress her, to smell her skin, to take their time. He didn't have the usual hot girl fuck fantasies about Zoe. He wanted to take care of her.

Question three of this survey was the worst. Justin preferred the tidiness of checking yes or no, or maybe a number from one to ten. But now he had to ask, "Are there groups of people that you are now more suspicious of, and if so, who?" He had to listen to their fear and paranoia, their stereotypes, their carefully disguised, shameful racism, their proud, firm convictions. The first day it had been interesting, but now it was just depressing. People were scared of everybody: Young people. Blacks. Arabs, ragheads, sand niggers. Homosexuals. Women who want to be men. Men who dress like women. Foreigners. Hippies. Anarchists. The homeless. Gangs. Poor people. Rich people. Yuppies. The kind of people who watch Jerry Springer. The kind of people who listen to NPR. Militia types. Our government. The liberal media.

At first Justin had been shocked by perfectly nice sounding people proclaiming bizarre fears and hatreds. Sometimes he fell into their feared categories: Men, college dropouts, guys with beards, liberals, people who don't own cars or houses. Once he'd been tempted to say, "Ma'am, I don't have a car and I'm sure you wouldn't be afraid of me." But how did he know? Everybody was afraid of anyone outside their immediate family and social strata. Walking on the streets he noticed the way he timidly smiled at people, especially women, trying to convey that they need not fear him. Sometimes they looked relieved. Sometimes they walked faster, never meeting his eyes.

After midnight, waiting for the bus, Justin noticed that people looked more suspicious than they had a year ago. He tried to pinpoint what kinds of people scared him. Successful people, if you measured success in accumulation. People who wouldn't want him to marry their daughter because he had dropped out of college and did phone surveys for a living and didn't even have a plan to make the future better.

Every night the bus took him back across the river to the east side of Portland. He could breathe better in his own neighborhood, where hanging out in coffee shops and bitching about the president was considered more productive than putting on a tie and building a stock portfolio.

Alone in his bed, three AM, Justin wondered if Zoe was still awake. Those rave kids she hung out with probably stayed up late. But Zoe had to be at the café so early. When did she sleep? He worried about her. She wasn't the healthiest looking girl. Maybe she didn't sleep enough. Maybe she did all those rave drugs with her friends. She needed someone to take care of her. Or maybe she already had someone, a handsome young rave guy. Then again, it could be a girl. That's how little he knew about her. He thought he'd never fall asleep, but of course he did.

CHAPTER FOUR

Things might have stayed like that forever, if something hadn't happened. But something always happens. Otherwise, we'd still be in our hometown with our pimply faced first love, working at our original fast food job. Circumstances shift, giving us the chance to muse to our friends, "Last November, I never would have believed I'd be working here in this petting zoo after eloping with a door-to-door silverware salesman."

In this case, everything was about the same for two more months, just progressively more intense. In the police state, increasing numbers of suspicious foreigners were detained without charges. Security at airports was put under federal control, and plane travelers obediently lined up to be searched at the X-ray machine and randomly re-checked at the gate. Police no longer needed search warrants to enter your house. Hardly anybody let out a peep, except liberals like Justin and his friends, whom it seemed lacked an audience. They continued to congregate at Jojo's Fair Trade World Coffee Café, where they ranted about the government while Zoe made their coffee. Justin continued to burn with passion for Zoe, who occasionally smiled at him. At the call center, he maintained his rank in the upper third of his colleagues. Both Justin and Zoe still lived with their respective housemates, who brought them fellowship, joy, annoyance and frustration. The delicate balance was maintained that allowed their paychecks, and that of their roommates, to stretch just far enough for everybody to remain living indoors and nobody to starve.

The thing that changed was Zoe's health. It was deep winter, two weeks past Christmas, drizzly chilled gloom outside. On a comparatively nice day, a radio commentator described the sky as "bright gray." And Zoe, who had always been skinny, was now even skinnier than T-Bone, formerly the skinniest of her friends. Zoe could hardly eat. Food held no appeal. T-Bone and Rex said she probably had Seasonal Affective Disorder, but Zoe knew it was something far bigger. She was weak, she wanted to sleep all the time. Her skin was sensitive, her mouth tasted like metal, and she awoke from terrible nightmares. It became progressively more difficult to open the café at six AM. At work, she slumped against the counter, trying to warm her hands over a coffee pot. She had never been overly friendly to her customers, but now she was like a zombie to all but her few favorites. If any of the customers wondered about the health of the girl who sold them coffee, they probably figured she was on heroin.

Justin was one of her favorites by now, though his frequent inquiries about her health embarrassed her. "What do you think you have?" he'd ask, concerned blue eyes locked on her face. "You must have some idea."

She'd shake her head. "I'm just sick, I guess."

"You've been sick a month," he'd say. "Haven't you seen a doctor?"

She smiled a bit at that. Seven dollars an hour plus tips just barely covered her share of the rent and utilities, plus the slack she picked up for her housemates. She had by far the best job. A doctor! Did Justin think she was rich? "Not yet," she'd say. "Maybe if I'm not better next week."

After several weeks of this, one morning Justin said, "Look, Zoe, I've made an appointment. I want to take you to see a doctor at 2:30, after you get off work. I'll pay. Just consider it like a tip." She was touched that he'd care so much about her health. She'd had guys offer her lots of stuff – money, a good time, the best fuck she ever had, a cum sandwich, cheap jewelry, bad poetry, an orgasm that would make a rhino scream, drugs, a modeling portfolio, dinner – but not a trip to the doctor. One tear welled up in her eye but didn't quite surface. She was moved by the fact of her own emotion. She wondered if she loved him.

But she couldn't accept the doctor because she didn't want anyone to confirm what she secretly knew: She was dying.

Zoe's illness didn't go over well with her housemates. She avoided telling them about her true condition, but they disliked the symptoms. It turned out that Zoe was the one who held the house together, although no one had really noticed before. There was Rex and T-Bone and a pair of raver twins named Peppy and Patty, and their friends who were passing through town, some of whom stayed long enough that, if they had been more mainstream, they would have gotten a job and their own apartment or at least have had the courtesy to be looking. The house only had two bedrooms, but the basement, the living room, even the kitchen, provided plenty of sleepable surfaces. The thing is, Zoe contributed a disproportionate amount of rent, and now she had called in sick three times in one month. She was also the only one who knew the location of cleaning supplies, or even of their existence. As the only resident with a checking account, she sent out all the bills. Now she was falling apart, and so was the house. The landlord had to come by in person to inquire about the late rent, because the phone was turned off. He didn't like the way the house looked, and placed them on warning. Nor did he like to see two cats on the premises when the contract clearly stated no pets. Not that the cats were attached to any particular person. No one knew where they came from and now that the bags of cat food were too heavy for Zoe to carry home from the store, the cats were spending more time at neighbors' houses anyway.

"Come on, Zoe, pull yourself together," Rex urged. He sprawled on the couch, stoned, a graphic novel open face down on his chest. "God knows jobs are hard to find these days. Don't blow it! You're just depressed. I'm sure someone around here has some Prozac or something. It's just all the rain. It's a bummer. We all know that. You'll be fine." He spoke slowly, his eyes drifting away from hers to examine intricacies in the ceiling. The room didn't get much light, even with the shades all open. The couches were old and clawed. Backpacks leaned against walls, mysterious piles of blankets on the floors, apparently where people had slept. Zoe slouched in a faded orange armchair, gazing about. A pile of blankets seemed to shift, and she saw a mid-sized brown dog curled in it.

"Where did that dog come from?" she asked. "The landlord's going to shit if he sees that."

"It's cool," Rex said, still looking at the ceiling.

Zoe was crying but Rex didn't notice. Everybody else was out, God knows where. Probably trying to scrounge up some food or cigarettes or drugs. Zoe hadn't felt like getting high on anything since she'd realized she was dying. And now, with Rex stoned, she felt alone. She felt a vastness in her chest, some pull to look inside herself. Just the sort of thing she had been resisting for the last five years by surrounding herself with so many people. This could drive a person crazy, knowing they were dying and being forced to analyze twenty-three years of a life where nothing of import had happened. She wanted to want to be high. Wouldn't that be the best way? Enjoying her friends, staying in sync with the meager life she had made for herself. No point in craziness or loneliness at the end. And no point in pity. She didn't want her friends to know.

"Or how about Welbutrin?" Rex asked dreamily. "I see that advertised on TV. The people are all doing shit outside, like walking in the sun and planting flowers. They look really happy." He turned and smiled in her direction, making her feel a bit warmer.

"Yeah, okay," she said. "I'm sure I can get my hands on some."

But still she avoided anything medical. Instead, she found herself drawn to the kind of mystical mumbo jumbo her former self might have noticed only long enough to laugh at with friends. One Sunday morning she felt compelled to walk in the cold rain. She wasn't the sort of person who went looking for exercise, nor did she relish the cold. But it felt like she was guided that morning as she left her bed, dressed, and walked more than a mile to the Aquarian Foundation. She couldn't remember ever seeing it before. But there she was, standing before the dingy storefront, staring at the purple neon never ending knot that hung in the window.

The door opened and a fat, smiling woman in a long rust peasant skirt took Zoe's arm, gently drew her in, and shut the door behind. Twenty-odd people were there for the Sunday service, sitting in rows of chairs and listening to a woman in a white robe. The fat lady guided Zoe to a seat, smiling the whole time. The woman in the white robe had a soothing voice. She led a song that everyone seemed to know. She gave a sermon or something on Ascended Masters. Zoe had no idea what she was talking about, and barely listened. She felt peculiar, more detached and more moved than usual, both at the same time. On the one hand, her body felt like it could have been sitting anywhere, in a hospital lobby or a meat locker, who cared. She sat very still. But also, she was crying. She wasn't listening or thinking, but the tears poured out.

After a while, she came back to her body enough to look around. The room itself was plain, but the Aquarians had jazzed it up with shelves of odd statuettes and lots of pictures of robed people, or maybe gods. These figures had halos and held their hands in stiff, formal attitudes whose significance escaped Zoe. The room's main feature was what might have been the world's hugest amethyst crystal, at least six feet in diameter, sitting on an ordinary wooden table. The rows of seats parted around it. Zoe was sitting just to the right of the crystal. She had to turn her head to look at it straight on, but she could feel its pull without looking. She blamed it for her tears. It had more force than the speaker or the congregation. Zoe vaguely wondered if the crystal had used its power to draw her out of bed and to the Aquarian Foundation. But why today? Surely the thing had been here a while. She could see the layer of dust on parts of it.

People were standing up. Apparently the service was over. Zoe stood too quickly and everything went black before her eyes. She slumped back in her seat.

Somebody took her hand. The lady in the peasant skirt, Zoe saw when her eyes flickered open. "Dear, your energy…" The woman trailed off. "Your aura…" Zoe couldn't remember anybody looking at her with such concern. Except Justin. Suddenly she wished she were holding his hand.

"I know," Zoe said. "I'm dying." Her voice barely came out. She felt so incredibly sorry for herself. She waited for the woman to contradict her, or ask her what disease she had. But the woman put her arms around Zoe. Her body was warm. Zoe cried for minutes, she didn't know how long. When the lady released her, Zoe hurried off into the cold air, too mortified to ever return.

CHAPTER FIVE

"We've got to do something about this shit!" Dale said, his hands flailing. Veins bulged in his skinny forearms. He bounced on the edge of his chair in Jojo's Fair Trade World Coffee Café, flanked by his girlfriend Xena, Justin, Gillis, Pete, and two of Pete's clients. Pete was officially working, which meant he had two residents from the group home along with him. Coats and hats littered the area around their table. Inside the café was warm. Justin peered out at gray drizzle. Freezing rain was in the forecast and he dreaded going outside. He looked over at Zoe, skinny and dear. He never wanted to leave.

"I'm going to throw it," one of Pete's clients said, picking up a plate that once held someone's cookie. No one paid attention. By now they realized that this middle-aged man with the shrill voice didn't carry out his threats.

"You know what's coming next," Dale continued. "Some kind of jihad." Xena sat beside him, a pale girl with a big nose. She nodded gravely. "And then, who knows? World War III. We got to roast these fuckers before it's too late!"

Justin was spending more time with Dale and his radical friends. He had twice gone along to deface billboards, though the height scared him and he opted to remain at the bottom as a lookout. Dale's anger and loud talk still embarrassed Justin, but he'd grown to admire him a lot. Dale had been there at the 1999 World Trade Organization demonstration in Seattle. He had locked elbows with other idealists and formed a human chain to stop WTO delegates from entering the building. And his commitment to nonviolence had been rewarded with pepper spray, rubber bullets and arrest. He had seen tear gas canisters thrown directly at medics. Riot cops had gassed a city bus. But what had hit Dale hardest was when he saw one of the Black Bloc anarchist kids – who had thrown a rock through a Starbucks window and rammed into police with a plywood shield – turn around and put handcuffs on another. The riot had been rigged!

Pete's other client, a slender woman who smelled like dirty underwear, talked to herself. "And then he said I couldn't get on the bus, but I had my pass and I told him Mary said the pass would take me home. So then he got on his radio…" She droned on with mundane stories about her days.

The other client shoved a water glass off the table and it shattered.

"Jesus!" Dale said. "Can't you make him behave?"

"I told you I was gonna throw it."

"That wasn't a throw," Pete said. "That was more of a shove." He stood to look for something to clean up the mess. Zoe was already trudging over with a mop and towels. She wore a baggy sweatshirt and loose pants. She was so skinny, Justin couldn't discern her breasts. It broke his heart to see her working in this condition. "Thanks," Pete said, taking the mop from her hand.

"I can do it," she said. "It's my job."

"No, I got it," Pete said, smiling at her. "It was my fault."

"I threw it," the client said.

"Hardly. That wasn't a throw at all," Pete said, bending to pick up the larger pieces of glass.

"Fuck! Don't encourage him!" Dale said.

The other client, who had gone on to detail something about her hairbrush losing its bristles, stopped in mid sentence. "Ooooh! You said a bad word. You get demerits."

"What the fuck are you talking about?" asked Dale. Justin didn't like the way Dale talked to these retarded people. But at least he talked to them. They made Justin so uncomfortable he usually ignored them completely.

"At their house," Pete said. "It's a demerit system when they don't keep up with their behavior programs."

"Jesus! Sounds like a microcosm of the police state!"

"Pretty much," Pete agreed.

"Don't they have rights?" Dale asked.

Gillis had been turning the pages of *Up Against the Wall, Motherfucker,* but now he looked up. "What's the point?" he asked. "It seems like Tyrell and Susan here are just going to be themselves, no matter what bullshit you put them through."

"Oooh! Demerit!" Susan said, clapping a hand to her mouth.

"I'm gonna throw it!" Tyrell had a fork in his hand now. Pete gently took it away, then finished mopping.

Dale rifled through his backpack, pulling out a stack of xeroxed pamphlets. "Okay, you fuckers got to read this and then put it up where you can see it when you need it. Maybe on the fridge, maybe next to the front door." He shoved pamphlets toward Justin, Gillis and Pete, never mind that they all lived together and had only one front door and one refrigerator between them. The pamphlet bore the ominous title "When An Agent Knocks." "Check it out. It tells you everything you need to know when the fucking feds show up on your doorstep."

"Thanks," Pete said, a twinkle in his eye. "You're a lifesaver."

Justin realized Zoe was staring at him, and he began to blush. His friends were good people with good hearts, but he was afraid they looked like a nerd pack to her. Zoe's friends were all so style conscious. He couldn't picture her joining his friends in one of their political discussions. He snuck a look at her odd gaze. She didn't look like she thought he was a loser. She looked intense, and she had almost a weird sort of glow around her, like a white taper candle with a big flame. Then she turned to help a customer.

Justin wondered if Pete had asked her out yet.

CHAPTER SIX

Everything had become too heavy. Rinsing out the big air pots that held the coffee, she felt like her wrists would snap. She had to rest on the way to the dumpster, dropping the smelly bags on the sidewalk and catching her breath. Rex had promised to come by and help her at the end of her shifts, but he hadn't shown. And her skin was sore and sensitive all over, especially her forearms and thighs. Even fabric irritated her.

The fifth day that Zoe called in sick during January, her boss told her she better get to a doctor. "You're a good employee, but unless you address your health problems, well, I don't know what we can do. I need to be able to count on my employees to show up and open the shop." All of Zoe's housemates – Rex, T-Bone, Peppy, Patty – had always claimed to envy her job. But could she get any of them to train so they could cover her shifts? When it came down to showing up at 6:30 AM, they laughed.

Zoe had promised not to miss another day. But a week later, on a Wednesday, she woke at six and felt like a huge pressure was holding her against the mattress. She tried to lift her body, but it was heavy as marble. She couldn't even make it to the phone to call her boss until eleven.

"What did your doctor say?" the boss asked sharply, less sympathetic with every work day missed.

Zoe couldn't even think of a good lie. "Pleurisy," she said, although she didn't know what it was.

"Pleurisy," said the boss. "I see. And how long does your doctor expect this pleurisy to last?"

"He wasn't sure," Zoe said feebly.

Her boss tried to can her right there, but Zoe pleaded until they devised a plan for Zoe to work the afternoon shifts instead of mornings. This meant fewer hours and way less in tips, but it was the best Zoe could get. She hadn't really thought about how much the café meant to her until her boss tried to take it away. Zoe opened that café five days a week. Brenda did the afternoon shifts, and her boss came in on the weekends, when she wasn't at her job at the escrow agency. But most of the time, it was Zoe's café. She unlocked the door, prepared the drinks, accepted and paid out the deliveries, handled the money, stocked the shelves. She knew what all her regulars drank, and started mixing their lattes when she saw them walking up the street toward Jojo's.

And what else did she do besides go to parties and hang out with her friends? She needed the responsibilities and order of the café. It was like her boss had pulled back a curtain to show the void of Zoe's life.

Zoe's housemates were unhappy when she told them that this time she wasn't joking, somebody had to get a job in a hurry. "Zoe," Rex whined over the techno music. "How could you lose all those hours? Don't you know how many people would kill for your job?"

"Don't look at me. I don't know how to do anything," T-Bone said, shrugging her skinny shoulders. "I barely made it through high school." Somehow T-Bone had managed to avoid employment thus far.

"Well," Peppy sighed. "We always threatened to do one of those twin acts. Maybe now is the time." In the past, Zoe had always thought it was a joke when the twins talked about being strippers. Twins were a porn cliché, but weren't they supposed to be blond and busty with rounded, high asses? Peppy and Patty were 5'1" with short, dark hair and next to nothing in the way of tits, waists or hips. Their pixie faces were cute, but overall they hardly seemed likely to inspire wet dreams.

Rex giggled, despite the seriousness of their financial situation.

"What are you laughing at, you pothead fuckface?" Patty asked. She had long differentiated herself as the foul-mouthed, verbally abusive twin. "We're gonna milk those motherfuckers." She made a vaguely obscene gesture that might have been intended to suggest a handjob. Zoe, too, began to laugh. "Fuck you, you underemployed bitch!" Patty said. She jumped up, pulled off her T-shirt and began to gyrate to the techno music. She wore nothing but dirty jeans and purple socks with one big toe poking through.

"Oh my God!" Rex howled.

"You've got to be kidding!" T-Bone said.

"I'm going to milk those fuckers!" Patty crowed, repeating her obscene gesture in time to the music. Actually she was a good dancer. This was hardly the first time Zoe had seen Patty suddenly undress, but usually the twin had the excuse of being fucked up on something.

"Come on, Peppy! Get your ass up here!"

Peppy stared, suddenly shy. "I think maybe this is more your thing."

"Don't give me that crap. The only thing I've got going for my dancing career is the twin angle. I mean, it's not like I have anything to shake!"

"She might be right," Rex said slowly. He had stopped laughing and was contemplating Patty's gyrating torso more seriously. "Let's see the two of you, Peppy. You might work up a decent act."

"What are you now, their pimp?" T-Bone asked.

"I'll dance with you," Peppy said, "but I don't know about taking anything off." She floated toward Patty and began to mirror her moves. After a few minutes, she lost her inhibitions and threw off her shirt, giggling. Zoe figured neither girl owned a bra. Their breasts were tiny mounds with big, flat nipples. Only their tattoos were different. A dragon wrapped around Patty's navel, while a monkey perched on Peppy's shoulder.

"Damn!" Rex said. "I think I'm getting turned on!"

T-Bone lay on the couch and put a pillow over her head so she wouldn't have to see.

Zoe had never before appreciated the twins' beauty, the strength or aliveness of their small bodies. "I'd hire you in a second," she said.

"Really?" Patty asked, stopping in mid-shimmy. "Are you shitting me, Zoe?"

Zoe was touched that they valued her opinion so much. They hadn't even commented on Rex's endorsement. "I mean it," she said. "You're good."

"You think we should do it?" Peppy asked, caught up in the admiration.

"Well, it might be gross. You know, the customers and stuff," Zoe said.

"No one's going to fuck with me," Patty said. "They get out of line, they're going to pay!"

Soon they were tearing through duffel bags, trying to find an outfit that might work for an audition. T-Bone offered a pair of red thong panties, given to her by a high school boyfriend and never worn. "Gross," T-Bone explained. "They totally gave me a wedgie."

"You said you never wore them," Peppy said.

"I put them on just long enough to get a major wedgie," T-Bone said. "Then I took them off and stuffed them in a drawer or something."

But the twins wanted to match. Zoe finally gave them two dollars so they could buy matching panties at the 99 cent store.

"How sexy are they going to be if they're at the 99 cent store?" Rex asked. "And won't they be dancing naked, anyway?"

"I think the job title is 'stripper,'" T-Bone said slowly, like she was talking to a kindergartener "And the job description is 'to strip.' Which means they have to take something off." Rex threw a pillow at her, and

T-Bone threw something back. Then everybody was giggling and the twins danced for all they were worth.

Zoe felt a rush of love for her friends, how they all banded together in difficult times like this. She hated the thought of leaving their messy, ramshackle house, whether by death or eviction.

CHAPTER SEVEN

Justin trudged toward the bus stop after another night of squeezing survey answers out of hostile telephone owners. It hadn't been a good shift. His response rate was down. He'd had a call from his parents earlier in the day, which might have had something to do with his poor performance at work. His dad had asked his usual questions: How much Justin was making now and what prospects for advancement did he have and how many credits was he away that from that B.A. he'd never finished and did Justin think maybe going back to school could help his prospects? His mother asked her typical questions: Was Justin healthy? What was he eating? Was he seeing someone special? Both parents' questions depressed him no end.

He reached the bus stop and took a book Dale had recommended from his backpack. Justin squinted at it beneath the streetlight. *Fucked up World: The CIA's Global Bloodbath*. This small volume from an independent publisher bulged with horrors: democratically elected leaders assassinated by CIA operatives, Brazilian street children abducted and used in nuclear tests, Central American farmers questioned then pushed out of airplanes. It didn't exactly lift his mood.

He really needed to go to the Goodwill and buy a warmer jacket. He pulled his Guatemalan hat down to his eyebrows and hugged his arms around himself.

When Justin's mother had asked him if he was dating anyone, he had told her about Zoe. "A girl who works in a café?" his mother asked doubtfully. "Is she a student? How old is she?" Justin's mother preferred to think of Justin as a person with a respectable office job rather than one of those parasites who harass you just as you're sitting down to dinner. As a respectable office worker, Justin should date a realtor or insurance agent, or at least a receptionist.

"I don't know, Ma," he had said uncomfortably. "I guess she's in her early twenties."

"A little young, hmm?"

"Well, I don't know."

"And you don't know if she's in school? How well do you know this girl, Justin? Have you even talked to her?"

God, it was demeaning. He wished he could tell his mother to fuck off. "I know her, Ma. I see her every day."

"Every day?" She laughed. "You go to this café every day?"

"Yeah. It's right by my house. Why?" he said testily.

"Don't you think that's a little obvious?"

"Well, probably. She probably knows I like her."

"Have you asked her out?"

"I'm going to ask her out tomorrow," he said, letting his mother push him into yet another promise of action.

"Good," she said brightly. "Do you want to talk to your father?"

Now Justin was stuck, cold and miserable and reading one of the world's most depressing books. Somewhere in his mind he equated his parents with the power-mad government, delighting in their manipulation of the weak. His mother would call him back next week and let him know he was a coward if he hadn't asked Zoe out, and a loser if she turned him down. He could lie and make up a date to tell his mother about, but that would just drag on and on.

It wasn't that Justin was a mama's boy, but he wanted his parents to be happy. He had let them down so many times – dropping out of college, neglecting to find a career, failing to marry and produce grandchildren. They'd bailed him out when he got in trouble with credit cards. They'd helped him when he was short on his car payments several times, back before the car got repossessed.

Justin rode the bus glumly. He couldn't think of a way out. Tomorrow he would have to ask Zoe on a date.

Justin could hardly sleep that night, so he got up at seven o'clock and decided to go right to the café. He wouldn't be able to think of another thing until he had talked to Zoe. He felt like his heart was a ball of modeling clay that she could smoosh with two fingers.

But when he got there, Brenda, the afternoon girl, was behind the counter. "Where's Zoe?" Justin blurted out. His interest had never before been expressed so nakedly.

The girl had dark curly hair and circles under her eyes. She had always seemed cheerful in the afternoons, but now her glance was practically vicious.

"I can't believe I tore myself out of bed at six AM to make coffee, and everyone acts stricken that Zoe's not here to serve them. What will it be?"

"Uh, a coffee," Justin said. "Please. But why isn't she here?"

"Schedule change," the girl said tersely, pumping the air pot so coffee spewed into a paper cup.

"Oh, I wanted that for here," he said, but she just glared and handed him the cup.

"Dollar fifty."

He counted out the money and dropped a quarter in her tip jar, even though she had been kind of mean. Justin took his coffee over by the window and tried to think how to talk information out of the harpy behind the counter. The coffee didn't taste half as good as when Zoe made it.

Justin had seldom been to Jojo's so early. He watched the parade of customers with interest. These were the people Zoe saw every morning. Lots of hip young people with commuter mugs, on their way to school or work. People in athletic gear, post-jog. He could overhear customers asking, "Where's Zoe?" and "Are you new?" He couldn't hear the answers, because the girl's voice had dropped to a low, menacing rumble.

A couple of people moved tables together, and soon a group of twelve clustered over coffee and muffins. Justin eavesdropped. One woman in her forties was going on about personal freedoms being taken away and urging her comrades to write letters to Oregon senators and congress people. Justin thought of Dale and imagined him sneering at the civility of writing letters. Dale would not be able to muster one "dear" or "sincerely" for the president. In fact, he refused to call the White House dweller "president."

The café's other seats were empty, except for a man with a mustache reading the *Oregonian* and a girl frowning at a textbook called *Political Economics and Today's World*. Justin felt a twinge, wondering if his life would be any different if he had finished school. But thoughts of college fell away as he tried to work up courage and strategies to ask Brenda for news of Zoe. Should he stick a five in her tip jar? Make up a story about how he lost Zoe's phone number and could she please give it to him? His chest and stomach hummed with disquiet, which eventually propelled him to his feet and up to the counter.

"Look," he blurted out, "I've been trying to get up the nerve to ask Zoe out for months and I promised myself I was going to do it today. I didn't mean to insult you like I was disappointed to see you–" he faltered, trailing off, then bravely forging on, "but, well, I couldn't sleep last night, I was so nervous."

"Well, that's kind of sweet," the girl said uncertainly, assessing Justin for signs of psychosis or an annoying personality or anything else that should prevent her from releasing sensitive coffee house scheduling information.

"Could you just tell me if she'll be in later?"

"I guess I can tell you that. I mean, you could just come by and look in the window, so it's not like a big secret."

"I'd appreciate it," he said.

"Okay. We're trading hours this week. She'll be here from two till six."

"Two till six," Justin repeated. "Oh, thank you." He was so relieved he stuffed two dollars in the girl's tip jar. What if Zoe had quit? How would Justin ever find her?

"You want some advice?" the girl asked, looking Justin over.

"I guess so," he said warily. "Does she have a boyfriend or something?"

She shrugged. "I was going to suggest shaving off that beard and getting a haircut. And not wearing that Guatemalan hat. Zoe doesn't really go in for hippies."

"I'm not a hippie," said Justin, who dressed like his friends and never considered what his look conveyed.

"Then try not to look so much like one," the girl said, smiling and turning to a handsome blond man who had walked up behind Justin. She made the blond a mocha and Justin drifted back to his seat. The political discussion at the next table was heating up. They were planning a demonstration against something or other. A woman said they should lock themselves together with bicycle locks inside some building in Salem. A girl asked timidly, "What if I have to go to the bathroom?"

A gaunt-faced guy with intense blue eyes answered her. "When I'm going to a protest," he said, "I wear an adult diaper, just in case. They're really quite absorbent."

Gross, Justin thought, was the guy serious? Then he wondered if Zoe thought he looked like a hippie. He thought his goatee was cool, but these girls were younger. His idea of style could be several years out of date. He hoped it wasn't necessary to spend money on a haircut. Seemed like he'd just had one a few months ago.

Justin finished his coffee, revising his plan for the day. Maybe he could take a nap? No, his heart pounded from nerves and coffee. He felt aimless. How could he fill the hours until two PM? His eyes drifted to the man with the mustache. It seemed like he'd been reading the *Oregonian's* Living section forever. It was a crappy paper, especially the Living section. Maybe the guy was an Ann Landers fanatic or was studying some craft project directions about crocheting a toilet seat cover. The political people were arranging a carpool to Salem now. The young girl closed her textbook with a sigh.

Justin used to go for long walks when he wanted to think, back when he was in college or back home after dropping out. That's probably the only thing he missed about Southern California, that it was warm enough to walk outside year round. He looked out at the gray misery plopping from the sky. He felt trapped, stifled by interiors. There would be at least a couple more months of this before he could rely on an occasional sunny day.

The political group moved their chairs back. Some left in a hurry, as though they had jobs. Others stood but still lingered, talking in twos or threes. The guy with the mustache finally put down the Living section. Justin, too, was about to go when Dale walked in.

"Hey," Dale said, charging toward Justin. Even at eight in the morning, Dale could electrify a room.

"What are you doing up so early?" Justin asked.

"There's a state to smash, bro!" Justin couldn't tell if he was joking or not. "Where's your friend?"

"What friend?"

"The girl you love!"

"Huh?" Justin asked warily.

"The skinny blond girl you always make eyes at!" Dale jerked his head toward the counter.

"What do you mean?" Justin asked, but Dale fixed him with a look that would brook no bullshit. "Christ, is it that obvious?"

"Uh huh." Dale changed course like lightning. "Did you hear what that fucker did yesterday?"

"Who?"

"The usurper! That unelected reptile! Now he's getting his stooges to track what books we're checking out of the public library."

"He can't do that! The librarians won't put up with that shit."

"They will if they don't want to go to jail," Dale said, shaking his head. "Something's got to be done. That fucker's going to ruin this country. I mean, really ruin it. Like get us bombed to shit or put dissidents in internment camps or Christ knows what."

"What can we do?" Justin shrugged, thinking about the political group organizing a letter campaign. He imagined the president laughing on a golden toilet, wiping his ass with their letters.

"It will probably take something more Malcolm than Martin, I can tell you that much," Dale said ominously. "Believe me, I've tried handcuffing myself to shit and going limp when the pigs break out the bolt cutters and drag me away face down. The pigs love that, man! They live for that shit. I'm done entertaining them."

Justin was already depressed enough. He stood to leave. "I was just on my way out," he said. "Maybe I'll see you later."

"Likely," Dale said. "I don't expect I'll be blessed with a job between now and then."

As Justin put on his jacket, he noticed that Mr. Mustache was reading the Living section again. At least there was one person with a sadder life than Justin's.

Justin rushed the two blocks home, sick of getting wet. Anybody, fashion conscious or not, would have to admit that the Guatemalan hat helped keep his head dry.

At home, Justin wiled away the day. He listened to some CDs, checked his email. Picked up a guitar and reviewed the five chords he knew. Days like this made him wish he had some artistic talent. He plucked books off the communal bookshelf and read five pages of *The Plague,* six pages of *The Lone Ranger and Tonto Fistfight in Heaven,* then got caught up in *1984.* Ain't it the truth, he thought.

Later, Gillis and Pete were in the kitchen eating toast when Justin went to get a glass of water. Gillis was talking about his plans to plant a rare kind of pygmy zucchini in the spring. Justin noticed that Gillis had a beard, smelled like pot, and definitely might seem like a hippie. Pete was clean shaven. Did Zoe think that Justin was more of a hippie than Pete was? Did she like Pete? Or maybe they were both pathetically uncool losers. Justin felt completely lost in his own kitchen.

He headed for the bathroom. Justin felt sentimental about his goatee, but a few swift strokes of the razor felled it. He peered at himself in the mirror. Was he more handsome now? Cooler? He had no idea. Then he trimmed his hair with a rusty pair of cuticle scissors.

"Does my hair look better?" he asked Sam when he heard him passing in the hall.

Sam shrugged. "Did you do something to it?"

"Never mind," Justin muttered, shutting the bathroom door so he could gaze at his reflection in peace.

At 2:30, Justin picked up his backpack and headed for Jojo's Fair Trade World Coffee Café. He would only have time to run in, ask Zoe for a date, then hurry to the bus stop. In a way, it was a blessing. He had a good reason for making a hasty retreat if she turned him down. Unless she didn't believe he was going to work, then she might think he was a coward, or mentally unstable.

Zoe glowed behind the counter, wispy and sick but with an intense heat coming off her. She smiled when she saw him and his heart leapt. A few people sat in the café, but not close enough to eavesdrop if he kept his voice low.

She had already taken down a mug for his usual coffee. "Uh, no coffee today," he said quickly, not wanting her to needlessly dirty a dish she would have to wash. "I don't have time. Got to go to work." Then he stared at her like a fool.

"No?" she prompted.

"Actually, I, uh, came to see you." Here he lost courage, his eyes flitted away, and when he spoke, his tone contradicted the casualness of his words. "I just thought, you know, maybe I could take you to a movie or something sometime. When you're not busy."

"Oh," she said, not exactly leaping at the chance. "Yeah, okay."

"Really?" he asked, still unable to look at her.

"I'm kind of busy right now, but maybe ask me in a couple weeks."

"That's great," Justin said, his eyes meeting hers for about half a second. Right then, Pete had to show up. Justin noticed that Zoe started making Pete's double Americano before he said a word.

"Thought you went to work," Pete said to Justin. "Hi, Zoe. You're looking beautiful today."

Justin noticed that Zoe smiled at Pete, the same smile she had given Justin.

"I'm on my way," Justin said. "Yeah, I'm just going to the bus." He waited for Zoe to give him a meaningful look or at least a farewell, but she was adding steaming water to two shots of espresso, and didn't look up until he said, "Bye, Zoe."

She half smiled at him and said, "See you."

That was it.

Justin marched through the rain, irrationally angry at Pete. Then he saw the tail end of the bus slip by in the distance, and he blamed that on Pete, too. When he reached the stop, he realized that not only did his date with Zoe need considerable firming up, he had failed to get her number! And Pete was probably lounging against the counter right now, trying to charm the pants off Justin's beloved.

CHAPTER EIGHT

The landlord was getting harder to put off. All the laws were on his side. Zoe and her crew were a month behind on rent and had final notices on electricity and gas. The phone had been off for a month. Luckily, the landlord paid garbage and water.

"We should double team him," Patty said lasciviously as they laid about on the ragged sofas.

"Damn, you're foul," T-Bone said. The landlord was one of those geriatrics that like to putter around the grounds pretending to fix things, hoping to catch a glimpse of young tit through an improperly closed curtain.

"That will be a strictly one-on-one proposition," Peppy said. "I don't want to see that old geezer in his boxers."

"I bet he wears high-cut bikinis," Patty said, pumping her eyebrows up and down.

"Gross!" the other girls chorused.

"It's not a bad idea," Rex said. T-Bone threw a musty couch pillow at him.

"Seriously," Patty said, "I like living indoors." Everyone sombered up at that. Not only had Zoe's hours and tips decreased dramatically, the twin act had been an awful failure. The better clubs had decided that Peppy and Patty lacked the "drop dead factor," so they'd wound up at a dive called Heartbreakers. When they'd met their junkie coworkers and the few cheap-ass customers, they realized the only hearts breaking belonged to the mothers of the girls working there. They had given up after two nights where their bar tabs exceeded their tips.

Zoe lay on the couch, wrapped in a blanket, staring at the ceiling. She thought of Justin. He had looked almost handsome today, since he'd shaved and cut his hair. But date him? Date anybody? She was on her way out. This was a solo journey.

"I bet he has a puckered old ass," Rex speculated about the landlord. Zoe didn't want to think about his sad, used up old body. What about her own wasting self? How would she look as death's hot breath singed her neck?

It was so tempting to lean on Justin. She knew he would do anything for her, she could see it in his gaze. But wouldn't it be cruel to accept his devotion, then die?

"Doesn't anyone have a rich relative to hit up for some money?" Patty suggested.

"My parents said they'd pay for me to go to school, but otherwise I'm on my own," T-Bone said.

"No way," Rex said. "I got cut out of the family fortune long ago."

"How come?" Peppy asked.

"They think if they give me money, I'll spend it on drugs." The others giggled. "I'd spend it on the house this time!" Rex protested. "What about you twins?"

"You know we're runaways," Patty reminded him. "Sexually abused and all that shit."

"Oh, yeah," Rex remembered.

They ran through other options: food stamps, welfare, crime. But no one could drag their ass off the couches to fill out a form or mug a senior. Zoe imagined how hard it would be to evict them. Probably the cops or sheriff or whoever was in charge of eviction would have to bodily remove them from the couches and drop them outside, still reclining, in the bushes.

"This is so boring!" T-Bone cried. "Poverty is so boring!"

Zoe fell asleep. She dreamt of huge, dark wings beating overhead. At first it was terrifying, then just creepy. In her dream, she was going about her business, working at the café, going to the store to buy ramen noodles. And everywhere, the wings flapped together, sometimes loud, close by her ear, sometimes retreating to a whisper. Eventually she got used to it and they became the wings of a companion glimpsed out of the corner of her eye.

She woke up. The wings were gone, her friends had disappeared. It was dark, maybe the middle of the night, and she felt dreadfully alone. She was crying.

Next day, their luck ran out. The landlord's wife brought the eviction papers. They had a month to clear out.

CHAPTER NINE

Justin managed to skip going to Jojo's Fair Trade World Coffee Café for one day. He didn't want to be a fool. Zoe obviously hadn't been biting her nails hoping he'd ask her out. She hadn't even volunteered a phone number. But pride could only overcome his desperate love for one day.

At three o'clock, Justin entered the café and sighed in relief to note Pete's absence. A couple of students sat in a corner, and the man with the mustache was in his favorite chair. Today he read the front section of the *New York Times*, raising him slightly in Justin's estimation.

"Hi, Zoe," Justin said, still shy about saying her name.

"Hi," she said. She wore a tight red T-shirt that accentuated her ribs and pallor.

"How have you been?" he asked, as though he hadn't seen her in weeks. She just shrugged. "Look," he said, "can I get your number? So I can call you about the movie?"

"Phone's not working," she said. Justin felt like she'd hit him over the head with an air pot. Talk about a lame excuse!

"Oh," he said. "Well, aren't you going to get it fixed?"

She looked away from him, color coming to her cheeks. "No."

Justin wanted to crawl in a ditch and die. He could feel a tear threatening to form. He loved her so much! How could she lie to him like he was just one more stupid guy? "Well, I have to go," he managed to say, turning abruptly so she wouldn't see his eyes.

He was almost to the door when she called his name. He stopped, but the tears were showing and he couldn't face her. "I didn't mean it like that," she said to his back. Her voice dropped so he could barely hear her. "This is embarrassing, but we're having a little trouble paying our bills. The phone got cut off last month."

Justin's heart soared. As he reached to wipe his tears before turning to face Zoe, Pete and two of his clients burst through the door. Pete, in his irritating way, immediately noticed Justin's tears.

"What's wrong with you?" he asked.

"Allergies," Justin said, wiping his eyes.

"I thought you just got those in summer," Pete said.

"It's some kind of winter allergy," Justin said, wanting to smack Pete. Why couldn't the fucker stay at work during his work hours, instead of dragging his bizarre charges into Jojo's whenever Justin might possibly be able to get a moment's peace with Zoe?

"I'm allergic to peas," said the client who had broken a glass the last time Justin saw him. The guy's shrill voice and greasy graying hair were enough to get on Justin's nerves even without his weird behavior. "They make me throw up."

"Well, see you," Pete said, starting to brush past.

"Huh?" Justin said. "I'm not going anywhere."

"Looked like you were heading for the door," Pete said, shrugging.

"No, I was just going to get a cup of coffee," Justin said.

"I think you order over there," Pete said, pointing toward the counter and laughing. He rolled his eyes at Zoe, as if to indicate that Justin was cuckoo. "Hey, Zoe," Pete sang out, striding toward the counter. "I love red. It's such a passionate color."

So Justin found himself, ten minutes later, sitting at a table with Pete and his clients, going over the conversation about Zoe's telephone, in his head, over and over. The poor thing! Couldn't pay her phone bill! No wonder she hadn't gone to the doctor.

The greasy-haired, shrill-voiced client busied himself with trying to knock over Pete's coffee cup whenever Pete looked away for a second. Pete deftly held the fellow at bay while chatting with Justin and Zoe. The other client, a creepy, brooding sort with a pinched looking face, said very little. He stared intently at the women in the café, alternating between the female student and Zoe. Every once in a while he'd catch the eye of one of the women and sneer, "Sneeze."

"He likes it when girls sneeze," Pete said. "Turns him on." The student giggled, but Zoe didn't seem to appreciate it.

They sat there for an hour, Pete and Justin trying to outwait each other.

"Gotta shit," said the sneeze enthusiast. Pete directed him toward the bathroom. Christ, Justin thought, he'd never inflict a foul character like that on Zoe. Pete damn well better go in afterwards and make sure there wasn't a mess left in the bathroom. But when the client returned, Pete didn't bother to check.

Another hour passed. Justin couldn't drink one more sip of coffee. The students and the mustache man had left. Finally, Pete stood up. "Well, guys, we have to go home and make dinner." He shot Justin an irritable look. "Shouldn't you be at work?"

"Day off," Justin said, smiling triumphantly.

It was almost closing time before Justin was rid of Pete. Zoe dumped coffee and rounded up dishes that needed washing. "Time to turn the sign around," Zoe said, reversing the open sign. "I have to lock the door." She took out a keychain decorated with a glow in the dark alien head, and looked at him expectantly.

"How about I stay and help you clean up?" Justin asked.

"Really?" she said, looking almost starry-eyed.

"Sure," Justin said. "It's no big deal."

"That would really help," Zoe admitted. "My housemates are always promising to come give me a hand, but they never seem to make it."

Zoe turned up the techno music, which made them work faster. Justin carried a heavy bus tray to the sink, hauled garbage to the dumpster, swept and mopped the floors, including the bathroom. Sure enough, Pete's client hadn't flushed. Justin tried not to gag. He didn't know how Pete stood it, being around people like that all day.

"I never knew how much work there was!" Justin yelled over the music. Zoe smiled without commenting. She looked much happier than usual.

It took an hour before the café was spotless. Justin didn't want to separate. "You want to get something to eat?" he asked.

"I'm not very hungry," she said, but when his face fell she added, "but maybe just a little something."

They walked across the street to Dots, which was convenient if not an original place for two young Portlanders to visit on a first date. As Justin slid into one of the glittering red booths across from Zoe, he couldn't believe his luck. Here they were on a date, and he hadn't had to spend multiple days of terror leading up to it.

A cute waitress with glasses and a tattoo of a long-necked cat on her arm brought them water. Zoe took off her coat, revealing the red T shirt. Justin would remember the overwhelming redness of this first date– Zoe's shirt, the booth, the flocked red bordello wallpaper, interrupted only by velvet paintings of big-eyed Indian children.

"You ever come here?" Justin asked her, grabbing at the first thing he thought of to say.

"Sure," she said. "Now and then."

He wanted to ask her everything, but at the same time he couldn't think of a suitable question. "Where did you grow up?" he asked after gawking at his good luck for another half a minute.

"Northeast."

"Oh yeah? Like New England?"

"Huh?" she asked. "By Fremont. Where the big Nature's is."

"Oh! Northeast Portland!" Justin exclaimed. "I thought you meant the Northeast. Like New England. Wow. I've hardly met anybody who's from Portland."

She shrugged. "I know lots of people from here."

"Yeah, but that's because you're from here. Trust me, this town's full of transplants."

The waitress returned, order pad in hand. "Ready?" The tattooed cat's collar glistened with glitter gel dabbed on like rhinestones.

"You know what you want?" Justin asked Zoe.

"Small salad, please," she said.

"Don't you want more than a salad?" Justin urged. "You can get whatever you want. How about some French fries?"

She smiled slightly, shaking her head. "I'll have the burrito," Justin said.

"Vegan burrito?" the waitress asked.

"Regular."

"The vegetarian one?"

"Yeah." The waitress walked off. Justin tucked their menus back behind the napkin dispenser. He wished Zoe would ask him a question, but she didn't seem like the kind of girl that ever asked anything. A Smiths album was playing. Cigarette smoke escaped the bar area and hung like fog over their table. He wanted to ask her why her phone was turned off, but that was too personal.

"How do you like working afternoons?" he finally asked. "Is it better?" She shrugged. "Are you going to school in the mornings?"

"No," she said. Silence.

"Hey, do you want a beer or something while we wait for the food?" She shook her head. He didn't know when he'd been so nervous on a date. Most of the girls he'd gone out with, you could hardly get them to shut up. And they had been so aggressive, startling him with a hand on his thigh under the table. But Zoe was self contained. She seemed to need neither talk nor touch.

The truth was, Zoe had been nervous on dates in the past, and had even occasionally chattered. But that was before she fell ill. There was no longer energy for little trails of talk that led nowhere. When she looked at Justin now, she saw him in his simplest form: a good heart. Sure, it helped that for once he wasn't wearing that stupid Guatemalan hat. But that was only a trapping. She heard the music, registered redness and his good heart, and that was the end of her energy. But when his nerves were about shot, she finally deemed it kind to make an effort at conversation, tiring as it was.

"Nice haircut," she said.

He looked astounded. "Thanks. I can't believe you noticed."

The waitress brought Justin's huge burrito and Zoe's petite salad.

"Please, have some of this," he said.

Zoe speared a lettuce leaf, chewed it.

"Is your family in Portland, then?" Justin asked.

She nodded. "Mostly."

"Mine's in San Diego," he said when she didn't elaborate. "They can't understand why I want to live somewhere so rainy."

"Why do you?" she asked him, because he was kind, because she should make the effort. She was exhausted after her shift and could hardly lift the fork to her lips. All she wanted was to lie on her sofa and stare at the stained ceiling of the living room that would soon cease to be hers.

"Oh, I couldn't live down there anymore. The traffic, the military, the phoniness. You ever been to Southern California?" She shook her head. "It's not worth the trip."

Justin told her about the poverty of Southern Californian culture. He tried to draw her out again and again, but, failing that, he told her about himself. She knew he wanted to hear about her life, and that later on when he was alone, Justin would kick himself for being such an ass and monopolizing the conversation. He wouldn't blame her for not holding up her end of the social bargain, though she was well aware this was her own failure.

Zoe was weighed down by fatigue, but also by a huge sadness. Because already she could see the next part of her story laid out before her. She could rely on neither friends nor family. None of her roommates would find a job and/or money in her lifetime. What was left of her family had their own problems. Her sister was an alcoholic, her mother the sugar mama to a verbally and economically abusive younger man. Neither was exactly equipped to install and watch over Zoe's death bed.

Instead, the eviction would close in on her, and Justin would be the one to come to her rescue. Zoe would live on his couch, and then in his bed. He would love her more deeply each day, and the more he loved her the more the life would drain from her body. These two phenomena would not be connected, but Justin would spend the rest of his life not only missing her and regretting not saving her, but blaming himself for sucking her last lifeblood like a vampire. It was a rotten legacy she would leave, hurting this decent man.

It's not how things ultimately wound up, but they started by limping along in that direction.

CHAPTER TEN

Zoe and Justin were together a lot after that night at Dots. He came to see her every day she worked at the café, and they spent evenings together on his days off. They both avoided bringing the other to their homes; Justin didn't want complications from Pete, and Zoe wished to avoid teasing. Justin was so different from her social circle and at first she worried that her friends would think he wasn't cool. But as she grew more tired and the eviction closed in and her friends failed daily to bail out their household, the need for coolness fell away. Zoe began to realize that each of her housemates would find someone else to leech off of.

Zoe knew that in all fairness she should tell Justin that she was dying. But the words had not formed since she told the woman at the Aquarian Foundation. She also needed to tell him about the eviction. It was three weeks off now.

On the one week anniversary of their first date, Zoe decided to tell Justin she was losing her home. She figured she better allow him several weeks to form the idea that she could live with him, clear it with his roommates, and get up the courage to ask her. She still had not kissed him. Maybe she should kiss him before mentioning the eviction? Or was it too cold-hearted to strategize?

Justin had the day off and they were spending the evening walking on Hawthorne Street. The shops were all aimed at their demographic: CDs, used books, specialty coffees, retro clothing, new clothing, stylish haircuts, cheap food. Zoe couldn't remember a time she had wanted so little. As they walked along looking in windows at the glittery, ephemeral consumer goods, she took Justin's hand.

Now in this modern culture where so many couples fuck on the first date and break up before the second, taking a person's hand might not be worth the ink to note it. But a couple of lukewarm tortoises could have outrun Zoe and Justin's love life thus far. Zoe could feel the thrill go through Justin's body when she touched his hand. As for her own body, she felt a pervasive, pleasant warmth, which is a good deal for a cold, dying person to feel.

Justin turned and looked at her, his face all happiness. They were passing a bead store and stopped to look in the window at necklaces and earrings. But really they were checking out the reflection of themselves, joined.

Once she'd taken his hand she had to wait a while to bring up the eviction, or it might seem an obvious prelude. They walked on. "Are you hungry?" he asked. She shook her head. As they passed a clothing store, Justin pointed at a shapeless off-white dress. Embroidered flowers circled the neckline. "I bet you'd look beautiful in that," he said.

She wouldn't look twice at a hippie dress like that, let alone leave the house in it. What if he started buying her stuff? "Not really my style," she said, thinking that better be made clear. Dying had relaxed her attitudes around coolness, but there was a limit.

"No?" he said, sounding disappointed.

"No." The incident with the dress discouraged her. Justin didn't understand her at all. How could he love her? Or who did he think she was that made him love her? Maybe he detected her essence, her soul, whatever, some timeless thing that lurked beneath her flesh? Or maybe her blond hair and skinny body attracted him? Did he even know why?

"Let's go in Powell's and warm up," Justin said, leading her into the bookstore. They wandered between racks of books that reached the ceiling. "What kind of books do you like?" he asked her.

"Oh, I don't know," she said.

"Do you like fiction or non fiction?" he prodded.

"Oh, not really," she said. Zoe couldn't think when she'd last read a book. It just didn't really pop into her mind, to pick up a book and read it. "I like magazines."

"Oh," Justin said. "Well, at least it's warm in here." She followed him to the political books. He picked up several, looking at them with great interest. She read a couple of sentences over his shoulder, had never seen anything so boring.

"I'm going to look around over there," she said.

"I'll come with you." He hurriedly closed the book.

"No, take your time. I'll be right over there."

She drifted away from Justin and the political section. As she tried for the hundredth time to think of a way to bring up the eviction, a subject category caught her eye: Death & Dying. "No way," she breathed. Half the length of one shelf was covered with these books. Zoe had never known such a book category existed. Some were psychology-based, but the New Agey ones were most compelling. She took a book called *You Don't Have to Die* down from the shelf. On its cover was a purple pyramid. Inside were graphs, diagrams of crystal healing techniques, incantations in God knows what language spelled out phonetically. She couldn't understand how this book could stop her, or anyone, from dying.

"There you are!" Justin's voice came from just behind her. She jammed the book back on the shelf, then pretended to be looking at the section below, which turned out to be Living with STDs, which wasn't much better. "What are you looking at?" he asked, a hand on her shoulder.

Before he could investigate Death & Dying or Living with STDs, Zoe spun around. "We're getting evicted!" she blurted out.

"What?!"

"Yeah," she said, looking at his feet. "It's kind of been on my mind."

"No! Why? When?"

"We have a few more weeks," she said.

"But how come? And what are you going to do?"

"Because life is expensive," she said. "And I guess I'll think of something."

"God, Zoe, I'm so sorry."

She started walking slowly, nudging him away from Death & Dying and Living with STDs. "It will be okay," she said, as though comforting him.

"Wow," he said. "I've never been evicted. What happened? You guys just didn't pay your rent?"

Zoe wished he would lower his voice and not ask questions. "We just fell a little behind," she murmured. She hadn't expected him to be so shocked. It was only her second eviction, but her housemates must have had ten between them. They had been more annoyed than surprised or concerned.

"Can you move back home?" Justin asked.

"Let's not talk about it. Something will turn up." She walked ahead of him now, hurrying toward the door. She didn't know where she was going but suddenly she wanted to be out of the store.

"Zoe? Wait up! Why are you in such a hurry? Did I say something wrong?" he asked from behind.

The evening had not gone right. Everything had fallen apart when she held that stupid book in her hands. Like a book could keep her from dying! She wanted to set fire to it, to see the stupid purple pyramid burn. She wanted to set fire to her disease and burn it out of her system. She felt a furious tear in her eye and hurried toward the dark night. Justin was so sensitive. He'd notice her every hurt feeling, each emotional misstep. Maybe she needed a stupid, selfish guy so she could retain her privacy and the right to her secret feelings.

Justin caught up to her just as she stepped into the dark. "Zoe, wait!" He slipped a hand around her wrist. "What did I say? I'm sorry."

"It's just embarrassing," she said. "I don't want to talk about it." Her anger exhausted her and now she seemed to be teetering. He slipped his arms around her to help her regain her footing, but then he was holding her close and she let him, right there on the sidewalk for anyone she knew to see. She pressed her head into his chest and listened to a heart that could easily beat another fifty years. Forty-nine years after I'm gone, she thought. She relaxed into him, surrendering for a few seconds. She couldn't stop death hurtling at her, or landlords who wanted her to clear out, or control her own body enough to keep her full time job. Justin was good. She closed her eyes and pretended no one could see them. She pretended they could stay like that for fifty years, a man and woman embracing until they died of old age. She had never realized what a sweet thought that was.

"Oh, Zoe," he said. "You don't have to be embarrassed. You're safe with me."

And against all the evidence life had shown her, in that moment she believed him. They kissed.

CHAPTER ELEVEN

Zoe moved into Justin's house two weeks later. They weren't lovers yet, and moving in together usually comes at a more advanced stage of a relationship, so they agreed that Zoe would sleep on the living room couch for now.

Justin could hardly believe his good fortune when Zoe consented to move in. He'd thought of the idea as soon as he heard of her eviction, right there at Powell's. But it took him another week to get up the nerve to ask her. He never thought she'd say yes.

Gillis was too mellow to mind another roommate, and Sam was never home. But Pete had been troublesome. Justin waited until they were the only two at home on a day when Justin had to leave for work in less than an hour. "Uh, Pete," he began, "I've sort of been seeing Zoe."

"Seeing?" It didn't register.

"Dating, you could say."

"Zoe's going out with *you?*" Pete was clearly incredulous.

"Yeah," Justin said.

"No."

"Really."

Pete sat heavily in a chair. "I don't believe it."

Pete was starting to piss him off, but Justin tried to suppress his anger. "And another thing. She has to move out of where she's living, and I told her it would probably be okay if she stayed here for a while."

"She's moving in with you?!"

"Well, it might be temporary. If it's okay with you. Gillis and Sam said they didn't care."

"I guess it's your room," Pete said tersely. A vein in his forehead began to throb and his fists clenched.

Justin could feel his cheeks reddening, and he couldn't meet Pete's eye. His gaze wandered to the front door, then at the "When An Agent Knocks" brochure that was taped up beside it. "Actually, she wants to stay in the living room."

"A girl is going to move in with you but sleep in the living room? What the fuck?"

Justin really didn't want to get into this part of the scenario. Of course he wanted her in his bed. But he would respect her wishes and not railroad her into something she wasn't ready for just because she needed a place to stay. Justin loved Zoe. He ached to sleep with her, but he knew he could wait a year if that's what she needed. "She needs some space."

"She hasn't even moved in with you and she needs space? Dude, that's not good."

"Look, I'm sorry, man," Justin said. "I wouldn't ask this but she kind of has to leave her old place in a hurry."

"Seems like she could have her space all day while you're at work, then sleep with you at night," Pete said. Justin focused on the brochure. He remembered feeling like a real radical when he taped it up. "You're not even fucking her, are you?" Pete cried, realization dawning. His face lit up to about ten times happier.

"Come on, man. Show some respect."

"For you?"

"For Zoe."

Pete smiled. "Sure, bring her home. I'll respect her choice to sleep in a different room from you. But if she gets cold on the couch, I have a nice warm bed."

Finally Justin's eyes jumped back to Pete's face. "I told you she's going out with me! We've been hanging out almost every day for three weeks now."

"Uh huh." Pete kept smiling. How Justin wished that he and Zoe were moving into their own place together. Maybe that would come next.

It only took two trips in Pete's car to transfer Zoe's belongings to the new house. Having to enlist Pete's help in the move had clouded Justin's day, but they needed a car. Sam was too busy to loan his, Gillis' van was broken with no money to fix it, and Justin, like Zoe and her former roommates, lacked a car.

Zoe tried to remain pleasant and appreciative of the moving help and her new rent-free residence, but inside she was freaking out. It was probably the closest she would ever come to being married off to another village, leaving behind everyone she knew for an unfamiliar culture and a bunch of weird customs. And inhabiting the living room would put her on display all the time. She knew Gillis and Pete only as customers. Even Justin, well, he'd been a customer a lot longer than he'd been whatever he was now. And was Pete going to ogle her 24/7 and annoy her with cheesy pickup lines?

Zoe felt demoted. In her former residence, she was the major breadwinner, the closest thing to a responsible adult. But now she was Justin's little girly, the leech on the sofa. She knew she would sleep her way into Justin's room soon, if only because she was too sick to live on the couch, where people would stare at her and expect her to chit chat.

Her first night on the couch, after Justin had kissed her and everybody had finally gone to their respective rooms, Zoe cried in the dark. She desperately wanted to go home. Her friends were still staying at the house, probably waiting for the law to show up before they'd budge. They hadn't understood why she was leaving already. The official eviction date was still almost a week away.

The blanket kept getting mussed up, and Zoe felt the scratchy couch on her face, then on her forearm. Every time she turned over, the blankets got more tangled, and the couch found more of her sensitive skin to scratch. It was a very long night, and she didn't get the hang of the couch until first light. Then she fell asleep just in time for various housemates to wake up and make noise. She kept her eyes closed while several people elaborately tiptoed through the living room. Way too early, someone sat at the end of the couch, just past her feet. "You awake?" came Justin's voice. She kept her eyes shut. "You like pancakes?" he went on, as though he knew she were awake. When she didn't answer, he just sat there, rubbing her foot in an annoying way that made her want to kick him.

"I don't really eat breakfast," she said when it seemed obvious he would never leave.

"You need to take care of yourself," he said in a gentle, motherly tone, ten times as maternal as anything Zoe's mother had conjured in a decade or two. "I want to take good care of you," he said softly, squeezing her foot.

"I don't need taking care of," Zoe said. "I appreciate you letting me stay on your couch, but I'm going to get my shit together and find a new place real soon." Zoe was so weak she could barely lift her head, and her skin felt like someone was sticking her with needles. She wasn't going anywhere anytime soon, and she feared that was obvious to both of them.

They fell into a routine for the first week. They spent the mornings together doing quiet things that required little energy, no money, and not having to leave the house. Outside was much too cold and wet for Zoe's condition. Sometimes Justin read to her. She didn't listen to the words, but liked the sound of his voice, his goodness and desire to please her. Other days, he read political books while she listened to music. They were extremely polite to each other. Justin insisted Zoe should listen to her CDs through his speakers, but she knew he secretly disliked techno, so used headphones. T-Bone called once, and another time the twins called. They were staying with Rex's friend that always got him high, but Zoe could tell they'd have to find somewhere else to stay before long. People can only take so much freeloading. The thought made her cringe. Poor Justin. Her friends couldn't do anything worse than what she was doing right now.

The word "dying" did not pass between them. Justin brought home library books on homeopathy, healing the immune system, fitness, diet, yoga, biofeedback, stress disease, fibromyalgia, chronic fatigue, psychic distress and healing with sound. He tried to hide the more diagnostic books. The piles of books reminded her of *You Don't Have to Die!* She wondered if it was still on the shelf at Powell's.

In the early afternoon, Zoe went to work for her four-hour shift. When she was through, Justin was already gone to survey people on the phone. This was the strangest time of day. It was a relief to escape the pressure of Justin's love. People in love think they are light, their heads full of helium, rising up into the air. But they are pressing against the beloved, and every lovey dovey glance is a prod, love me, love me, please love me back! Yet other times, Justin's love was a pillow to float upon. Zoe couldn't explain it. In short, her evenings were free of Justin, but this wasn't always good.

The best thing about the evenings was that if she wanted to be alone, she could go into Justin's room and close the door. She could lie on his bed and close her eyes and drift in her pool of fatigue, having dreamy dreams like she was smoking opium. Or she would look at Justin's room and try to understand the life of the person who had taken her in. His room was tidy and bright, with peach walls and a white comforter. Had he cleaned it up for her? Was he really a neat person? On his walls hung art prints – Picasso and Chagall. She wondered if he'd had the same prints back when he was in college ten years ago or whenever, because the edges of the pictures were stained yellow from old tape.

He actually lectured her on education! He blushed when he told her he had dropped out of college, and grilled her about why she had never gotten past one part-time semester of community college. It was sort of cute, but surreal. Nobody in her family, no guidance counselors or teachers, had ever encouraged her one way or another about college. And here Justin was, caring as usual, and failing to see that the couch was her deathbed. This girl's college days were over, no matter that those days only added up to six credits of general ed at Mount Hood Community College.

Zoe felt grateful, but not sexual. Justin gave her everything– a roof, food, attention, tenderness, a surfeit of maternal concern. But who wants to fuck her mother?

Ever since that night at Powell's, they held hands often, and exchanged tentative goodnight kisses. But he was waiting to see when and if she would escalate their contact. Zoe had never found sex very satisfying, and now it seemed more inconvenient than important. She wished she could muster more interest, because how else did she have to repay him?

CHAPTER TWELVE

On Zoe's sixth morning in the house, Justin overslept. When he saw the clock, he moaned. Ten AM! He had wasted a precious hour or two he could have spent with her!

He pulled on his jeans and a clean blue T-shirt. The house was freezing because they were always trying to conserve on the bills. Zoe must be turning to ice in the living room. He'd have to find her more blankets or pay extra for some heat. He pulled on his red hooded sweatshirt. Was it ugly and unfashionable? He had no idea. He went in the bathroom and pissed, brushed his teeth, shaved too fast and cut his chin. "Shit!" he muttered. Then he rushed downstairs to see the girl he loved.

Zoe and Pete sat side by side on the couch. Zoe balanced a plate of scrambled eggs and tempeh bacon on her lap. Pete strummed his acoustic guitar, his empty plate on the floor. Justin hadn't seen much of Pete for the last few days. He figured his housemate had been sulking. But Justin overslept one day, and the motherfucker was moving in on him!

"Well, aren't we spiffy," Pete said, grinning.

"Huh?"

"Looking good for first thing in the morning."

"Thanks," Justin said acidly. "Where did you get that food?"

"I cooked it," Pete said. "Where do you think I got it?"

"Since when did you learn to cook? I've never seen you cook anything in my life!"

"You want my eggs?" Zoe asked, holding her plate toward Justin. "I'm pretty full." Her pale wrist stuck out of a green thermal underwear top. Her eyes met his with an apology for being in enemy camp.

"No," Justin said. "You eat them. You need your strength." She took another bite of the fake bacon, chewing mechanically like all food tasted the same to her.

"Sit down," Zoe said when he continued to stand awkwardly, like a moron, in his own fucking living room. So then they all sat in a row and Justin couldn't think of a single conversational topic.

"How do you sleep on this thing?" Pete finally asked. "I think I've got a spring in my ass."

"It's fine," Zoe said. She didn't look like she had been enjoying Pete's attention, but what did Justin know about girls? Then, like a miracle, she set her plate on the coffee table and took Justin's hand quietly in hers. A warm wave of relief flooded his body, though a few seconds later it occurred to him to see if she was holding Pete's hand, too. She wasn't.

"You going to work today?" Justin asked Pete.

"Nope," he said, strumming a C chord, one of the few that Justin knew.

Justin wondered what he used to talk to Pete about. It seemed like in the past, they got along fine. Why hadn't he ever noticed Pete was the smarmiest, most annoying guy on earth? Cooking eggs and tempeh bacon, for Christ's sake! Usually Justin saw the oaf eating straight out of cans.

"Thanks for cooking," Zoe finally said. "Do you mind if I lie down in your room for a little while?" she asked Justin.

"No, of course not. Are you okay?" She looked more delicate every day, despite his attempts to care for her. "Can I do anything for you?" he asked hopefully, sick of feeling powerless.

She shook her head and smiled sweetly. She leaned all her weight on him as she struggled off the couch. All her weight felt like a bird skeleton. She moved slowly toward the stairs, seeming simultaneously like a waif and an old person. They heard Justin's door close softly behind her.

Justin looked stonily at the coffee table. Pete started laughing. "You should see your face, bro! Jesus, I made the girl some eggs!" Justin shook his head, not looking at Pete. "Do I need to point out that the girl is still sleeping on the couch? I always heard lovebirds like to share a nest." And then the bastard made revolting cooing noises.

"Fuck off."

"She's in your nest right now. That was a come on if I ever heard one!"

"Fuck off! Can't you see the girl is really, really sick?" Justin turned a tortured face to Pete, who stopped laughing.

"Look, man, it's very nice you're trying to provide her with a healthy environment and all that shit," Pete said soothingly. "But she won't get off the smack unless she's good and ready."

"What? She's not on smack!"

"Open your eyes, man! She's skinny and weak and strung out! It's very touching that you love her and you know I like her a lot, too. But if any of us owned anything worth stealing, I'd say no way could she stay here!"

"You are so wrong," Justin said, hating himself for trying to picture her arms in T-shirts. "Have you ever seen a needle mark on her?"

"Lots of girls shoot up in the ass and thigh so no one sees. You seen her ass and thighs yet, buddy?"

"Fuck you."

"I'm not saying she's a bad person. She's young. She hangs out with all those little druggies. Maybe she'll straighten out. But watch yourself, man. You're taking all this really, really seriously."

After that conversation, Justin went through an ugly suspicious phase where he noticed how often Zoe went to the bathroom and how long she stayed in there. Nothing seemed out of order about her bathroom usage, and she surely wouldn't shoot up in the living room. No, it wasn't drugs and he'd known that all along. He hated Pete.

About this time, more reports popped up on Indymedia about police harassing local activists in their apartments. Cops would show up at the door and insist they could come in without a search warrant. Everybody was confused about legality. Search and seizure was now A-OK with the government, as far as anyone could tell. Dale ranted to Justin and Gillis and whoever else would listen, telling stories of cops dropping by the homes of activist leaders, finding one joint and locking them up. Justin didn't know any of these people personally. It was hard to know what to believe. Anybody could post on Indymedia, and who was to say whether it was really true? Dale seemed more paranoid every day.

Justin had been disillusioned by the U.S. government long ago. He wasn't one of these innocents who think the president cares about the average Joe in America, let alone the nameless brown hordes of the Middle East, Africa, or the Mongolian Steppe. Now he was shocked to find that he could still be shocked. He hadn't wanted to believe that libraries, video stores and booksellers could be forced to disclose patrons' borrowing or buying records. He didn't want to think federal agents could come into his house while he was at work, look through all his shit, and he'd never even know they'd been there. He thought the name "Homeland Security" sounded awfully *1984,* and he would not be bullied into snitching on his neighbors' every slightly suspicious activity. Justin had heard and read enough to believe that his government would do just about anything in other countries, but it was harder to get used to the shit going down here. But the scariest part was, nobody except marginal characters like Justin and his friends seemed to care! The newspapers reported it all in laudatory terms, as though the citizens were now safe. Even if they could be safeguarded, nobody asked whether it was worth losing the rights that used to set Americans apart from the citizens of most of the world. And how could a country that ranted about democracy and freedom convince everybody in mainstream America that dissent was unpatriotic, perhaps even a terrorist activity? Ultimately, Justin was angry that people could be stupid enough to believe the government, or apathetic enough not to care.

Most everybody Justin knew felt that something was about to give, and the media stoked this suspicion. Every other week they warned the citizenry to be on "orange alert." Government drones released vague documents about how people needed to be especially careful for the next three days. But how to be careful was never explained. Justin heard that one man had been detained for *not* having an American flag on his property, but he was 90 percent sure that this was untrue.

Sometimes Justin tried to talk to Zoe about politics, but she was completely unmoved. He found her apathy unnerving, and disliked her acceptance of her own powerlessness. Everyone else he knew wrung their hands in frustration. They foresaw glaciers melting, land disappearing beneath expanded seas, whole countries overheating past the point of sustaining life, society dissolving into warring tribes who would compete for whatever food could be grown in the depleted soil, educated people reduced to savagery in a single generation. But talking to Zoe, one would think the world were as peaceful as a postcard of a placid lake, blue sky and pine trees. A few times, Justin had disloyal thoughts, wondering if she wasn't smart enough to care. But mostly he told himself that she was very ill, that exerting the energy to rant was the privilege of the healthy. Then he thought what a shitty person he was to judge Zoe when he should be appreciating how lucky he was to have perfect health.

Late one night when Zoe had been staying on the couch for about a week, she and Justin were lying on his bed. She flipped through a rave fashion magazine called *Trip*. Justin studied his voter's guide for Portland's latest mail-in election. Justin wasn't sure how frequent the elections actually were. They seemed to happen every three months. "Is your ballot still going to your old place?" Justin asked, bored of reading pros and cons on a tax measure for social services. He knew he would vote yes, but he always felt compelled to read these things thoroughly. Besides, it only raised the property tax, and house-owning yuppies could certainly afford to cough up a little something for the less advantaged.

"Huh?" she asked.

Justin glanced over and saw *Trip* was open to a fashion spread. A pale, skinny boy in black and a pale, skinny girl in pink were looking hot in the desert. "Your ballot. For voting."

"Oh, I don't vote," she said absently.

"At all?" Justin asked. She shook her head. "But surely in the presidential elections?"

"I've never voted. Not even once."

He stared at her, wondering why he was surprised.

She laughed. "You look like I said I like to molest children," she said.

"Sorry. I just, well, I guess I was raised to think it was important. I don't think I've ever missed an election."

Her eyes softened. "That's really cute," she said. Then she leaned over and kissed him. For real this time, with her hands around the back of his head and her lips parting. He pulled her against him and she was tiny in his arms, like a wishbone. Her kisses were slow and tender. He caressed her hair and back. She felt sacred to him. She touched the front of his jeans.

"Not yet," he whispered. He didn't want to go too far tonight; he was afraid his heart would explode, or he would break her into pieces. "Let me just hold you tonight. Sleep in my bed with me." He meant forever, but he wouldn't let on to her.

Suddenly he imagined a whole future for himself, so fully formed that it must have already been lurking in his subconscious. He would nurse Zoe back to health. They would get their own place together. He would find a better job and support her while she finished her B.A. They would marry. He even foresaw children, something that had never seemed relevant before. It blew his mind, this vision. It was so square, so fifties! And who wanted children these days, when Earth would only be inhabitable for another three decades, tops. But suddenly he knew in his heart that all this was exactly what he wanted. Pretty much what his parents had, without the descent into alcoholism or the dubious improvement of recovery.

"What's wrong?" she whispered, her hand lingering on his belt. "Don't you want to?"

"Well, yeah, of course. But do you really want to? Don't you think we should wait?"

"For what?" she asked. He couldn't say till we're engaged or have our own place or come up with names for the children. He tried to think of the right words, but she already had his belt open and was starting on his zipper.

"Well, uh, isn't it kind of sudden? And aren't you pretty sick?"

"Ssh." She kissed him. He gave in.

It wasn't like with anybody else, ever. Her aggression was spent by the time she'd unzipped his pants, so it was up to him. She was quiet, except for ragged breathing. Most of the girls had moaned, cried out, scratched his back, surprised him with nasty talk, told him exactly how they wanted it, or all of the above. Either that, or they had been young girls when he was a young guy, all ignorance and awkwardness. But Zoe's passivity wasn't cold or uncomfortable. It was yielding. He felt subtle currents of energy running through her body. She was definitely engaged in their lovemaking, even if she wasn't hollering. He thought again of how she reminded him of a postcard, placid lake, blue skies and pine trees. This was like diving into that lake, and it was every bit as perfect and refreshing as it looked on the postcard.

Zoe slept in Justin's room from that night on.

CHAPTER THIRTEEN

When Zoe started having a hard time getting to work at two in the afternoon, she knew her condition was worsening. She told herself that it was only four hours a day, and she badly needed the money, so there was no way she could be too weak for this little job. Justin walked her to work every day, and if the morning girl had left the place messy, he would wipe tables, straighten chairs and take out the garbage. On his days off, he stayed for her whole shift and did almost all of the cleaning. Her job had never been half this easy, and she wasn't ready to admit it was still too much.

Her regular customers were patient, but sometimes strangers fidgeted in line or sang out, "How long is my mocha going to take?" She used to be quick without trying. Now she got short of breath just grinding coffee. And she had become clumsy. She broke two plates, a mug and a saucer in a single shift. Things slid from her fingers, maybe because her hands were often numb.

In just a few weeks, Zoe's feelings toward Justin had altered radically. She hated to imagine what would have become of her without him. Her friends didn't call anymore, and her family didn't have her new number. Would she be sleeping on the streets if he hadn't come along? But she felt more than gratitude. She was awed by his kindness and generosity, and his patience with her. He made her wish she had been a better person, someone who truly cared about the world's unfortunates. She brewed fair trade coffee all day at Jojo's, but she hadn't known what that meant until Justin educated her about the global coffee business and the lives of the workers. He knew all about pesticides and cancer, babies with too many fingers, rich companies that denied a doctor's visit to loyal workers. Zoe felt unworthy of Justin's love. She realized he had probably assumed she was more socially aware because of her workplace. But in fact she had seen the help wanted sign at Jojo's and put in an application the same day she had applied for nine other low paying customer service positions, including one at Starbucks. She vowed she would never tell him about that. And what if Starbucks had hired her? She never would have met Justin. And who would have caught her when she fell ill?

One afternoon Zoe watched Justin, Gillis, Dale and Xena discussing the president. It was afternoon at Jojo's, grayness outside the windows, cozy within. Only a few other customers were there: a high school couple holding hands while they shared a mocha with extra whipped cream; two middle-aged ladies who came in every week and earnestly discussed their recovery from alcoholism, oblivious to customers who couldn't help overhearing; and the quiet fellow with a mustache who seemed to spend more and more time reading in the same chair.

Today Dale was as impassioned as a TV preacher. "Something's got to be done," he cried. Zoe saw Xena pull her hand out of Dale's, and wondered if he was squeezing the shit out of it in his fervor. "There's got to be some way to get to him. But the goddamned Secret Service, who's a match for them?" His face was red. He was standing now, his long arms swinging wildly. Zoe wondered what it would be like to burn with passion about a political issue, or anything else, for that matter. The high schoolers and the alcoholic women stared openly. The mustached man pretended to keep reading, but Zoe could see him watching Dale from the corner of his eye. Xena tugged on Dale's shirt, coaxing him to sit back down. But Zoe really didn't care if they heard Dale all the way to Gresham. She enjoyed this display of passion like others might enjoy the opera.

Dale rattled off the possibilities, and the dangers in each of them. Of course, letter bombs were out, he said. How could you ever get to the chief executive through the mail? Hopeless. And guns were out; none of them could shoot as well as the Secret Service.

"How about you hire a pro golfer as an assassin?" Justin asked. "All those kind of people golf, right? Well, my father took up golfing a while back, and Mom had a fit. Said it was dangerous because if someone hits you right here between the eyes, that's it." Justin winked at Zoe, making her feel included, sharing his joke with her. "So we just need to find a left-wing golf pro."

"That is the dumbest thing I ever heard!" Dale thundered. "Fuck! Your bourgeois roots are showing again. You sure you're not a narc?"

"Come on, man," Gillis said, holding his hands up. "Justin's cool."

"You fuckwads don't take this shit seriously! Well, we're going to have to do something. Either we go to Washington, or we're ready to act when that buffoon comes here."

"He's coming here?" Justin asked.

"Sooner or later," Dale said. "Those fuckers always come around trying to influence right wing motherfuckers or squeezing money out of them or lying to the people or some shit. But how much more shit is he gonna do while we're waiting for him to come to us?" Then Dale barked at Justin, who had stood up, "Where are you going?"

"Getting more coffee."

"How can you think about your pathetic little desires at a time like this? We're coming up with a plan here."

"It will help me think," Justin said, walking toward Zoe with his empty mug. At the counter, he leaned over and kissed her on the cheek. "He's gone off his nut," he whispered. "I'm not sure how to get him out of here without him throwing something or trying to beat us all up."

Zoe shrugged, smiling. "I like listening to you guys talk."

Justin laughed. "I don't think this can be good for business."

"It's slow anyway," she said. The high school kids were giggling. To them, this was entertainment. The guy with the mustache came in all the time, so he certainly knew what to expect. And the two women, it was probably good for them to get their minds off alcoholism now and then.

"I hope you don't think I'm as crazy as Dale," Justin said.

"I don't think any of you are crazy. You're passionate. You have a cause, something to live for." She felt a stupid tear of self pity and had to pretend she was pushing her hair back to rub it away. Maybe she was dying because she had no impact on anything. She was obsolete, a ghost. Maybe she was dead already. She forced herself to smile at Justin. "You want a mocha or a latte or something?" she asked. "No charge."

"Just coffee, Zoe. And you know I can't let you give me things for free. I couldn't endanger your job."

She refilled his cup. She loved him.

CHAPTER FOURTEEN

Justin made appointments with three doctors, an acupuncturist and a chiropractor in the month that Zoe lived with him. But she refused his every attempt to diagnose or heal her. He worried he was doing something wrong because despite his love and attention, she was not getting better. If only he had a car, it would be so much easier to trick her into visiting a doctor.

Pete still thought Zoe was on heroin. And although Justin had now seen all of Zoe's body and knew she had no track marks, he decided it was easier to let Pete think what he wanted. Cause wasn't it even worse to have a girlfriend who was wasting away from unknown causes and wouldn't see a doctor?

Was it anorexia? Bulimia? Cancer? Lupus? Leukemia? AIDS?

But he couldn't pressure her. Whenever he asked the least intrusive question about her condition, she withdrew far into herself. Not until the subject was thoroughly changed would she revert to being normal, sweet and loving.

There came a day when Zoe had to stop and rest on their two-block walk to the café, even though she was leaning most of her weight on Justin. "I feel a little dizzy," she said, smiling at him in a way he recognized was supposed to ease his mind. He wondered if inside she was scared shitless. She sat on someone's retaining wall, not noticing that it was wet and muddy. Her hair hung in her face, her breath made quick puffs of white in the chilly air. Rain splatted on her head.

Justin couldn't let her sit there, helpless. So he scooped her up in his arms.

"What are you doing?" she protested.

"Taking you home."

"No!" she howled with surprising force, right in his ear. "No! I'll lose my job!" She sounded desperate. "She'll fire me."

Justin couldn't take her distress, so he carried her to Jojo's. He knew it was stupid. A girl this sick should be home in bed or maybe in the hospital. "I'm sure she wouldn't fire you," he muttered.

"Yes she would. Switching shifts was my last chance."

"Oh," Justin said, pieces falling together in his head. He called his work and told them he would be two hours late. He had to watch it or he'd be fired himself. He stayed with Zoe and did just about everything except handle the money and work the espresso machine. Then he took her home, put her to bed, and took the bus downtown to work.

All through his shift, Justin juggled numbers. When he couldn't make them add up in his head, he jotted columns on a notepad. He would have to support both of them. She wasn't expensive because she hardly ate and didn't strain their utilities. But the things he wanted to buy her! That was something else entirely. Most of all, he wanted to buy her an engagement ring. No, medical bills and then a ring. Or would that look as if he had no faith in her getting well? Hell, he'd give her the ring in the waiting room. If she'd ever go to the doctor. If he ever had money.

His voice sounded mournful as the calls rang through. "Just a few quick questions tonight," he said. "First, would you say that the current rate of inflation will make people's social security benefits obsolete in thirty years? How about in twenty?" People hung up less than usual. Maybe it was better to sound sad than phony. Justin often thought of the word "phony" and wondered if it sprang from these sort of telephone calls. Or was the word older than telemarketing? Maybe it referred to how old telephones distorted voices. If they did. "And the last question tonight is how much money would you contribute annually to an IRA if it would be entirely tax deductible?" Some people just laughed. Justin wasn't the only one without enough money.

When the last few minutes finally ticked past, freeing Justin from his prison of measured time, he rushed to the bus stop. He had retired the bright Guatemalan hat and now wore a plain black stocking cap. It wasn't as water resistant as his previous hat, which he secretly missed.

As he waited for his bus, he caught a glimpse of a figure across the street, lurking in a doorway. So what, he told himself, fighting against an inexplicable case of the creeps. People were always lurking, that was the nature of every big city downtown. People lurked all the time and it didn't bother Justin. He had a feeling like this character was watching him. Justin kept an eye toward the doorway across the street, but nothing moved. Now that he thought about it, he'd had a prickly feeling since the day before, when Dale had told him about the new network of surveillance cameras that were being installed downtown. Maybe they were already in place. Maybe he had the creepy feeling of being watched because somebody in a control center somewhere really was watching him. Dale said that New York already had 150 public cameras, allegedly designed to stop terrorism.

The bus arrived, bright and warm and welcoming. Justin had an impulse to tip the driver, then realized that would look funny. But to whom would it look funny? He found himself glancing suspiciously around the bus, which only a few seconds ago had felt safe and wholesome. Then he worried that the seven other passengers would notice his furtive glances and think he was some paranoid tweaker looking to follow them at their stop and bash their head in for a few dollars to buy more meth. He tried to look out the window, but just saw his reflection staring back. Instead, he looked down at his knees.

He ached to get home to Zoe. And at the phrase "home to Zoe," warmth shot through his body. She was home to him now, a safe harbor. His skinny, sickly girl felt like protection from everything wrong with society. Is happiness protection? Or just the opposite? He took his fearful, scattered mind in hand and told it sternly that tonight he would believe in love and happiness as the best protection from the nameless gray dread that looked for every crack through which to seep.

Maybe I'm insane, he thought, but at least I'm in love. It would be sadder to be insane and loveless.

At home, he found her asleep in his bed, the light on his nightstand still glowing. He kicked off his shoes and climbed in bed with his clothes on, too eager to hold her to undress. She moaned, mostly asleep. He held her too tightly, feeling the flutter of her heart, the quick risings and fallings of her chest.

In the dark, holding the sleeping Zoe, Justin experienced at least thirty minutes of full on peace and well being. All the bad parts of his mind shut down and the purest part of himself, which he had never even known was there, bloomed silently in the night. Later he would hold onto this as the most perfect time in his life. But then he fell asleep, and when he awoke, his mind was working in its usual way, plaguing and irritating him.

Justin and Zoe lay on his bed that morning. While gazing out the window at the rain, Justin suddenly put down his book about CIA operations in Latin America and asked her to quit her job.

"Huh?" She cocked her head like a dog.

"Then you can rest as much as you need to. To get better." He wanted to pet her hair, but she looked so adult and remote all of a sudden.

"But Justin, how would I live?"

"I'll take care of you."

"You're already doing way too much." Her mouth drew down and her forehead creased. Was she angry at him? "I'm already too dependent on you."

"It's okay to depend on me until you get better. It makes me happy when I can help you." Her breath was getting shallow again. He had to make his case, somehow. "I'm afraid you're working yourself to death," Justin said. It slipped out, just an expression, but it seemed to hit the bed between them like a cannon ball. He looked away, distracting them with more talk, not knowing what he'd say and surprising them both. "I want to marry you."

"Huh?" Panic crossed her face, then she was looking around the room and moving toward her shoes. "I've got to go out for a while," she said.

Justin remained on the bed, jaw clamped tight despite his urge to protest, shocked by his stupidity. Had he really mentioned death and marriage in the same ten second span? He realized he was silently repeating some sappy bumper sticker that had been popular a decade or two ago: *If you love something, set it free. If it loves you, it will come back to you.* Or something like that. He told himself that's why he didn't try to stop Zoe from putting on her second shoe. But honestly he didn't think she'd get past the stairs in her condition. He didn't have much chance of losing the one he loved, because she was too sick to get away. He felt a pain in his gut, wondering if he ever would have got this far with the girl if she hadn't been sick. Not in this lifetime, you sorry sack of shit, said the voice in his head. It sounded like his mother's, but more direct.

Zoe made it down the stairs and out the door. Justin heard it thud gently behind her. "Shit," he said, laying back on the bed and covering his eyes.

CHAPTER FIFTEEN

Zoe wasn't dressed for the weather. She had not stopped long enough to put a jacket on, so wore only the sweatpants and light sweater she'd slept in. The pants were designed to be tight hiphuggers for a skinny girl, but since Zoe was way past skinny now, she had trouble keeping them up. Every few steps she tugged at the waistband, hoping her crack didn't show. She had no clue where to go. She felt seriously freaked out.

What was wrong with Justin? Was he pathologically nice? It's not normal to want to marry a dying girl. Did he love her? Or did he love her dying, her need, her dependence?

Rain plopped on her hair, which was thinner now. Her scalp felt each drop like a little ice pick. Every step felt like it drove shards of glass through her veins. She wanted to be at her old house, bullshitting with Rex and T-Bone and the twins. She plodded along, nowhere to go. Her feet automatically took her to the café. Brenda stood behind the counter, scrubbing the milk steamer with steel wool, her back to the customers. Zoe stood in the doorway of the apartment building next door, peering around to look in the window. This had been her shift for almost a year, the longest she had held any job. Her hours, her money, her customers. The alcoholic ladies sat in the middle of the café, talking earnestly. A cute young college student, whom Zoe always felt shy around, read an art history book. Dale and Gillis were in there early, drinking coffee, Dale's hands gesticulating and Gillis' saying whoa, man, calm down. The man with the mustache sat reading the front page of the *Oregonian,* whose headline read, "President Visits Portland." Zoe smiled, figuring she knew what Dale was ranting about today. She had this nostalgic feeling looking at the café tableau, maybe like someone in California feels when she gets a Christmas card with a beautiful snow scene and it reminds her of her childhood in Kansas. Zoe hung by the window feeling mothlike, a forgotten ghost.

Dale and Gillis stood up. Zoe didn't want them to see her pathetically lurking about, so she grabbed a copy of *Just Out,* the gay paper, that someone had discarded on the apartment steps. She noticed the guy with the mustache stand up, too. Usually a model customer, he left his mug and his crumb-covered plate on the table instead of bussing it. All three seemed to be leaving, so Zoe backed into the stairwell and held the paper up in front of her face. She was staring at an article on a gay Filipino singer– "the thrilla' from Manila" – when she heard the man with the mustache say, "Excuse me, I'm with the FBI. And I need to ask you both some questions." Zoe stood rigid behind the newspaper. She stifled a gasp.

"What's this about?" Gillis said, sounding scared.

"I think we should talk somewhere else. Come with me, please," the man said. Zoe yearned to peek past her paper and see if the man had a gun on Dale and Gillis. She couldn't imagine what else would keep Dale from going apeshit. But Zoe didn't dare move. As it was, she was just out of their line of vision. She squeezed her eyes shut, willing them to walk in the other direction. If they walked by her doorway, she didn't know what the man would do to her. She got the feeling that Dale and Gillis were supposed to just disappear.

None of the three said anything else. Zoe heard their footsteps walking away from her.

Zoe's heart pounded so fast she saw only black for a few seconds. She worked to slow her breathing. I won't pass out, she told herself, I can slow my heart like those guys in Tibet or India or wherever. She heard a car start up and drive off, but was it the right one? What if the FBI agent just questioned them in his car, right there on Clinton Street, and saw her leaving the doorway? She made herself count ten long, slow breaths. Then she lowered her newspaper and peered over it. Nothing out of the ordinary. Just act cool, she told herself. She folded the newspaper and tucked it under her arm in case she needed it again. She stood slowly, her hand on the wall so she wouldn't faint. She stepped out onto the sidewalk.

Terror after terror chased through Zoe's head as she hurried home. What if they had come for Justin, too? What if she came home to find the house empty? She had always found their political talk cute and harmless, healthy in its optimism that nobodies like them could do anything about the government. Never had it occurred to her that anybody important would take them seriously. Now they gained a new significance in her mind, a kind of glory. Nobody ever took Rex or T-Bone seriously. They had never done anything of import, even in their fantasies. A federal agent wouldn't have any cause to ask Rex or T-Bone a thing, except maybe the time. No, Rex and T-Bone wouldn't even know that.

The sharp energy of fear ran through her body, fueling this vital errand. She covered the two blocks home almost as fast as a healthy girl.

She burst into the living room to find a scene of tranquility. Pete sat on the couch, eating cereal out of a mixing bowl and thumbing through a Victoria's Secret catalogue. "Hey, where you been?" he said, using the bowl to cover his reading material.

But Zoe raced past him, taking the stairs two at a time, and burst into Justin's room. "The FBI took Dale and Gillis away!" she cried, panting.

"Huh?" Justin asked. The room was dim, but Zoe could see Justin face down on the bed. She got the feeling he had been crying.

"At the café! The guy with the mustache who reads the *Oregonian* for half the day." She had to stop for breath. "I was outside, they didn't see me," she gasped. "He said, 'I'm with the FBI and I have to ask you some questions' and they went away with him."

"The FBI? The fucking FBI?" Justin sprang out from under the covers. "What would the FBI want with them? What has that crazy bastard done now?"

Zoe shrugged, helpless. Already her body was telling her she was going to pay a toll for hurrying it like that. She lay down on the bed, trying to preserve what little strength she had.

"I mean, it's not just the police," Justin said. "The police all know Dale. But the FBI doesn't come for billboards, does it? What else has he been up to?" Justin paced as he talked. Zoe closed her eyes; his pacing made her dizzy.

"You think Pete knows anything?" she asked.

"Is he here?" Justin asked. Zoe nodded. Justin strode toward the stairs. "Pete!" he called down.

"Yeah?"

"Come up here. Fast." Justin's voice made Pete obey. He appeared in the bedroom in about five seconds.

"What's going on?" he asked, sleepiness fighting panic on his face. "Did she O.D.?" He still held his spoon.

"No! Zoe saw an FBI agent taking Gillis and Dale away."

"What?!" Pete said, then started laughing. "What is this, April Fool's?"

"No, you idiot, it's barely even March!" Justin snapped.

Pete stopped laughing, but looked far from convinced. "Surely you saw some kind of joke," Pete said to Zoe. "Some friend of his playing a prank. I mean, what would the FBI want with a pair of clowns like them?"

Zoe told him exactly what she had seen. Her voice was quiet and strained by chest pains.

"Jesus," Pete said, his face going pale. "Jesus. I know just who you mean. Definitely not a friend of Dale's. I thought he was some down on his luck, laid off middle management type. I figured he spent his unemployment checks on lattes."

"Mochas," Zoe said feebly.

"Huh?" Pete said.

"He drank mochas. Single shot, extra chocolate."

"Fucking Christ," Justin said. "That explains how he could spend so much time looking at the *Oregonian*. He wasn't reading the fucking thing."

"The *Oregonian*," Zoe said, remembering the headline. "Did you know the president is coming to Portland?"

Pete and Justin stared at each other. Justin's jaw dropped open. "You don't think he was planning something," Justin said slowly.

"Wait," Pete said. "Wait." He sat on the edge of the bed beside Zoe, holding his head like it ached. "I don't like the sound of that. Planning something. I mean, it wasn't really a plan. It was just a bunch of bullshit talk. Letting off steam. Wasn't it?"

"I wish I could remember what he said. What we said. I can't think straight. I wish I had it on tape and could go back and listen to it."

"Somebody probably has it on tape," Pete said.

"Oh, Jesus. What did we say?" Justin implored Zoe. "Do you ever pay attention to what we're talking about while you work?"

"Well, killing the president. Mostly," Zoe said quietly. "You talk about whether you should go to Washington, DC or wait till he comes here."

"No! But that's just a bunch of bullshitting! Just guys talking," Pete said. "And it's mostly Dale. Do I ever say anything?" Pete asked Zoe.

"I don't remember anything. I don't think so."

"What have I said?" Justin asked hopefully.

"Well, you were joking about killing him with a golf ball just the other day. Do you think they know that's a joke?"

Pete and Justin both groaned. "They're not famous for their sense of humor." Pete's tone was light, but his face showed real concern. Zoe had never seen that look on Pete's face before, especially not when he was looking at Justin. She felt her world dropping away.

Justin was terribly pale and his body trembled. "What the fuck am I going to do? What's going to happen? Do you think they'll want to question me?"

"Maybe it's not what we think," Pete said. "Maybe Dale's up to something else, in which case they'll probably want to question all three of us." Zoe's eyes widened in alarm. She had felt a premonition of loss, but hadn't thought about having to talk to those people. "But if we're not just being paranoid, then you're in big trouble and I might be, too." Zoe couldn't help admiring how calm Pete was, still able to function and think. "Since we don't know if you're in trouble or not, I think you should go on a vacation."

"Vacation?" Justin asked, surprised. "A vacation where?"

"Underground." Pete turned his attention back to Zoe. "Try to remember if you ever heard me say anything incriminating while that guy was around. Think hard."

Zoe tried to remember. "I don't know," she said. "I don't usually pay that much attention. And I can't hear a thing over the espresso machine."

"I don't think they have anything on me," Pete said. "Except guilt by association."

"That's all they need these days," Justin said sourly. "They can detain you for years, just for that."

"I'll take my chances," Pete said. "We can't all disappear."

"Disappear?" Justin echoed.

Pete stood now and began to pace Justin's room. "We have to act fast. They might show up any time. Justin, you're going to go away, at least for a few days till we see what's going on. I'm going to stay here, go to work as usual. Zoe's not going to miss a day of work, either."

Justin felt Zoe's whole body trembling where she lay. He gathered his courage together. "You think I'm going to go hide somewhere and leave Zoe? Jesus, Pete, I can't do that!"

"And I can't go to work," Zoe whispered.

"You'll go at two today, as usual."

"Look at her!" Justin cried. "Look how ill she is! Don't boss her around."

"You'll be fine," Pete said to Zoe.

"You're crazy!" Justin said. "None of us is fine. And we have to stick together."

Justin was starting to rally, to steel himself to face whatever was coming his way. Zoe needed him. But when they heard the knock downstairs, how could they know it was only a pimply-faced nineteen year-old who was trying to quit meth and reconstruct his battered life by selling the *Oregonian* door to door? All Justin knew was the absolute terror of huddling together in the closet, their three hearts pounding. They must have stayed there for fifteen minutes, worrying that the agents would break the door down when nobody answered.

Finally they spilled out of the closet and collapsed on the bed, gasping for air. Pete recovered quickly, pretending he hadn't been scared. Justin had barely managed to control his sphincter, and Zoe had briefly fainted. "Okay," Pete said. "I have a plan. Justin, throw together a couple of changes of clothes and your toothbrush. How much cash do you have?"

"I don't know, maybe twelve dollars."

"That's not enough. I'm going to go see what I have. Zoe, give Justin all your cash."

Zoe didn't hesitate to contribute her thirty-two dollars, though Justin tried to refuse her money. Pete found two twenties in his room.

"Any money in the bank?" Pete asked.

"A little," Justin said.

"Okay. You're going to take the bus downtown, get as much money out with your debit card as you can, then get on a Greyhound."

"I don't know where to go. Where should I go?" He sounded pathetic, but couldn't help himself.

Pete glanced at Zoe. "I'll tell you on your way out. Zoe's not going to know."

"What?" Justin cried.

"It will be easier for her when she's questioned."

Zoe gulped. "He's right," she managed to say.

"So I have to put my life in your hands?" Justin asked Pete.

"No," Pete said. "You're free to come up with any plan you want. I'm not the one who's in trouble here." His expression was the slightest bit mocking, as though he were infinitely more competent than Justin. And in many ways, Zoe could see that he was.

"What do you think?" Justin asked Zoe.

"Trust him," she said, closing her eyes.

CHAPTER SIXTEEN

Twenty minutes later, Justin was taking the bus downtown. He had thrown clothes, books, toothbrush and razor into a backpack. Pete had instructed him to empty his wallet of everything but his license, debit card and cash. No business cards, no scraps of paper with people's numbers. Nor did he bring his address book, which Pete promised to hide.

Justin tried hard not to look shifty. His armpits were wet and he glanced behind him about ten times as frequently as a normal person. Never had he been so hyper-aware, able to report that the bus held sixteen people, six males and ten females, including the driver. Everybody was white except for two black girls and one Asian man. The agent with the mustache wasn't on the bus, but surely they didn't work alone. Any of these people, at least the adults, could be the agent's partner.

Leaving Zoe had been awful. Already he knew that it would be one of the worst memories of his life. In five years, ten, twenty, if he lived that long, he would remember her scared eyes, his cracking voice saying goodbye, his shameful fear so obvious. The awful pit in his stomach, roiling with bile, knowing he left everything to Pete. He was such a coward, he had run away and left Zoe with that buffoon. Why had Zoe said to trust him? Did she lack confidence in Justin's ability to take care of himself, to take care of her? Or maybe she wanted him out of the picture, to be left alone with Pete?

The bus crossed the Hawthorne Bridge and Justin looked at the gray river below. If only the bridge were higher, jumping might be worthwhile.

He got off at Broadway. Already his furtiveness seemed ingrained. He felt like he'd been a beady-eyed, rat-faced man for years. He spotted an ATM and thought fuck it, he wasn't going to worry about the three dollar bank fee today. He cleaned out his account, removing all hundred and eighty dollars. He didn't know how he was going to pay his rent, but Pete had said to withdraw all the money.

A blond woman stood behind him at the money machine. He imagined he could feel her eyes boring into his back, that he could sense a badge and gun inside her jacket. He looked back at her three times during his transaction. She looked away. What did that mean? Did she feel caught? Or was she just a normal citizen, and he was creeping her out by looking at her so much? Did he seem too suspicious, like someone she should report to bank security?

The machine produced nine twenties and spat out his card and receipt. He grabbed everything and stuffed it all in his pocket.

The bus station was only eight blocks away. He covered the distance in five minutes, trying not to look noticeable. In fact, Justin was a very average looking Portlander. His hair was a bit shaggy, his pants faded, his face that of a good person, neither stunning nor ugly.

Pete had told him to buy a one-way ticket to Seaside. In five days, on Tuesday at two o'clock, Pete would meet Justin at the Seaside bus station to give him further instructions.

The ticket only cost twenty dollars, so Justin had almost two hundred and fifty left. He didn't know if that would even pay for a motel and food. He had been to Seaside once, with a girl, during summer. They had walked on the beach boardwalk, bought saltwater taffy, sat in the sand, browsed shops full of useless and tacky shell souvenirs, played air hockey in the arcade and ridden the Tilt a Whirl. It had only been a day trip, and they had done just about everything there was to do. Justin didn't know what he'd do with five days there, worry eating a hole in his stomach.

The bus didn't leave for half an hour. Justin sat on one of the metal chairs that were attached in rows, back to back. He looked in his backpack to see what books he had packed. One was about eighteenth and nineteenth century imperialism in Africa, another about the sorry state of democracy in the U.S. The other two were criticisms of political policies in the Middle East. He groaned. He'd always scorned people reading genre novels for escape, but now he saw the point. What safety in the certainty of a happy ending, a solved crime!

He saw a discarded heap of newspaper down the row of chairs and went to retrieve it. Turned out to be that piece of shit *USA Today.* He couldn't fathom that people could produce a newspaper even worse than the *Oregonian,* and folks all over the country would eat it up. The cover story was about the president visiting Portland on Monday. He was coming for a thousand-dollar-a-plate fundraiser for Oregon's own right-wing senator. Justin snorted. How many people could afford that sort of lunch? Who had voted for this asshole?

Justin looked around the station, at the face of the American underclass: the crazy woman talking to the Coke machine; the man trying to sleep in the seats, metal arm rest digging into his ribs, a dirty jacket cushioning his head; stoic mothers with young children; angry mothers snapping at their kids, threatening to spank their butts all the way to Cleveland if they didn't shut their mouths right now, by God. Surely these people hadn't voted for candidates who held thousand-dollar lunches?

Unable to sit, Justin prowled the station. In the newsstand, he shook his head at the saddest collection of periodicals he had ever seen. The only newspapers for sale were *USA Today* and the *Oregonian.* The magazine selection was limited to *People, Soldier of Fortune,* and six different *True Confessions* magazines, including *True Confessions Romance,* and *Sexy Hot True Confessions.* A rack of Christian paperbacks completed the choices. Ten minutes ago, Justin wouldn't have thought it possible to be more depressed. But faced with this assortment of shit, his heart sank below his knees. Was there no hope for his country people? Weren't the riders of the Greyhound the poor, the under-represented, the Americans with the most valid complaints, cynics who understood the failure of the American dream? In short, the revolutionary class? But how would they ever think of revolution when their heads were full of this stupidity? Between TV news, *People, USA Today,* football and Christianity, it was like the culture itself was giving citizens a mass lobotomy.

"Seaside, now boarding, gate two," came the voice over the loudspeaker. As he walked through gate two, it hurt to think Zoe would still be in this city and he would be a hundred miles away. It felt like he was leaving something important behind, like his spleen, a part of himself.

The bus wasn't crowded. No surprise there, as early March on the Oregon coast is notoriously unpleasant. Justin had two seats to himself, two hours on his hands to worry before he got there, and five days once he arrived. And that was just the beginning.

He pictured Zoe's face and her wasting body. He hated himself for not being a man and staying by her side.

CHAPTER SEVENTEEN

Pete walked Zoe to work that afternoon. "I want to call in sick," she had protested, but Pete was firm.

"You have to go to work every day," he said. "Now more than ever."

"Who made you in charge?" she asked.

"Justin did. By failing to act on his own. Look, Zoe, if you care about the guy at all, you have to act as normal as possible."

She sighed in reply. They had spent the hours since Justin's departure waiting for a knock or a ring.

"What did Gillis ever do?" Pete had asked three or four times. Zoe answered that Gillis had done nothing. "Then why hasn't he come home? How can they hold him?"

At least Pete didn't hang around her work this afternoon. She needed a break from his thinking aloud and his pacing.

The café felt strange to Zoe. One minute she would be comfortably steaming milk and watching espresso flow into tiny silver cups, the next she would be reliving her horror when she saw the mustached man leaving his mug on his table and following Dale and Gillis.

Pete didn't return to help her close, so Zoe had to do the exhausting work of carrying trash and sweeping the floor by herself. She thought painfully of Justin, who had always helped her. Where on earth had Pete sent him? And what sort of connections did Pete have? It was like he thought he was part of the Underground Railroad.

After counting the money, which she always did last, Zoe locked the café and stepped onto the sidewalk. A woman she had never seen strode toward her. She looked awfully professional for that neighborhood, her beige coat flapping open over a wine colored skirt that fit tight and tailored. "Excuse me," she said, stopping in front of Zoe, reaching into her coat pocket, extracting a wallet, and flipping it open to show a badge. "I need to ask you a few questions."

Zoe gulped, her eyes growing huge. "We're closed for the night," she said stupidly.

"This should only take a few minutes," the woman said firmly.

Zoe had every intention of being cool, but now her knees buckled and she felt her body falling away into darkness.

She awoke to find herself sitting on a chair in the café. Only one light was on, apparently so the agent could stare into Zoe's face, which was what she was doing when Zoe opened her eyes.

"Feeling better?" the agent asked. Her voice was neutral, as though the process would go more smoothly if Zoe was well, but the agent had no real concern either way.

"How did we get in here?" Zoe looked around.

"I used your key. Then I carried you inside and sat you in that chair." The agent might be pretty if she smiled, Zoe thought. She had curly brown hair and green eyes with lines at the corners.

"You carried me?" It was too creepy, to be toted about, unconscious, by an FBI agent.

"Yeah. You only weigh about ten pounds. Are you ill?"

"Yeah."

"What do you have?"

Zoe shrugged and looked away.

"Do you know why I'm here?"

Zoe shook her head, not looking at the agent's face.

"Are you sure you don't know?"

"Why don't you just tell me." Zoe suddenly felt too exhausted to be scared. She closed her eyes and wished she was in Justin's bed, her head underneath the covers.

"All right. We're trying to locate Justin Allen. Do you know where he is?"

Zoe shook her head, her eyes still closed.

"Do you think you could open your eyes and answer my questions aloud?" the agent asked coldly.

"No," Zoe said, opening one eye and shutting it again.

"No, you can't open your eyes and answer my questions?"

Zoe opened one eye again. "No, I meant that I don't know where he went."

"Where he went," the agent repeated. "So he went somewhere."

This bitch was too slick for Zoe. "Well, he's not here, so he must have went somewhere," Zoe said.

"Did he leave town?" the agent asked.

"I don't know. Maybe."

"You're his girlfriend?"

No one had called her that before. Was she Justin's girlfriend? "Something like that," she said.

"You live with him," the agent said, like she already knew.

"Uh huh."

"How long have you cohabitated?"

"Not long. A few weeks, I guess."

"Do you know his friends?"

"Some of them. Some of them are customers here." Obviously they already knew that.

"Do you know anything about their political activities?"

Zoe shook her head.

"Please speak up," the agent said.

Zoe realized she was probably being recorded. Her heart sped up. It was so easy to say the wrong thing. That's all Justin had done, and look where it had got him. "No," Zoe said clearly.

"Have you heard them discussing politics in here?"

"I can't hear anything over the espresso machine."

"Does Justin talk to you about politics at home?"

"I'm not very interested in politics," Zoe said. "I've never even voted." Justin had made her feel guilty about not voting, but now she felt terribly relieved. No one could accuse her of participating in the political system at all.

The agent gave her a hard look. "It doesn't sound like you have much in common with Justin Allen. What's the attraction?"

"I guess it's sexual." Zoe found herself smirking at the agent, whom she hated.

The agent pulled a business card from a jacket pocket. "Don't leave town," she said. "And if you have any change of phone numbers, or receive any kind of correspondence from Justin Allen, you are to call me and let me know immediately."

Zoe took the card and dropped it in her purse without a word.

"Do you understand?"

"Yes," Zoe said, too loudly, too clearly, conscious of the hidden tape recorder.

CHAPTER EIGHTEEN

The bus crept into Seaside at a few minutes past three. Justin reluctantly got off the bus, half expecting agents to be waiting for him.

The wind came up from the ocean, making it feel twice as cold as Portland. He walked into the bus station to get out of the rain. It was a tiny station, full of derelicts lounging in the metal chairs. A guy in a dirty blue denim shirt cleaned his nails with a pocket knife. A man who looked Native American rhythmically kicked the snack machine, saying, "Jesus! Shit! Jesus! Shit!" punctuating each word with a kick.

Justin felt conspicuous. He considered buying coffee out of the machine, to give himself a purpose. But of course it would be undrinkable. He looked at advertisements pinned up on a cork board. Three of the ads promoted local lodgings. The King Neptune boasted, "TV in every room! Ice on premises! Off season starting at $200/week!" Justin was dismayed to see that he couldn't afford the Motel Six at $41.95 per night for a lousy single room. The third option was the Seaside International Hostel, which sounded too good to be true at twenty bucks a night. The flyer advertised an espresso bar, gardens, decks, lounges, movies every evening and Internet access. Justin had never stayed in a hostel. He didn't know if a dorm room would be a good idea. Wouldn't he have to talk to people? What if they wanted to know about his life?

His eyes darted between the King Neptune and the hostel, trying to weigh the risks without knowing exactly what they were. The guy in the blue denim shirt finished cleaning his nails and licked his knife. Justin's face must have shown his horror, because several of the derelicts burst out laughing. "Hey, buddy!" called the knife licker, like a long lost friend. "The King Neptune! I lived there last winter! They'll treat you right!"

"Yeah, okay," Justin said. "Uh, thanks." He memorized the hostel address and got the hell out of the bus station. He heard more laughter behind him.

The town was small. Soon Justin was walking down the mostly deserted main street. He passed the big building that housed the neglected Tilt a Whirl, then the locked arcade. The Pig & Pancake was open, so he ducked inside to ask directions. The food smelled great. He decided to sit in a booth and ordered a real American breakfast-all-day meal: eggs, hash browns, sausage links and a pancake. One voice in his head told him to conserve money. Another voice said fuck it.

The waitress reminded him of his mother, something around her eyes and forehead that made her look like she was waiting to be disappointed, again. He'd been trying to keep thoughts of his parents out of his mind. This latest development would eclipse all the other ways he had let them down, about a thousand times over.

The waitress brought all the food and set it on Justin's table. He asked her for coffee, too, because the little silver cream pitcher on the table suddenly made him nostalgic for the restaurants his parents took him to as a child.

He gazed at his food, realizing how the government could snatch him up at any time. And if they did, he could no longer order pancakes and sausages and hash browns or even just one egg, scrambled. If they found him out here on the coast, they could grab him and lock him up, and nobody would know where he was. They could keep him as long as they wanted, torture him or not, feed him or not, and decide every single thing in the world.

His shaky hand reached for the ketchup. He wanted to use all the condiments, even the ones he didn't much like. He put salt, pepper and ketchup on his hash browns; A-1 on his sausage; syrup on his pancake; Tabasco on the eggs; cream and sugar in his coffee. The Pig & Pancake seemed to Justin like the world's best restaurant. It tasted like freedom itself.

The waitress turned out to be friendlier than she looked. "The hostel?" she asked, after giving him directions. "What are you, visiting from the Midwest? You don't have much of an accent."

"Yeah," he said. "Sure. Kansas. We talk the same there. Pretty much."

The restaurant was deserted this time of afternoon. The waitress leaned against the booth, the lines in her face relaxing. "Get lots of those hostel people in here. Germany. Australia. Do you know, they get six weeks of vacation time there?"

"Yeah. That's what I heard."

She peered at him. "You look a little low. Some girl break your heart?"

"Uh, how did you know?"

"Thought so. They always do that to the nice young men, and you look like a nice one."

Justin had a fleeting feeling of unease. Was she trying to pick up on him? But unease turned to inspiration. "I'm trying to get over her. That's why I took this trip."

"Good for you!" the waitress said, smiling and reaching out to ruffle his hair. Somebody cleared his throat and she drew her hand back. "The cook," she said, wrinkling her nose. "Always giving me a hard time for hitting it off with the customers. He's been divorced three times. He's jealous of me because I get along with people." Justin smiled at her. He really did appreciate somebody being friendly. "Well, you come back to see me. I'm here all the livelong day! You going to be around for a while?"

"A few days, I think."

"Bravo! Now you just bring this up to the register when you're ready," she said, pulling his check from her pink apron and placing it beside his elbow. She walked toward the kitchen, perhaps to argue with the cook.

The hostel was only three blocks away. The sky was so gray he couldn't tell if the sun had set. The hostel overlooked a river, he didn't know which. He walked up the front stairs of the two story building. An old purple couch and two red easy chairs sat on the porch, empty and mildewed. The door was unlocked. Inside, the décor was mismatched but cheery. He found the front desk and was prepared to tell the girl sitting there that he was from Kansas, but luckily he saw the sign saying "All guests must show ID" before he embarrassed himself.

"Hi," said the girl, who was in her twenties with shoulder length brown hair, a brown cardigan, and tortoise rimmed glasses. She was cute and looked smart.

"Hi," Justin said. "I'd like to stay for a few days."

"Are you a member?"

"No," he said, feeling suddenly panicked. Visions of a sordid week at the King Neptune flooded his brain. "Do I have to be a member?"

"No," she said, smiling to ease his distress. "Don't worry. It's just a little cheaper if you are." She had him fill out a form and looked at his ID. He braced himself for questions about why he wanted to leave Portland to visit Seaside in the bleakness of winter, and didn't he have a job and who was he, anyway. But she asked none of these. "You'll be upstairs in the men's dorm. We're not too busy right now. You only have a couple of roommates so far. Australian guys." She handed him a sheet that was stitched together on three sides, which apparently he was supposed to sleep inside like an envelope. He walked upstairs to see his temporary home.

The dorm room held four bunk beds. A dirty backpack sat on one, a purple towel hung from another. The other two looked unoccupied. He contemplated upper bunk versus lower. Lower was more cave like, good for hiding in, but also felt more trapped. Upper was more exposed, but if someone came in looking for him, he could jump atop them and maybe knock them out. He puzzled over the problem for five minutes, feeling a creeping helplessness and fear. Eventually he flung himself on the lower bunk, because it was easier.

When Justin woke up, he had the impression that it had been dark but was now extremely light. "Sorry about that, mate!" said a big Australian fellow.

"It's okay," Justin muttered, closing his eyes and rubbing his forehead. "Jesus, I didn't even know I was asleep. What time is it?"

"Half past six."

Another fellow came in behind him, this one skinnier and blond. "Oh, hello," he said.

"Hi." Justin felt too vulnerable, lying on the bed, too bleary to defend himself. Memories of the awful day rushed back. "You guys are Australian, huh?" he said before they could ask him anything.

"Yep. Come to see your country in the off season. Sure is dreary!" said the blond one. "And bloody freezing!"

Justin felt surprisingly defensive. "Well, it is March."

"At least it's cheap," said the bigger one. "And seems perfectly all right. My mum didn't want me to come, said we'd be blown up." His face looked young, maybe twenty, and Justin wondered if he still lived with his parents. "Oh, sorry, mate," he said when the other one jabbed him in the ribs. "I should mind my manners."

"It's okay," Justin said. "How long you been in Seaside?"

"Too long!" said the blond one. "About two days. This place is dead."

"Yeah. It seems kind of boring," Justin agreed.

They asked him where he was from and he said Portland. They wanted to know why he would leave a relatively happening city for Seaside. He practiced his new story. "Trying to take my mind off a girl."

The Australians laughed. "Best way to do that is find another girl," said the big one, as though he'd written the book on sex relations. "Come on out to the pub with us and we'll find you a new one."

It wasn't like Justin was doing anything else, so he agreed he'd meet up with them later, after they returned from dinner at the Pig & Pancake.

So he found himself at the Anchor, a dingy local bar, at ten PM on a Thursday night in Seaside. He never would have believed he could miss his job, that he could feel nostalgic about heaving himself out of his desk after a depressing night of phone surveys to go freeze his ass off waiting for the bus. But oh, at the other end of the bus ride, Zoe.

The big Australian jabbed him in the ribs. "Got your mind on that girl again, eh?"

"How did you know?"

"Looks like you're about to cry!" He ordered Justin another beer.

Some slickly produced country song came on the jukebox. "What's with this music? Everywhere we go in your country, they play sentimental cowboy songs," said the big Australian, who had drank a lot of beer and was talking loudly.

"What do you guys listen to?" Justin asked. He didn't like country music either, but he was getting sick of the guy insulting American culture. Not like Justin thought it was so great, either, but his head hurt and he had a lot of problems and the Australians were getting on his nerves. He tried to think of Australian bands to somehow return the limited view of another culture, to see how they'd like it. "AC/DC? Midnight Oil? INXS? Olivia Newton John?"

"Yeah!" the blond guy roared, laughing. "Now you're talking, mate!" He slapped Justin on the back, and Justin had to laugh, too, at the idiocy of it all. At least he wasn't alone on his bunk at the hostel, where he would have quickly lost his mind.

"You play darts?" the blond guy asked.

"Sure," said Justin, who had vague memories of a dart board at a cousin's house when he had been in junior high.

They got darts from the bar, then walked past two pool tables to find a dart board on the far wall. Justin soon learned that he indeed didn't play darts, and that the Australians were on a dart team back home. After losing ridiculously for a couple of games, he relaxed and let himself play the clown without embarrassment. It was satisfying just to throw something sharp, even when the dart gave the board a wide berth. The Australians kept buying him beer. He tried to buy a round, but they wouldn't hear of it. "Oh, no, mate, we couldn't take your money," said the big guy, holding his side because he had a stitch in it from laughing so hard. The more Justin drank, the worse his aim. The blond Australian said he hadn't had so much fun since arriving in America. They picked out potential dates for Justin, to help take his mind off Zoe. Each woman seemed more farfetched than the last. Justin laughed along with them, the alcohol numbing his panic and heartache.

Of course, he felt much worse when he awoke in his bunk the next morning. The Australians, who were about ten years younger than Justin, had already gone somewhere for the day. Justin rolled over, groaning, tugging the pillow over his head to blot out daylight. He had absolutely no idea how to spend his time in Seaside. Who knows how long he would have stayed right there, if he didn't have to piss so bad.

Four and a half days till Pete arrives with a plan, he thought to himself as he sat on the toilet, too done in to stand up.

CHAPTER NINETEEN

Back in Portland, Zoe had no idea how to spend her time, either. Justin's bedroom felt creepy without Justin, like he had died. She missed him more than she would have expected. They still hadn't heard from Gillis, so now she lived with Pete and Sam. Her status had become tenuous. Without Justin, without paying rent, she had no claim on a room in their house. But Pete and Sam were much too shook up to kick her out yet.

Zoe spent a lot of time lying on Justin's bed, contemplating disappearance. Somehow death was less scary. There was a body, it was clear cut. But where was Gillis? Was he in a regular jail in Portland? Or a secret detainment center in Washington, DC? Or that military base in Cuba? And what on earth did he do all day? She imagined him sitting in a small, dark cell in solitary confinement. Or having nothing to read but the bible. Or maybe he was in a crowded holding cell, playing checkers with a tattered bunch of men speaking Arabic. And then, once or twice a day, did some guard take him to another room where they attached electrodes to his scrotum? And what could they possibly think he knew? He was just a stoned hippie from Southeast Portland. Couldn't they see the only danger he posed was to himself?

Sometimes Zoe got out of bed and fooled around on Justin's computer. She hadn't lived anywhere with a computer for almost a year. She tried to check her email, but had lost her free account from disuse. She set up a new account, then realized that her address book had been lost along with the old account. She stared at an empty message, trying to remember a single address she could type into the top line. There was no one. Instead, she downloaded some free music from a techno site.

Pete had insisted Zoe keep going to work, and she had complied. But the café she had so loved was tainted now. She couldn't go there without remembering the agent who took Dale and Gillis away, or the agent who questioned her. She couldn't seem to relax her muscles; she kept finding her shoulders up around her ears. Every afternoon she was more tired than the last, and could do nothing for the rest of the night but lie on Justin's bed or sit at his computer. One day she realized she had not been to a grocery store for more than a month. She ate only at the café, or if Pete offered her something at home. This didn't help her condition, since the café sold nothing but muffins, cookies and croissants. Such a diet would probably kill anybody, Zoe thought miserably as she stared at Justin's ceiling.

She wished she could tell him that she truly missed him. He was probably not even sure if she'd been using him for a place to live. Maybe it had started out that way, but he was the only person who meant anything to her anymore.

Every day she considered asking Pete where Justin was, and if she could go to him. But she was so weak. If the agent caught her before she reached Justin, how could she know she would keep his secret? Even if she reached him safely, a dying girl is a liability. She was certainly no good on the run.

Pete would not let Zoe talk about Justin at home or in the café. He assumed both places were bugged. If she even looked like she was going to say his name, he would clear his throat or shake his head or, ridiculously, tap his nose. Zoe thought if anybody was listening it was more suspicious that they never talked about how two-fifths of the household had gone missing.

The only chance she got to talk to Pete was on the days he walked her to work. Then he kept an arm around her and talked quietly near her ear. This is how Zoe knew what Pete said to the agent when she questioned him. He had played it casual, characterizing Justin and Gillis as "some harmless clowns I live with because it's cheaper than getting my own place." When they asked him about all the hours he spent with them at the café, he claimed that he and Justin had been rivals for Zoe's attention, but Justin had won out – marginally and briefly – when Zoe had been evicted from her old place. He carried it off perfectly and easily since it was more or less the truth.

Zoe was relieved that they hadn't carted Pete off, too, and left her alone in the house with the elusive Sam. But she didn't like the agents knowing about her private life. It embarrassed her that she had failed to pay her bills, and made her feel like a whore and a freeloader that she only moved in with Justin because of her eviction.

At least Pete didn't try to get with her now. Maybe he doubted his ability to perform with his bedroom bugged.

So time passed. While Zoe worked and rested, Justin spent the days reading his bleak books in a café, walking on the blustery beach, and visiting the Pig & Pancake every day until one night, terribly drunk at the Anchor, he made out with the Pig & Pancake waitress and was too mortified to ever return to the restaurant. Luckily, that was Monday night, and Pete was due with a plan the following day.

During these five days, Pete was ten times busier than Zoe and Justin put together. In addition to his usual duties at the group home, he was thinking profusely, preparing phony documents and making bogus phone calls. He was also busy alternately congratulating himself for being a total fucking genius and worrying that his plan was impossible because Justin would surely blow it.

Working on his plan replaced the excitement he had lost when the competition for Zoe's affection had ended. Without Justin on the scene, Zoe wasn't so enticing. She was a skinny kid, languid and a little dim, and her junk habit or whatever was wrong with her was kind of pathetic. Still, Pete liked her and wanted everything to come out okay for her and for that useless clown Justin, who was basically an okay guy.

CHAPTER TWENTY

By Tuesday, Justin fit in better at the Greyhound station than he had upon his arrival in Seaside. Scruffy and hung over, he sat on a metal chair and waited for Pete. Usually he wasn't much of a drinker, but he had been alternately too afraid and too bored every night in Seaside to do anything else.

As Justin waited, he skimmed through a discarded *Oregonian* he found on the floor. The president had visited Portland without major incident, according to the paper, nothing but the usual pepper spraying and a few arrests. That newspaper never told the truth, so Justin became increasingly jumpy and suspicious. What had really happened to Dale and Gillis? No mention of them in the *Oregonian*. And was Pete purposely making him sweat? Or, worse, maybe Pete had bailed on him and run off with Zoe. Or, worse, maybe Pete had been detained and right now was being held somewhere by Homeland Security ogres. Or, worse, maybe Pete was being detained and had talked, and right now agents were on their way to apprehend Justin. Ridiculously he imagined the agents stepping from the next Greyhound, their guns drawn.

Justin was surprised to see Pete enter the station with the 2:15 load of passengers. He had expected Pete to drive up in his dented blue

Mustang. Justin was so relieved that Pete had arrived and so happy to see someone he knew, someone with news of Zoe, that all his bile evaporated and he wanted to throw his arms around Pete and squeeze. But Pete was in full spy form. When Justin moved toward him, Pete stopped him with a slight shake of his head. He touched his nose and jerked his head toward the exit door. Justin didn't know what the nose business meant, but he gathered he was supposed to act like he didn't know Pete and meet him outside.

Justin waded through the crowd of bus passengers, reaching the door minutes after Pete had disappeared through it. He could see him a block away, headed for the beach. A vicious wind had kicked up. Justin sighed and hurried after Pete, scorning himself for being such a baby that he really wanted a hug.

Justin caught up with Pete two blocks from the beach. "What's going on?" he asked. "You weren't followed, were you?"

"Well if I was, they've obviously seen you by now." Pete hiked a black backpack higher on the shoulder of his old army parka.

"How come you took the bus?"

"My car's way too easy to spot."

Pete's paranoia seemed like a bad sign. Justin hadn't allowed himself to believe that Pete would say it was all a false alarm, Dale and Gillis were back, the agents were sorry, their mistake. But more than a sliver of hope had hidden in his heart, counting on good news.

"How's Zoe?"

Pete shrugged. "She mostly just stays in your room and fools around on your computer. Still goes to work. Something's wrong with that girl. She has no pizzazz. No offense."

Hearing Pete insult Zoe was better than thinking he was seducing her while Justin was away, but it didn't help Justin to like him. "Any word from Gillis or Dale?"

"Nope."

"You talk to Dale's girlfriend?"

"Haven't seen her."

"You think they nabbed her, too?"

"Probably."

It gave Justin a chill. Being bored with obnoxious Australians and making out with the Pig & Pancake waitress suddenly seemed pretty good. Oh, forgive me Zoe, Justin thought, I am so not a man!

"You okay, old man?" Pete asked. "You look a little green."

Justin nodded. They had reached the beach and now had to shout over the wind to be heard. Shouting on the beach felt indiscreet to Justin. He grew more dubious about Pete's spy techniques every minute.

"I didn't tell them anything, and neither did Zoe. Although she gave them the impression that you left town. Good thing she didn't know where to find you."

"They questioned Zoe?" Justin felt sick thinking how scared she must have been.

"Don't worry. It was okay. And it should work to our advantage, them thinking you left town."

"Why is that an advantage?"

"Because you're coming back to Portland."

"I am?"

Pete had a maniacal twinkle in his eye. Justin hadn't heard the plan yet, but he already knew he didn't like it.

"Ever done any acting?" Pete asked.

"Acting?"

"School play, maybe?"

"Well, I had the title role in *The Murky Monster* in the fourth grade."

"You played the murky monster?" Pete burst out laughing.

"It was a good play!"

"Well. The murky monster. What the hell is a murky monster?"

"It was a marine story," Justin said stiffly.

"You played a Marine?"

"No. Marine as in ocean. I was a sort of sea monster that bullied the other sea creatures."

"Oh, okay. I get the picture. This is going to be a little different."

"Obviously. I mean, you can't expect me to hide in the ocean."

"Of course not. You'll live in a house and all of your needs will be taken care of." Pete's face was serious now, but he still looked to Justin like he was laughing just underneath the surface.

"Oh?"

"It's a brilliant plan, Justin, but it will take a certain amount of work on your part. And some patience, and maybe even some sacrifice."

"I'm listening."

"I thought of someplace they'll never look." He paused.

"Where's that?"

"In a group home."

"You want me to work in a group home? Not really my sort of thing. And wouldn't they find me there? I mean, don't they fingerprint the staff?"

"Uh huh," Pete said, watching Justin intently like he was waiting for him to figure it out. But Justin wasn't figuring.

"I don't get it."

Pete sighed as though Justin wasn't very bright. "You're going to live in the home. As a client."

Justin's jaw dropped open. "No."

"It's brilliant."

"No it's not! It's horrible!"

"I've worked my ass off forging forms and making phone calls," Pete said. "You're supposed to arrive at our home in Gresham on Thursday. You lived in Ohio with your mother, but she died recently. You have no more family in the Midwest, but a sister on the Oregon coast. In Lincoln City. She has shirked her family duty long enough. She wants you nearby so she can visit you on holidays."

Justin was shaking his head. "No way."

Pete shrugged. "Like I said, I worked my ass off for you. But if you have a better plan, be my guest. It's a free country," he said, laughing.

Justin realized he had depended entirely on Pete, forming no alternate plan of his own. "That's what I'll do, then. My plan."

"Fine. Let's hear it. Unless it's a secret."

"Well, I'll just go somewhere else. Start over."

"Uh huh. You got money? Fake ID? How are you going to live?"

"I'll get something under the table."

"Pick grapes with the Mexicans? Clean houses? Be a nanny? You'll fit right in with all the other educated young white men clamoring for those jobs."

"There's other jobs. Maybe I could wash dishes."

"Or you could rob people. Or sell drugs or pimp girls. Come on, Justin, this is the cushiest option. Not only do you not have to work, hell, you don't even have to wipe your own ass!" Pete slapped his thigh, he was laughing so hard.

Justin thought he was going to throw up. This was the plan he had been waiting for? Maybe he should just kill himself. "I can think of a better plan than that," he said softly, as if to himself.

"Suit yourself, old man. You're not due at the home till Thursday morning. That gives you tonight and all day tomorrow to work on your plan. But listen closely. You have to take the earliest Greyhound to Portland on Thursday. It's due in at 7:50 AM. I am going to pick you up at the station in the van. Then I'll hand you over to the staff of your day program. Then a bus will pick you up at the end of the day and take you to your new home. But don't worry about remembering that part. They'll tell you what to do. Your job's just to stay in character. But you have to arrive on the early bus or it's all fucked up. That's the trickiest part of the plan, your arrival. Supposedly you're staying with your sister now. But instead of delivering you to the group home in the evening, which would be more normal, she's this high maintenance type who travels a lot for business and she couldn't be bothered to bring you to the home at an appropriate time. So I'm supposed to meet her for the hand off at the Washington Square Starbucks on Thursday morning before she jets off to God knows where. That's been the worst of it, trying to figure out how to deliver you without introducing the sister."

"You love this idea!" Justin burst out. "How would you like to go live in a group home?"

"Hey, I'm not the one who made stupid comments in a public place about offing the president."

"Oh, come on! You weren't any smarter than I was, hanging around Dale."

Pete just smiled. "I've got to get back and do an overnight shift. Not in your new home, by the way. We don't have any space in the home I manage, so I've arranged accommodations in one of our other ten homes." He opened his backpack. "I've brought you a copy of your file, so you can get into character. It is imperative that you memorize everything and burn it afterwards."

"I'm not doing this."

Pete held the folder out to Justin. "Take it. Then you have freedom of choice. You can read it and reject it or accept it. You can do anything you want. I'll look for you Thursday morning at 7:50."

Justin's traitorous hand accepted the folder. "I guess I'll look at it," he said reluctantly.

"Fine," Pete said, starting to turn away. "So either I'll see you Thursday morning or otherwise, well, good luck."

"Wait," said Justin, confused. "If I don't see you Thursday, I'll call..." his voice drifted off.

"Better not call," Pete said. "Phone's bugged." They stood there for a moment. "Well, see you," Pete said, not laughing for once, before heading for the bus station.

"Bye," Justin said. "Thanks." But his voice was soft and the wind loud, so Pete probably didn't hear him. Justin stood alone on the beach, an immense weight of desolation and abandonment holding him down on the shifting sand. The sinister gray sky began leaking rain.

Who ever heard of such an ugly beach? It wasn't supposed to be like this.

CHAPTER TWENTY-ONE

The Australians had left for Seattle, and no other travelers had been dumb enough to come to the freezing beach town, so Justin had a night alone in the dorm room. He lay on his bed, brain spinning, determined not to break down and open the file Pete had left with him. His mind ranged over imaginary maps, looking for a safe space. Would the FBI have alerted the airports? Was leaving the country a possibility? He supposed he could go live in the woods somewhere, build a shanty, roast rabbits over a campfire. But he could barely start a fire, let alone construct a dwelling or catch live food. Unless he could find a hermit apprenticeship program, he probably couldn't survive a single winter.

Nor would he expose any relatives, no matter how distant, to possible repercussions. How wide was the FBI's net? How much time and effort could they possibly expend on such a stupid case? Justin had heard lots of hard to believe stories in the last year. Innocents disappearing, examples made. If Pete had told him that Gillis had been released, Justin would have gone home. Taken his chances, maybe been locked up for a few days and questioned. He could deal with that. But indefinite detention? Maybe he'd be thrown in with real terrorists. He imagined a cell block full of young Muslim fundamentalists. What would they do to someone like him? And what if they learned his only crime was a stupid joke about offing the president with a golf ball? They'd probably tear him limb from limb.

He wanted to call Zoe so badly, he could barely bring his mind back to focus on a plan.

Justin felt like he had been at the hostel forever. This led him to his first idea: Maybe he could stay here in exchange for cleaning or working the desk. Well, why not? They wouldn't have to pay him anything. He would find a way to eat, somehow. It might even be fun, when the weather warmed up and more people came. He turned over the possibilities for fifteen minutes, feeling like a genius, relieved that he wouldn't have to live his life as a retarded person. But when he heaved himself off the bed, the girl at the front desk shot him down. "As you can see," she said, smiling, "there's not much to do around here at the moment. But if you're interested in coming back in summer, I'll give you an application." She reached into a drawer. "It takes a little while to do the background check, anyway."

"Oh, never mind," Justin said, his voice heavy with dejection. "It was just a whim. I'll probably have another whim before summer."

Back in his bunk, he continued thinking. How about joining the carnival? He'd seen those ride operators drinking out of paper sacks, grinning their missing tooth smiles at underage girls. He'd bet all the money he had left that no one ran background checks on those characters. But where is a carnival when you need to run away with one? Certainly not on the Oregon coast in cold and gloomy March.

The image of the Pig & Pancake waitress popped into his head. She seemed to like him a lot. Could he be a kept man? Maybe he could go live in her trailer park or wherever the hell she lived. Make love to her at night. Have the days to himself while she waited tables. He could do some sort of solitary hobby while she was gone. Woodworking, maybe? He could learn to carve duck decoys and sell them to the tourists.

Jesus, it was like his brain was defective. Sometime past midnight, he broke down and opened the file on Jacob Arnold.

Jacob Arnold was the same age as Justin, and their physical descriptions matched, except for eye color. Doesn't that motherfucker Pete know what color my eyes are, Justin wondered. Blue, not green! Jacob's IQ was estimated at twenty-three. He spoke only six words: dog, pop, no, coffee, fire and paper. Partially toilet trained. Never known to be violent. Compulsive masturbator.

Justin groaned. Leave it to Pete to take away his speech, make him piss his pants and play with himself in public. No wonder Pete had had that sadistic gleam in his eye. Justin slammed the folder shut in disgust. No way. NO WAY!

Thus he passed a long night in the hostel, thinking until he was sick with fear, reading the file till furious, casting it off, brooding, opening it once again.

By daybreak, he knew all there was to know about Jacob Arnold. The youngest of three children. Parents deceased. Grown up in Columbus, Ohio. Diagnosed as autistic and severely developmentally disabled at age three. A lifetime of special schools, alternative work programs. Lived with his parents until a year ago, when their age and illness precluded caring for such a difficult son. Moved to a group home in Columbus, made a fair adjustment. His biggest problems in the home were not respecting other people's property rights, and his frequent, inappropriate masturbation.

Justin skimmed through Jacob's health records, an ordinary collection of rashes, toothaches, a broken arm, colds and flu, and their corresponding lotions, fillings, and medications. It didn't seem like a good idea to mention dental records. Justin went into the bathroom to count his fillings in the mirror. Five. He was astounded to see Jacob's chart matched his own mouth. How had Pete got his dental records? And how had someone brilliant enough to obtain his dental records failed to notice something as obvious as his eye color? Justin would never understand the guy.

Between bouts of reading Jacob's file, the brainstorming sessions weren't going so well. Justin seemed to lack all skills and talents that might help him now. If only he could support himself through day labor construction jobs, or petty crime. He considered defecting to Cuba or North Korea or Iran. He daydreamed about Cuba for a while.

What if he sent a letter to Castro, explaining his situation? Cuba was sunny and if there was any food, everybody got some of it. And the island was crawling with hot girls in scanty tropical outfits. He'd seen pictures. But he couldn't figure out the logistics of getting Castro's attention and arranging transportation. As far as North Korea and Iran, he was almost certainly better off in the group home.

Justin slept from seven AM until noon, then awoke from bad dreams, sick to death of being inside the hostel room, alone. He threw on his hat and jacket and stalked out to the beach. As usual, it was gray and drizzly with a ripping wind that tore into his ears like it would infect them with death itself.

There's no telling what Justin would have done, other factors remaining relative. Maybe he would have evaded Pete's plan, tried one of his own half baked ideas, not got on the Thursday morning bus to Portland. But when he arrived back at the hostel that evening, the girl at the desk told Justin that a man had stopped by and asked questions about him. Six feet tall, a bit rough looking, in his forties, not friendly. Of course Justin couldn't know that the waitress from the Pig & Pancake had an estranged boyfriend who drifted in and out of town. Justin couldn't know that this boyfriend liked to hoist drinks at the Anchor with all his friends, and that the Pig & Pancake waitress had only used Justin that night so that word would get back to her quasi boyfriend that she was seeing someone new, someone young and mannered. Justin did not even get the satisfaction of indignation at being used. And the estranged boyfriend would never know the incredible revenge he would have on Justin. All Justin knew was that the FBI was onto him, that he had to get the fuck out of Seaside, and that Pete's plan had an immediacy and cohesion that his own plans lacked.

CHAPTER TWENTY-TWO

When Justin arrived in Portland at 7:50 AM, Pete greeted him with a big grin. "Have a nice bus ride, Jacob?" he asked, reaching for Justin's backpack.

Justin held only his few possessions. "I can carry that myself."

"You won't need it where you're going," Pete said, and it sounded like Justin was dying and going to hell.

"I think I'd like to hold onto a few things, just in case."

"Dude, you're not fully understanding the situation." Pete jerked the backpack from him and walked briskly towards the door.

"Wait up! My keys and my wallet are in there. I thought I'd hide them someplace."

Pete shook his head, not looking back. "And this is the last time you can be out of character," he said when Justin caught up. "Once our van ride is over, you are Jacob Arnold."

Justin had not felt good for a week now, and the last twelve hours since he thought he had learned the FBI was onto him had been especially hellish. He had left the hostel as soon as he could throw his stuff together, gotten the first Greyhound out, taken it halfway to

Portland, then skulked around some miniscule town for half the night, including a brief stint of sleeping beneath a bush. The Greyhound had smelled like piss and vomit and he'd had nothing to eat since lunch the day before. He had been so distracted by immediate discomforts that the reality of his new role had slipped away from him.

"Man, there's no way I'm going to jerk off in the living room. I don't care what that file says."

Pete slid open the van door. "You have to sit back here," he said. "Safety regulations. By the way, you did burn the files, didn't you?"

Justin obediently slid into the backseat. "And I am *not* pissing my pants."

"Speaking of pants, I brought you some clothes to change into."

"What's wrong with my clothes?"

"You don't look like Jacob in that old sweater. People in our homes are taken care of." Pete handed Justin a yellow polo shirt, an Izod knockoff with a tiger instead of an alligator; a bright red acrylic V-neck sweater; and a pair of stiff new jeans. Justin groaned. "Go on and change now. Oh, and I almost forgot." He dug through a duffel bag till he found a pair of sparkling white briefs.

"What the fuck?" Justin said, limply holding the briefs and staring with horror at Pete.

"What? Those are perfectly respectable. Don't tell me you only wear velvet boxers or some shit." Still Justin stared at him. "Go on! We don't have all day. I'll sit in the driver's seat. Don't worry, no one's watching."

So Justin resignedly stripped and changed into the new clothes, none of which he would have ever bought for himself. Except the underwear. He actually did favor white briefs, but didn't appreciate receiving a gift of underwear from Pete.

"You ready back there?" Pete asked in a bright voice.

"Uh huh."

Pete started up the van. "But really, you have to piss your pants now and then or it might be suspicious. And you want to fit in, don't you?"

"You are such an asshole," Justin muttered.

"How can you say that? I'm saving your life!"

"You don't even know what color my eyes are."

"Of course I do. But do you know what kinds of clowns work in these places? If your file was entirely accurate, that would be highly suspicious."

Justin groaned. "These clowns are going to tell me what to do all the time?"

"Relax," Pete said, careening out of the parking lot. "It will be surreal. I'm really curious. Someday when you can talk again, you'll have to tell me all about it."

"Tell me about Zoe."

"Nothing new. Work. Mooning around the house. Fooling around on your computer. Pretty boring, really."

"See if you can get her to go to a doctor."

"A doctor? Who's got money for that?"

"I'll pay–" Justin began, then reality slapped him upside the head again. "I'll pay you back later. In the future," he finished lamely.

"Don't worry about anyone but Jacob Arnold. I'm really going out on a limb for you here. You blow this and Jesus, am I ever fired with no future references! In fact, this is probably fraud or some shit that could land our asses in jail."

"Not my ass. I'm just some retard," Justin said.

"Developmentally disabled. Please!"

Pete seemed perfectly cheerful, despite the possibility of jail. But Justin's stomach ached with dread and stage fright. How would he remember to not talk? To appear as though he understood nothing?

"I'm going to give you a crash course in appearing developmentally disabled. It's like an altered state. You no longer have to worry about anything practical like making a living or getting a date or not losing your keys. You can form grotesque attachments to any person or thing you want. If you find an old shoe in the street, you can carry it around until someone tries to take it away from you, then scream and cry and hit them. If you're hungry and someone else has food, you can grab it and eat it yourself. If you're horny, whip it out of your pants. If you have to take a whiz, go for it. Really, it's a pretty good way to live. Simple. No more landlord coming after the rent. No electric bills. No concept of time. Do whatever you want. Just remember you're disabled and don't blow it by acting too normal. Remember, you don't want to appear merely mute. You have to act up some." Pete drove with one hand, the other arm thrown back over the seat like a playboy giving tips on picking up girls.

"What have you told Zoe?"

"Nothing, naturally. She can't know."

"Could you bring her a note?"

"Nope. Too dangerous. I'll give her a verbal message."

Justin reddened. He hated this sadist. He could just imagine Pete relaying his message in a mocking tone, one eyebrow lifted. But he had to say something. He had no other way to tell her anything. "Tell her I love her and I miss her. And one day I'll make it up to her."

"Okay," Pete said, slowing the van and pulling it into a parking space in front of a dismal building on Sandy Boulevard. "We're here. No more talking. I've packed a few possessions for you." Justin reached for the duffel bag. "No, I'll carry it. The staff are your bearers. We carry everything. We provide." Pete looked him in the eye. "Good luck. Do me proud. Now I'm going to come around and open your door, and lead you in by the hand so you don't dart out into traffic. Knock 'em dead." Then he leapt out the driver's side door and came around the van to lead Justin into his strange future.

The room where Jacob Arnold would spend his days looked like it had been an industrial space, or maybe a garage. The ceiling was unfinished, wiring and pipes clearly visible. The floors were concrete, with drains, which made Justin wonder if they hosed it down every time one of the retards let their bladder loose. He'd always fought not to think of Pete's charges as "retards," but now that he was one, he gave up that struggle.

About two dozen of his new comrades gathered around long picnic style tables. Some sat on the benches, some were in wheelchairs, and a few wandered around clutching Styrofoam cups of what Justin would learn was weak, decaf coffee. The oldies station blared from a radio, mixing with the noise of the people. Two fat women argued shrilly. One's most prominent feature was crossed eyes, the other, crooked teeth. A guy with a bowl haircut and protruding tongue sat alone on the floor, rocking and moaning an eerie tone that cut through the rest of the noise. Justin's palm was sweating in Pete's hand as he followed his ex-roommate through the crowd.

"Pete, I made a wind chime!" said the cross-eyed woman, who was skinny and looked to be in her forties. She seemed to be attempting a coy look, but with the crossed eyes it was hard to say.

"Pete! Pete! Pete!" cried a small, shrunken fellow. Pete greeted his fans by name, smiling.

"Who's that?" asked the woman with the crooked teeth, eyeing Justin narrowly.

"Jacob Arnold," Pete said.

"Hi, Jacob," the woman said.

Justin automatically opened his mouth to answer, then remembered that "hello" was not one of his six words. So he said "aaaa," then closed his mouth. Pete squeezed his hand approvingly.

"He doesn't talk, either?" the skinny woman asked, exasperated. "Pete, bring someone that talks."

"I'll see what I can do, Mary."

Justin didn't see any staff as Pete led him to the back of the building. Were these people left to their own devices all day? What would happen to Justin in this mayhem?

In a small office in the back, a man sat at a messy desk, drinking coffee from a commuter mug. He looked about forty, with dark receding hair. He wore a tweed jacket, a light blue shirt and a bow tie. The man put his mug down. "Pete, I heard you were bringing me a new worker." He extended his hand to Pete, but didn't stand up.

"Marvin, this is Jacob Arnold. He'll be living at the 187th Street home in Gresham."

"Hi there, Jacob, nice to know you."

Again Justin's mouth opened automatically, and again he caught himself in time to merely say "aaaa."

"Jacob is a man of few words," Pete said, letting go of Justin's hand.

"Well, he looks very alert. I'm sure we'll find something for you to do around here, Jacob," Marvin said, enunciating clearly and showing all his yellow teeth.

"I've got to hit the road," Pete said. "Did they send Jacob's file over to you already?"

"I think it's here somewhere," Marvin said, indicating the mess on his desk. "Anything I need to know up front?"

"Nah, Jacob's an easy one," Pete said. "A few inappropriate behaviors, but no harm to himself or others."

"Just what I like to hear." Marvin picked up his commuter mug, which was crusted around the top with coffee past. But before he could take a sip, they heard screeching from the workshop, and what sounded like chairs being thrown. "Oh, shit," Marvin groaned.

"I'll go check it out," Pete said, rushing out to the front room. Justin followed along after Pete, panicked at letting him out of his sight, leaving Marvin gazing at his coffee cup.

In the workshop, a tall, skinny boy with black hair was letting loose an unearthly scream while tugging at the UPS delivery man's beard. Justin watched, impressed, as Pete deftly unlocked the boy's hands from the man's chin. The screeching continued, but dropped a few notches.

"What the fuck?" the UPS guy was yelling. "What the fuck was that about?"

"I'm very sorry," Pete said. "Linus doesn't react well to beards. Our usual delivery person knows that. We're awfully sorry." Pete held Linus by one shoulder. The UPS man held his chin. Justin glanced around and saw that everyone in the room was clean shaven.

"I'm just delivering a box. Fuck! This is my first week on the job." The UPS guy was pale, except for the red, irritated skin around his beard.

"If you have to deliver here again, you can just set the box on the sidewalk and ring the bell," said a man in a wheelchair. He spoke perfectly. Justin realized he was staff, and probably hadn't been able to save the UPS guy because of his handicap. Lazy-ass Marvin surely must be thanking his lucky stars that Pete had stopped by at that moment.

Linus made another grab for the beard, but Pete was too quick. "I'm out of here," said the UPS guy, rushing through the door.

"Thanks," the guy in the wheelchair said to Pete.

"No problem."

Linus' screeching stopped abruptly once the beard was gone. Pete slapped him on the shoulder. "Good going, keeping the workshop beard free."

"Don't encourage him," said the guy in the wheelchair.

"I don't think it makes any difference," Pete said. "I'm hitting the road, Rick. Bye, everybody." A few scattered goodbyes answered from around the room. Pete's eyes flickered over Justin's, then he was out the door.

Justin heard himself gasp. Already Rick was wheeling his chair towards him, and Justin was seized with stage fright. "So, Jacob, we've been expecting you. Welcome."

Justin didn't know where to look. Should he recognize his name? How alert should he appear? He wished like hell he'd paid more attention to Pete's charges when he'd brought them to Zoe's café. He settled for an indifferent gaze in Rick's general direction. If he was a real retard, he'd probably piss his pants right about now. He wondered where the restroom was. Obviously he couldn't ask. Damn, he should have gone in the Greyhound station.

"We're making wind chimes for a gift shop on the coast," Rick said, coming to a stop in front of Justin. He looked about fifty, and had gray hair and a shriveled leg. "I wonder if you would like to string them together? Or perhaps put the finished product in plastic bags?" He was like a person who lives alone and talks to their cat all day, as though it could understand or would care if it did. "Let's try you on stringing first. It's a little harder, but if you don't like that, we'll move you over to packaging."

"Argh!" Linus cried, making Justin jump. None of the other clients flinched.

"Shut up!" cried Mary. "That's dummy noise!"

"Come over here," Rick said to Justin, who remembered to be slow to understand. "Come with me," Rick repeated, beckoning. No response. He sighed and reached a hand out to Justin, who could tell it was difficult for Rick to guide him and steer his wheelchair. Justin decided to catch on.

"Aaa," he said, because his own non responsiveness spooked him. He took a step in the direction Rick indicated.

"Good," Rick said. "That's right. Come with me." Justin shuffled along, taking a few steps in the wrong direction only to have Rick patiently steer him back on course. "That's good. This way. Over here." He led Justin to a table piled high with pre-cut lengths of plastic string and metal pieces shaped like coyotes. Rick sat Justin down in a chair and modeled how to thread the string through the holes in the coyotes. Justin wished Pete were there to advise him. Could Jacob Arnold learn to tie a knot? He thought back to the file. Nothing about knots, but supposedly he had decent motor skills. And it seemed like a pretty good gig, since he'd have his own work space with his back to most of the commotion. He decided to demonstrate just enough ability to keep his new post.

"Excellent, Jacob," Rick said when Justin finally tied a half assed knot. "Splendid work!" Some kind of tussle seemed to be going on behind them, but Rick was intent on teaching. Justin liked the guy and felt sort of bad about deceiving him. And Rick was probably feeling proud of himself for teaching Justin. Had he ever managed to teach a retard to tie a knot before? Justin doubted it. Then he realized he had just felt superior to the others because he had learned to tie a knot. Was he cracking up already, feeling proud about being the smartest retard?

Something whizzed by his head and landed on the pile of string. Half a peanut butter sandwich. Rick wheeled away to investigate. Justin stared at the peanut butter fouling up his string. How the fuck good were his wind chimes going to be if the string was greasy and smelled like peanut butter? Calm down, he told himself, they're disabled. But how would he respond if he were really disabled, too? And in a flash of understanding he yelled, "Aaaa!" He seized the smashed sandwich, turned in his chair, and lobbed it at the first retard he saw, which happened to be the girl with the crooked teeth. She screamed. Rick wheeled from person to person, soothing them. Marvin didn't emerge from his office, though he must have heard the hubbub. Justin turned back to his desk and pulled a clean string from the bottom of the pile. He concentrated on knot number two while the battle continued behind him.

Justin stayed in his chair till lunch. Rick came by with occasional encouragement, but as the only staff he was too busy to provide Justin much support. Justin sneaked glances over his shoulder to try to familiarize himself with his new work situation. There seemed to be only a handful of major players in the workshop. Out of the twenty or so folks present, about half were eerily absent. Never had he seen such vegetative states: the wheelchair bound, the drooling, the staring into space, the waxing and waning of individual stenches. Some didn't let out a peep, while others groaned, keened, hissed or chortled. Speech was a rare gift here. Only three of his coworkers carried on something like conversation. A few sang out random words with the seeming intelligence of parrots.

Justin concentrated on working slowly and tying poor knots. When his mind wandered, his hands became too competent. It was awfully boring to have to think, "Slow, slow, bad knot, bad knot." Some strings he tied only once, neglecting the second tie that would form a knot. Already he disliked Jacob Arnold's incompetence. What if he learned quickly, and became the first person to be cured of mental retardation? But that would call way too much attention to Jacob Arnold.

By lunchtime, Justin really had to piss. There was no way he was going to let loose in his pants. He didn't think he could, even if he tried. But a speechless red-haired girl saved him from further worry about this humiliation. She thumped her upper thighs with both hands, grunting. "Good, Raquel," Rick said. "Good telling me you need to use the bathroom." He escorted her to a rear corner of the workshop, a door not far from Marvin's office. When they returned, Justin stood, heart racing, and moaned to get Rick's attention.

"What's going on, Jacob?" Rick asked, wheeling toward him.

Justin thumped himself the way the red-haired girl had.

"Well!" Rick said. "Don't we have a mature group here today! Makes my life easier. Come on." And he headed for the restroom, Justin trudging behind.

But Justin wasn't prepared for the help he was expected to need. When Rick reached for Justin's belt buckle, it was all Justin could do not to slap the man's hand away. Instead, he groaned in an agitated way.

"What's wrong?" Rick asked. Justin fumbled with his belt. "Oh, you want to do it yourself? Very good." Rick took his hand away and Justin gracelessly unbuckled, unzipped, and took out his dick. Never had it seemed so flaccid. He pointed at the toilet. "Hold on," Rick said, reaching out to flip the seat up.

But Justin couldn't go. He glanced back at Rick and groaned again. And God bless him, the man was an intuitive genius. "Hey, take your time. I'm not looking." He wheeled off to wait in the doorway.

Eventually, Justin took his first piss as a retard. He vowed to drink and eat as little as possible from now on. He didn't know how the hell he was going to take a shit in front of someone when the time came for that.

Everybody else had brought a lunch and Justin felt an irrational stab of anger at Pete for not thinking of that. A second staff person waltzed in at noon, which was lucky since half of Justin's coworkers needed help eating.

"Dude, sorry I'm late," said a big, handsome guy who looked like an Asian surfer. He had shoulder-length black hair and an easy-going face. He couldn't have been any older than Zoe, and stood about six feet tall.

"We managed fine," Rick said, but Justin sensed his annoyance.

"Did Marvin help you out?"

"You kidding?"

"I talked to him this morning," the surfer kid said, "and he said you two could cover it."

"Oh, so you called," Rick said, relaxing a bit.

"Of course I called, dude! Didn't Marvin tell you?" The surfer guy casually removed his jacket and a bright orange wool hat, dropping them on the floor as he spoke.

"Never mind," Rick said. "Let's get everybody fed."

The two staff began unloading lunch bags off the backs of wheelchairs. Justin smelled bologna. "Hey, who's this?" Dave asked, noticing Justin. Not knowing what else to do, Justin had kept tying knots. He wasn't much for staring into space, the preferred pastime of his comrades.

"This is Jacob Arnold," Rick said. "He just joined us today. He's from Ohio, if I remember correctly."

"No shit," Dave said, striding up to Justin. Rick cleared his throat. "Sorry, dude. I mean, no kidding."

Justin turned to look at Dave when he heard him behind his chair. "Aaaa," he said in greeting.

"Well, hello yourself. I'm Dave. Where's your lunch, Jacob Arnold?"

Justin liked Dave immediately for noticing his lack of lunch. "Aaaaa," he reiterated.

"Rick, didn't Jacob come with a lunch?"

"Now that you mention it, I don't think so. Go ask Marvin, will you?"

Dave had a relaxed, slacker sort of walk, but his legs were long so he covered ground quickly. He returned from Marvin's office a minute later. "No lunch," he said. "What clown brought him here with no lunch?"

"Pete brought him in."

Dave groaned. "Figures."

Rick was spooning something creamy into the mouth of a bulbous-eyed man in a wheelchair. Half of the slop dripped back out. Justin looked away. "I think there's some more of this in the fridge," Rick said.

"Sick!" Dave said. "You can only feed that to paralyzed people cause they can't hit you." He turned to Justin. "You like burgers? There's a Wendy's across the street. My treat."

Justin hadn't eaten a burger since he read *Fast Food Nation.* Of course he didn't approve of the decimation of the rain forest due to cattle farming, or the corporate hegemony running America, or the low wage, no benefit service jobs of the fast food empires, or the way chain restaurants put locally owned independents out of business. But now that he was retarded, how could anyone expect him to have any standards? And a burger sounded damn good after not eating for twenty-four hours, especially knowing that the alternative was the glop he had just watched slide down the face of the guy in the wheelchair.

"Aaaaa," Justin said hungrily.

"Okay, my man, a burger it is."

"Why does he get a cheeseburger?" Mary asked, grimacing at a sandwich made on Wonderbread.

"You're going to start an uprising," Rick said.

"Come on, people, the man doesn't have a lunch! Be right back," he said to Rick, who groaned in exasperation.

The burger was the highlight of Justin's day. He wondered if it would be the best thing to happen all week, all month, or even for the rest of his life as a retard. The meat was square, the bun tasted lightly buttered. He'd forgotten how tasty processed cheese slices were, if you could ignore the ingredients. He ate in little bites, making it last. Dave also brought him fries and a Coke.

"We haven't seen his file," Rick lectured, confiscating the Coke. "We don't know if he can have sugar or caffeine. We don't know what meds he's on!"

Dave shook his head in disgust. "Dude, one soda is not going to hurt anybody. I don't care what their IPs say."

Justin was chilled by Rick's words. No caffeine? Meds? He spent the afternoon trying to tie knots slowly while his mind whirled. Escape would be easy enough. All he had to do was quit acting like a retard and no one would take him for one. His thoughts slipped back into the well-worn grooves he'd carved at the hostel. Where could he go? How would he live? When would he ever see Zoe again?

"Dude, look at you go!" Dave had snuck up behind Justin, whose thoughts had strayed from maintaining incompetence. He was tying knots like any normal person. "Rick, this guy is fast! He can really use his hands."

Rick scooted over to check out Justin's work. Justin slowed down, not knowing how to react at being caught out.

"Well," Rick said. "I guess we know who gets the jobs requiring hand-eye coordination." Rick picked up some of the strung coyotes and examined the knots. "Perfect," he said, dropping them back into Justin's pile. "Good work, Jacob," he said, smiling.

Justin started breathing again. He mentally kicked himself. Any retard could do a better job of passing for a retard, he thought. It was such a stupid thought, he laughed. But instead of the staff asking why he laughed, like a friend would if you suddenly let out a chortle, Dave and Rick barely noticed. Justin had the first inkling of the liberation that was now his. His moods were his own business, and could be expressed publicly whenever he wanted. Nobody would pry into their origins, since they didn't know he could talk. Justin's emotions would be both more public and more private than ever before.

The workday ended at four PM. "Jacob, time to go home," Dave said. "Come on, we're going outside to get your bus. Come on, Linus." Dave led Justin and Linus out to the corner, where a gray van was pulling into the loading zone. Dave handed the driver Justin's duffel bag. "Okay, see you guys tomorrow," Dave said. Justin's terror returned. The awful thing was about to happen: Justin would live in a group home.

"Aaaaa," Justin said tremulously, surprising himself.

"It's okay, dude. See you in the morning." Dave gave him a friendly push into the van, then turned to the driver. "This is Jacob Arnold. New guy for the 187th Street home."

"All right," said the driver, an older black guy who turned out to be very quiet.

The doors shut behind Linus and Justin, the only two passengers in the van. Great, Justin thought, he got to be confined in a small space with the crazy fucker who didn't like beards. Suddenly he didn't miss his goatee anymore. Justin examined Linus. He could have been a handsome kid, except for his abnormally large mouth, which hung open, and the vacancy in his eyes. His whole face was slack. Justin figured this guy for a born goth, if he had been born normal. His slender build, black hair and pallor would have wowed the goth girls.

Linus caught Justin staring, and something hostile flickered in his otherwise empty eyes. A rumbling sound came from deep in his chest. Justin quickly looked away. Jesus! It was like looking at a junk yard dog, the way they take a stare as a challenge. Or maybe any wild animal. Justin didn't know, since he'd always been very urban.

As they drove toward the suburbs, Justin switched his focus to the driver. The man must be pushing sixty. He had a short, strong neck and graying hair. He hadn't said a word since the door of the van closed. Justin imagined he was a man who disliked words. Perhaps he had sought out a job with the nonverbal so that no one would engage him in useless conversation. The man's eyes flicked toward the mirror to check on his charges. No change in his face when he caught Justin staring. The man's gaze returned to the road, satisfied that Linus and Justin were as intact as when they'd boarded.

They made one stop on the outskirts of Portland. A couple of blocks off Burnside, in what looked like a residential neighborhood, they picked up Justin's other three new housemates. The driver parked in front of a mustard colored ranch house and honked the horn twice. A young woman emerged, followed by the trio of retards. Of course, Justin wouldn't know their names until later, but they turned out to be Billy, a short, rotund Asian man with a protruding tongue; Sally, who had pretty green eyes but wore her brown hair in an ugly bowl cut; and Nancy, the only verbal resident, who was tall and red-haired and suffered from echolalia. Or rather, made the staff suffer by repeating whatever phrases she heard.

The staff person was a cute hippie girl in her twenties with long brown hair hanging loose. Justin could discern big breasts inside her baggy purple sweater. She smiled at the driver. "Hi," she said. "Everybody's had a good day."

"All right," he said, his glance flicking her way, both hands still on the wheel.

Sally caught sight of Justin, and began whimpering. "Oh," said the hippie girl. "Who's this?"

"New one for the house," the driver said.

Sally was shaking now. "It's okay," the girl said gently. "This is your new housemate. No worries." She turned to the driver. "Sally hates change. Is it okay if she sits up front with you? I think she'll be less nervous." The driver sighed heavily, not looking at the girl, who took his annoyance for assent. "Thanks, Lester. You're a peach." She led Sally into the seat right beside the driver. Sally kept looking over her shoulder at Justin, then whipping her head back to face the windshield, shuddering. Justin felt like shit. He wasn't ready for this shift from retard to villain. He didn't want either role.

Everybody else sat on the long benches facing each other in the back. The girl made sure that all the seatbelts were buckled. Justin hoped she was coming to the house with them, but she jumped out of the van and next thing they were racing toward Gresham.

Justin had never been so far down Burnside. He'd never imagined the street went on for so long. On one side, the MAX train tracks stretched beyond sight. Gresham was a land of boredom, full of chain stores and tacky houses. Never before had he had a reason to come out here.

Justin's new home was one of several one-story beige buildings that shared a cramped lot. He was surprised there was no sign out front. It looked like any of the other ugly residential structures they had passed. It could just have easily been a meth lab or the home of twenty Russian immigrants packed in together, or the headquarters of the Gresham KKK. The only landscaping was gravel between the buildings and a few scruffy rose bushes beneath the windows.

Lester honked his horn twice. Nothing. He honked again. When still nothing happened, he sighed and parked the van. Somebody began to moan.

It must have been fifteen minutes before an old VW bug turned into the driveway. Justin heard the gravel crackle beneath its wheels. A very young girl scrambled out. She looked fifteen, though later Justin would learn that you had to be at least eighteen to work in the home.

"Sorry! Sorry! Sorry!" the girl sang out, running toward the van. She was petite, with black hair tied back in a ponytail. Lester started the engine before the girl opened the side door. "Sorry!" she said again, sounding out of breath.

He shot her a chilling look.

"I said I'm sorry," she said meekly.

"Sorry ain't the same as on time."

The girl had no answer, so she began undoing seatbelts and helping people down from the height of the van. "This the new guy?" the girl asked after a minute.

"Yep. Jacob Arnold."

"Come on, Jacob," the girl said in a cloying voice. Justin let her take his hand and lead him out of the van. The contact was nice so he tried to hold her hand longer than necessary. "Now, Jacob," the girl said. "You have to let go so I can help Linus."

"Aaaaa," Justin said, still holding on, testing his new powers as someone outside the norms. She put up with his hand until they heard the van pull away, then she escaped with a painful little twist of the wrist.

Inside, the floors were covered with red indoor/outdoor carpeting, so profusely stained that at first Justin thought all the blotches were its intended pattern. The couch was old and green, and looked like the sort of thing that would scratch your thighs if you sat on it in shorts. The house smelled of urine, pine cleaner and rose air freshener.

As soon as the door shut behind the clients, the staff girl's voice lost its sweetness. "Jacob, this way," she said, suddenly no nonsense. She grabbed his arm roughly and led him down a dark, short hall. "This is your bed," she said, throwing his duffel bag on one of the two twin beds. A ratty brown chenille cover was on the other bed, but his was bare, except for a plastic cover that fit tightly around the mattress. "The fucking morning person," she growled. "You'd think they could make up the fucking bed." Justin noticed that the girl wore braces, making her seem all the more like a junior high student. Her chest was practically flat beneath her little pink sweater.

They heard a cry from down the hall. "Fuck!" she said, glancing wildly around. "Sit here for now." Her arm shot out abruptly, knocking Justin on his bare mattress. The plastic cover crackled beneath his ass. She hurried out of the room.

Justin looked around, taking in the impersonal nature of his new habitat. He had never seen such an uncluttered room. It seemed curiously uninfluenced by his roommate's personality. What could you learn from the ugly bedspread and the scratched dresser? On the wall above his roommate's bed hung a framed copy of the Lord's Prayer. But even that said nothing. Justin's big-tongued roommate was certainly not a Christian. Perhaps his parents had requested it be hung on the wall, or some religious zealot who worked at the home had stuck it there. Where monastic living meets incontinence, Justin thought, lying back on the creaky plastic.

He heard screams down the hall, some altercation between Linus and the staff person. His first impulse was to get involved. But on whose side? Linus was so slack-jawed and unlikable, and the girl was obviously a mean little bitch. Then Justin remembered he was retarded and didn't have to do anything. He relaxed on his bare mattress and wondered how long before he'd be comfortable masturbating in public.

CHAPTER TWENTY-THREE

But what of Zoe? While Justin hid out in Seaside drinking with Australians and making out with the Pig & Pancake waitress, then spent his days tying knots for coyote wind chimes and learning the etiquette of the disabled, how are we to imagine her? Endless glum hours sitting in Justin's room, enlivened only by weak trips to work and occasional hounding by FBI agents? What about the cost of living when she was only working twenty hours per week, and could barely hold onto that? Wouldn't there come a day when her boss would have to fire her? The customers were complaining. Zoe was too slow. Spots of coffee remained on the floor, unscrubbed. Trash languished in the wastebasket. She was so exhausted, she felt constantly on the brink of hallucination. She thought something really stupid would happen soon, like maybe a customer would order a latte and suddenly his face would appear to turn into a dragon and she would run him through with the bagel knife.

One night, after Justin had been gone two weeks, Pete told Zoe that he and Sam were looking for new roommates to replace Justin and Gillis. He looked embarrassed, his eyes on the floor. "You can still stay in the living room for a while," he said lamely. "And you don't have to clear out of Justin's room until we find a new roommate."

There was also the unpleasant ringing of the telephone. All too often, relatives of Justin or Gillis blabbered on the other end. The FBI had talked to Justin's family; Gillis' were freaking out, not knowing why he hadn't answered their calls for two weeks. Zoe couldn't bear the hysterical tone of Justin's mother, who somehow sounded like her lifetime belief that Justin would fail had been realized once and for all. Zoe stopped answering the phone, which was hard, because she desperately wanted to talk to Justin. Then again, their phone was tapped, so if he called, he was stupid. All this shit gave Zoe a headache, on top of dying. She really wasn't up to it.

One night while she was fooling around on the Internet in Justin's room, unable to think of anything else she wanted to investigate online but too tired to move from the chair, Zoe viciously typed "fuck dying" into a search engine. Mostly it brought up web logs of depressed teens. But as she scrolled down, she came to something called fuckadyinggirl.com. The homepage showed a thin, dark girl reclining on a bed. Her eyes were sad and soulful, her black lacy nightgown disheveled. Zoe guessed it was a goth porn site, but she was intrigued by the girl's eyes. Zoe skimmed through the disclaimer: over eighteen, live in a state where such sites are legal, blah, blah, blah. She clicked on "enter."

Pictures of four girls popped onto her screen. One was Asian, the rest were white. All looked young, all were pretty but sickly with dark circles under their eyes, pale, little or no makeup, looking sad or brave. Zoe clicked on the picture of the dark girl she'd seen on the home page, who's name was Deni. Her menu options were bio, web log, gallery, and make a date. Zoe began with bio. It said Deni was nineteen, her family had been killed in a car crash two years ago, and last year she had been diagnosed with leukemia. She used to enjoy playing basketball and riding horses. She loved to make new friends, and would like you to write to her.

Zoe wasn't an experienced porn connoisseur, but this seemed kind of out of the ordinary to her. She clicked on gallery and waited patiently while rows of small photos loaded. They started with Deni lounging in bed in a nightgown. As Zoe moved down the rows, she saw the nightgown come off to reveal a red satin bra and panties on Deni's wasting body. The girl's hair changed dramatically from photo to photo. Zoe realized Deni was wearing wigs. As she scrolled down, Deni lost her bra and panties, then her wig. But the photos were taken at teaser angles, so you could never see her nipples or her crotch, though you could count her vertebrae. The girl couldn't have weighed more than ninety pounds. In the last row of pictures, a guy knelt at the side of a bathtub, giving Deni a bubble bath. A banner popped up at the end of the photos, saying that if you wanted to see what happened next, you had to become a member of the site for $100 a month.

Zoe stared at the bald girl with the big, haunting brown eyes. Deni looked so wise, like she would understand whatever Zoe told her before she even finished speaking.

Zoe spent the next two hours poring over everything on the site. She read their web logs twice. They wrote about their illnesses, treatment, giving up hope, spiritual grapplings, their relationships with the other girls on the site. Zoe cried steadily. Her alienation left her for minutes at a time. She felt no separation between herself and these girls.

When she got to the end of the Asian girl's web log, suddenly the font shifted and changed color. In fuchsia letters: "Jasmine passed away on February 18. She is in all of our hearts." Zoe had to hurry to the bathroom, where she dry heaved for five minutes before throwing up the half a muffin she'd eaten that afternoon.

After she'd rinsed out her mouth, she went back to Deni's page. She clicked the make a date button. New options popped up: phone date, live cam date, or email me. Zoe hit the email button, which turned out to be the only free option. She typed without thinking, "Deni– I'm sick, too. Alone. Don't know what to write. This is so scary. Zoe." She was going to delete it because her message sounded so pathetically idiotic, but she hit send by accident. Her face burned. What would Deni think of her?

Zoe turned off the computer and lay down on the bed. Her dreams were full of the dying girls. They were all in her bed, languidly eating crackers. Then she was kissing Jasmine. In the dream, Zoe thought Jasmine was alive, but then realized she was dead, her flesh cold and unpliable. Zoe woke up crying. It was three AM, a chilly death time. The house was cold and quiet. Zoe needed to pee, but was afraid to leave the warmth of the blankets and step into the dark hall.

She lay awake, worrying. When would Pete and Sam find a new roommate? Where would Zoe go? For the first time, Zoe wished death would hurry up already. What was she supposed to do now? She couldn't see herself reading the classifieds, calling households of cheerful twenty-somethings about their rooms for rent, going to their houses to be interviewed by a panel of potential housemates. It would be much easier if she could die in her sleep in Justin's bed. Maybe tonight. Hopefully before a new roommate demoted her to sleeping in the living room. Zoe really didn't see herself dying on the couch.

The dying girls in her dreams comforted her up to a point, but then they crowded in on her, leaving no room for her own diminished body in the bed. She was falling in space, the floor a long way from the bed, and Justin was falling beside her. She wanted to hold him, but she couldn't reach and anyway, it didn't seem practical.

She hit the bed and her eyes popped open. It was light out. She propped herself on an elbow, dismayed to feel the amount of energy that simple movement took. Outside was grayness, but a lighter, softer gray than February. Yesterday she had seen a daffodil on her way to work.

Footsteps passed her room, quick and deliberate. That would be Sam going to school or to one of his jobs. His energy embarrassed her. She sank back into the bed.

Zoe realized that she desperately wanted to check her email, but she was scared she'd be overwhelmingly disappointed if Deni hadn't written back. And why should she? Deni probably got lots of mail from her admirers. And how was Deni to know that Zoe wasn't just another pervert pretending to be a sick girl? Deni probably got mail like that all the time. And anyway, Zoe had just written the night before, and didn't even know what time zone the dying girls lived in.

Six empty hours stretched between now and two o'clock, when Zoe would report to work. She closed her eyes, promising herself that she wouldn't check her email until after she returned from the café. If Deni hadn't written back, the disappointment might. . . what, kill her? She moaned to herself, remembering those perfect days when she was dying by Justin's side. She most regretted not agreeing to marry him.

Because all this would have happened anyway, he would still have had to disappear. At least she could have given him that.

At seven PM, after working at the café, coming home, and lying helpless with exhaustion in Justin's bed for an hour, Zoe made it across the room and turned on the computer. There were eleven new messages in her email box: three to enlarge her penis, three to enlarge her breasts, four to lose weight, and one from deni@fuckadyinggirl.com. Zoe's heart sped up. Would Deni be telling her to go to hell? Asking what did Zoe think she was, a charity, so why didn't she shell out the money and join the site?

But no. Deni wrote: "Zoe– I was real scared, too, but now I have the other girls so it's not so bad. What do you like to do? I'm stuck in bed a lot, so I read mysteries and do word searches. And email with my fans. Gotta go, write me and send a pic. Deni."

Zoe didn't know what to make of it. She read the message six times. Word searches? Send a pic? Deni didn't sound goth, or depressed, or mystical, or any of the things Zoe would have guessed. She sat for a long time, wondering if she should answer or if she would be bugging Deni. But ultimately, Zoe couldn't help herself. She had no one else to talk to. She wrote: "Deni– Thanks for writing me back. I don't do very much. I used to work full time at a coffee place. Now my hours are cut back to half time, but I'm afraid I'll get fired soon because I can't do the work fast enough anymore. Sorry this is so depressing. I'm attaching a pic that was taken of me last year at a rave, before I got sick. Take care, Zoe."

She attached a picture of herself from a Portland rave website. She looked young, carefree, happy. Her green eyes were shiny, her blond hair flattened under a multi-colored wool cap. Smiling. She didn't look much like that anymore.

Their emails continued all week. Zoe felt better than she had since Justin had gone underground. The correspondence gave her enough energy to get through her shifts at the café. Every day that she wasn't fired felt like a triumph.

Zoe learned some important things about the dying girls. They lived together in a house, and made their living from the website. Best of all, by a miracle of fate, the house was in Portland.

On Friday evening, after five days of corresponding with Deni, Pete knocked on the door to Zoe's room. "Uh, can I talk to you for a minute?" he called.

"Just a sec," Zoe said, minimizing the fuckadyinggirl site. "Okay. Come in."

He opened the door and glanced around the room like he was expecting to spot a syringe. "Uh, you know how we've been looking for new roommates?" He sounded flustered.

"Yeah." Heart slowing. It was over. She better die fast, before she had to pass away on the living room couch.

"Well, we found them. They're moving in next week."

"Oh."

"You can stay on the couch for a while."

"Thanks."

"Don't you have some family or something?" His eyes met hers for a second, then flicked back to his shoes.

"Don't worry about me," she said. "There's lots of places I could go."

He stood there in the doorway for an awkward length of time. "Okay, good. Good," he said, then shuffled backward and closed the door behind him.

Her mind felt unexpectedly calm. She would check her email one last time, send Deni a note, then lie back on Justin's bed and will herself to die. She would just stay there, not eat, not drink. She was so weak already. Surely she would slip away before the new roommates arrived.

Zoe turned back to the computer and found a new message from Deni in her inbox. "Zoe– Why don't you come out to the house and meet the girls this weekend? I'll send my friend to pick you up. Give me your address and tell me what time is good for you."

What was that feeling on Zoe's face? A smile? Her fingers tripped over each other writing back. She could die any old time, she told herself. She'd wait till after she met the other dying girls.

CHAPTER TWENTY-FOUR

From Justin's first day in the group home, his life became a series of failed ultimatums. Conditions were always just on the verge of driving him to run away, plan or no plan. But then he would decide to hang in a little longer.

At dinner the first night, a strong odor suggested that one of his compatriots had fouled his or her pants. If they think I'm going to eat one bite of tuna casserole with that stench hanging over the dining table, well, fuck it, Justin thought, I'm going to leave tonight. Instead, he sat staring at the salt and pepper shakers, which were green and shaped like smiling dragons. Occasionally Justin blurted out "Aaaa!" in frustration and protest. His discomfort upset Sally, the timid green-eyed woman, who began to cry and whimper.

"Ah, for fuck's sake!" spat Claudette, something black showing in her braces.

"Fuck's sake," echoed Nancy ponderously, prompting Claudette to shoot her a look of even more disgust. Sally's tears grew louder.

Claudette sat at the table with the residents, a frozen burrito on her plate. Everybody else had the nauseating tuna casserole, a runny mess of mayonnaise and uneven celery chunks. Billy ate steadily without looking up. His protruding tongue made polite eating impossible. Glops of tuna dropped back to his plate. Justin didn't see how the hell Claudette could eat.

Then Linus started rumbling, like he was on the brink of another fit. Sally kept glancing at Justin, her eyes red now. "Eat your casserole," Claudette snapped at Sally. "Who cares if what's his name doesn't eat?"

Could they really be so sensitive? Was he causing the others to freak out? The only thing on the table besides the casserole and Claudette's burrito was a stack of dented Wonderbread on a plate. Justin reached for a slice. He didn't want to eat it, or anything else in this dump. He had an irrational fear that consuming the food of the retards would make him shit his pants, masturbate in public, and erase his abilities to communicate. Sally watched him intently. Slowly, Justin bit into the bread. It tasted normal for Wonderbread, as far as he could remember. Usually Justin bought organic seven-grain bread.

When Justin took a second bite, Sally stopped crying and picked up her fork. A minute later, Justin noticed that Linus had stopped rumbling. Now they ate in silence, except for the slurping and open-mouthed chewing.

After dinner, Sally and Nancy sat on the living room couch and stared at the TV. Billy sat on the kitchen floor, picking up the lid of a coffee can and dropping it repeatedly. Linus paced, making a circuit around the living room, down the hall, around his bedroom, then back through the hall to the living room. Claudette put dishes in the dishwasher and talked on the phone to what sounded like a boyfriend, then another boyfriend, then a girlfriend, then her mother. Justin wasn't used to TV, and that noise alone would have been jarring enough, but added to Nancy's echoing of commercials– "Gets your shirts cleaner," she said in a clipped, precise way, then, "Changes your mood. Ask your doctor" – and Claudette's phone calls: "I told that motherfucker he better not think he can play me like that!" she squealed at what must have been a girlfriend – Justin wanted to scream, "Shut the fuck up! Shut the fuck up!" Instead, he sat down in an armchair and fumbled around for the lever to make it recline. It took a minute to find the lever hidden deep inside a fold of upholstery, but eventually the footrest popped out on its metal arms and Justin propped his feet up. He tried to focus on the show, to give his racing mind a rest. But the show was a sitcom about an ex-football player who gets stuck coaching his sassy little daughter's ballet class, and was so pitifully stupid that soon Justin's mind was whirling in vain, desperate for an escape plan.

Claudette walked in, cordless phone stuck to her ear. "Can you believe I'm the only staff on again? It's ridiculous! I have to do everything around this fucking place." Then she stopped talking and stared at Justin. "No way! One of the retards just got this chair to recline! It's been broken for like six months!" She kept staring at Justin while her mother or whoever it was chattered in her ear. "What difference does it make what I call them? It's not like anyone around here understands English. Hey, maybe he's one of those idiot savages or whatever who has special talents. Maybe he knows how to fix things! I'm going to bring in that busted CD player!"

She was overreacting. Anyone with a grain of motivation could have felt around for the latch. Nothing was wrong with the chair. And Justin sure as hell knew nothing about electronics.

"That was my favorite chair!" Claudette continued. "I think some folks are going to bed early tonight so I can sit in it in peace. After a good disinfecting." Pause. "I told you, no one speaks English!" She wandered out again. Sally laughed, maybe at Claudette or something on TV or something in her head, Justin couldn't say. Her laugh transformed her face until it looked pretty, almost normal. Justin smiled at her, but she immediately stopped laughing and looked at the floor.

He didn't get to enjoy the recliner for long. It couldn't have been past 8:30 when Claudette began dragging everybody into the bathroom, one by one. First Billy, then Linus, Sally and Nancy. Justin's anxiety mounted. Finally Claudette came to him. "Okay, Jason," she said, and he was surprised how offended he felt at her getting his fake name wrong, "time for tooth brushing." She talked in her sweetie pie voice now, like he was an unfamiliar dog that might bite as soon as wag its tail. "Come on, now, Claudette's exhausted working by herself all night." She pulled him gently by the arm. As he got out of the chair, he folded the footrest with his feet. The chair popped back to upright. "No!" she shrieked. "Damn! Why did you go and close that up?"

He knew by now that his housemates were sensitive people, and the only appropriate reaction to her yelling in his face was to spaz out. "Aaaaaaooooooeeee!" he wailed, his voice rising with each vowel. He saw from the look in her eyes that the power was finally on his side. She was a tiny thing, and couldn't be very strong.

"Okay, Jason," she said in a suddenly calm voice. She put her hands out to face him like she was saying "whoa." "It's okay. It's okay."

He got in a couple more hearty yells before he let himself be soothed. He hadn't felt so good all day. But then it was off to the horrors of the bathroom.

The bathroom had two sinks, side by side, and harsh fluorescent lighting. She led Justin to a closet that stood open, a padlock dangling off its handle. A stack of brightly colored tackle boxes sat on the top shelf. Each had the name of a resident written on its side. "We'll have to put together a box for you," she said. "But for tonight…" She raided the other boxes for toothpaste, soap and, oh Christ, a toothbrush! She took the toothbrush from Billy's box. Justin flashed back to his roommate's big tongue and the tuna casserole glopping from his mouth onto the plate. No way. This was it. He was not brushing his teeth with that Mongoloid's toothbrush.

But Claudette didn't hand the toothbrush to him. Instead, she marched him to the sink, turned on the tap, and said, "Open your mouth." He didn't. She sighed and squeezed his nostrils shut with two hard little fingers. "Come on, open up. Nice and minty," she said in her sweet voice.

A lot of thoughts raced through Justin's brain. He thought of strangling her, and what kind of person that made him that he wanted to. He thought of talking. He considered complying. And then he thought of Gandhi, and decided to do some passive resistance. He dropped all his weight back, and sat on the floor with such force his tailbone would hurt for days.

"Oh, for fuck's sake!" Claudette spat. "I can brush your teeth down there, too."

But the force of his falling body had helped him escape her grip on his nose, and now all he had to do was curl up into a fetal position and the bitch had no chance in hell. He curled.

Her breathing was ragged with fury and defeat. "Do you know how much they pay me? Do you? Seven fucking dollars an hour." A couple of random cries from the bedrooms made Claudette drop her voice before everybody started freaking out. "Seven dollars. To clean shit off people's asses while they try to bite me. Fuck it! Do you think I really give a shit about your oral hygiene?" She started slamming toiletries back in their boxes, then locked the closet door. "Let your teeth rot. Fine with me." And then she walked out and left Justin curled on the bathroom floor.

Justin remained in the fetal position for who knows how long, crying. He felt like he'd die if he couldn't hold Zoe. Right now. Right now. He cried himself to sleep on the floor. When he awoke in the night, cold and stiff, he clambered through the dark house onto his own twin bed. Nobody had bothered to put blankets or sheets on it.

The first morning he awoke in the group home, and for some days thereafter, Justin didn't know where he was. And it was with a horrible thump of his heart that he traded dreams of Zoe for the smell of Billy's piss-soaked bed and the horror of a staff person yanking the sheet from his morning hard on.

The first morning, some guy Justin had never seen woke him with, "Up and at 'em, buddy." Then, without giving Justin a moment to wake up, he grabbed his arm and led him toward the bathroom. The guy had a gentle vibe, quite unlike Claudette. He tested the water in the shower to make sure it wasn't too hot or cold. "Step on in, buddy," he said. Justin had taken his own pajamas off before the guy could try to undress him. He slinked into the shower, blushing from head to toe. Never had anyone looked at his body like it was an object. It was sort of like going to the doctor, but a hundred times worse. At the doctor, you can assert yourself, ask questions, show the mind behind the medical condition. But now he felt like a car in the carwash.

The water was colder than Justin would have liked. He looked around for the soap, but it was already in the staff person's hand. Oh, shit, Justin thought. Like some bad porno movie, the guy started scrubbing Justin with a washcloth, lifting his arms to reach his armpits, soaping his chest, working down methodically to wash his groin and balls. Justin stood meekly, a feeling of total defeat. If Zoe could see this, he thought, if Zoe knew this, could she ever want me again? Take me seriously as a man? He imagined what his mother would think, what any woman in the world would think, of his extreme humiliation and cowardice. What if he had said to the FBI agent, "No, I don't like the president. What are you going to do about it?" Would jail be worse?

The staff person guided him to turn around and face the green tiled wall. Justin relaxed a tiny bit when he felt the washcloth on his back. But when it slipped down to his ass crack, he silently began crying. He had never felt like less of a man.

After Justin's shower, his caregiver led him to the kitchen table and sat him down. Sally and Billy already sat over bowls of cold cereal. "I found this guy sleeping in his clothes, in a bed that hadn't been made up," the staff person said to Claudette, in a pleasant tone of voice designed not to upset the clients.

Claudette poured cereal into Justin's bowl. She looked up and spoke in her phony voice, like she had in front of the bus driver. "Did you kick off all your blankets, Jason? What did you do with your bedding?"

"Isn't his name Jacob?"

"That's what I said."

"No, it isn't what you said. And he didn't kick the sheets off. And why was he sleeping in his clothes?" Justin could tell this guy wanted to slap the stupid bitch, though he kept his voice calm.

"He doesn't have any pajamas," Claudette said triumphantly. "We'll have to buy him some today. Would you like some orange juice, Garth?" she offered sweetly.

"Isn't that his duffel bag in there by his bed?"

"Huh?"

"With two pairs of pajamas in it."

"I was working by myself all night," she said, her face changing, her lower lip petulant. "I had to do everything!"

"Yeah, whatever." Garth glanced at the clock. "The van's going to be here in twenty minutes. I'm going to get the others ready."

"You're not going to say anything, are you? It was just a little mistake." She sounded sort of whiny now, like she was trying to play the girl card. Garth just sighed and left the room. Claudette turned her mean little face to Justin, as though he had snitched on her. For a second he thought she was going to throw his cereal at him, or maybe spit in it.

Everyone else got meds with breakfast. Garth distributed them after he'd showered Nancy and Linus. "Doesn't Jacob get anything?" he asked Claudette, as though she would know. He thumbed through some charts. "It looks like he just came with vitamins."

"He probably needs some thorazine or something," she said. "He's temperamental," she added.

"Temperamental," Nancy echoed knowledgeably.

"Thorazine! Jacob doesn't need that. He's a lamb."

"Not last night. He threw a fit when I brushed his teeth."

"Oh, yeah. I meant to ask you where his toothbrush is. I couldn't find it when I showered him."

"It must be in there someplace," she said, wiping the table.

"I looked all over. Do you remember what color it is?"

"Green? Or maybe purple. I don't know. I was so tired I was about to drop dead," she whined.

"What, your hands were tired from wearing down the touch tones?"

The van beeped its horn. Justin realized he could hardly wait to get to work. Much as he enjoyed hearing Garth give Claudette a hard time, Justin was dying to get out of the group home.

After a good deal of rushing about to find lunches and sweaters, Claudette and Garth marched the whole crew out to the bus. "Morning, Lester," said Garth. "How's it going?"

Lester nodded curtly.

"Hello," Claudette said in her phony voice, but Lester apparently thought one nod was enough. He stared ahead while Claudette and Garth buckled everybody in.

Justin was surprised by the relief he felt as the van cruised down Burnside. Since Lester didn't talk at all, and paid no attention to his charges as long as they remained in their seats, it was almost like they were free of staff. Justin breathed liberty in deeply, until he caught the stench of one of his comrade's accidents.

At the workshop, Justin spent the day tying knots and keeping to himself. He had a weird kind of privacy there. Most of the nonverbal people seemed to exist in their own worlds. The few talkers interacted with each other, but Justin was of no interest to them. Except for constant low level surveillance by staff, people barely looked at him. I have really disappeared, he thought. Even the people in this room don't see me. And all because he had ceased speaking. A vision of his eleventh grade English teacher popped into his head. Mrs. Sherwood, a big, loud woman with heavy makeup and lots of curly red hair, used to stand before the class, hands gesturing, eyes wide, and orate about "the power of language." She must have used that phrase three hundred times while Justin was in her class. But now he realized she didn't know the half of it. By forfeiting speech, he had slipped out of his own life.

Dave talked to Justin more than anybody else did. "Hey, Jacob, how's it hanging?" he asked affably, popping up behind Justin to glance over his pile of half-assed knots. "Looking good, man, looking good." Justin got the feeling Dave was a natural born back slapper who was resisting the impulse in favor of professionalism. And Justin realized that he yearned for that kind of reassuring, warm physical contact. Gillis used to be a shoulder rubber. When he remembered that, sadness welled up in his gut. Poor stoned, unemployed, bad luck Gillis. Such a good, gentle guy. So kind to Dale when that wiry little fuck would overheat, spewing spittle and invective.

"Hey, you okay, man?" Dave asked, looking closer.

"Aaaaa," Justin said. He knew he had six words, but he wasn't sure if he remembered them correctly. Besides, six words were such little consolation. It wasn't like six dollars being infinitely better than none. Six dollars would buy you lunch. But six words?

Dave lay a big hand on Justin's shoulder. "You're doing great. Don't worry, you'll love it here. You'll fit right in." Then he rushed off to check on some other facet of the wind chime project.

Left on his own again, a tear slid down Justin's cheek, then another. The kindness did him in. He hadn't cried in public since grade school, but just when the mortification began to creep in, he remembered that retarded people did much, much more embarrassing things than crying in public. This wasn't shit.

Through the long, bleak, knot-tying afternoon, his thoughts ran, as usual, to alternate plans. He couldn't deal with Claudette for long. Nor could he imagine week after week of knot tying. Suddenly it seemed like the only logical thing to do was to hitchhike to Mexico. He'd been to Tijuana a half dozen times when he lived in Southern California. Back then, at least, nobody cared who went into Mexico. They only worried about who came out. Of course, he didn't know about extradition laws. In old westerns, the outlaws were safe once they crossed the border. At least, safe from the U.S. government. But now, with NAFTA, could the U.S. suck people out of Mexico like it sucked out cheaply produced goods? Still, wasn't it the best idea?

Justin wouldn't have admitted it to anybody, but he was afraid of Mexico. His mother used to go into such a panic about Mexico and Mexicans. He'd run into a bit of trouble there already, drunk off his ass in high school. Once a pickpocket had stolen his wallet. Another time, a Mexican cop took all his money when he caught Justin drinking on the street. Of course, this time he'd keep his wits about him. He'd be fine.

Justin's spirits lifted in the late afternoon, buoyed by a wave of optimism. It would work out. He would reach Mexico safely. He felt so good, he even managed to take a dump while Rick sat in his wheelchair nearby. "Don't forget to wipe yourself," Rick said hopefully. And both men were very happy when Justin proved competent at the task, even flushing the toilet himself. "Bravo, Jacob, bravo!" said Rick. "An excellent knot tier and a self toileter. Just the kind of worker we've been needing around here."

That evening, Justin was thrilled to find that Claudette was not in the group home. Instead, Garth greeted them when the van pulled up in the driveway. "Good day, everybody?" Garth asked jovially.

"Good day," Nancy replied.

"Aaaa," Justin threw in.

"Tacos tonight," Garth said. Justin's heart lifted. First, because no way could tacos be as gross as last night's tuna casserole. And it seemed like a good omen, what with his Mexico decision.

A second staff person was on duty that night. Lenny, who wore a baseball cap and looked about twenty-two, sprawled on the plastic-coated couch, watching TV, his filthy shoes on the cushions. He was watching a talk show about redneck guys who find out their best hunting buddy is gay. "But that fucker is flaming!" he yelled at the TV. "You're telling me you didn't know? What did you think when that guy was sucking your dick?" Lenny seemed oblivious to the residents, except when Garth suggested tasks for him.

"Can you get some plates down?" Garth would ask and Lenny would answer yeah, sure, craning his neck to see the TV while performing the task, scowling with the concentration of simultaneously listening to the stupid show and doing some monkey-brained thing.

Dinner kicked ass: chicken tacos with black beans, salad and guacamole. Justin noticed that the empty cans on the counter had held organic beans. He wondered how quality food had made it into the shithole he now called home.

"Do you really need the TV on during dinner?" Garth asked Lenny.

"You sound like my mom!" Lenny snorted. "It's *Jeopardy,* man!"

"Jeopardy, man!" Nancy said.

"Okay, okay," Garth muttered.

Garth served blander versions of dinner to the residents. Justin coveted Garth and Lenny's pico de gallo and cilantro, though Lenny didn't even want his. "Lettuce in the beans?" he asked, confused.

"Cilantro," Garth said.

"Oh. Where's the margaritas?" Lenny asked, then laughed a big, stupid laugh. "Ha. Ha. Ha."

Justin remembered Pete had told him that retarded people would take someone else's food if they wanted it. Justin couldn't bring himself to pull the shreds of cilantro out of Lenny's beans. Instead, he pointed at Garth's pico de gallo and said, "Aaaaa!"

"I don't know if you want this stuff, buddy," Garth said. But Justin kept pointing and eventually Garth shrugged and stood up. "Try it if you like." Justin pointed at the cilantro, too. Garth brought both items over and put them on the table. He served Justin a small spoonful of pico de gallo and a few cilantro leaves. Justin ate them in two bites and reached for more.

Linus rumbled with jealousy. "I know you won't like this," Garth told him. One of Linus' long arms shot across the table and he managed to scoop a handful of pico de gallo out of the plastic tub.

"Foul!" Lenny cried. "That dude puts his hand in his own shit. You better throw that out, man."

"Throw that out, man," Nancy echoed.

Linus shoved the salsa in his mouth before Garth could grab his hand, then he began howling. He struck out, hitting Sally in the side of the head.

"They don't pay me enough for this shit!" Lenny said. But before the words were out of his mouth, Garth had already wrestled Linus out of his chair and was leading him down the hall to his room. Justin could see why Linus had been given a room to himself; he'd probably kill a roommate, maybe *had* killed roommates in the past. "Check on Sally, make sure she's okay," Garth called to Lenny.

"You're okay, huh?" Lenny asked, glancing in Sally's direction. Her pretty green eyes were full of tears, and she held a hand to the side of her face where Linus had hit her. But almost immediately, Lenny's attention was sucked back to the TV set. "Dodgers!" he cried out. "Who are the Dodgers! You moron!"

Billy continued to eat, completely unfazed. Justin thought maybe Billy had to tune out all distractions in order to consume his food in the allotted time. Since at least half of his every mouthful landed back on his plate, it must take him twice as long to eat. Justin followed Billy's lead and took this opportunity to help himself to a handful of cilantro leaves. He would have liked more salsa, but was dissuaded by the image of Linus touching his own shit.

Garth returned a minute later, looking grim. "Linus is cooling out in his room. How's Sally?"

"Huh?" Lenny said. "Oh, fine."

"Did you give Jacob all that cilantro?"

"What? No." Lenny turned his attention back to the table and looked at Justin's plate. "We got a gourmet on our hands. Ha. Ha. Ha."

"He's got good hand-eye coordination," Garth said.

"He looks almost normal," Lenny said. "I say put him on a bike going downhill, he'd snap out of it and start pedaling. Ha. Ha. Ha."

Garth ignored Lenny and ate his dinner. The category on *Jeopardy* was Reptilian World and the clue was "Tennessee Williams movie set in Mexico." Justin yearned to scream out, "What is *Night of the Iguana?*" It was that almost impossible-to-stifle urge you get when you know a *Jeopardy* answer and no one else does. Lenny said, "Uh, uh... *Godzilla?*"

Garth admitted he'd been listening by responding contemptuously, *"Godzilla!* That's about as far as you can get from Tennessee Williams!"

"Well, it's a movie and it's a reptile!"

"It's Japanese," Garth pointed out.

"Oh, yeah. I know that. Tennessee, not Japan."

Justin stuffed taco in his mouth to keep from blurting the answer.

Garth served everybody seconds, except Billy, who was diligently scooping up food that had already fallen out of his mouth at least once. If only Garth cooked every night, Justin thought. He wondered if Lenny ever had to cook. He couldn't imagine him doing more than opening a bag of Doritos and letting them fight over it.

"You want to clean the kitchen tonight or get everyone ready for bed?" Garth asked.

"Kitchen," Lenny said.

Garth found a new toothbrush for Justin, who watched him remove it from the packaging. He let Justin brush his own teeth. "Good job!" Garth said encouragingly.

Everybody was in pajamas by eight o'clock, which made Justin feel off, like he was an overgrown child, or ill, or, well, retarded. He remembered his phone survey job with a surprising pang of loss. This would be the time he might get up for a second cup of the wretched office coffee, just to escape his desk and trade a few words with the cute, sarcastic girl in the eyeglasses.

"Well, I'm out of here," Lenny said as soon as the clock hit eight.

"Okay." Garth turned off the TV before the door closed behind Lenny. His face relaxed. Justin was 90 percent sure that Garth was cool, not like Claudette, who turned into a frightening harpy without another staff person to keep her in line. "How about the radio?" Garth asked, and turned on KBOO. Now Justin was 100 percent sure about Garth, because KBOO was the community radio station everyone in his old world listened to. Justin sat back in the recliner, closed his eyes, and pretended he was back home.

The living room opened into the kitchen. Justin could hear Garth scrubbing things in the kitchen while they listened to the radio. After a while, Justin leaned forward till he could peer past the refrigerator and see what Garth was doing. He was furiously scrubbing all sides of an electric can opener with steel wool. After that, he took down the ceiling fan and started cleaning it blade by blade. Justin wondered if Garth was obsessive compulsive. Regardless, he was about ten times better than the rest of the staff of this madhouse, especially since he listened to KBOO.

Justin fantasized about confiding in Garth. Surely Garth, a KBOO listener and consumer of organic beans, would be on Justin's side. Then, whenever Garth was alone on duty, Justin would stay up after the other clients went to bed and they could talk. It had only been thirty-six hours since he'd gone retarded, but it seemed much longer. Just think what comforts Garth could offer him: conversation, news of the world and of his people in it. Maybe Garth would deliver a message to Zoe! And bring one back from her. Maybe Garth could let

Justin's parents know that Justin was all right. And then there were personal favors, like maybe he'd bring Justin a good beer now and then, or give him real coffee in the morning, instead of decaf like the other clients got.

But then doubts crept in. What if Garth couldn't keep his mouth shut? Pete's job would be on the line, not to mention Justin's freedom. And Pete would be locked up, too.

And what if Garth was angry at being fooled? Justin suddenly flashed back to Garth wiping his ass crack with a soapy washcloth. He felt like he was going to vomit. No, he could not tell Garth.

Then the news came on and Justin listened with growing nausea to a long report on U.S. detainees caught in the war on terror. The horrors of enemy combatants at Guantanamo Bay had already been well publicized. But Justin listened with a more personal dread to stories of the estimated twelve hundred people detained in the continental U.S. Not that these stories were fleshed out, as hardly anything was known. Identities of detainees not released. Secret sites. No access to legal counsel. Handcuffs. Leg irons with heavy chains. Lock down. And no charges, so nothing anybody could fight against. In short, no hope.

Suddenly the Mexican border seemed much farther than a thousand miles away. Infinite chances per mile to be caught.

Then the commentator's sweet, compassionate voice was talking about a CIA interrogation center in Afghanistan. "Prisoners' heads are covered by black hoods," she said, "and they are bound and left in excruciating positions for hours. They are thrown against walls, or made to stand or kneel overnight. They are alternatively tormented by bright lights, loud noises, foul smells, and brutal beatings. At least two detainees have died. The Red Cross is banned from the interrogation center."

Justin looked around from where he relaxed in the recliner. Billy lay face down, asleep on the carpet, peaceful as a child. Sally had returned to the couch, where she sat beside Nancy, looking at a picture book of kittens. Justin tasted defeat. He was not an enemy combatant, dying for a cause, spitting in the face of fascist American soldiers. He had no nationalism, no religion, no convictions that made him itch to pick up a gun and point it at anybody. He was not even Dale, a leader in the defacement of billboards, a champion political shit-talker. Justin had stood at the bottom of the billboard. Justin had made a stupid, half-assed joke about offing the president with a golf ball, eyeing Zoe the whole time and only yearning for her. Justin was no sort of American male that anyone admires, not the clear-eyed, well-trained soldier supporting the establishment, not the revolutionary tearing it down. He felt taco rising in his throat as he realized he was too gutless to venture beyond his soft prison.

CHAPTER TWENTY-FIVE

Zoe awoke Saturday morning feeling better than she had in months. This afternoon she was going to meet the dying girls.

She had barely thought about clothes since she got sick. But today she deliberated over what outfit to wear for at least half an hour. Finally she decided on an aqua T-shirt and black pants. Usually she wore baggy sweaters because her body held little heat. But Deni had said one of the best things about their house was that they kept the thermostat set at eighty. The dying girls always ran cold.

Zoe was nervous, of course, but knew she was rushing to meet destiny. In her dreams, the dying girls visited, perched on her bed like birds, and the set of black wings fluttered overhead, fanning their faces.

At 1:30, Zoe went downstairs to wait for her ride. Pete sat on the living room couch reading *A Field Guide to Outdoor Erotica,* and seemed to have a hard on. When he heard Zoe, he put the book down quickly. "What a surprise!" he said.

It was true she never ventured downstairs, unless she was going to work. Sam was hardly ever there, so Pete probably felt like he lived alone. "I'm going out," she said. She couldn't help smiling at seeing Pete flustered for once.

"Oh?" he said, expecting more.

"What are you reading?"

"Nothing. Just some junk I picked up at a garage sale."

Then they didn't talk. What could they say? Zoe wasn't about to tell him about the mysterious house of the dying girls. He didn't want to talk about *The Field Guide to Outdoor Erotica.* And they couldn't discuss what really plagued their days, the disappearance of their roommates.

Pete found another book to pick up. Zoe sat, her eyes unfocused, her overriding sensation one of anticipation. It felt so foreign and exotic to her. After a while, the doorbell rang, startling them both. None of the house's inhabitants ever used the front door, and there hadn't been many guests lately.

"I'll get it," Zoe said, floating toward the door. Maybe she still had a little slice of future waiting to be lived.

George was a nice looking guy in his thirties, with golden hair and tanned skin in March. His eyebrows were thick and high, giving him a surprised look. He wore a blue sport jacket, like he was taking her out on a yuppie date. "Zoe?" he asked, his warm brown eyes taking her in.

"Yeah."

"I'm George."

Zoe could feel Pete craning his neck behind her back, trying to see who the hell had lured Zoe out of Justin's room. Zoe didn't know if Pete was in contact with Justin, but she'd rather give him the fewest details possible. Besides, no new friend would appreciate walking into a bugged house.

"Let's go," she said softly, smiling.

Zoe thought she heard Pete call something to her, but she was already out the door. George took her arm and she leaned on him a little as she walked down the unfamiliar front steps to his car, which was dark blue. He opened the door for her. Inside, the car smelled like plastic. Unlike the few cars any of her friends had ever managed to own, this one lacked rips in the seats and trash on the floor.

"It's sort of a secret where the girls live," George said as he headed east on Division Street. "Usually I blindfold visitors. But I don't need to do that with you, do I, Zoe? You're not going to tell anyone." He looked over at her and smiled. In that instant, Zoe realized why he looked familiar to her. She had seen him on the dying girls' website. He had been in Jasmine's section, giving her a bath. And maybe in Deni's, too, feeding her cake. The focus hadn't been on the man. The man was always a prop in the shadows, hovering on the edge. But she was sure George was one of the guys on the website. Suddenly she felt uneasy. Zoe had been thinking of these girls like her sisters. She had dwelt more on the feelings she had in common with them than about this obviously being a porn site. It dawned on Zoe that the dying girls might have some expectations of her.

"Who would I tell?" she said, smiling weakly.

"I don't know," he said, smiling back. "Who would you tell?" His eyes regarded her steadily.

"Nobody," she said, her voice coming out a whisper.

"That's the right answer," he said, laughing. "No blindfold, then." He turned the radio on low to *Prairie Home Companion.* "Best show on radio," George said, settling back into his seat for the drive.

The trees were getting their first leaves now, and Zoe saw masses of daffodils and a few tulips. It seemed like she should have died in winter. It was wrong to die in spring, when everything else was coming to life. Zoe had questions she wanted to ask George, like how did he know Deni and how long had they been friends. And what had gone on between him and Jasmine and was it awful when she died or had everybody somehow accepted it? And who was he, George, and where on earth was this house and what would happen to her there? But these were all the sorts of questions that a person has to wait and watch unfold around her.

They turned onto 82nd Avenue and headed south. George let out the faintest groan. Zoe turned to look at him and saw his face had grown grim. Two vertical lines creased the skin between his big eyebrows. He noticed her looking at him and smoothed his face out.

"It's just this neighborhood," he explained. "It's so low class. You girls–" He broke off, catching his slip. "I mean, the girls should be somewhere nicer. I'd like to see them over in the Northwest hills. But out here, people don't ask questions."

Zoe absorbed this information. She supposed a house full of dying girls with a sexy website would raise questions in some neighborhoods. But SE 82nd was glutted with ugly businesses: car lots with three-door heaps that cost five hundred dollars, cut rate furniture and appliance stores with garish banners, lingerie modeling shops that everybody knew were hooker parlors, and the kind of strip clubs that even Peppy and Patti had too much pride to dance in. Zoe had to agree with George that the dying girls should have a better view on their way out.

George passed yet another strip mall containing a liquor store, pawn shop, strip club and check cashing place. "Almost home," he said, turning onto SE Dora, a weird one-block stretch of residential neighborhood backed up against skanky 82nd Avenue. The houses weren't big, but they looked fairly respectable. They had probably been built before all the shitty businesses had moved onto 82nd, Zoe guessed. Most of them had small squares of neat lawn out front. Only one house looked ominous, its dirt yard strewn with chipped toilets and three reclining pit bulls.

George stopped in front of a neat two-story house painted light yellow and trimmed in white. The front stairs were dark blue.

"It's so pretty," Zoe murmured.

"Thanks." George smiled. "I painted it myself last summer, when the weather was good. Hell of a job! Mother picked out the colors."

Of course by now Zoe was growing very curious about the relationship between George and the dying girls and the house they lived in. And what was this about his mother? Surely she didn't know her son was involved with a death row porn website.

Faces looked out the window. Zoe couldn't see them clearly behind the glass, but they seemed to be waving in a friendly way.

"You ready to meet the girls?" George asked, looking Zoe over happily, with a hint of proprietorship. She nodded and reached for the door handle. "Wait for me to come around and open the door, Zoe. It's time for you to be treated with the respect and consideration you deserve." He smiled at her tenderly. His whole demeanor said he wanted to take care of her. Zoe felt the tension in her stomach ease. She smiled at him. "That's my girl," he said, smiling back.

On the way up to the yellow house, George hooked his arm solidly through Zoe's. She felt okay now, more excited than nervous, despite the fast pulse and the flutters in her stomach.

George opened the door, which wasn't locked. He led her into the living room. She had only a quick impression of spotless elegance: blond hardwood floor, Persian rug, furniture that had come as a set. Mostly she was captivated by the sight of the girls. Deni in real life – frail, huge luminous eyes, a cobalt scarf wrapped around her bald head – rushed towards her. "Oh, Zoe, I'm so happy you're here!" She hugged her tightly. Zoe closed her eyes and sank against the bony girl. She felt her own face smiling, while a tear of joy trickled out of her left eye.

When Deni let go, Zoe smiled at the other two girls. They weren't her pen pals, so they just said hello and looked friendly but didn't hug her. Candi had frizzy auburn hair and freckles. Brenda's hair was dishwater blond and she looked plainer in her sweatpants than she had on the website. Candi and Brenda were both very pale, but Deni's skin was darker, like maybe she was part Indian or Central American or who knew what.

"You look nice, Candi," George said, looking over her emerald dress, her pearl choker. "You're not going out, are you?"

"I have a date with Frank at three."

"But Zoe's here!"

"I'm sorry," Candi said. "But Mother said I should go. Frank will be out of town for two weeks."

The two lines between George's eyebrows had reappeared. "Why don't you girls take Zoe's sweater for her? Candi, could you come help me in the kitchen?"

It was awfully warm in the house. Zoe didn't think she'd felt such heat since last summer. She pulled her baggy sweater overhead and caught George's eyes flicker over her T-shirt before he and Candi left the room.

Brenda reached for Zoe's sweater and dropped it on the couch. Then she and Deni started giggling. "Take your sweater! King of subtlety," Deni said.

"Never mind George," Brenda said. "Come sit down."

The couch was wine-colored velvet, sumptuous and expensive. Zoe thought she had seen it online. She wondered what kind of antics had taken place right on this plush sofa. Suddenly the mystery of just what members got for a hundred dollars a month loomed up, overwhelming her so she couldn't begin to think of small talk.

Brenda helped her out. "Who do you live with?" she asked.

"Some guys," Zoe said, realizing she couldn't mention Justin or the FBI.

"Boyfriends?" Brenda asked.

"No. Just roommates. I work in a café," she added, for something to say.

"You work?" Brenda sounded shocked. "But I thought you were, you know, dying," she said. Nobody had put it so bluntly to her. Zoe couldn't answer.

"I told you that!" Deni said. "Zoe's written me all about the café. I told you!"

"No you didn't!"

"You never remember anything!"

"Fuck you, Deni! You know I'm not well," Brenda said, sounding on the verge of tears. But a few seconds later, they started giggling again. Zoe felt left out.

"Brenda's medication makes her forgetful," Deni explained.

"And Deni's makes her a bitch!"

They shoved each other lovingly. "What do you have?" Brenda asked.

"Huh?" asked Zoe, taken aback.

"I told you! She doesn't know! It's a mystery," said Deni.

"Hell, maybe it's just mono or something," said Brenda.

"But she has the dream! About the wings." Deni looked at Brenda significantly.

"Oh," said Brenda.

They were all quiet while Zoe wondered why Deni hadn't mentioned in her emails that she also dreamt of the black, beating wings.

Candi walked back through the room, glumly headed for the stairs. "Where are you going?" Deni asked. "Come talk to Zoe!"

"George says I have to change," said Candi.

"What?!" Deni and Brenda exclaimed.

"I look too well," Candi said.

"Oh," Brenda said, understanding. "He used to tell Jasmine that, too." They all nodded.

"No blush," Deni said. "Rule number one for dates." They nodded again.

"I'll be right down," Candi said, trying to smile at Zoe like a good hostess.

"We like seeing you dressed up," Brenda said. "You can dress up for us anytime."

"Thanks," Candi said, trudging up the steps.

"I'm confused," Zoe admitted.

"Oh, who cares about any of that?" Deni said dismissively. "You wanna see my photo album?"

"Sure, I guess," Zoe said. Except for customers at the café, Zoe had had almost zero interaction with people since Justin disappeared. Her body felt exhausted and yearned to lie down, but her mind wanted to learn all the girls' secrets. Deni hauled a green photo album out of a bookcase. She sat very close to Zoe and opened it over their laps. Deni had a kind of electricity coming out of her spare body that excited Zoe where their thighs touched.

"These are from my childhood," said the nineteen year-old, as though childhood was very far away. "I grew up in Phoenix."

Zoe had never been to Arizona and the photos struck her as exotic. Deni as a scrawny little girl in cutoff jeans, toy gun in hand, staring at the camera while the sun set over spiky cacti. Other little kids that looked just like Deni, only slightly bigger and smaller, naked, being hosed down by a scowling man.

"What's going on there?" Zoe asked.

"Bath time," Deni giggled. "After Mom took off and left Pops with five kids, he found ways to keep house more efficiently."

"But who took the picture?" Zoe asked, perplexed by anybody hauling out a camera at such a sad sight.

"I don't know," Deni said, unconcerned. "Probably one of Pops' girlfriends. It's amazing, but he never had trouble getting women, even with five kids! You can't really tell in that picture, but Pops had lots of sex appeal." She flipped a few pages forward. "I know you can see it in some of these." She stopped and pointed to a picture of her father in a black cowboy hat, staring into the camera in a sultry way.

"Is he Indian?" Zoe asked.

"Yep. Sioux. Grew up on a reservation in the Dakotas." Deni stared lovingly at the man. Zoe could imagine him stomping around a ranch, breaking chickens' necks for fun. He was the sort of man they were talking about in *Cosmo* articles titled, "Why We Love Bad Boys." Zoe had never related. He looked like the sort who would come to a bad end, so Zoe didn't ask Deni what her father was doing these days. But the dark girl volunteered the information.

"Died in prison," she said, turning the page. "That's my foster sister." She pointed at a red-haired girl with cleavage spilling over a pink minidress, endless leg emerging beneath. "My first love. Damn hot stuff. Everybody thought so. Probably why she got raped and died in a ditch."

"Deni!" Brenda cried. "You're a terrible hostess!"

"It's okay," said Zoe, who felt very ill.

"Excuse me," Brenda said, rising from the couch and picking up a walking stick. "Try to be a bit more cheerful." She strode slowly from the room.

"She goes to the bathroom about twenty times a day," Deni whispered. "Her medication, I think." They were too close to face each other and talk, so Zoe stared straight ahead. She felt Deni's breath on her cheek. "I don't mean to be a downer, Zoe," Deni said. "Of course I used to be real upset about their deaths, but now I'm glad. I know it's selfish, but it would be awfully lonely to be the first one over. It's like that for some girls that die so young. But not me! I know loads of dead people. When I'm dead, I won't be lonely at all. There's Pops and Julia, my foster sister. And Jasmine and Rachel and Tracy and Cindy, they all lived here, too, before Brenda and Candi. I've been here the longest."

"You think they're really waiting for you somewhere?" Zoe broke in. She didn't believe in anything.

"Yes! I feel them!"

"I guess you're lucky, then. I don't have anybody, you know, dead." Zoe felt peculiar even talking about this.

Deni grasped Zoe's hands. "I'm bound to go before you, Zoe! I've been dying for ages! I'll wait for you over there. You won't have to be scared about being alone." And then they were embracing. Deni stroked Zoe's back while she cried with relief, even as another part of her sat aside, unmoved, saying why am I so relieved? I don't believe any of this.

Over the course of the afternoon, Zoe learned the basics of the house of dying girls. George's mother owned the house, and George had grown up here. He had moved away to Seattle or Vegas or somewhere – parts of his story seemed to conflict – and fallen in love with a waitress or a realtor or maybe a college student. But the girl had gotten very ill and George had quit his job to support her 24/7, because he loved her too much to entrust her to a nurse. At this part of the story, Brenda looked dreamy and Deni giggled. Candi was gone on her date at that point, her cheeks paled down and the emerald dress put aside for her burial, Brenda had confided, so Zoe didn't know how Candi felt about this tale of George's devotion.

George's mother had been living alone at that time, right here in this house, with some big deal position at a dotcom that produced interactive tours of nursing homes for prospective residents, or, more likely, for the children of prospective residents. She worked twelve and fourteen hour days, and invited George to live with her rent free while he nursed his fiancée. So what happened? George found out that he loved caring for his sick girlfriend. He greatly preferred it to his former career in restaurant management or video poker machines. "It was fine dining," Brenda said. "With white tablecloths. Trimmed in lace. And silverware that matched. And was polished!"

"No," said Deni, her eyes shining but the sag of her shoulders revealing fatigue. "It was poor slobs losing the rent money in poker machines and having to explain it to their old ladies."

But neither girl disputed that dotcoms had crashed and George's fiancée had died.

"She died?" Zoe asked, sucking in her breath.

"Yeah," Brenda said. "In my room. With George holding her hand. It was so romantic."

Deni rolled her eyes. "Of course, that was before we were here," she said. "We don't really know the particulars."

George and his mother were left with a house, a mortgage, one unemployment check, and a lot of experience in computers and caretaking.

"But how did it all come together?" Zoe asked, gesturing at the house around her. "How did he come up with the idea? And what exactly is the idea? And how did he find you girls?"

Deni and Brenda both looked embarrassed. Brenda ventured an answer. "Well, you probably noticed that the site is sort of...erotic."

"It's a porn site," Deni interjected.

Brenda ignored Deni. "It's kind of hard to understand, maybe. But I think when George was taking care of his fiancée, he found everyday activities sort of sensual with her."

"They'd had some bang up sex life," Deni said. "Lots of S&M and vinyl nurse outfits and stuff up the ass."

"She just makes stuff up! Watch out for her. I just mean all the normal stuff like eating lunch or taking a bath or getting dressed. Maybe they couldn't have sex anymore so that became sexy."

"I think he liked her needing him so much," Deni said. "The power."

Both the girls were obviously stumped about why someone would find it erotic to care for a dying girl. But Zoe knew people got turned on by all kinds of weird stuff– feet, little kids, whips. Maybe dying girls were just another fetish for some people, no worse than wanting a girl to be blond or to have big tits. At least, she tried to tell herself this.

"Weird," Zoe said. The three sat in silence for a minute, contemplating themselves and their illnesses as fetish objects.

"Whatever," Deni finally said. "Now I have a house to live in. I can go to the doctor, get pain pills when I need them. George will get me anything I need. Drive me anywhere I want to go. People read my journal online. I'm a celebrity, sort of. And a year ago I thought I was going to have to die in a squat in North Portland! Maybe it all seems weird, but I'm not complaining."

Brenda put an arm around Deni, who was breathing shallowly. "We've been up for a long time," she said. "Usually we take a nap by this time in the afternoon."

Zoe felt like she'd unconsciously overstayed her welcome. "Oh, I should go home," she said, though it was the last thing she wanted to do.

"Don't you want to take a nap, too?" Brenda asked Zoe. "You can sleep in Jasmine's bed. There's clean sheets. It's real nice."

"Okay," Zoe said uncertainly.

Jasmine's room was a pale, delicate pink. Nothing personal was left, but still Zoe felt some sort of lingering inhabitance, like she was a visitor in someone else's room. The oak desk held a computer and nothing else, not even a stray piece of paper. The thick, rose-colored carpet muffled Zoe's footsteps as she crossed the room to close the window. The cold air coming in made the room about thirty degrees cooler than the rest of the house. Outside, a tree just beyond the window grew its first leaves of the year.

"Rest as long as you like," said Brenda, who had brought Zoe upstairs. She closed the door behind her, and Zoe was alone in the dead girl's entirely clean and quiet room. She tiptoed across the carpet to the white dresser. It was a nice piece of furniture, well made and the sort of old that comes from an antique shop, not the Goodwill. It was dust-free, and the brass drawer pulls shone like somebody had actually polished them. Zoe had never lived anywhere that people would think to polish a drawer pull.

She slid open the top drawer. Not a thing was left inside but the scent of roses.

Zoe was so tired. She eyed the bed, made up tight with a pink and white quilt and more pillows than anyone could put under her head. Nobody had said where Jasmine died, but Zoe suspected the girl had drawn her last breath right there. If she wasn't so exhausted, it would be too creepy to even be in this room. But she drew the line at the bed. Instead, she lay on the carpet and looked up at the frosted white light fixture. She wondered if Jasmine was hovering above her right now. She glanced at the bed, imagining Jasmine laid out there in death.

As she turned her head, something caught her eye, something that seemed to be sticking out of the box spring. She looked closer and saw the corner of a piece of paper. At first she thought it was maybe a gum wrapper, but that seemed awfully out of place in such a neat room. She reached out nervously and pulled the paper from its hiding place. It was a note, written on stationery with a big pink "J" on top, and smelling like roses:

Hi, New Girl– It's me, Jasmine, writing from beyond the grave! George probably gave away Inanna, but it's your job to get her back. Or else! I *will* haunt you! This is Inanna's home, so here's what you better do: Tell George I came to you in a dream and told you about Inanna and that I'm going to curse him and Mother if Inanna isn't restored to her room. ASAP. – Jasmine

P.S. Hope you're not allergic to cats! If so, tough. I hear there are some shots you can get.

P.P.S. Good luck. Don't worry, it's only dying. Ha ha.

Zoe's first thought was what the hell kind of name is Inanna? Her second was thank goodness Jasmine had died instead of one of the other girls, who seemed much nicer. But then she tried to censor her thoughts because maybe Jasmine could read minds now that she was dead.

Next, Zoe wondered if the new girl would successfully restore Inanna to the house. Zoe hoped so, because dying was bad enough without being haunted along the way. She carefully slid the envelope back into the bed frame, making sure it stuck out a good deal so the new girl would find it. Zoe had a feeling that Jasmine would haunt the girl for not retrieving Inanna even if the new girl never found the note.

The note made her nervous, but exhaustion won out and soon Zoe was dozing. Images of Jasmine filled her head. She saw George holding the girl in his arms, her blue/black hair flowing, her eyes closed, her pale eyelids bluish. Then they snapped open and stared hard at Zoe.

She awoke with a start, and was further surprised to find she was on the bed. She tried to figure out how she got there, but sleep pulled her under again. Justin appeared, crying, in the distance. Then a black cat was staring at her up close, its yellow eyes boring into her face. Then she was working in the café, but she was well, and she mixed mochas and cappuccinos faster than the customers could order them.

The next time she woke up, the room was dark. She clambered out of bed and searched for a light switch. She didn't like groping around in the dark, half expecting some creature from her dreams to grab her fingers. But she found the switch and was overwhelmed by bright light. The room was just the same as it had been earlier, and didn't look creepy at all.

"Zoe?" A tap on the door. "You up?" It was Deni.

Zoe tried to answer, but was so mixed up from the dreams and Deni's sudden presence that she couldn't talk. Instead, she opened the door.

"What's wrong? You look a fright," Deni said.

"Weird dreams," Zoe rasped.

"Tell me about it! Mine are never anything but weird. I dreamt of a garden where these humongous zucchinis were growing. Like four feet long! I don't know what it means."

"Yeah. I don't know."

"So, what did you dream?"

"A bunch of things. My old boyfriend was in it, and my job, and a black cat, and Jasmine and George. It was kind of a jumble."

"You saw Jasmine?" Deni whispered. Zoe dropped her eyes, wondering if she shouldn't have mentioned her. "What did she say?"

"Nothing. She just looked at me."

"She didn't say anything?" Deni said, sounding peeved.

"Not a thing."

"Nothing, for example, about dying? Or how that went? Or where she is now?"

"No."

"Well, how did she look?"

"The same as in the pictures I've seen. Really pretty. Her eyes were big. She looked sort of pissed, I guess."

"Hmm." Deni's jaw was clenched and her eyes narrowed. "She was my best friend. Wouldn't you think she'd show up in *my* dreams? No offense, but you didn't even know her."

"Probably cause I was sleeping in her room," Zoe said gently. "Maybe if you slept in her bed, you could see her in your dream."

Deni was silent. Her jaw and shoulders relaxed. "Yeah. Maybe I'll try that." She took Zoe's hand. "Are you hungry?"

"I don't know."

"Come on. Valentina has dinner ready for us." Zoe followed obediently, reassured by Deni's touch. "Do you want to brush your hair or anything?" Deni asked, stopping outside the bathroom. "You can use anything you like in there."

"Okay," Zoe said uncertainly.

"I'll wait for you. Then we'll go downstairs."

Zoe slipped into the peach-colored bathroom, wondering what was expected of her. No one had suggested she brush her hair for years. But when she looked in the mirror, she understood why. Although the lighting was soft and should have been flattering, Zoe looked much worse than she expected. Her cheeks and eyes were sunken and skull-like, her skin too gray. Her T-shirt was loose where there should have been breasts. She tried smiling at herself, but looked scary as a jack-o-lantern. Worse, her gums seemed to be receding. She groaned, opening a drawer in the vanity to find a brush.

The drawers were full of things to delight pretty young women who aspired to be prettier. Lipsticks and eyeliners, hairclips and ribbons, nail polish and curling irons, and surprising amounts of sexual lubricants. Deni had said to use whatever, so Zoe tried to improve her face with concealer and blush. She brushed beige eyeshadow on her pallid lids. She dragged a comb through her limp hair, and frowned to see a blond clump leave with it. When she had done all she could, she peered at herself in the mirror. She couldn't tell if she looked convincing, or like a made up zombie.

"Zoe?" Deni called from outside the bathroom. "You okay?"

"I can't tell if I look better or not," Zoe said, opening the door.

"Better," Deni said decisively. "But let's tone the blush down." She brushed past Zoe, dampened a washcloth, and passed it over Zoe's cheeks. "There. We don't want you to look *too* vibrant. You're about to meet Mother."

Zoe had gathered that Mother was sort of like a boss. "She's here?" Zoe felt unreasonably nervous. Mother wasn't *her* boss. Why should she care?

"Oh, she'll love you," Deni said. "She prefers blondes," she added, a faint acid note in her voice.

Downstairs, everybody already sat around the table. Zoe had passed through the dining room earlier, but the lights had been off and she hadn't paid much attention. Now a chandelier blazed over a table set with white tablecloth and white cloth napkins.

Mother sat at the head of the table, auburn and heavily made up. Mascara-stiff lashes surrounded sharp green eyes. Her hawk nose looked regal above full magenta lips. Her hair was short and heavily moussed. When she saw Zoe, Mother backed her chair up and rose with grace, straightening up to her statuesque five feet, ten inches. She stood still, but seemed to pull Zoe towards her with personal magnetism.

"You must be Zoe." Everything about her screamed power, from her booming voice to the shoulder pads in her purple blazer. When Zoe reached her, Mother clasped her big hands around Zoe's. "Call me Mother. Everybody does."

Zoe looked down at Mother's hands, which were ruddy but well-manicured. "Okay," she squeaked, unable to find her normal voice. "Nice to meet you."

Mother looked at her so thoroughly that Zoe felt Mother knew her shoe size, bra size and IQ in one glance. Zoe imagined Mother could see her whole life: trailer kid, raver, dying girl. A short and pitiable little life, like a fly's.

"Sit down," Mother said. "Sit down, Zoe."

Zoe's place was beside Deni, across from Candi and Brenda. George sat at the foot of the table. While the silverware shone and the napkins had perfect accordion folds, no food was in sight.

Mother cleared her throat. Zoe saw that everyone else had bowed heads and clasped hands. "Lord," intoned Mother, loud enough so that heaven could hear, "thank you for another day." Deni elbowed Zoe under the table, as if to indicate this was a big joke. Later, Deni would tell Zoe that Mother's religion was capitalism and that her fake Christianity at strategic moments was a ploy to keep the dying girls calm and controlled by believing in Christian heaven. "We thank you for the love and security you provide us with each day, and the opportunity to serve you by supporting each other. Bless these precious young girls whom you saved, through me, from degrading deaths on the street." Another good jab from Deni startled Zoe against the table edge. Her fork rattled. Zoe could feel Deni shake with silent laughter. Mother cleared her throat again. "And Lord, let us remember to have respect and gratitude for those who do so much for us."

When everybody had said amen, Mother slapped her spoon against her water glass. Immediately a woman in a movie-perfect maid's outfit – black dress with white apron and cap – swung into the dining room, carrying trays of food. Deni shot a look at Zoe to gauge her reaction, and squeezed Zoe's hand under the table.

The maid had dark hair and eyes, high, wide cheekbones, and an expression that managed to be both severe and melancholy. She silently set out a huge bowl of white rice, a vat of chicken curry, and plates of what looked like party hors d'oeuvres. Then the maid soundlessly retired to the kitchen.

"Candi, serve me some rice, please," Mother said, handing her plate down to Candi. The red-haired girl looked tired. Her makeup was washed away, and her salmon-colored T-shirt gave her a sickly skin tone.

"How's that, Mother?" Candi asked.

"Perfect, dear. Thank you."

Everyone else passed their plates to Candi. Zoe would come to realize that whenever Mother set a precedent, even in the smallest things, the girls would know to follow.

Zoe gazed at the chicken curry and rice on her plate. She didn't know if her stomach could digest real food anymore. She'd eaten nothing but muffins for weeks. She reached for a Ritz cracker adorned with Cheese Whiz and an olive, unsure of protocol, afraid her hand might be slapped away.

"I hope you don't find the menu odd, Zoe," Mother said. "The girls like to nibble small things, mostly. That's why it looks like food for a cocktail party, not a proper dinner."

"It looks delicious," Zoe said awkwardly.

"Good. Now let's hear about Candi's date with Frank. Where did he take you, dear?"

George leaned forward, as though eager to hear the details. Brenda and Deni exchanged a glance.

"We went to the rose garden," Candi said. "It sucked."

"The Rose Garden? Did you see a concert? And please, we're trying to refine our language."

"Not the Rose Garden. The rose garden in Washington Park." Candi pushed a stuffed mushroom around her plate with a fork. "I told him the roses wouldn't bloom for months, but he said he wanted to photograph me with the rose bushes anyway. But they're all cut back to horrid thorny stumps. Not a leaf on them. They look dead."

"And then afterwards?" Mother asked, her eyes gleaming.

Candi shrugged. "You know, we stopped by his place."

"Stopped by?" Mother persisted.

"Look, I'm awfully tired," Candi said softly, poking the tines of her fork into the mushroom so little streams of liquid dribbled out.

"Did you leave him happy?" Mother asked.

"Would you like some mushrooms, George?" Brenda asked, picking up a plate and thrusting it toward the foot of the table.

George accepted the plate from Brenda with his eyes still on Candi. "Thanks," he murmured. "Did it go better this time?" he asked Candi. "Like I told you, think passive. Did you remember?"

A strange look had come across Mother's face, and when she spoke, her voice was even louder than before. "They don't come to us because they're looking for trampy vixens eager to spread their legs or chomp their– "

Deni surprised everybody by interrupting Mother, whose face had grown flushed. "Hey, we have a guest! I would like Zoe to come over again, so could you please not weird her out?"

There was a tense silence as everyone waited to see how Mother would react. She visibly collected herself, then laughed. "I'm sorry, Zoe," she said. "Sometimes I get carried away. I have a great fondness for hearing about the exploits of the young." Deni couldn't stifle a giggle, and this time Mother gave her a decidedly dark look, but didn't say anything.

The rest of the dinner was more normal, with Zoe giving stilted answers to questions about her life, her job, her housing, her family. The maid returned to refill water glasses, then again to clear plates. She brought glass dishes of sherbet and fresh fruit for dessert. Nobody talked to her, and she said not a word.

After dinner, the girls hugged Zoe. Mother shook her hand. "Well, are you ready to go home?" George asked. Zoe nodded, though she didn't want to leave.

On the way home, they said little. George asked her if she would like to come over again. She said yes and he promised to be in touch. When they pulled up in front of Justin's house, Zoe feared George would kiss her. Instead, he walked her up the front steps and shook hands. "We'll call you very soon," he said almost formally.

Inside, Zoe found that Justin's things were partially boxed up. Maybe tonight would be her last night in a bed. Soon the new housemates would arrive, and then Zoe would be on the couch until–until what?

She slept on her side of the bed, pretending Justin was still on his.

CHAPTER TWENTY-SIX

After two weeks in the group home, Justin suspected he was developing a mental illness. It had to do with the split between his inward life and outward manifestation. The first few days took a huge amount of effort just remembering not to talk, not to appear like he knew how to do a thousand simple tasks on his own. But by the end of a week, the effort had lessened considerably. It seemed as though his real self had drawn inward, compacted itself into a very small parcel, and hidden behind his ribcage. It scared him to think his real self would retreat so willingly, surrendering his body to the whims of staff people. He kept remembering Dave's ominous words on his first day at the workshop: You'll fit right in.

Justin had not adopted any of the personality quirks noted in Pete's original report. He had not slipped into public masturbation, nor had he peed his bed even once. The most he could muster was an occasional loud belch. But the staff had no reason to suspect anything. Except for Claudette, who seemed to hate everybody equally, Justin was a particular favorite at the workshop and in the home because he was so little trouble.

As he spent his days knotting cord, Justin gleaned information about the workshop and his coworkers. Some had come to this building every workday for the last ten years! As far into the future as Justin stayed, his life could remain thus. It reminded him of childhood, but without ambition. In the first grade a child can expect to be provided for: a roof, clothes, food, a daily schedule. But the parents have their own expectations: get good grades, clean your room, join the soccer team, be smarter than the neighbor's kid. In his new life, Justin had found the advantages of childhood without any expectation to grow up. It was eerily peaceful, if you looked at it a certain way. Maybe it was what people get out of meditation retreats, Justin thought. An appreciation of being, rather than accomplishing. For the first time in his life, Justin could drop the burden of trying not to disappoint people. No questions from his mother about where is her daughter-in-law, the incubator for her grandkids. And no queries from his father regarding the potential upward mobility in Justin's bullshit job. Justin had not done well at pleasing his parents, at rising in the dog-eat-dog world of moderately well educated white guys from middle class families. But as a developmentally disabled person, he was a top citizen: a self-toileter who had never yet attacked the staff.

Of course, this was only one of Justin's moods, the bright side of defeat. Obviously there were the problems of not seeing Zoe, not holding Zoe, not sleeping with Zoe, not feeling her breath on his skin or hearing her voice. He also missed talking, reading, and the right to scrub his own balls and ass. Free rent or no, this new life wasn't paradise.

And where was Pete? Where the fuck was Pete? When would Claudette or Garth or Lenny catch the flu and need to call in a substitute – Pete – to spend a night bringing news of Zoe and listening to Justin speak and maybe coming up with a new plan? Justin hated himself for this last thought, for his ongoing failure to fix his own problems.

At home, as long as everybody remained calm, the other residents pretty much ignored each other. They reminded him of a pair of male cats his family had when Justin was a kid. These cats lived their lives as though each were the only cat in the house. They were invisible to each other unless one got in the other's way, in which case teeth pierced necks and claws engaged. Justin's roommate, whom Justin thought of as Billy the Tongue, seemed not to notice that Justin moved in. Nancy's main interest in others was echoing their words. Since none of the other residents spoke, she was oriented toward the staff. Linus' overtures were truculent: glaring, growling and attempting to bite. Justin had an ugly scratch in his arm from Sunday morning, when he and Linus both wanted the last pancake. Garth had cleaned Justin's arm with betadine while telling Lenny he hoped Justin wouldn't get staph infection from Linus' nails. Lenny had been confused, saying he thought only staff could catch that.

Sally was the only housemate Justin liked. She was no longer afraid of him, sometimes even smiling when she saw him looking her way. She didn't seem dumb; her green eyes were alert. She had nice skin and a decent body. Justin wanted to kick himself for checking out a retard. He fantasized that she was hiding underground like he was. Or maybe she was in some top-secret witness protection program. Or traumatized as a child so she never developed normally. Or deaf-mute. Or something, because she was starting to look sort of good.

The second weekend turned out to be a break from monotony. Billy the Tongue's family came to retrieve him, leaving Justin with his own room. He used his privacy to catch up on masturbation and to read a *Portland Tribune* that he smuggled in from the living room. The front section pissed him off with its glorification of his country's bombs, boasts and bullying. But he was amazed by his pleasure in the arts section. He read about a jazz pianist who played hotel lounges, an art installation made entirely of found shoes, and a one-woman play about chocolates, sponsored by Godiva, with seats starting at $42. None of these articles would have held his interest three weeks ago. Was he starved for the act of reading? Or suddenly fascinated by the lives of normal people, so frivolous and free?

That second Saturday, Claudette said to Garth, "Jacob's hair is awfully shabby. Where are those scissors?"

"In the safe box," Garth said, continuing to sweep the hall. "I wish they'd fix the vacuum already." He frowned at the red indoor/outdoor carpeting, which looked about as clean as it would ever be since the stains obviously weren't going to come out.

Justin felt his heart pound as Claudette climbed on the kitchen counter to reach the safe box, which was kept on top of a cabinet. How could he keep the little bitch from cutting his hair? One of the problems with being retarded was you couldn't put people off by acting busy. No one's going to believe you're truly busy if you're repeatedly picking up and dropping a coffee can lid, or staring at a TV that isn't on, or pacing the hall and moaning. A staff person can grab hold of you at any time and make you submit to just about anything.

Garth hummed "Beauty School Dropout" as he swept. Claudette monkeyed her way down from the cupboard, scissors in hand. "Hey, why didn't you finish cosmetology school?" Garth asked.

"It was gross," she said. "I like doing hair, but you have to study about foot fungus. And people come in with nasty toenails and you have to give them pedicures."

"So you got a nice non-gross job at a group home." Garth laughed.

"Well, after my mom said I had to move out, everything changed. If only I'd stayed in school, she probably would have kept letting me live there rent-free! But it was too late. I'd dropped out. Living ain't free."

"Yeah, I've noticed that," Garth said.

Claudette and the scissors were getting closer. Justin's only chance to save his hair was to throw a fit or piss his pants, or maybe to faint. But the house was so peaceful this morning. Claudette and Garth were in good moods. Linus hadn't bit anyone for days. Justin didn't have the heart to send everyone into an uproar.

He knew his hair was a shaggy mess anyway. "Aaa," he said tentatively as Claudette came closer. At least with Garth here, she couldn't stab him.

"Now, Jacob," she said in her sweetie pie voice. "Don't worry. We're going to give you a nice haircut." Then in her normal voice, to Garth, "Can you get me a towel or something?

Claudette steered Justin toward a kitchen chair. "Aaaa," he said, but without conviction. He was 90 percent inclined to comply. Garth came back with two towels and a comb. One towel he spread on the floor beneath the chair, the other he wrapped around Justin's shoulders.

It felt nice when Claudette combed Justin's hair. He closed his eyes and pretended Zoe held the comb, though they had never shared an intimate hair combing moment. Why hadn't they? There were so many things he wished he'd done with her.

Fortunately, Claudette had a better touch with hair than with brushing teeth or dressing people. Justin wondered if Claudette's circumstances had been different and she had finished beauty school, would she be happy instead of evil?

"You look like you know what you're doing," Garth said, sounding surprised.

"I'll do yours next."

"Uh, that's okay," he said.

"Hey, are there any clippers around?" Claudette asked.

Garth found the clippers. Justin closed his eyes, resigned. "I can't believe he's putting up with this," Garth said. "He should win some kind of prize."

"Hey, I'm not hurting him," Claudette snapped, sounding more like herself.

When she finished, she and Garth examined Justin from every angle. "Damn, I'm good," Claudette said.

"Uh huh," Garth agreed. "Good job."

It was the only time Justin could remember that someone had cut his hair but not given him a mirror to see for himself. He didn't get the chance to admire his new look until that afternoon, at the Pioneer Place Nordstrom's.

Apparently, the staff was required to take clients on outings to simulate the normal life of non-retarded people. Garth and Claudette tossed a coin to see who got to decide on today's expedition. Claudette shrieked with joy when the quarter landed heads up. "Nordstrom's!" she screeched.

"No," Garth said. "Oh, no."

"Oh, yes!" Claudette cried. "Oh, yes! We went to that revolutionary nutcase bookstore last time! And we had to pick up trash with your ecology Nazi buddies the week before that! It's about time I got to pick somewhere normal."

"But Claudette, I can't go into Nordstrom's," Garth said.

She looked him over. "They'll probably let you in," she said doubtfully. "Try combing your hair. That might help."

"That's not what I meant." Garth's fingers clenched, probably dreaming of tightening around Claudette's scrawny neck. "Nordstrom's is a leader in the Portland Business Alliance. They're one of the foremost voices in getting the city council to vote against the resolution proclaiming Portland anti-war." Claudette stared at him blankly. "Everybody's boycotting Nordstrom's! KBOO was encouraging people to go leaflet outside today."

"Who?" Claudette asked.

Garth sighed. "I'll tell you what. You take the girls to Nordstrom's. I'll take the guys to Pioneer Square while you shop."

"You take Nancy. She talks too much. I'll take Jacob."

"Fine. As long as I don't have to go in that stupid store."

And so Justin found himself in the Nordstrom's lingerie department an hour later, while Claudette attempted to return a bra and panty set given to her by one of her boyfriends.

He had caught the first glimpse of his new look as they passed the ladies' department, but Claudette, who held one of his arms in her right hand and one of Sally's in her left, had yanked him along. Now, as she argued with the salesperson, Justin could examine his reflection at leisure. First, the clothes. They had dressed him in primary colors, like a little boy. He wore bright, new, no brand blue jeans, a red windbreaker over a sweater of a different red, yellow high tops, and a red baseball cap that said "SPORT" crowning the whole getup. Cautiously, he took off the cap to see his haircut. It wasn't just new, it was downright new wave. He fluffed the long front part, then turned to try and see the back, which had been trimmed to the scalp with the clippers. If he knew how to play an instrument and wasn't retarded, he could probably get a spot in a Duran Duran tribute band.

"I'm sorry, but underwear is simply not returnable, even with tags," said the saleslady, one of those perfect but interchangeable girls in their twenties who seem to have been raised for such jobs.

"Honestly, this panty set screams 'skag.' I was surprised to find out it came from Nordstrom's," said Claudette, her lips set in a tight, mean line. "It looks like Frederick's, or worse."

"Yes, but that doesn't change our return policy," the girl said, unruffled.

Justin noticed Sally standing before a rack of lace underwear in dozens of colors. She fingered a pair of white panties, smiling to herself. Gentle soul as she was, she often seemed to smile when Claudette was unhappy.

"I would like to speak to your manager. Can I speak to your manager?" Claudette demanded.

"No," said the salesgirl, her face passive, her eyes glowing.

A snort of laughter escaped Justin, but he pretended to be responding to a display of mannequins wearing underwear made of blue and purple feathers.

The saleslady turned back to her work of tagging tiny, sheer thongs. "Excuse me," Claudette said. "Excuse me." But the girl was done with her. She could see at a glance that Claudette wasn't a real Nordstrom's customer– cheap clothes, crooked teeth. There was nothing left for Claudette to do, short of rioting. "Bitch," she spat, then roughly seized Justin and Sally. "Come on!"

On their way out the front door, Justin saw a Jojo's Fair Trade World Coffee Café customer handing a leaflet to someone about to enter the store. He looked down the sidewalk and saw eight or ten other folks with stacks of leaflets. They ignored him and Sally and Claudette, maybe because they were leaving the store, maybe because they were retarded. Did everybody know? The way he was dressed, Claudette's grip on his arm – that of a guide, not a girlfriend – did that give him away?

"Nordstrom's wants Americans to keep consuming, and not think about what we are doing to other countries!" boomed a voice. "Folks, your tax money is killing people in countries you can't even pronounce!" The voice was so familiar, Justin caught his breath. Then he realized it was one of the KBOO deejays, a man whose voice used to wake Justin up every morning when his clock radio told him it was time to get up and visit Zoe at the café. He could feel those days in his gut– the excitement mixed with doubt that she would even notice him. The anticipation of simply seeing her, regardless of her reaction to him. It seemed like decadent languor now, the way he could loll in his bed and hit snooze if he wanted, no staff to interrupt his morning idyll with a jerked back blanket and a shower that was always too hot or too cold. That deejay's voice conjured up his old life: The goofy roommates. The stupid job. His vexing parents. It all seemed lovable and nostalgic now, like a seventies sitcom.

"Aaaaa," Justin exploded, like a true retard. The noise came pouring out of him and with it, the tears.

"Oh, for fuck's sake!" Claudette said under her breath. "Jacob," she said in a louder, cloying voice, "Now, now, sweetie."

"Aaaa!" he screamed, breaking free of Claudette and running blindly toward the Don't Walk sign. Brakes screeched, people stared. He made it across the street unharmed. "Stop him!" Claudette shrieked, and Justin was surprised he could hear her over a Saturday crowd at Pioneer Square.

He ran without a direction in mind, not sure what he was trying to escape. His old life? His new life? Most likely, himself. He tripped down the brick stairs, vaguely aware of a protest and counter protest. Signs, flags, shouts, stares. Not looking where he was going, his flight was short-lived. Suddenly he tripped over a sprawled body and fell on his stomach, the wind knocked out of him. His head wasn't working right and he couldn't breathe, so the scene around him registered slowly. He was lying in the midst of twenty people dressed in black or camouflage. At first, they were lying so still they seemed to be dead, an impression amplified by liberal quantities of dried blood on their faces, arms and clothes. But one by one they stirred, turning to look at him with hateful eyes.

He couldn't meet their gazes. He slowly rolled over onto his back and stared at the drizzly sky. From this perspective, the protestors he had run past were upside down. A guy with a sign proclaiming "God loves the USA" pointed at Justin and laughed. As Justin's brain slowly began working, he realized he had fallen into the middle of a die-in, a bunch of people playing dead to symbolize the deaths in other countries where American soldiers were dropping bombs. He heard an angry buzz, then saw a group of anarchist kids stomping towards him. They wore black clothes, except for the vinegar-soaked bandanas covering their mouths and noses. In addition to providing a disguise, these were supposed to lessen the effects of the pepper spray so popular with Portland cops. Slowly it dawned on Justin that the anarchists were coming for him, that they must have thought he fucked up this solemn protest on purpose. They didn't know he was retarded.

Who knows what would have happened if Garth hadn't run up just as the anarchists closed in on Justin. "Hey," Garth gasped, "leave him alone."

"Fuck you!" yelled an anarchist in a purple bandana. "You think bombing people is funny?"

"He's devel–" Garth began, but realized there wasn't time. "He's retarded, okay? He freaked out cause my coworker made him go in the Nordstrom's." Garth stopped, trying to catch his breath.

"Aaaaa!" Justin said, because this was sure as hell the time to act retarded. He saw the look in the nearest anarchist's eye soften.

"I'm really sorry," Garth said. "Believe me, I'm on your side. He didn't mean to mess up your protest. He didn't mean anything. He doesn't take a side. Let me just get him out of here."

Justin was terrified and helpless. This was just the sort of place the FBI stooges were sure to be. He felt warmth on his leg and realized he had peed his pants in public for the first time since adulthood.

Back in the van, the mood was dark. Linus grumbled and gnashed his teeth. Sally whimpered. "What set him off?" Garth asked Claudette.

She changed lanes without signaling and a horn honked. "Oh, piss off!" she said to the other motorist. "I don't know. What sets any of them off?"

"I've never seen Jacob act out like that," Garth said. "Something must have triggered it."

"Maybe that cunt in the lingerie department," Claudette said.

"Cunt in the lingerie department," Nancy echoed.

"Smells like someone peed their pants," Claudette said, rolling down her window.

Justin sank toward catatonia. What was left to do? If his extreme cowardice hadn't already turned him into a nonperson, now he had wet himself in the middle of Pioneer Square.

Garth had to practically drag Justin back inside the group home. Justin had given up. He had no intention of cooperating in any way. "Come on, buddy," Garth grunted. "Give me a little help here. You ever hear of a slipped disk?" Inside, Garth steered him toward the bathroom. "I think a shower and some clean clothes will help fix you up." For once, Justin didn't undress himself. He let Garth do everything– tugging at his wet jeans and briefs, pulling the stupid red sweater over his head. "What's with you, buddy?" Garth asked, annoyance and concern vying in his voice. "What happened back there?"

Once Justin had been thoroughly washed, Garth dressed him in his pajamas. "Why don't you lie down, okay? Maybe you're getting sick." He left Justin alone in the room, staring at the ceiling.

The catatonia wore off by dinnertime, leaving shame, sadness and a rumbling stomach. "Zoe," Justin whispered into his pillow, pretending his face was pressed against her shoulder. He hadn't spoken for two weeks.

Things were normal at dinner time. Claudette's macaroni and cheese was too soupy. She and Garth sniped at each other throughout the meal. Justin was glad Billy the Tongue was home with his parents. This was just the sort of food that would slip from his roommate's mouth as fast as he shoveled it in.

"Maybe we should put him in an adult diaper next time. Just in case," Claudette said, looking at Justin critically.

"Diaper next time. Just in case," Nancy repeated.

"We should put them all in diapers all the time," Claudette said. "Less laundry. Less disgusting."

"And we could lock them all up in a rubber room and just throw a loaf of bread in once a day," Garth said sarcastically. "Christ, Claudette, we're trying to make their lives as full and normal as possible. That's the whole point of having them live in a house in the middle of a regular neighborhood."

"Yeah, I went through the training, too. But no one's fooled. Do you see the neighbors coming over to borrow a cup of sugar?"

"I don't think the neighbors eat. I think they run a meth lab," Garth said.

"So much for your regular neighborhood," Claudette snorted.

Linus had quietly slipped a hand in his pants and suddenly Justin noticed Linus' forearm moving rhythmically.

"Not at the table, Linus," Garth said firmly.

"Oh, for fuck's sake!" Claudette said.

Sally smiled down at her plate, her fork poking holes in a piece of macaroni.

"Uhhhh," Linus moaned, his hand suddenly still, his body relaxed.

Justin ate his macaroni. It was better than it looked.

After dinner, Garth and Claudette argued over listening to the radio versus watching TV. "You get to go home in an hour, but I have to stay all night," Claudette complained.

"So?" Garth countered.

"So I get to pick!" She won because he would be out of earshot, getting everybody ready for bed. Garth and Linus disappeared into the bathroom. Claudette turned on a reality TV show, dialed a number on the cordless phone, then cleaned the kitchen with one hand. Justin sat on the couch, avoiding the soggy end where Nancy habitually pissed. Someone should do a reality show set here, he thought, as he watched scantily clad twenty year-olds lounging on their houseboat.

After all teeth were brushed, Garth left the residents alone with Claudette. A news program about new trends in underwear followed the houseboat show. Male and female models strutted about in thongs, bikinis and fake smiles. Their bodies looked shiny, like they were molded out of plastic.

Justin entertained himself by trying to guess who was on the phone. One was her mother, then possibly a sister, if you could imagine anything as gruesome as multiple Claudettes. Then a boyfriend, then a guy who might be auditioning for auxiliary boyfriend. Claudette's voice got high and giggly when she talked to him.

"What's so funny?" Claudette said into the phone. "What channel? I want to see." She grabbed the remote just as the only attractive model, a tall Brazilian girl with masses of black hair, was about to model what had been hyped as "a revolution in panties."

"Oh my God!" Claudette screeched. Justin watched in horror as a brightly clad figure ran straight toward what looked like dozens of dead bodies, tripped over one, and flew headlong into the supine crowd. The colorful figure lay still, though some of the nearby corpses resurrected to glare at him. Then, as he slowly turned over, the camera zoomed in to clearly show Justin's face, his mouth opening wide as he said, "Aaaaaa!"

Claudette broke into laughter, then abruptly stopped. "Oh my God, I hope my boss doesn't see this." Then she was explaining to the guy that the famous retard was one of her charges, that in fact he was sitting right there on the couch right now. She smiled at Justin, as if to thank him for conferring celebrity upon her. "You really think so?" she asked. "The funniest thing *ever?* I don't know about that. But don't you think his hair looked good? I cut it myself this morning." Justin had lost his cap when he fell on his stomach, revealing all his new wave glory.

At least you can't tell I peed my pants, Justin thought in his first shocked moment. His next worry was Zoe. Would she see this? She would think he had gone insane! His clothes, his haircut, his dive into the landscape of bodies, none of these would add up to her planning a rosy future with him.

And what about Pete? He would shake his head at this latest proof of Justin's ineptitude, his inability to do anything as simple as lay low and have all his needs provided for.

It took Justin another thirty seconds to think of his real problem: the FBI. But they had no reason to watch local news. Did they? What did they do at night in their corporate hotel suites, paid for, no doubt, with Justin's own tax dollars? What if they were bored of pay-per-view TV? What if they were flipping channels and happened upon

Justin's yelling face? Perhaps they had informants who monitored such things, who would call the FBI on secret numbers and say, "Turn on channel six, Agent So and So."

When Claudette finally got off the phone, her mood began to slump. "If Garth had stayed with the others, and I'd run after you, maybe I would have been on TV," she said, eyeing Justin jealously. "You probably didn't even recognize yourself. You know, my mom's dog doesn't know his own reflection in the mirror." She leaned back, stretching her skinny body and sighing. She looked tired. "What are you still doing up, anyway? It's after eleven."

"Aaaaaa," Justin said.

"Well, go to bed already," she said. She pointed toward the hall and slowly repeated, "Go to bed."

He decided to understand her words tonight. Slowly he stood and ambled down the hall. Maybe fifty years from now he'd be an old man in pajamas, toddling around the halls of a nursing home with some young bitch like Claudette giving him orders.

No. He'd shoot himself first.

CHAPTER TWENTY-SEVEN

Deni called Zoe the day after Zoe's visit to the house of dying girls. Zoe sat on the couch in Justin's house, trying to make herself smaller as the new roommates carried in load after load. The roommates were a couple, big blonds that looked like siblings. Zoe wouldn't have answered the phone if they hadn't given her such a strange look as she sat ignoring the ringing. "Zoe, you were in my dreams last night," Deni said when Zoe answered the phone.

Zoe felt better hearing the other girl's voice. "Really? You were in mine, too." She couldn't remember anything specific, but the dying girls had been with her in dreams since she first saw their website a couple of weeks before.

"Really? What are you doing?"

"Just sitting on the couch. Some new roommates are moving into my room," Zoe said, feeling detached. The inertia of dying had set in. She no longer worried about Pete and Sam's discomfort at having to evict her. Let them try! She was too tired to worry about finding a new home, and had no plans to go anywhere.

"Really? How many of you are going to live in your room now?"

"Huh?"

"They're moving in your room with you?"

"No, I moved out," Zoe said.

"Where are you going to live?"

"Right here."

"On a couch?"

"Sure."

"Zoe, are you okay? You sound so far away." Zoe didn't answer. She felt okay, but not talkative. "Zoe? What's going on? You can't live on a couch."

Zoe wondered if the new roommates were from a farm family in Nebraska, brother and sister suffering beneath the weight of forbidden love. They looked so happy. Zoe didn't see anything wrong with it.

"Zoe? Zoe?"

"Yeah. I'm okay, Deni. Just kind of tired. But happy to hear your voice. Really happy." A tear rolled down her cheek as she said this, though she didn't feel sad. Weird. First her physical self had mysteriously broken down. Now maybe her emotions were going haywire.

"Zoe. You just stay there and rest. I'm going to call you back in a little bit. Okay?"

"Yeah. Okay, Deni. Okay."

Zoe hung up and counted the blond couple's trips in and out, U-Haul to house, to and fro. Dressers, boxes, lamps. She counted six trips before she dozed off.

The wings beat over Zoe as she lay on the couch, comforting her like white noise. Nothing else was going on in her dream. It was very peaceful. Then a light touch on her shoulder. Deni? But the voice was male.

"Zoe? Zoe?" She opened her eyes and there was George: handsome, solid, only slightly sinister. "That's good, honey. Is this your stuff?" He gestured towards six shopping bags, the paltry belongings she had moved with her out of Justin's room to make way for the blonds. She nodded. "You're coming with me, okay? Deni told

me you need some looking after, and I'm going to take care of you."
His eyes were moist. "Okay, Zoe? Will you let me take care of you?"

She wasn't sure if she was awake or asleep. How had he gotten in?
Surely the doorbell would have woken her. She must be asleep,
because she could still hear the wings beating. She smiled at him.
"Okay," she whispered, then closed her eyes and dozed while he
carried her bags to his car. He gently roused her and she leaned on his
shoulder as they left the house. She said goodbye to no one, and no
one saw her go.

George's car was warm. Zoe sank into the seat, listening to
seventies light rock playing on the radio. Was it the Little River Band?
Zoe remembered this song from her childhood, or this feeling, at least.
There had been a time when Zoe felt safe, warm and comfortable with
her mother, who favored just this sort of music. Zoe remembered a box
full of cassettes that all sounded like this song.

"Mother thinks you're very pretty," George said, and it took Zoe a
moment to realize he was talking about his own mother. "And the
other girls think you're nice and friendly. You'll fit in perfectly. You'll
be very happy." He looked over and smiled at her. With one hand on
the wheel, one stretched over the back of the seat, he seemed so
comfortable and natural, so reassuring. She smiled back, sending him
her gratitude. Now she would not have to die on the couch.

George didn't try to make her talk like Justin had. George
understood dying girls. Zoe realized with a pang that Justin wouldn't
be able to find her now, if he returned, if he tried. But she would spare
him her death.

At the house, the other girls gathered around and Deni almost
knocked Zoe over giving her a hug. "Zoe needs a little rest," George
said, shooing them off her. "I know she's happy to be here, but she
needs to lie down right now."

Zoe smiled at the other girls. She was happy, but George was right.
The room spun. "Just for a few minutes," she said. "Lie down." She
saw concern on Deni's face. The girls moved back, letting George lead
Zoe upstairs, stopping to rest every few steps. He guided her into
Jasmine's room, then sat at her feet to remove her boots. He gave each
foot a squeeze, and didn't mention the missing heel in one sock and
missing toe in the other. She gasped when he undid her pants, but she

let him slide them over her bony hips. When he had stripped her down to a T-shirt and underpants, he pulled back the blankets on Jasmine's bed. The pink flannel sheets were soft on her sensitive skin. George kissed her forehead. "Sleep as long as you like, dear," he said. She drifted off while he sat on the edge of the mattress.

Zoe woke several times during the afternoon and night, but lacked the strength or will to move. She didn't feel fully conscious again until the gray morning light seeped through her windows. She had a lingering impression of a yellow glow, like the moon, like two moons. A black cat's eyes. She had seen that same cat before, in a dream, in this same bed. She shook off the memory of its intense gaze.

Deni tapped on Zoe's door around eight. "Zoe," she whispered. "You awake?" Zoe told her to come in, and Deni entered wearing a sheer black nightgown. Wide straps stretched over her thin shoulders and the long skirt brushed the floor. Her cinched waist was so tiny. Zoe imagined George's two hands encircling it. Had she seen that in one of the website photos? Deni's chest was almost flat, her big nipples visible through the gown. Her eyes were made up with black eyeliner and a dusky plum eye shadow. She wore a black scarf around her bald head.

"What are you wearing?" Zoe asked, confused. "Is it goth day or something? And isn't it like eight in the morning?"

Deni laughed. "We dress up whenever we feel up to it," she said. "Our fans live all over the world."

"Huh?"

"The webcam! I've been chatting with fans on the webcam." Deni sat on the edge of Zoe's bed. "It's a hoot. You'll love it."

"Oh," Zoe said, her brain beginning to work. She hadn't planned on earning her care. She figured she'd just come with George and die. In fact, what was she doing alive and awake?

"You're not shy, are you?" Deni asked. Zoe shrugged. "You ever dance or turn tricks or anything?" Zoe didn't answer. "It doesn't matter. This is easy. Believe me. Our members, they treat you like a fucking princess. This guy in Holland I was talking to today, he's going to send me some diamond and emerald earrings."

"Why?"

"To show his love! He's halfway around the world. What else is he going to do, give me a foot rub?"

"You look pretty," Zoe said.

"You think so?" Deni's face lit up. "You can come on my webcam with me. Until you have your own set up."

"My own?"

"George will have you all set up by the end of the week. He'll take a bunch of pictures of you. Don't worry. You'll look great. And he'll make it all easy for you."

"I don't have clothes like that."

"Oh, you will soon enough. Probably by the end of the day. George is a genius at shopping. Everything fits, and it's always the right color. When I first came here, I thought I'd get some dead girl's hand me downs. But George isn't tacky like that. He might pass down jewelry. Real stuff, you know, diamonds and shit like that. But the clothes go straight to United Cerebral Palsy. I think he had a cousin or something with cerebral palsy, cause he always gives them good stuff."

"Wow," Zoe said. "I wonder what he'll buy me."

"Oh, it won't all be stuff like this. We just try to give some variety. Like today I'm dying goth queen, but Candi will be on later and maybe she'll be dying cheerleader. Sometimes the fans request a look, or George or Mother has an agenda, or we just choose."

"Did you choose that?"

"Yeah. I wanted to look good on your first morning. I'm so happy you're here, Zoe. We're going to have so much fun together!"

"Fun?" Zoe said. "I was just hoping for a warm place to die." Her blood surged to hear herself say aloud the words she thought. But Deni just laughed.

"Don't be in a hurry," she said. "You have to outlast me, remember? I'm supposed to get there first so I'll be holding my hand out to you when you stumble down the tunnel of light." Deni looked deep into Zoe's eyes and all was silent for a minute. Then she smiled.

"Move over." Zoe scrunched herself toward the wall and Deni slid under the sheets. She kissed Zoe on the lips, a soft warm kiss, then held the blond girl in her arms. "I'm so happy, Zoe," she murmured. Zoe felt curiously stirred. Both girls were skinny as birds, their hearts beating fast together.

They lay in the bed, both smiling, Zoe feeling complete. They were quiet a few minutes, then a tapping came at the door. "Zoe?" George called. "You awake?"

"Uh huh," she said, but not loudly enough for him to hear, so he pushed the door open.

"Oh, lovely," he said when he saw Deni in Zoe's bed. "Where's my camera?"

"Let the new girl eat breakfast first," Deni said. "Anyway, the outfits don't go together. Vampirella meets girl next door doesn't work."

"I'm not so sure about that," George said. "But okay, okay. How did you sleep on your first night?"

"Fine," Zoe said brightly, trying to show her gratitude. "Great."

"Mother and I are going to get you some things today." George beamed at her with his dewy eyes. "You need anything, just ask the other girls."

The girls had a leisurely breakfast in the dining room. Zoe really wasn't hungry, but the novelty of being waited on intrigued her even more than it embarrassed her. Who was this Valentina – dressed in her spotless maid's outfit and not saying a word – serving them coffee and sweet rolls? While Valentina was in the kitchen fixing Candi's special caffeine-free tea with lime juice and grated ginger, Brenda whispered a story about the maid's tragic life in America. She had been a doctor in one of the Soviet states before the end of communism, fallen on tough times, come to the U.S. as a mail order bride, been horribly abused by her American husband, reduced to turning tricks on 82nd, and saved by the wonderful George. Deni rolled her eyes and shook her head. Zoe was about to question them, but Valentina returned, stony-faced, with Candi's tea.

In midmorning, Zoe realized she was due at the café in three hours and that her new lifestyle was totally incompatible with her job. The café was approximately eighty-five blocks away now instead of three. And she hadn't merely moved to a new house. More and more she was seeing that she had landed in an entirely different culture that would swallow any vestiges of her old life. It turned out that even calling her boss wasn't simple here.

"Where's the phone?" Zoe asked Brenda and Candi as they sat in the living room listening to some sort of mainstream alternative rock station that Zoe found abysmal.

"Who do you need to call?" Brenda asked.

Zoe thought this was a nosy question, but maybe Brenda was bored. "Just my job," Zoe said. "Tell my boss I can't make it."

"He'll notice when you don't show up," Candi said. "Why call?"

"If I call now, *she* might be able to cover for me so she doesn't lose business. I've worked there a whole year. I'm not just going to blow her off."

"George doesn't really like us to use the phone," Candi said, not meeting Zoe's eye.

"We talk to members," Brenda said.

"Well," Zoe said carefully, thinking this was the creepiest thing yet, "after this, I don't think there will be anybody left to call. So where's the phone?"

The other girls looked at each other. "George's office," Brenda said. But as Zoe started to get off the couch, Brenda added, "It's locked. He locks it whenever he goes out."

"What if there's an emergency?" Zoe asked, but the girls shrugged. "Payphone close by?" Zoe probed. "Like maybe on 82nd?"

"82nd," Candi said, wrinkling her nose. "I never go there. It's trashy."

Zoe sighed. The house was warm and she was tired. But she still had the resolve that had sustained her for the last few months. Was she going to let it fizzle out now and not even call to quit her job? Laura had been more than decent to her, trying to keep Zoe employed despite all the days she missed.

Ten minutes later, Zoe was dressed in her coat, hat and gloves and had located one dollar in quarters. Deni was on her webcam, so she didn't comment on Zoe's expedition. The other girls acted like she was a raving eccentric. Zoe had a moment of panic when the front door stuck and she thought they were locked in. But then she saw the deadbolt was engaged. "I'll be right back," she said to the girls, who looked nervous.

"Hurry. You should get back before they do," Candi said.

"They're awful worriers," explained Brenda.

As Zoe walked the half block to 82nd Avenue, a peculiar thought flitted through her head: that she'd have a better reference from her café job if she called and quit than if she disappeared without a word. But what did she need a reference for? Part of her still denied reality and expected a future.

A tulip lit up one scruffy, weed-filled yard. Full and red, it stopped Zoe's breath. Her last spring, her last season of tulips. Quitting her job was final, it meant she was on her way out. Because she had loved running Jojo's Fair Trade World Coffee Café. Nowhere felt more like home to her. A year ago, if some guy had asked her to quit her job at Jojo's to come live in his house and do God knows what on camera for strangers, she would have called the cops. Or at least told the guy to fuck off. Zoe liked to take care of herself. Besides, she had no interest in other people's sexual thrills.

By the time Zoe reached the corner of 82nd, she was exhausted, cold, and had tears on her cheeks. Worse, she didn't see a payphone. Across the street were used car lots. To her right, the sign on a bright pink mobile home said Beauty Spa. To her left, a strip mall contained a liquor store, nude bar and XXX video rental. She tried the liquor store.

"You have an ID, honey?" asked the man behind the counter. He had a face like a Bassett hound.

"I'm looking for a payphone."

The man jerked a big thumb at the wall to his left. "They got one next door."

She hesitated outside Tina's Hideaway, but the wind whipped her cheek so she pushed open the door and entered a nude bar for the first, and she supposed the last, time ever. Inside, it looked like any rundown bar with neon beer signs and overflowing ashtrays, except for a small stage where a big-breasted woman idly shook her hips to "Maggie May." A few men were sprinkled about in the shadows, hunched over their drinks and paying minimal attention to the naked woman.

The bartender, a guy in his fifties with slicked-back hair, polished cocktail glasses with a stained towel. His gaze slid over Zoe, and she imagined he had appraised so many potential dancers that he could see the contours of her body despite her big coat. "Not hiring right now," he said. "Not like we have a crowd here. Christ, take a look around."

"I'm trying to find a payphone," Zoe said, but couldn't project over the music.

"What? Christ, you work in a place like this, where does your hearing go? It goes!"

Zoe stepped closer. "Payphone?" she asked, mimicking a receiver held to her ear.

"One by the ladies room is busted. These dancers! Do they wreck things!" She must have looked dejected, because his face softened. "Hell, you look like a girl I once knew a long time ago. I could be your daddy! Do you know your daddy?" Zoe nodded. "Oh well. But it's one thing I regret. Not having kids, as far as I know. Yeah, you look just like her, best I can remember. Hell, kid, why don't you use the bar phone?" He shoved it toward her.

Zoe thought the noise level might improve after "Maggie May" finished, but next came Alice Cooper's "Welcome to my Nightmare." Well, she was quitting anyway. She picked up the phone and dialed Laura's number.

"Hello?" came her boss' wary voice.

"Hi. It's Zoe," she said loudly.

"Zoe! Where are you? The caller ID says Tina's Hideaway. I almost didn't pick up."

"It's a bar. I don't have a phone right now."

"No phone? What happened?"

Zoe felt a spark of annoyance. What did she think happened? She was the one who halved Zoe's hours and demoted her to a practically tip-free shift. "Listen, Laura," Zoe started, but she was all choked up.

"What? Zoe, I can't hear you. Maybe they could turn the music down?"

"I can't make it in," Zoe managed.

"Did you say you can't make it?"

"Yeah."

"But your shift starts in two hours," Laura said, that familiar testiness creeping into her voice.

"I have to quit," Zoe forced herself to say.

"What? Can't they turn down the music?"

"I quit!" Zoe said loudly. "I'm too sick," she added softly.

"What! I wish you had given me more than two hours notice. You've been a good employee up till recently, Zoe, but–"

Zoe hung up. She had done the responsible thing, but she felt like shit.

"I feel like saying that every day," the bartender said. Zoe looked at him, confused, till she realized he must have heard the "I quit" but not the "I'm too sick." "What are you going to do now, kid? You got another job lined up? Cause we're not hiring here. You know what they like here? Breasts. Big ones. It's not like downtown where they hire lots of skinny dancers. No offense. I ain't saying nothing about you. So you got a new job?"

"Sort of," she said.

"Or maybe a new man?"

Zoe didn't answer. That might be more correct than calling being a professional dying girl a job. "Thanks for the phone," she said, leaving in a hurry.

The journey to Tina's Hideaway and the sorrow surrounding her resignation from Jojo's exhausted Zoe. She dragged herself back to the house of dying girls, past Brenda's worried inquiries, up the stairs, and into Jasmine's bed. She slept for three hours.

Once again, Zoe awoke feeling like she had sunspots from staring into two bright yellow orbs. Her dreams had left her with a feeling of an animal, a bright-eyed, black furred animal. And then it hit her. Inanna! The cat in Jasmine's note. It had to be. But instead of Jasmine, it was Inanna herself who had come to haunt Zoe, because she was the new girl to whom the note was addressed. Zoe groaned. The creature from her dream was stronger and more threatening than a normal cat. Did she want it for a roommate?

Zoe got up to go to the bathroom. "Zoe?" Deni called to her when she heard Zoe in the hall.

"Just a sec," Zoe said. After using the bathroom, Zoe walked into Deni's room. Deni had changed out of her goth outfit and was resting on her bed in baggy blue pajama bottoms and a black tank top, a word search book propped on her knees and a pen in her hand. Zoe lay down beside her, gazing idly at Deni's rock collection. It was just out of camera range, something personal that the fans never saw. Deni had lovingly shown Zoe the rocks and gems of her native Arizona: malachite, amethyst, turquoise, peridot, petrified wood.

"Were you sleeping?" Deni asked, tossing the word search to the floor and reaching out to stroke Zoe's hair. It was nice, but Zoe felt a twinge of guilt for having hair when her friend was bald.

"Yeah. But every time I sleep, that cat's in my head. Its big yellow eyes."

"What cat?" Deni asked, her own eyes widening.

"I guess it must be Inanna," Zoe said. "Or however you say it."

"Inanna! How do you know about Inanna?"

"Jasmine left a note. She said she'd come back and haunt me if I didn't get Inanna back." Zoe shrugged. She didn't think Jasmine would have much luck haunting her. Zoe imagined herself lying on the mattress in her usual exhausted state while the black-haired girl prowled around the bed, rattling chains and yelling, "Boo!" Zoe would lack the energy to react. Pretty soon Jasmine would be yelling, "Pay attention, bitch! I'm haunting you!" And that wouldn't exactly be terrifying.

But Deni looked freaked out. "Oh, shit. I hope George knows where to find that cat."

"What do you think Jasmine could do?" Zoe asked, catching a smidgen of paranoia.

"I don't know. She was my best friend, but she could play mean tricks. But really, if it's her last wish and her only wish, well, what if it isn't fulfilled and she keeps roaming around the earth with the living? What kind of life is that? I mean, afterlife."

"Well, I'm sure she'll get bored eventually and go wherever spirits go."

"But how long will that take?" Deni sounded almost whiny.

"What's wrong?" Zoe asked, seeing the scared look on Deni's face.

"She's supposed to be there for me," Deni whispered. "Sure, I know lots of dead people, but she's the only one who said she'd be waiting for me. She knows I'm coming soon. I mean, there's got to be lots of dead people with all of history behind us. I don't know how long it takes to find people over there. It might be lonely or scary at first."

Zoe wrapped her arms around Deni, who was shaking "What can we do?" she asked gently.

"You have to tell George right away! Tell him about the dreams, and about Jasmine wanting Inanna back."

"Maybe you could tell him?"

"No! He'd think I was just fucking with him, making stuff up."

"Okay," Zoe soothed her. "Okay. What kind of name is Inanna?"

"Oh, it's some ancient goddess type thing. Jasmine was into all that. Magic, you know, and goddesses and stuff to do with the underworld." A tear rolled down Deni's cheek.

Oh, to be loved and missed like Jasmine, Zoe thought enviously.

Zoe suffered through another strange dinner with Mother presiding. "We decided on a high class look for you," she said to Zoe.

"You have a look like an ill Victoria's Secret model. Less bust, of course, but with those upscale cheekbones and vacant eyes. You look pliant."

Zoe didn't know what was upscale about her cheekbones and it didn't sound like a compliment about her eyes. She nibbled at a Vietnamese salad roll. The cilantro and peanut flavors seemed sharp after her steady diet of muffins. She sensed that everybody was waiting for a response, so she mumbled, "Okay."

"You might need some lessons in articulation and etiquette before conversing with our members," Mother said. Deni squeezed Zoe's hand under the table, but nobody spoke up on her behalf. Mother sighed. "It's a unique mission I have in life," she said, "helping such needy, uneducated young ladies." Then she ignored the girls and talked to George about specifications of computers and video streaming that Zoe had no knowledge of or interest in.

After dinner, George got out the camera. "How about a few pictures, Zoe?" he asked. "I'd like to get your page up by Friday so our members can meet you." He smiled reassuringly.

"I'm kind of tired."

"Of course you are!" he cooed. "Just a few pictures. You don't have to do anything special. You can lie in bed. Deni, why don't you help Zoe with a little eye makeup? You know how I like it."

"Do I ever!" Deni said. "Come on." She took Zoe's hand and pulled her towards the stairs. "We'll call you when she's ready."

All the girls crowded in front of the mirror. Brenda and Candi were getting ready for a two-girl live cam show for some members. Candi wore emerald bra and panties, which made her hair look redder. Brenda wore a sheer pink nightie. She was the only girl whose illness had left her more than an A cup. Zoe's eyes kept straying to Brenda's breasts, which looked like life. "You like girls?" Brenda asked, catching Zoe's eyes in the mirror. Zoe blushed and shrugged. "It's okay. I like girls, too. And guys."

"Listen," Deni hissed. "You won't believe it. Jasmine came to Zoe in a dream. She wants Inanna back!"

"No!" Brenda and Candi both said, makeup applicators freezing in midair.

"She said she's going to haunt us if that damn cat doesn't come home."

"But it's probably been put to sleep by now," Candi said. "Didn't George take it to the Humane Society?"

"Maybe someone adopted it," Brenda said. "I'm sure George wouldn't let it be put to sleep."

"Adopted the world's creepiest cat?" Deni said. "No one in their right mind would adopt Inanna."

"How do you think she'd haunt us?" Candi asked, looking nervous. "I mean, what would she do?" She looked at the brush she had just dipped in face powder like she didn't know what to do with it. "George is going to freak."

"You have to tell him when he comes upstairs," Deni said to Zoe. "You have to tell him tonight."

"Okay," Zoe said, though she didn't understand the hurry.

"Are you ready?" came George's voice from the base of the stairs.

"Almost," Brenda called back when Deni couldn't seem to answer.

"I'm coming up in two minutes," he said.

Deni's hands were shaky, so she instructed Zoe on her makeup application. Zoe's eyes looked huge, framed with brown mascara and eyeliner, a dusting of gold shadow shimmering her eyelids.

Then George stood in the doorway. "Four good looking girls!" he exclaimed, aiming his camera where they gathered before the mirror. And thus the first picture was taken before Zoe knew what was happening.

"I wasn't ready," she said.

"They'll all be just that easy," he smiled. "Now let's put you in a better outfit. Mother and I bought you a few things today." Sure enough, when Zoe, George and Deni walked down the hall to Zoe's room, Zoe found three shopping bags on her bed. "Like Mother said, your wardrobe will be classy," George said as Zoe peeked into a Victoria's Secret bag. "Nothing flashy. No sequins, glitter or that sort of thing. What do you think?"

Zoe had never owned such underwear. Silky and beautiful beneath her hands, cool as water. She pulled out camisoles and panties in blues, greens and gray. "Wow," she said, strangely moved. She realized that George was doing this for his own profit and jollies. He and Mother were perverse, maybe dangerous, so she hadn't expected to be touched. But only her mother had ever gone shopping for her. On a good day it would have been Target, on a bad day, the Goodwill. Her mother had never bought her silk or anything else that would require hand washing. "Thanks, George. Everything is beautiful."

His smile was warm and genuine. Behind him, Deni was mouthing something, but Zoe didn't understand what. "Try something on," he said.

"Okay. What should I wear first?"

"How about the pale blue camisole? And the matching tap pants."

"What pants?"

"Those little shorts that match the camisole," George said. "They're called tap pants."

"I never knew my lingerie terminology before moving in, either," Deni said. "You'll expand your vocabulary around here."

"Hey, why don't you be in a few pictures, too?" George asked Deni. "Go change into that coral teddy."

Deni sighed like he was asking a lot. She mouthed something at Zoe again.

"Huh?" asked Zoe.

"Tell him," Deni said, exasperated. Then she went to get the teddy.

"Tell me what?" George asked. He looked concerned.

"I'm supposed to tell you Jasmine wants Inanna back," Zoe said as though she were delivering a phone message. "That's all. Jasmine said you'd better bring Inanna home, or she's going to haunt us."

"Huh?" George said, struck ineloquent himself. His winter tan drained from his face. Deni returned, holding the teddy. "Did you put her up to this?" he asked the bald girl sharply.

"No! Do you think I liked that creepy cat? But if Jasmine wants it back, I hope you know where that cat is."

"Was she here?" George asked softly.

"Inanna?" Zoe asked.

"No! Jasmine."

"Oh. No. Well, just in a dream."

"Hmm." He walked to the computer in the corner of the room and started fiddling with it.

Deni caught Zoe's eye and shook her head and rolled her eyes around like George was a case. She seemed very relieved now that the message was delivered. "Change your outfit. I'll take the first few pictures," she said, picking up the camera.

Zoe quickly changed into the camisole and tap pants while George's back was turned. She knew he'd see all of her before long, but right now she was grateful he was occupied with his worries.

"Damn, you look hot!" Deni said. "Let's start with you lying on the bed." Zoe lay stiffly on her back. "No, no. Dying, not dead. That's a different website. Roll over on your side. Sort of delicate and fetal. Yeah, that's better. Just relax. Don't worry about looking at the camera yet. We'll do those later." Deni walked around the edge of the bed, taking photos of Zoe from different angles. Zoe closed her eyes and pretended she was dreaming.

"How about caressing yourself a little. Like stroke your thighs or your breasts. Yeah, that's perfect. Artistic and tasteful."

Lying on the bed with her eyes closed, it was easy to follow Deni's instructions. It felt like nothing. Each click of the camera made it matter less. Lying in her own little room with dear Deni was a whole different reality than what would become of the pictures– available for infinite reproduction, weird men spilling their salty cum on computer keyboards.

At some point, Deni handed the camera to George and crawled in bed with Zoe. At first Deni embraced Zoe, then she kissed her neck, her cheeks, her shoulder, sweetly and tenderly. Zoe couldn't say at what point it turned sexual, because it all felt like comfort. The kissing of lips and breasts, the stroking of thighs. But when Deni's fingers were in her pussy, Zoe had to admit to herself she had become a porn model.

Zoe lacked the energy to come. When the digital camera was full, they stopped. Zoe had kept her eyes closed almost the whole time, but when she opened them now she saw George's wide smile. "What a great first session!" he said.

It was easier to become a porn model than Zoe had ever suspected. She fell in with the house, and her new life unrolled as naturally as a potato bug.

George was never forceful, and Mother wasn't around much during Zoe's first week. It was Deni who goaded Zoe along to each new step. "Ooh, let's take a shower together, Zoe," Deni would suggest at the breakfast table, and a minute later George would follow with the camera. "You're kidding! You've never tried a vibrator? I have a drawer full. Come see." Sometimes Zoe wondered if this seamless coordination between Deni and George was planned. But mostly she figured it was a combination of Deni's loneliness and the business of the house. Deni had discovered Zoe. It was Deni to whom the new girl had sent those first emails. Besides, Candi and Brenda had each other. Everybody got along, but Deni didn't do two-girl shows with Brenda or Candi. The relationships were like the intense pairings of adolescent girls. If they had known each other outside of this house, they might not have thought of each other sexually. But here, everything was sex and death, with cameras tracking both.

By Friday, George had 500 photos on Zoe's website. Non members could access twenty-five pictures. If they wanted to see 475 more, then had to cough up the money.

Zoe's photos disturbed her. She had always considered porn fake. The women in the few magazines and videos she had seen looked like they'd just as soon be standing in line at the grocery store. Or they overplayed it, turning themselves into caricatures of arousal. But Zoe's own photos transcended her surface. The ones Deni had taken of Zoe seemed like art photos that captured loneliness and alienation more than anything sexual. The two girls together looked more porn, but their faces and poses were natural and joyful. When Zoe saw the photos, she wondered for the first time if she was in love with Deni.

But didn't she still love Justin? Everything was fucked up, sped up, because he had disappeared and she was dying.

Towards the end of Zoe's first week, she napped pleasantly one afternoon. For once, Jasmine and her cat let Zoe dream about something forgettable. But when Zoe awoke and opened her eyes in the near dark, two golden glowing orbs looked back, not three feet away. Zoe shrieked. Inanna curled a lip at her, but stood her ground.

"Zoe, what's wrong?" Deni cried, pushing the door open and flipping the light on. She wore only shorts and a sheer navy tank top. "Inanna! What the fuck!" The cat turned her head slowly to sneer at Deni. "How did she get here?"

"I, I don't know. I just woke up and she was staring at me. I didn't mean to scream like that." Zoe had always liked cats, had even fed the one that moved into her old rave household. But she'd never seen such an intimidating cat. Gingerly she took a hand from beneath the covers and slid it toward the hulking black feline. Inanna leaned forward and noisily sniffed Zoe's fingers. Then she curled her lip again, looking right into Zoe's eyes, and let out a demanding meow. "Was she like this with Jasmine?" Zoe asked.

"Nope. All purrs." Deni laughed. "I bet George brought her back. You scared the shit out of him the other day. I bet he's been trying to track this cat down all week." Deni looked relieved herself.

"All purrs, huh?" Suddenly Zoe felt a surge of competitiveness. Here she was in Jasmine's room, Jasmine's bed, even, with Jasmine's cat and Jasmine's old housemates. Zoe's own web page would probably be taking up Jasmine's old web space. Even Deni had more or less been Jasmine's girlfriend. Zoe knew she wasn't as pretty or tough as Jasmine, nor as well-loved by George, and now not as well-liked by Jasmine's cat. Zoe glared at Inanna and had the stupid conviction that she would make this cat like her if it was the last thing she did. Inanna met the challenge in Zoe's eye with another meow.

Deni laughed nervously. "I don't know how you'll get on as roommates. I tried to keep Inanna in my room after Jasmine went, but we had some trouble."

"Trouble?"

"She kept meowing and keeping me awake. I swear, she saw things I couldn't see. Gave me the creeps. So I threw her out in the hall. But then an hour later I hear this awful noise and there's Inanna's big yellow eyes, staring through my window. She was yowling like a fucking siren, and her claws in my screen were the only things holding her up. I don't know how she got there. It was like magic. Like she had flown. It freaked everybody out."

"Maybe she climbed a tree."

"There's no tree under my window."

"Jumped?"

"No way! Twenty feet off the ground?"

"Hmm. And then George got rid of her?"

"The next day. I wasn't the only one Inanna woke up that night. She even woke Mother."

Zoe was surprised by a tear in her own eye. Inanna's devotion to Jasmine, followed by the cat's cruel exile, reminded Zoe of Justin. How he had loved Zoe! And now he was sent who knew where?

"Hey! What's wrong?"

Zoe shook her head. "I just missed my boyfriend for a second."

"Yeah, you got sick and he took off, right? Tell me about it!"

"It wasn't like that," Zoe said softly.

"Sure it wasn't." Deni rolled her eyes. "Anyway."

At dinner, Deni asked George about Inanna's return. "What?!" George said, dropping a serving spoon into a casserole of candied yams. "That blasted cat is back?"

"That fiend?" Mother echoed, her eyes narrowing.

George shook his head. "Wow. It must be one of those *Incredible Journey* things," he said. Deni snickered.

Zoe awoke to a knock on her door the next morning. Inanna, who had been cuddling by Zoe's feet, leapt away as soon as the girl stirred. The cat resumed glaring.

"You ready to meet your fans?" George sang out as he barged through the door, carrying a video camera and a tripod. Inanna hissed and dove for the closet.

"Huh?" Zoe asked. Her feet felt unusually warm.

"Time to set you up with your own webcam. The fans have been asking the other girls when they can meet you."

Zoe closed her eyes again. "I'm tired."

"That's okay," George said, opening the tripod. "I'll just get everything set up." He bustled about, humming "How Deep is My Love."

The camera was set up within thirty minutes. Zoe had dozed off, but heard the sound of the computer turning on. "We have to test it out," George explained.

"I'm not really awake."

"We'll just make sure it's connected right. If any fans are lurking about, you'll just say hi."

"But I must look awful!"

He smiled at her. "You look pretty good." She wore an outfit he and Mother had bought her– gray silk pajama pants and a teal cotton T-shirt. They had bought the top in extra small so it would fit snugly. Whenever her old clothes went to the laundry, Valentina seemed to misplace them. Zoe hardly had anything left from her former life.

A few clicks later, the camera and computer were running. "Hey, there's six members logged on right now!"

"Who's doing a show?" Zoe asked, confused.

"Well, no one so far. They're just hanging around in case one of you girls come on." This struck Zoe as monumentally sad, at best. "Wave at the camera!"

"They can see me?" Zoe asked, her eyes wide with shock.

"Come on, just a little wave."

She picked up her right hand and fluttered her fingers.

"They're writing to you already!"

"Well, what do they say?" She was too far from the monitor to read the screen.

"One says, 'Good morning, beautiful Lorelei, from your new fan in Phoenix.' Another said, 'How are you feeling, Lorelei?'"

"Who? What are they calling me?"

"That's your new name. To protect your privacy."

"I don't even know how to spell it! Who picked that name?"

"Mother chose it." He turned to look at her, his smile shrinking. "Don't you like it?"

"I guess. Yeah." As a young girl, Zoe had yearned for a solid, traditional name, like Alice or Elizabeth. Lorelei sounded like what someone in a trailer would name a daughter she had big dreams for.

"Smile at them, Zoe! They're watching you." She tried. "You want the keyboard, or shall I type in a message?"

"You."

"I'll write, 'Hi, I'm happy to meet you. I know we'll get to know each other real well,'" he said, clicking away at the keyboard. "Oh, they're already asking who's typing. They can see you're not using the keyboard." He briefly stepped in front of the camera and waved, which brought a torrent of insults from the fans, like, "We want Lorelei to write, numb nuts," and "Who's the ugly chick?"

George's fingers clicked on the keys. "I'm just telling them that I'm teaching you to use the equipment, that we're testing it out."

The monitor was set up on a cart, which George managed to wheel close enough for Zoe to see. "Sit up," he urged, then propped the keyboard on her lap. She didn't complain, although she needed to pee. "They insist on hearing from you directly," he sighed, as though he hadn't seen that coming. He showed her where to see how many members were logged on. The number had suddenly jumped to twenty-three. She wondered how they knew. It was like they could smell her, nervous and naïve, exhausted by the thought of learning this equipment and communicating with God only knew how many creepy losers.

"But I can't type very fast," she said.

"Just hunt and peck," George encouraged.

The text messages poured in:

"Lorelei, my dear, could we please see your ass?"

"What disease do you have?"

"Could you shave your pussy for me?"

"If you marry me, I will take care of you."

"How long do you have to live?"

"Can that guy feed you on camera?"

"Please show ass."

Each member was identified by a fake name, such as Serve U, Dr. Feelgood, and Horse Hung.

"What's wrong? You look scared," asked Sick Girl Lover.

"Relax. Try to look like you're having a good time," whispered George, who was standing off camera, but close enough to read the messages. "Here's a remote control for the camera. When you don't want to show your face, like if you need to sneeze or yawn, you can pan down your body and zoom in on your breasts or thighs. Try not to let them see you yawn."

Zoe tried the remote, accidentally zooming in on her knee. Flustered, she couldn't figure how to zoom out.

"What is that????" asked Sick Girl Lover.

"Nice ass," said Horse Hung.

"Give me that," George said, deftly zooming out, panning up, and zeroing in on Zoe's chest.

"Lift T-shirt!" demanded Cum 4 U.

"Please! Please!" echoed Serve U.

"Are u gonna show titz or am I wasting my time?" asked Sergeant Big Balls.

"Well?" George said.

"What?" Zoe asked.

George sighed. "Come on. Make your fans happy."

So Zoe lifted her T-shirt, glad the members couldn't see her gloomy face.

"They're excited cause you're new," George said. "But don't worry. They respect all you girls."

If she had had more energy and passion, she might have hated the members. They were like little boys, whiney and demanding, wanting to see a tit, ogle her pussy, stomping their feet and abusing her when she refused. She wondered how representative these guys were of men in general. Was she seeing naked, primal desire? These were their wants without the social conventions of dating, without sexual harassment laws. They expected that their anonymity and membership fees gave them the right to demand anything at all.

Brenda was flattered by the attention, and even Deni seemed to feel she had some star cachet. Candi was more like Zoe; they called the men "members" or "customers," while Deni and Brenda called them "fans." Fan denoted a symbiotic relationship between adorer and adored. Members or customers sounded less personal. In Zoe's mind, the customers were simply "them," and the thought of them stirred both sadness and contempt.

Zoe did as little as possible on cam. Instead of trying to engage her fans, she played up her illness as an excuse for conversing so little. After the first few sessions, she hit on her formula. She would wrap a sheet around her naked body, not bothering with her face or hair beyond some lip gloss and a quick combing. After saying a simple hello, she told the members she wasn't feeling well and was going to lie down. She would lie on top of the sheet, exposing her nakedness. She ignored them. Sometimes she closed her eyes. She took herself out of the equation. She practically forgot about the men. They could count her ribs and jerk off to their hearts' content.

Some of the members complained about Lorelei, but some loved her. She was just what they had been looking for, they wrote. They knew she needed them, she was so frail, they would come take care of her. Zoe guessed her admirers were the sickest of the sickos, the ones who really wanted to fuck dead girls but reassured themselves that as long as they stayed with the dying, they were one step above necrophiliacs.

Life was the time Zoe spent with the other girls. Late at night, when they were presumed asleep, or anytime George and Mother left to do errands, the girls congregated in one of their rooms. Zoe's room was the least popular, probably because it reminded the other girls of her predecessor. Or maybe because they all seemed to attribute diabolical powers to Inanna.

Zoe liked Candi's room best. Candi had filled it with dolphin décor, from scientific charts comparing their sizes and diets, to New Agey tie dyes and batiks. Sentimental dolphin figurines with googly eyes lined her windowsill.

The dolphin theme stopped abruptly where camera range started. George had banned Candi from showing pictures of, or talking about, dolphins on camera, a rule she broke regularly. "Our members simply aren't interested in dolphins," he'd said at the dinner table at least twice since Zoe had arrived.

"Dear, that's a different demographic," Mother would add, giving Candi the evil eye.

"I just feel so good when I'm with the dolphins," Candi said to the other girls, late at night. Her voice got breathy when she spoke of dolphins. "It's the most amazing feeling, floating, but more than floating. Like I'm buoyed up by the warm water, but also by their intelligence, and, well, on their love." Every night the dolphins came to Candi in her dreams. They bobbed with her in a warm sea, rubbing their smooth sides against her affectionately, and tapping her with their snouts till morning. She was certain they would be waiting for her when she died. She expected to be amongst them always, perhaps as their queen in human or dolphin form, maybe in another reality, or in Heaven. If she was reincarnated here on earth, she hoped to live off the coast of Santa Barbara, or perhaps in Hawaii.

Deni laughed openly, and Brenda stroked the dolphin lover's head in an indulgent but disbelieving way. Candi spoke on, enraptured by her dolphins, not giving a rat's ass what the other girls thought. Zoe lounged on the floor, her body relaxed but her mind in rapt attention. She thought she had never met anyone so unafraid of death.

Deni and Brenda's views on death coincided, mainly lifted from a 1973 paperback Brenda kept hidden under her mattress. Such books were contraband. Mother preferred the girls to take a straightforward Christian view. Deni swore that once Mother had gathered the girls for a special lesson on the matter, opening with, "Now I want us all to be on the same page about Heaven."

The cover of Deni and Brenda's book, *I Died a Short Death,* pictured a vague body-shaped outline flying above a flatlined patient in a hospital cot. Zoe had won the girls' trust quickly, and they showed her the book on her third night there. It felt familiar to Zoe, like she'd seen these ideas on TV or in a movie. "Look," Deni whispered reverently as she turned to a line drawing, "the tunnel of light." The book was full of testimony by people whose hearts and/or lungs had stopped for anywhere from thirty seconds to several minutes. "First you float above your body. You feel absolutely no pain. You're free," Deni whispered, her eyes huge.

"You don't understand at first, because you still feel sort of like you have a body. Just a different kind of lightweight body," Brenda added, equally awed. "Except I wonder if maybe we won't be surprised. I've read this book about twenty times. I feel well prepared."

The light body floated around for a while, maybe confused to see its former, grosser body beneath it, maybe figuring it out. Before long, there was a great light, and a tunnel, and sometimes a loud noise. The noise could be a whirring or a pop. Zoe figured she would hear the beating of wings. She wondered if Candi was right that the dying girls' dreams were preparing them for death.

In *I Died a Short Death,* the people all came back to life, as promised in the title. But what about the long death, Zoe wondered? What about six hours later, three days, a week, a month, ten years? What if the sensations of the tunnel and light and noise were hallucinations, or settling of the body, or the senses' last hurrah?

But the girls didn't always talk of death. Sometimes they made scathing jokes about the members, or told funny stories about their childhoods, or cried for lost boyfriends, girlfriends, siblings, parents, pets. Sometimes they held each other, sometimes kissed. One night they all fell asleep together on Candi's floor, but luckily awoke at first light, before George came upstairs to coax one of them onto camera. Having sex with another girl on camera was good business, but staying up late and telling each other their life stories wasn't. Mother said excessive closeness was unwholesome, and staying up late led to bags under one's eyes.

After Zoe had been on camera for a week, George came upstairs one morning with a message from Mother. "She wants to see you in half an hour, at 9:30," George said, as if this were a business appointment Mother had jotted down in her day planner. George looked Zoe over critically. "Wear your blue T-shirt. And that Almay lipstick, tingling beige."

"Uh, okay," Zoe said, still surprised that George would know the names of their lipstick colors, though she shouldn't be. She joined Candi and Brenda in the bathroom. The other girls were doing their eye makeup. Zoe examined the lipstick holder, which held about thirty lipsticks. "Why would Mother want to see me?" Zoe asked.

The other girls didn't meet her eyes. "Maybe she just wants to see how you're doing," Brenda said brightly.

"Why would she schedule an appointment to see how I'm doing?" She couldn't remember if George had said tingling beige or blushing beige. There was one of each.

"Mother has her own way of doing things," Candi said, and quickly started talking about her latest night of dolphin ecstasy.

Zoe felt her stomach knot. Mother was going to throw her out. She wasn't nice enough to the members. Anyone could tell she thought they were losers. Maybe they had complained, demanding that a friendlier dying girl be installed in Jasmine's room.

"Where's Deni?" Zoe asked. Her question sounded rude, cutting off a magical moment of riding a dolphin, or leaping from the water under a rainbow, or something like that.

"She's on cam, hon," Brenda said, in a tone that sounded like pity.

Zoe went down the hall and tapped lightly on Deni's door, which you weren't supposed to do when someone was on cam. "Yeah?" Deni called out.

"Can I come in for a minute?" Zoe asked.

"Yeah," Deni said. Zoe entered the room and gasped when she saw the darker girl propped on one forearm, ass in the air facing the camera, anally penetrating herself with two fingers. She smiled at Zoe. "What's up?"

"Uh," said Zoe, momentarily forgetting why she'd come into Deni's room. She never did anything like this for the members. This was probably the kind of thing that would have saved her from getting fired. "Mother wants to see me. I think she's going to throw me out."

Deni laughed and reached for a mid-sized dildo, which she turned to slowly lube in front of the camera. Then she returned to her former position and slid it into her ass, gasping. "Nothing like the first dildo of the morning," she said to Zoe. Once she'd established a slow rhythm, she said, "She's not going to fire you. Believe me."

"How do you know?"

"I've been here a while. Hey, why don't you type a hello to the fans?" Deni said, jerking her chin toward the keyboard.

"What does she want?" Zoe asked, watching Deni's face. She got the feeling all the girls knew something she didn't. "Is there something you haven't told me?"

"No. Type in a greeting to the fans. They'll get even more excited if they know you're watching me, too."

"I don't care about the stupid fans!" Zoe said in an uncharacteristic loss of temper that exhausted her immediately.

"Don't be scared, Lorelei," Deni said. Zoe winced, even though all the girls called her Lorelei now when they remembered to, as Mother had ordered. "Just go see her and then talk to me afterwards. Really, there's nothing to be scared of."

Zoe walked out of the room without saying a word to the members. She went downstairs to get it over with.

George sat reading the *Oregonian* on the living room loveseat. The clock above him told her she was ten minutes early. He looked up, frowning slightly. "I said *tingling* beige."

"Should I go back up and change it?" she asked, intending sarcasm.

He seemed to ponder. "No. Blushing beige is okay on you. Want some of the paper?" She sat in an armchair. He gave her the choice of business or local news, and she picked local. "I've got to run an errand," he said, not looking at her. He fumbled in his pocket for car keys, then walked out the door.

In the local section of the *Oregonian,* an article detailed the controversy over a local TV station that had sold footage to *America's Funniest Videos.* The footage was of a severely retarded man who ran amok during a political protest, falling into the midst of young radicals impersonating the battlefield dead. Because everybody was interested in the possibility of an upcoming war, America's Funniest Videos had managed to put it in circulation without their usual six-month lead time. And because millions of cable watchers thought it hilarious and no one had seen anything like it, lots of news stations around the country aired the thirty-seven-second clip. Of course, the anchor people had to keep straight faces and talk about the shameful exploitation of the handicapped, tsk tsk. The *Oregonian,* claiming a high moral stance, omitted the name of the young man and resisted the temptation to print the now famous picture of him lying on his back, screaming, surrounded by furious young anarchists.

But Zoe was too worried to read the paper, instead holding it limply in her hands. And since there was no picture or name, even if she had seen the article she couldn't know it was about the man who loved her more than anybody else in her life ever had or would.

She heard tiny popping sounds as the minute hand jumped forward. When it was time, she rose, mouth dry, and started down the hall to Mother's office.

Mother sat behind a massive, dark wood desk. Heavy navy blue curtains hung around the windows behind Mother, who wore a fuchsia suit. Her auburn hair looked stiffer than usual. She gestured Zoe into the straight back chair across the desk. "Good morning, Lorelei,"

Mother said, smiling with teeth that looked strong enough eat young, dying girls for a midnight snack. "You've been here a while now. I thought it was time we had a little chat. Is your room satisfactory?"

"My room," said Zoe, feeling dazed. Dying put a person at a horrid disadvantage. Mother's plentiful body chugged along faithfully, and her brain swelled with vital energy, aiding her schemes and calculations. But it seemed to take all of Zoe's energy just to keep her heart thumping, her lungs expanding and contracting. "Yeah. It's nice."

"You're well fed?"

"Of course." Zoe had never had access to such good food.

"The other girls treat you right?"

"Yes. I like them."

"You seem to be making friends with them?"

"Yeah."

"Good." The smile widened. Mother's mouth seemed exceptionally big. "I'm glad you make friends easily. Because you're about to meet a new friend."

Zoe stopped breathing, the better to listen.

"And I know you will grow very fond of him. He's already fond of you."

"Him?" she asked with a sharp intake of breath. "Who?"

"He watches you every day on cam. He says you're just the girl he's always dreamed of meeting. Isn't that sweet?" Mother's smile faded when Zoe didn't answer. She looked at the girl with shrewd concern. "Why don't you lie down for a few minutes. You look strained." Mother came around the desk and helped Zoe onto the navy couch that ran along one wall of the room. "You can lie down while we talk. But don't fall asleep. We have a few points to go over. Your new friend will be here in half an hour. So pay attention, because you need to know how to behave. You hear me, Lorelei?"

"Yeah," Zoe whispered. So this was it. What a fool she'd been! Of course, Candi had gone on a date the first day Zoe came over, and Brenda and Deni had each been out once since she'd moved in. But she had assumed these were voluntary. She figured if the other girls were lonely for men and wanted to go out with losers they met on cam, that was their business. She had never realized she couldn't opt out.

"There are a few important points. Number one, I negotiate everything. Before you see your friend, I will tell you what is expected, what is allowed. If they try anything else, say, 'You have to talk to Mother.' Sometimes they try to trick you. They might imply I made a mistake or forgot part of the arrangement. But I don't make mistakes." She tapped her bronze lacquered nails to emphasize these last words. "You understand?"

"You don't make mistakes," Zoe breathed.

"Now this isn't a big deal," Mother sighed, annoyed. "I thought you would be pleased to meet a friend. Sometimes you girls don't seem to appreciate what my son and I give up to devote our lives to caring for the terminally ill."

"Sorry." Zoe had become so used to the name of the site, she had forgotten what the words meant. Fuck a dying girl. Well, that meant Deni or Candi or Brenda. Or her, Lorelei. Obviously.

"You need to adjust your attitude, Lorelei. Don't think your attitude toward your fans has escaped my notice. You don't have to love them, but you need to hide certain feelings a little better. When a friend comes to visit, never look bored or unfriendly. If you have a problem, you tell me afterwards and I will handle it. But while a friend is present, never argue, never insult, never raise your voice. Fans don't like the word 'no.' Instead of no, what do you say?"

"Maybe?"

"No! You smile sweetly and say, 'You'll have to talk to Mother.' If someone is really disagreeable, your best course of action is to use your illness to your advantage. Tell them you feel weak, that you need to lie down. Or simply faint. Our members love weakness. They do not like contrariness, sass, cynicism, political involvement, feminism, or many other traits of the modern girl. So steer clear of those arenas."

Zoe lay still and tried not to think about a stranger's hands on her body.

Mother sighed. "You must not look frightened. Your new friend wants to be your champion. You absolutely cannot look afraid of him. No matter how weak you are, you need to cultivate a friendly and tender facial expression. Your new friend wants to be called Sir Robert. You will spend one hour together today. He will give you a bath in the downstairs bathroom, including undressing you before the bath and dressing you after. He is allowed to touch your body in the normal course of washing. He is not allowed to remove his clothes. He is not allowed to penetrate you with anything but his finger. One single finger at a time," she emphasized, holding up her index finger. "He will help you up the stairs afterwards and tuck you into bed. If he still has time enough remaining, Valentina will fix you a cup of hot chocolate and Sir Robert will feed it to you with a spoon. Do you have any questions?"

Where was Justin, Zoe wondered.

"Lorelei? You've been listening, haven't you? You're not asleep?"

"No questions," Zoe said. Mother sighed again and turned her attention to some paperwork on her desk. Zoe closed her eyes. In no time, she heard the front door opening.

Sir Robert wasn't ugly like Zoe expected. When George led him into Mother's office to meet Zoe, Sir Robert looked almost normal. He was about five foot ten, and on the skinny side. Flyaway light brown hair framed his clean shaven face. The only remarkable thing about him was his intense gaze, which was trained on Zoe as soon as he entered the room.

"This is my mother," George was saying.

"Hello," Sir Robert said, his voice thick with emotion, his eyes still on Zoe.

"And of course you recognize Lorelei," Mother said in just the sort of tone she had forbidden Zoe to use. Disgust emanated from her as she watched Sir Robert's instant devotion bloom forth for a stupid, weak girl whose only distinction was her inability to hold onto something as basic and free flowing as life. Look at them all! The disgusting girl, the sickening admirer, the vile panderers who had brought them together!

But Sir Robert probably didn't notice Mother's attitude, and if he did, certainly he did not care.

"Lorelei," he whispered tenderly, kneeling on the floor beside the couch and picking up a pale hand that lay almost lifeless beside her. "Oh, Lorelei."

She lay looking back at him, her eyes blank, thinking oh, Jesus. Then she thought of Rex and T-Bone and the twins, how they would pee their pants laughing if they could see this scene. The thought animated her face enough for something to flicker across it, a something Sir Robert embraced as recognition of his soul.

"It was fate. I never look at, you know, that kind of stuff on the Internet. I was searching for Russian novels in translation, and I somehow stumbled upon your website." Behind Sir Robert, Mother coughed, a sharp, derisive sound.

"I don't feel so good," Zoe whispered.

"I know, precious baby, I know. That's why I've come to take care of you."

In the bath, his soapy hands on her arms, her back, her legs, weren't so bad. When he got to her crotch, she closed her eyes and pretended his finger was a fish darting in and out of an underwater cave. Nothing to do with her, really. He didn't linger there nearly as long as she had expected. That didn't seem to be what he was after. Mostly he tried to hook her gaze onto his, which in a way was more exhausting. If she was a regular whore she would have to put up with him fucking her, but he probably wouldn't be trying to suck her soul out through her eyes. As Mother had suggested, she sought privacy via frequent lapses into her illness, closing her eyes and withdrawing for minutes at a time.

He toweled her off lovingly with a plush pink towel, pressing it gently into her flesh like gauze into a wound. "I brought you something, precious baby," he said, bringing a bottle of lotion out of his pants pocket. For a second she thought it was lube and he was about to propose something off limits. But it was merely moisturizer, tea rose scented, which he smoothed carefully into her breasts and thighs.

He looked about Justin's age. Zoe didn't get it. What could have brought him to this, thirty years old and paying God knew how much to tend a dying girl?

"Would you like some hot chocolate, Lorelei?" He said her name shyly, as if it were real. She didn't want any, but what could she say? He still had twenty paid minutes.

When he led her upstairs, all the other doors were shut and Zoe suspected the girls were hiding from her. "Down here," she said. "This is my room." When she opened the door, Inanna stared from the bed like a stern chaperone.

"Oh," Sir Robert said. "Your familiar?"

"Inanna," Zoe muttered. The cat watched them both with wary yellow eyes. She looked like she'd seen it all, a jaded cat, transcending the gauche world of humans.

Sir Robert held a hand out to Inanna, who sniffed briefly but didn't hiss. Zoe wondered if Mother had even paid off the cat.

Valentina brought up the hot chocolate as soon as Zoe was under the covers. This was the worst part of all, being fed like a baby or an invalid. The brown spoonfuls came faster than she could swallow; the clock was ticking. She thought she might throw up or start screaming at him. To make things worse, he began reciting something in a language she couldn't understand. After a few minutes of this, he explained that had been a Russian poem about love and hardship.

Zoe couldn't see a clock and of course couldn't ask the time. But Sir Robert seemed to be winding down. "Lorelei," he whispered tenderly when the hot chocolate was gone. He had tucked her under the covers and his face hovered just over hers. "My girl. My one and only. Can you tell me I'm your one and only?"

He waited expectantly. Zoe had never been much on lies, but now that she was dying, they really seemed a waste of time. She felt a flash of hate toward Mother for getting her into this stupid mess. His smile shrunk a millimeter.

"You're my..." she began slowly, barely audible. She couldn't go on, she felt too sick. She pretended to faint, which seemed less a lie than saying the words.

"Oh, sweet baby Lorelei," said Sir Robert, remorse in his voice. "I've tired you out. I'm sorry." She couldn't tell if he thought she could hear him or not. "I just felt jealous. I'm sorry. I want you all to myself. Mother said I would be your one and only, but I wanted to hear it from you. I shouldn't have tired you out." He sounded like he was crying. Fucking psycho, Zoe thought, her face sweet in feigned sleep. He hung around for a few minutes, breathing audibly, then kissed her forehead. "I'll come back soon. I 'd come every day if I could, but—" he trailed off, embarrassed to say he couldn't afford to.

Zoe listened to his footsteps walking down the stairs, strained to hear the front door close behind him. His visit would have been prepaid; Mother was a businesswoman.

Zoe had never felt so disgusted by humanity, her own or that of others.

Late at night, in Candi's room, the girls tried to downplay it. As they lay on the floor under blankets, shadows cast by candle light played over the tie-dyed dolphin sarong. Zoe wouldn't let Deni hold her hand.

"At least you didn't have to fuck him," Candi said.

"It was just a bath and hot chocolate," Brenda said. "I mean, you have to bathe anyway. And you like hot chocolate, don't you?"

Zoe wondered where else she could go. She imagined limping down the walk with a knapsack full of cam clothes. Bound for what?

"I told George you shouldn't have to go on dates," Deni said. "I told him you're not like the rest of us."

"What do you mean?" Zoe asked.

"Yeah, what do you mean?" Brenda echoed.

"Well," Deni said, "take me. I was on the street for a while. Nowhere to sleep. Doing the cam shows and a couple of dates a week, this is a fucking holiday for me! And Candi, you turned a few tricks in your time."

"True enough," Candi agreed.

"But Lorelei was always respectable," Deni said. "Working in a café."

Zoe had never thought of it that way. She had never felt respectable, because she had never felt respected. A rave kid making so little money, living in a house full of kids on drugs. But it was relative, wasn't it? She held that job for a whole year. Until she got sick, the bills were paid.

"Hold on!" Brenda said. "I was a cashier, you know. I'm not exactly in your street whore category."

"But you used to answer those personal ads for kicks." Deni turned to Zoe. "In the *Willamette Week*. You know, 'Help me give my boyfriend a birthday present he'll never forget.' Threesome ads. For a hobby!"

"There's nothing wrong with enjoying sex," Brenda said, almost primly.

"You sucked more dicks than me and Candi put together. You just didn't have the sense to get paid for it."

"Maybe I didn't want to be a whore."

"A whore's just a slut with the brain to demand some cash for her efforts," Deni said. She and Brenda were raised up on their elbows now, looking like they were about to start punching or pulling hair.

"Hold on, you two," Candi said. "You girls save your strength." They settled down, though Deni's breathing was ragged for a couple of minutes. The candle light made the dolphin look like it was shimmying on the sarong. "Were you ever molested, Lorelei?" Candi asked, breaking a long silence.

"Huh?" Zoe asked.

"Your dad? Uncle? Mom's boyfriend? Brother? A babysitter?"

"No. I don't think so."

"See, that's why it's hard for you. All the shit in life is easier to face if you were molested early enough. You don't expect so much."

"What a disgusting theory!" Brenda said. "You make it sound like it's good to be molested."

"Not good. It just sort of sets the tone. Helps you not be so surprised later."

"Might be something to it," said Deni. "Me, I never had it half as good as I do now. Haven't been so happy since my foster sister was alive."

"Personally, I would have been happier if my father had kept his pants zipped," Brenda said.

Zoe hadn't realized the other three had all been molested. She felt guilty for being so disgusted by her interlude with Sir Robert, but the disgust remained. "So," Zoe said, "how often do we have dates?"

"As many as they can arrange," Deni said. "That's the most lucrative part of the business."

"Oh, it won't be that many, hon," Brenda said. "Don't scare Lorelei, Deni. George wants us all to be happy. He won't load you up on dates."

"George wants to buy rental property," Deni said. "So we can all expect a few more dates."

"How do you know that?" Candi asked.

"I watch him read the paper."

"You're just paranoid," Brenda said.

"Yeah, maybe he circles real estate classifieds for entertainment," Deni said.

"More than twice a week?" Zoe asked, trying to get an answer to her question. "The dates. More than two per week?"

"You just have to wait and see, hon," Brenda said. "We don't get much warning around here."

Zoe said she was tired and headed for her room. She felt like more of an outsider than she had since the first day she'd visited. She was the nice girl, the non-molested. They had all picked up on it, even George and Mother, who had bought her classier cam clothes than the other girls wore.

Soon after she turned out the light and slid between the sheets, she felt a soft thud on the bed, then a great warm cat tucking itself in beside her. She didn't move at all, not wanting Inanna to know she was awake. Zoe could swear she heard a faint rumbling, and she felt just enough warmth and comfort to get her through the night.

CHAPTER TWENTY-EIGHT

"Dude, you're a celebrity!" Surfer Dave walked into the workshop twenty minutes late, his shirt buttoned crookedly. He strode over to Justin and clapped him on the back.

"Aaaa," Justin said, not smiling. Dave was his favorite worker, but Justin had spent the last two days increasingly frazzled.

Rick wheeled over. He wasn't smiling, either. "It's not funny, Dave. Those TV stations are lousy."

"Sorry I'm late, man. Bus passed right by me."

"Right by your apartment when you were still in bed," Rick muttered.

Dave smiled. "There's people out there."

"People?"

"With cameras. They wanted me to comment."

Rick groaned.

The workshop was the same as usual: same concrete floor, same fluorescent lights, same screams and groans from the nonverbal. Mary talked incessantly to herself, Linus was always on the verge of a new eruption. But now Justin saw that security was short lived. Ever since that stupid camera had photographed his stupid fall at the die in, his world was on the verge of collapse. Outside the group home, outside the workshop, Justin had seen people straggling about. Reporters. Hello, FBI.

Justin sorely regretted losing his cool in Pioneer Square and becoming a famous retard. Now, as he tied knots in the lengths of plastic, he thought each knot could be his last. The back of his neck was hot, as though the law was breathing down his crew neck sweater.

Justin was so caught up in his troubles, it took him a minute to realize that Dave and Rick were discussing Pete. "Yeah, man, I didn't even know they'd let you have a leave of absence," Dave was saying. "But with his dad gone now, and his mom has asthma or diabetes or something like that."

"Asthma and diabetes aren't much alike," Rick said.

"Dude, that's not my point."

"Well, I'm sorry to hear about Pete's father. But it's not like he got much work done. So I suppose we can do without him until he can work something out for his mother." Rick wheeled over to soothe Linus, who was beginning to simmer.

Justin stopped tying knots and stared at his hands. So, Pete had taken off. Hot tears of abandonment burned Justin's cheeks. Shame overwhelmed him as he realized he'd unconsciously been waiting for Pete to tell him what to do next. For Pete to fake papers and ship him off to a group home in Florida, or to sneak up to his window at night and give him an address where he could hide with friends of friends in Kalamazoo. But Pete had cut Justin loose and run away on his own. And where was Zoe? Had she run away with Pete? The poor girl was so sick, someone had to be taking care of her. It all bubbled up in Justin. He used his new retard skills and started to yell. "Aaaaaa! Aaaaa! Aaaaa!"

Rick and Dave were at his side immediately. "Jacob, dude, what's wrong?" Dave asked, concern on his sweet face.

Rick was more worried about de-escalation than causation. "Hey, Jacob, it's okay," he said in a professionally calm voice. "Sssssh. It's okay."

Dave took Justin by an elbow and gently pulled him out of his chair. "Let's go for a walk. Come on." Dave guided Justin toward the far end of the building, back towards Marvin's office. "Chill, dude," he said. "Just chill out." Justin wasn't screaming now, but tears poured down his face. Dave's grasp on his elbow was so comforting. He longed to ask him for help. But should he drag anybody else into it? And if he started talking, would Dave scream like a person might if his dog suddenly confessed to posing as a pet to hide from the CIA? He couldn't decide. He finally had to admit to himself that Pete was smarter than he was, and Pete had already disappeared from the group home scene.

Instead of talking, Justin let Dave walk him the length of the workshop six times. He focused on the warmth of Dave's hand on his arm, the solidness of Dave's tall, sturdy body beside him. Then Justin returned to his station and tied more knots. He tried to calm himself by concentrating on simple things, like knotting the strings slowly and not very well. He couldn't believe he'd been tying these strings for going on three weeks now. How could there be such a demand for ugly wind chimes? Had people already bought the ones the workshop had been churning out in the previous weeks? Or was there a whole warehouse somewhere, full to bursting of these crappy wind chimes, destined for the landfill?

No one came for Justin that afternoon except Lester, the driver, at the end of work. On the van ride home, Justin felt jumpy. His head turned furtively, his eyes darted about. He couldn't seem to control his suspicious behavior, and his housemates immediately picked up on it. Linus tried to attack Claudette twice before dinner. Sally cried and hid in her room. Claudette was on the pissed off side of frazzled, cursing at the clients while cleaning the kitchen. "Fucking understaffed again and you all are driving me up the fucking wall. I'm going back to school next semester and then you retards will be sorry."

Garth came in at eight to relieve Claudette. A reporter tried to follow him through the door. Garth stood just inside, blocking the writer's entry with his foot. "What do you mean, the story? There is no story! A developmentally disabled man tripped. Why don't you go write about something real, like this government's imperialistic policies in the Middle East? It's obvious you only want to show our client falling down to mock citizens who want to prevent the government from starting another unjust war."

"What the fuck are you doing?" Claudette asked, yanking Garth backwards. "We're not supposed to talk to them." She stood smiling on the threshold, apparently hoping to be blinded by a few flashbulbs. When nothing flashed, she slammed the door, muttering, "Pigs."

Garth threw his backpack on the couch, then clapped Justin on the shoulder. "How ya doing, buddy?" he asked sympathetically, like he knew the reporters were getting Justin down.

"What's the idea, talking to them?" Claudette whined. "You already got to be on TV." Which was true, because when the stations showed the uncut version of the clip, America saw Garth save Justin from the anarchists by informing them about his mental state.

"Aaaaaa," Justin moaned. He felt like he might vomit or hyperventilate or perhaps suffer some other dreadful physiological consequence he didn't even know about.

"They're all fucking keyed up tonight," Claudette complained. "But that's your problem now." She was already putting on her coat, which was pale blue and made her look like a little girl. "I am so out of here!" She showed off her braces and pointy teeth in a grotesque metallic smile.

Everybody went to bed promptly, including Justin. He lay in the dark, listening to Billy the Tongue slurping and snoring. Justin had to leave, there was nothing else to do. He had nowhere to go. But if every news outlet knew where to find him, the FBI couldn't be far behind.

Justin waited what seemed like ten hours, but was probably only two. His pajamas stuck to the nervous sweat on his chest. The radio still played in the living room, a women's reggae show on KBOO. But Garth often fell asleep listening to the radio. Was he asleep now? Justin couldn't postpone his departure any longer.

He crept out of bed and tried to find normal, matching clothes in the dark. Billy the Tongue moaned. Justin had to give up on matching and settle for piling on as many layers as possible. He would have no money, no ID, just the clothes on his back.

Justin eased open the bedroom door and slipped into the hall. For once he was grateful for the stained, ratty carpet; it muffled his footfalls. He saw Garth lying on the sofa, a blanket covering his body, one arm flung over his face. He looked asleep. Justin wished the lights weren't on. He tiptoed by the couch, holding his breath. It wasn't until Justin turned the doorknob that Garth woke up.

"Hey," Garth said, confused. "Jacob! Wait, buddy, what do you think you're doing?" Garth sprang from the couch faster than Justin thought possible. Too late, he realized that Garth was a professional who had doubtlessly woke to countless emergencies before. Justin fumbled with the deadbolt, succeeding when Garth was no more than five feet away. Justin leapt out into the dark, forgetting the three steps and tumbling down. Garth caught him before he regained his footing. By now, Justin was desperate. Garth held him in some restraining hold, probably meant to be as humane and painless as possible. Justin thrashed in his arms, but couldn't get free. He hated himself for waiting so long, then making such a pathetic attempt at escape. 'Fucking let me go!" Justin cried in utter frustration.

Garth lost his hold, stunned. Both men crouched in the driveway, breathing heavily. In the crucial moment, Justin was too surprised by his own voice to take advantage of his freedom. By the time he collected his wits enough to run, Garth had the presence of mind to grab his leg and tackle him. And once Justin was down, Garth jumped on his chest, all thoughts of humane holds forgotten, and pinned his arms to the asphalt driveway. "Who the fuck are you?" Garth hissed. "What the fuck is this?"

"Please let me go," Justin whispered. "Just let me go."

"What kind of sick fuck are you?" Garth said, his voice climbing. "Jesus Christ, I showered you!"

"Ssssh," Justin said. "Please. I'm supposed to be underground. I blew it. I'm all over the fucking TV."

"Are you some kind of criminal?" Garth asked, holding Justin's wrists tighter.

"No! No. It's all stupid. The FBI, they think I want to kill the president. It's totally stupid."

"Oh my God! With a golf ball? Was that it?" Garth asked.

"What? How did you hear about it?"

"Jesus!" Garth breathed. "You're one of the Portland three!"

"The what?"

"They got the other two," Garth said. His grip had loosened. "You better come back inside and talk to me. Hope those reporters all went home."

Justin groaned. Garth yanked him up hard, not forgiving him for all those showers and trips to the toilet, all those glimpses at Justin's morning hard-ons.

Inside, Garth made Justin's first cup of real coffee since Justin had been retarded. They sat at the kitchen table. Garth kept shaking his head. "I've never even heard of anything like this happening. God! I never even suspected you were acting."

"Well, why should you?" Justin said, trying to comfort him. "It's not like people are lining up to be treated like the developmentally disabled."

"It's too weird. I can't get used to you like this. How the hell did you get in?" Justin stared at the table, which was perfectly clean from Garth's scouring. It didn't take Garth long to figure it out on his own. "Pete! That sneaky bastard! He's the one who brought you to the workshop that day. And now his dad just died and he left..." he stopped, putting it together. "God, he's hiding now, too!"

"Uh, Garth, I'm sorry. You were way the best staff here, and the best cook. I'd like to stay and talk to you more, but I really have to go."

"What? You can't go."

"What do you mean I can't go? The FBI's going to figure this out any second. I have to get out of here."

"Wait till tomorrow," Garth said. "Run away from the workshop."

"No way! They'd be looking for me in two minutes!"

"This job might not seem like much to you," Garth said, "but I happen to like it. And I think the residents here need me. At least, the rest of the residents. And I think I'm good at it. And jobs are very hard to find right now."

"Yeah, you're good at it," Justin said impatiently. "And of course they need you. To protect them from Claudette."

"Have you even thought about what will happen to me if you disappear on my shift?"

"Uh, I guess not."

"I'll be fired, Jacob! Or whatever the fuck your name is."

"It's not your fault."

"Yes, it would be my fault, if you were really disabled and you got away!"

Justin didn't have an answer to that, because it was true and he hadn't given Garth's job a thought at all. He sat down. He'd already cost Pete his job, and maybe a lot more. But if only Garth would fall asleep, Justin would still run away. Every minute he delayed, his panic grew like cancer. "Any suggestions?" he asked.

Garth wiped doggedly at a miniscule piece of food on the tabletop.

"Have you heard anything about my friends?" Justin asked when Garth didn't answer. "Have you heard if they've been released?"

Garth shook his head. "Seems like I would have heard. And I haven't."

"What if the FBI shows up right now?" Justin said, shifting in his seat like he had crabs. "They could show up any minute."

"I guess I'll pretend to be disabled, too," Garth said.

"It's not a joke! Christ! They're going to lock me up!"

"Ssh. I wasn't joking. It seems like the best way not to implicate myself. Let Nancy be in charge."

Justin imagined Nancy repeating everything the FBI agent said. "Fugitive from the law," she would say ponderously. "Killing the president."

"Are you going to try to stop me from leaving?" Justin asked.

"Didn't I just make that clear ten minutes ago?"

"Is it really so important for you to keep this job? Important enough to chance an innocent man going to jail?"

"That was a rotten trick you played," Garth said. "Can't you even try to put yourself in my place?"

"Can't you put yourself in mine? I couldn't think of a single plausible idea, and they were after me! So when Pete came up with this, I hated it, but I couldn't think of anything. And he loved it, trying to make me into a chronic masturbator!"

"I saw that in your files and wondered why you had stopped," Garth said, sounding irritated. "I thought maybe it was anxiety from the move to Oregon. Why would Pete have put that in there?"

"A girl. We liked the same girl," Justin sighed. What a shit he was! He couldn't believe how easily he'd just ratted on Pete, barely noticing as he spewed confidential information. What if the FBI got him? All they had to do was say canary and he'd sing. Apparently he was just that sort of person.

"Where did you plan on going when you ran out of here?"

"I haven't a clue," Justin said. "But even if I did, it wouldn't do either of us any good if I told you."

"Move to another city, maybe a bigger city. Get some fake ID. Get a job. Start over."

"Yeah. It sounds easy," Justin muttered. It was all the in between stuff that was hard. He didn't want to stand on the cold highway, sticking his thumb out and hoping someone nice stopped and drove him wherever. Once he got there, he had no desire to creep around dingy alleys, looking for people who know how to fake birth certificates and driver's licenses. He wasn't Jack Kerouac. Hell, he wasn't even Dale. He was bourgeois, hopeless, and consistently too paralyzed with fear to act. "Do you think if I turned myself in, would they really do anything to me?"

"Are you kidding?" Garth's forehead wrinkled in surprise. "Buddy, they got you for treason, conspiracy to assassinate the president, hiding from the law, I don't know what all. I'm sure living here constitutes fraud, especially since we're partially supported by county and state money. If I were you, I would stay underground. At least till the next presidential election. The people can't be stupid enough to elect that son of a bitch twice, right? And then you should be home free. Or, well, in a better position."

"Oh," said Justin, pale and full of dread.

"Maybe Canada. Go up to Canada, get some fake ID up there says you're Canadian. Vancouver's nice and Montreal is supposed to be really cool. Hell, it's all better than here these days."

"Do you know where to get fake ID?"

"Me? What would I need with fake ID? That's one of those things you figure out when you live underground."

Justin didn't point out that he had been living underground for going on a month now, and instead of gaining survival skills, he seemed to have lost any that he might once have had.

"Well, I guess we can't do anything till the morning," Justin said, faking a yawn. "So we might as well get some sleep." He stood up.

Garth eyed him skeptically. "You're not getting away tonight. Either I'm staying awake or I'm booby trapping the door. If you somehow get away, I'm calling the police immediately. I won't say who you really are, but I will report you missing and give the cops photographs. This job is important to me. I sympathize with your situation, but not enough to lose a good job over."

"I'll be a political prisoner! That's worse than losing a seven dollar an hour job!"

"Buddy, you're hardly a political prisoner. I mean, come on. Killing the president with a golf ball? The only kind of crime that is, is criminally stupid."

"It was a stupid joke!" Justin suddenly felt too weary to defend himself. Besides, there was no defense. In retrospect, it certainly did seem criminally stupid to say such a thing. "Oh, never mind. Don't worry, I won't try to leave. You made your point."

Warily, Garth returned to the couch, and Justin to his bed, neither intending to sleep. Justin lay fretting in the dark, trying to think of ways to evade Garth, but before he did, worry gave way to sleep.

Everything was different in the morning. Justin knew it was his last day in the group home. Garth woke him before the other residents with a light punch to the shoulder. "Go take a shower," he said. For the first time since the Seaside hostel, Justin set the water temperature and soaped himself. It felt like heaven for a moment, till his mind wandered toward the future and he wondered what the circumstances of his next shower would be like. A gang shower in a prison? Or maybe solitary confinement in a detention center, guards in black hoods leading him down a dank hall to his monthly shower.

He dressed himself in several layers of clothes, planning to ditch the top layer when he went missing. Garth didn't meet his eyes during breakfast. Justin looked around the table at the other residents for the last time: Billy the Tongue slopping milky cereal back into his bowl, Nancy sitting stiffly, listening to KBOO and occasionally repeating something that caught her ear. "The president and his gang of thieves," she said carefully, her brow furrowed. Linus examined a piece of toast, his goth face young and beautiful in a lull between rages. And Sally, Justin's favorite, such a sensitive, gentle person. He had lived with them three weeks, but did he know them at all? And would they even recognize him on the street? Suddenly he felt he had failed in some way, that he should have considered their humanity more. And now he would be leaving.

They heard the van pulling up. Garth stepped close behind Justin's chair. "This is all I have on me. Good luck, man." He slipped a twenty and a ten into Justin's hand. "Don't say anything. You're not supposed to talk, remember?"

Justin smiled at him gratefully, tears welling up in his eyes. Garth gave his shoulder a squeeze.

"Okay, everybody," Garth said. "Off to work." He busied himself with jackets and lunches, then herded them all towards the door.

Thus began Justin's eagle eye search for opportunity. He contemplated leaping from the van at a red light, but by some miracle they all turned green at the van's approach. Lester pulled up in front of the workshop before Justin had a single chance for escape.

Rick was already inside, but Surfer Dave was late as usual. Justin watched Rick, waiting for him to get absorbed in one of the scores of distractions that happened in the workshop every day. When Rick bent over someone's cut hand, and then wheeled to the back of the room to get the first aid kit, Justin headed for the exit. He was five feet from freedom when the door opened and Dave burst in. "Hey, dude, don't you have any knots to tie?"

"Aaaa," Justin said, turning and walking a ways in the other direction, pretending to be pacing.

Mid-morning, Justin went to take a piss. Since he had a solid reputation as a self-toileter, he was allowed to go alone now. As he walked into the bathroom, he saw the window. He had noticed before that the bathroom was always colder than the rest of the workshop, but he had never considered why. It was because of this window, this glorious window, separating him from escape with just a thin screen. He was sure it was big enough.

Even self-toileters weren't supposed to close the bathroom door, but nobody was nearby so Justin eased it almost closed. The window was over the sink and a little to the left. All he had to do was climb on the sink, bust the screen and hoist himself out. The climbing was easy, the busting not bad. But the hoisting was problematic. He tried twice to lift himself delicately, but he couldn't get enough momentum. The cheap walls were hardly thicker than cardboard, and Marvin was sitting right on the other side. It seemed the only way Justin was going to get through the window was to swing the full force of his body upwards, kicking the wall in the process. He was running out of time. Desperate times call for desperate measures, he thought, annoyed that he didn't know where that quote came from, that he didn't know anything, that he was a total fucking loser to have wound up standing on a sink in a workshop full of retards, trying to get out a small window to a fucked up, wholly unknown destiny. All his fury and loathing went into the next jump. He hit the wall hard with his shoes, but his upper body went through the window. He heard Marvin call out, "Come in," as though he thought the thud was someone knocking on his office door, and then Justin was falling headfirst toward the ground, trying to get his arms in front of his face to break the fall. One wrist buckled on impact, but didn't break. Two pieces of gravel embedded themselves in his right hand, and his left knee bled from a broken Budweiser bottle. But as he stood up he found his body basically unharmed. He was in a mostly empty parking lot, close to a dumpster. He pulled off his top outer layer, the ugly and conspicuous red sweater, and threw it in the garbage. Underneath he wore the most low profile shirt he could find, a long-sleeved navy blue T-shirt. Then he ran like fucking hell towards a bus that was just pulling up a half block away.

On board, panting, Justin reached into his pocket and pulled out the ten and the twenty. "Uh, does anybody have change for a ten?" he asked the half empty bus. The people in the front seats looked too old, deaf or crazy to answer. Those in the back, too indifferent. "Anyone?" he repeated pathetically. A girl in a black hat with cat ears shrugged. A sweatsuited young man shook his head dolefully. Justin sighed. He didn't know when he'd get any more money, but escape was escape. He started to slip the ten into the money slot.

"Hey, what are you doing?" asked the bus driver, a petite woman in her fifties with curly blond hair. She covered the slot with her hand. "Don't you know I can't give change?"

"I really need to get somewhere on time," Justin said quietly, trying to push the bill past her fingers.

"There's another bus in ten minutes. Go get change and you'll save eight dollars and forty cents."

"I don't care. I need to take this bus," Justin said through gritted teeth.

"Young people today don't know the value of money," the bus driver said.

"Ain't that the truth," threw in a blind black woman in a wheelchair whose hearing, apparently, was still keen.

Ordinarily Justin would be pleased that someone still considered him young, but this wasn't the time. "Please move your hand so I can pay," Justin said. "I want to ride your bus, I don't care if it costs ten dollars, and it's my money."

"I can't let you pay ten dollars," the driver said, sighing heavily. "I can't stand to see that kind of waste of money."

"Hey, are we gonna move, or what?" came a man's voice from the back.

"Hold your horses," barked the driver, suddenly fierce. "Sit down," she said to Justin. "And please get change first next time."

"Thank you," Justin breathed. He found a seat near the middle of the bus. Glancing out the window, Justin saw Dave standing on the sidewalk, concern and terror on his face. Justin slumped in his seat and turned his face away. The bus pulled into the street, the workshop fading behind them.

Justin wondered where the bus would take him. He didn't know what route he had stumbled on, but he had no idea where to go, so it didn't really matter. So far, this bus was heading north.

How long would Dave search for him before he gave up and called the cops? Not more than two hours, Justin guessed. He had to make a plan, but his mind was entirely blank.

The bus kept heading north until the streets looked unfamiliar. Justin had hardly deviated from his routes in Southeast Portland and downtown the whole time he had lived here. Now he looked out the bus windows at what seemed like a different city. Small houses, built in the forties or fifties, with unpicturesque patches of grass and chain link fences. He didn't know where he should get off. The bus slowly emptied of people until Justin was one of five left.

The bus turned again and they were on a business street Justin had never seen. It looked like an old-fashioned downtown. "End of the line!" the driver announced. Justin wanted to ride the bus until he thought of something, but that would look too suspicious. He trudged down the aisle, last one off. "Thanks for the ride," he mumbled.

"Don't forget! Correct change next time."

About half the businesses on the street were quaint: the faded blue stucco of the Bubble Bar, neon bubbles lit up on the sign; the Ladies' Foundation Store, a mannequin modeling a beige girdle in the window. Two diners. The other businesses looked like more recent additions to the neighborhood: a bookstore with a window full of New Age titles, a café selling wraps, and, to Justin's delight, a hip looking coffeehouse with a banner boasting of fair trade coffee.

Perhaps caffeine could stimulate his brain to make a plan. Inside, the walls were a mossy green with huge purple leaves painted on them. Mismatched couches, ratty but comfortable looking, lined the walls. A woman breastfed two young children on a purple couch. A young guy, maybe eighteen, dressed all in black, sketched at a table.

The rich smell of coffee, the scattered newspapers, the girl behind the counter, the droning music on the stereo, all these combined to flood Justin with memories of Jojo's. His heart hurt. The girl was nothing like Zoe – black hair, busty, with a tattooed leopard running up one arm, apparently chasing a parrot down the other – but watching her pump his coffee into a mug brought Justin close to tears.

"Room for cream?" she asked.

"Please." He could barely answer.

At the milk and sugar counter, he paused to survey the bounty: lowfat milk, soy milk, half and half, brown sugar, white sugar, turbinado sugar, honey, cocoa, cinnamon, nutmeg, Sweet 'n Low. In the group home, it had been weak decaf with Coffeemate. He settled on half and half with a dash of cinnamon.

Justin had barely seen any news for three weeks. He was starved for it. He grabbed an abandoned paper and took his coffee to the couch. Even the spectacle of the woman nursing two children at once couldn't distract Justin from the front page.

Well, the world was still in a bad state. The U.S. was on orange alert, again or still, Justin wasn't sure. Three people had made it through PDX security yesterday with sharp objects: one with knitting needles, two with manicure scissors. A pop star had run off with another pop star, even though he was married. A state legislator had committed suicide. The president was puffed up, threatening to bomb three more countries if they didn't "shape up," a threat terrifying in its vagueness.

Justin didn't notice the kid with the sketch pad staring at him. Eventually the kid crossed the room and sat beside him on the couch.

"You look like someone," the kid said.

"Huh?" Justin looked up from the paper, his heart immediately pounding.

"You look just like somebody else." The kid was skinny with black hair and sharp features. He wore a silver ankh around his neck.

Justin thought of asking who, but that seemed dangerous. Instead, he settled for, "So?"

"I study faces," he said. "I always have. When I was a kid, I planned to go into forensics. But later I realized that meant working for the cops. Which is fucked."

"Uh huh." Justin stared at the kid, hoping he would go away.

"Now I mostly draw. I'm an expert at faces."

"Uh, I guess that's helpful. For drawing."

"I could swear I know your face," continued the kid, his intensity never wavering. "But the person you look like doesn't talk or read. He's mentally impaired."

Justin could feel his face reddening. "Oh?" He didn't mean for it to come out as a question.

"I saw your face on TV. The guy at the demonstration. The retarded guy. But you're not. Retarded."

Why had Justin taken a bus directly to the place where a precocious facial expert hung out? "I don't know what you're talking about."

The kid shrugged. "Like I said, I know about faces. Let me see you do this." He opened his mouth wide, as if he were yelling.

"No!" Justin said, angrily and too loud. The girl behind the counter looked up.

"Derrick! Don't bug the customers!"

"My sister," Derrick explained.

"Go away, okay? I'm trying to read the newspaper in peace," Justin said, bolstered by the sister's command of the situation.

"I'm just saying, I know faces. And it's pretty fishy if you're retarded on the news, and not retarded in person. I'm better at faces than almost anyone, but your face has been on the news a lot. You know what I mean? A lot." He kept his dark eyes boring significantly into Justin's face. "So I was thinking, if you don't want to seem fishy, you need to change how you look."

"How I look," Justin repeated. "How do you think I should look?"

"Not like a famous retard. Unless there's a good explanation."

Justin wondered if the kid wanted to blackmail him. Somehow he thought Derrick wanted to help, but he wasn't sure if this was a good intuition or his usual desperation. He held Derrick's eyes for a few moments longer, then gave in. "There's not a good explanation," he said softly.

Derrick smiled, pleased with himself. He had white square teeth. Justin figured Derrick had a dozen arty little girlfriends. "You should change your hair, at least. Before someone else notices." When Justin didn't answer, Derrick went on. "You don't have to tell me anything. I just like to help people, and you look kind of lost. I take it you're hiding from something. That's cool. I'm not going to ask a thing about it." He'd been leaning forward, intent. Now he sat back. "So, do you want help?"

Justin nodded. "Can I get more coffee first? And finish the paper?"

"Later," Derrick said. "You're much too recognizable right now." He stood. "Come on."

Justin stood uncertainly. "What will your sister think?" he asked. "You know, me just leaving with you?"

"Oh, she won't think anything. I deal ecstasy, so she'll just think you're another customer. Come on."

Derrick opened the driver's side of a beat up 1982 Dodge. Shouldn't a dealer have a better car? Maybe Derrick was fucking with Justin, and really had a minimum wage job at Kinko's or Dairy Queen.

"Uh," Justin said, standing on the sidewalk, paralyzed by second thoughts.

"Get in!" Derrick said, smiling big.

So Justin opened the door and gingerly slid into the low, ratty brown seat. Junk littered the floorboards. He kicked a cardboard box and something rustled, and kept on rustling. "Uh…" Justin began, almost as vocally inept as Jacob had been.

"That's just crickets. For my snake."

"Oh." Justin half heartedly felt for a seatbelt, then thought better of putting his hands where his eyes couldn't see.

"You got any money?" Derrick asked.

Justin realized he should have expected this. "Twenty-eight dollars," he admitted. "But that's all I have."

"Hmm. We'll have to keep costs down. For your new look." Derrick accelerated, pulling away from the curb in the line of a honking car. He flipped it off and turned up the tape player.

"What's this?"

"Sisters of Mercy!" Derrick exclaimed in a way that made Justin feel stupid for asking. The song was about a black planet. Justin briefly wondered if the color referred to the planet's terrain or people, but then his mind was too occupied with fear for his life to ponder song lyrics. "Well, fuck me!" Derrick yelled at another honking car.

Justin wondered if the word was out to look for him yet. What if a cop stopped Derrick? Would they recognize Justin? But mostly he kept his eyes closed and pictured Zoe. Where was she right now?

"Here we are," Derrick said a few minutes later, squealing to a stop. "I think it's still early enough they can fix you up. Come on." Justin saw they were parked in the lot of something called Fredia Foreman's Institute of Beauty. "Best deal in town," Derrick said as they walked up the brick steps to the entrance. Justin was still disoriented. He had never seen this street. "I know a couple of the girls here. Let me do the talking, okay?" Justin nodded. It was a relief to surrender to Derrick's will. After three weeks of a retardo-monastic lifestyle, Justin's brief stint of self-determination had been heady, but look where it got him: Recognized the first place he went. More interested in drinking coffee and reading the paper than planning his next move. He obviously wasn't prepared for a life underground.

Inside the beauty institute, a skinny dark girl sat at a reception desk. They could see behind her into the salon, a large room full of frenzy. Women and a couple of guys in white smocks clustered around their victims, people too poor or cheap or perverse to go to a regular salon. The students gathered in knots of two or three around each customer, seeming to debate every movement of scissors.

"Hey, Sugar. Can you get my friend in?" Derrick asked the girl behind the desk. Justin flinched at the tacky familiarity, but then he saw that the girl's nametag said Sugar. Derrick smiled at her and she smiled back.

"Well, sure, Derrick," she said in an intimate tone. "What does he need?"

"Whole new look." Derrick turned to Justin, examining his hair and face as though Justin were nothing more than this collection of features. "New haircut, short. Dye his hair and eyebrows dark brown."

"My eyebrows!" Justin exclaimed. He didn't want beauty students wielding dye so close to his eyes.

"We don't usually do eyebrows," Sugar said doubtfully. "But I guess, for your friend…" She pulled out a clipboard. "But I need him to sign this waiver."

Derrick shook his head slightly. "We can't sign anything," he said quietly.

"But…" she began.

"But you and me, tomorrow at four," Derrick said, pinning her with his dark eyes. To Justin's utter amazement, Sugar placed the clipboard back on the desk.

"Four-thirty," she croaked. "That's when I get off. Of work, I mean." And she started to blush.

A woman stood behind them, clicking her long nails against her clutch purse impatiently. Derrick flashed one last smile at Sugar, then steered Justin toward a bench to wait.

"How did you do that?" Justin asked in awe, his eyebrows forgotten.

"What?" Derrick said. He picked up a hairstyle magazine and began to study the pictures.

Before Justin could explore Derrick's mysterious seduction technique, two Asian women came out to the reception area. "Cut and color?" asked the younger of the two, whose hair flipped up at the ends in a disturbing, artificial way. Derrick nudged Justin, who stood up.

"Oh, that's me," he said.

"This way, please," the younger woman said. Justin followed her into the salon area. It wasn't until he was sitting in the styling chair that he noticed Derrick had glided along behind him. The kid was like fog, seeping through any barrier. Derrick smiled at the Asian women and the younger one giggled. Frankly, the kid was getting on Justin's nerves.

Next came a round of consulting with the supervisors, a black woman and a white woman, both around fifty and wearing suits. They talked about Justin's skin tone, his natural hair color, how dark they should go. Justin felt like a wig on a Styrofoam head. He felt even more like that when the older of the two Asian women began to comb his hair. As she almost raked Justin's ear off, he wondered if his was the first human head upon which she had been set loose.

The hair students, the supervisor, and Derrick all leaned over a book of color samples. "How about the G6S," Derrick suggested.

"Well, I think you have quite an eye," said the black supervisor, drawing back to give Derrick an appreciative once over. Justin watched them in the mirror, smiling at each other.

"This is so eighties," said the white supervisor, lifting the front of Justin's hair and laughing. "Oh, sorry," she said, remembering there was a person attached.

Nobody asked Justin's opinion. Soon the two students were mixing a bowl of dye and speaking over his head in what he guessed was Vietnamese.

Justin looked at a hair magazine while the dye was processing. He turned the pages, scrutinizing women in the before and after pictures. He imagined maybe getting up the nerve to ask some of the before girls on a date. But after? No way.

When the students finished with him, Justin could hardly believe his transformation. Staring back from the mirror was a guy whose hair was short and almost black. He had a few bangs, which were gelled to points. The darkened eyebrows gave him a slightly brooding look, not unattractive, and made his blue eyes gleam like sapphires. Even his cheekbones were more prominent.

"Hey," Derrick smiled. "That's a lot better." Derrick quietly reminded Justin to tip his student stylists, then they were heading for the door, a wink for Sugar on the way out.

At least my corpse will look good, Justin thought as Derrick wove through the evening traffic amidst a deluge of horns and raised middle fingers. "So," Derrick said. "Tonight, you'll stay with us. Tomorrow, maybe somewhere else."

Justin, lost in his own city, said nothing.

They were on a street of scabby lawns and barred windows. Derrick stopped before a blue cottage, its patch of weeds protected by a chain link fence. A butt ugly dog stopped pissing on the dandelions and began to bark.

"Isn't that a pit bull?" Justin asked.

"That's Man's Best Friend. He's a sweetheart." Derrick reached over the fence and the dog licked his hand, barking giving way to snorts and wheezes. His dark, greasy brown fur was streaked with gray and white. He cavorted on three legs; the fourth was tucked up at his side. There had been a kid at the workshop with an arm like that. Cerebral palsy, Justin thought. A pinkish growth stuck to the dog's side like raw hamburger.

"What's wrong with him?" Justin asked, hesitating to follow Derrick through the gate.

"Nothing. Jesus!" Derrick's face screwed up in an offended scowl. Justin followed him inside and slammed the gate behind. Derrick leaned down to kiss the hideous, barrel-chested creature.

Justin tried to take an interest in the dog so Derrick would forgive him. "What's his name?"

"I told you! Man's Best Friend."

"That's his name? I thought that was just an expression."

"It's his name and it's true!" Derrick, who now crouched on the damp ground rubbing the monster's belly, glared at Justin.

"Uh, he's great."

"Don't patronize us. Go inside. I'll be there in a minute."

Justin trudged toward the door, which was unlocked. He tentatively crossed the threshold, stepping into a living room like none he had seen. A ten foot tall painting of a sarcophagus, done mostly in metallic gold and blue glitter, stood against the wall directly across from the door. In case anyone failed to notice the art, two spotlights lit it from above.

The living room was divided clearly into halves. The half with the sarcophagus was spotless. Two turquoise Naugahyde chairs and a matching loveseat surrounded a shiny red and silver boomerang table. Chrome gooseneck lamps loomed over each chair. Black and white photos of models in front of the Eiffel Tower hung on the walls. The girls in the photos had lank hair and big, black-rimmed eyes looking soulfully out from the sixties.

The other half of the room looked like its décor had come from the dumpster behind Goodwill– ratty tan furniture, beer cans, cigarette butts overflowing ashtrays, a scratched coffee table held up by three legs and a coffee can. A huge gray cat peered at Justin through one yellow eye. He couldn't tell if the other eye was closed or missing. Beneath the cat slept a lumpy form, apparently human.

Derrick and Man's Best Friend came in behind Justin. Man's Best Friend sat on the graying rug on the dirty side of the room. He whined at the cat, who bared its teeth.

"Time this fucker got a job," Derrick said, striding to the couch. He clapped his hands loudly over the head of the snoozing form.

"What the fuck?" a male voice muttered.

"Your time on the couch is up. We have a new tenant tonight."

"I don't want to inconvenience anyone," Justin said.

Derrick glared at him. "I said, time's up."

"Hey man, be cool. Darla said…"

"Darla's a soft touch. Your time is up! You've been here five days. Hup, hup, hup," Derrick said, kicking the side of the couch.

"She said she'd help me," the guy whined.

"God helps those who help themselves."

The mystery guy sat up suddenly, knocking the cat onto the dog. Justin couldn't see what happened in the mess of fur, but Man's Best Friend whimpered.

"I'll show you around," Derrick said, walking out of the room. Justin followed. "Kitchen. Want a beer?"

"Okay."

Derrick gave him a Pabst Blue Ribbon. As Justin took the first sip, he realized he hadn't had a beer since the night he made out with the Pig & Pancake waitress. He felt a pang of longing for her. She was so much easier to understand than Derrick, and probably would have let him stay longer than five days.

After pointing out the bathroom, backyard, and a room described as off limits, Derrick headed for the front door. "Later," he said.

"You're leaving?" Justin asked.

"Don't sound so shocked. We're grownups. Hey, read a book. Watch TV. Hasta la vista." And the door closed behind him.

The guy whose time was up still sat on the couch, which Justin realized was supposed to be his bed now. "Who'd you fuck to be king around here?" the guy muttered now, rubbing his head, which was covered with long brown hair.

"Pardon?" Justin said.

"You make me sick."

"Whatever." Man's Best Friend kept looking at Justin, who couldn't determine if the dog wanted to be friends or to tear him a new asshole. He'd never been intuitive. Maybe that was the source of his problems, he thought now.

"You think you can just come in here..." the guy began, rising. He looked like the kind of guy who crawls under your car to huff glue. The door opened and Darla sauntered in. "That little bastard told me I had to go!" the guy said before Darla could even put down her purse, which was pink with a picture of a little cat with rhinestone eyes.

Darla yawned. "See ya." She turned her eyes on Justin and slowly looked him up and down. "Well, that's a lot better. Want a beer?"

"Uh, okay." He hadn't finished the last one and hoped she wouldn't notice. She was a good looking girl. He didn't want to turn down what she had to offer.

The long-haired guy stomped off to sulk in the bathroom. Darla returned from the kitchen with another PBR. She brushed Justin's fingers when she handed it to him. He took in her stately bust, the way her black hair fell over blue eyes.

"What's your name?" she asked, opening a beer.

"Uh, well…"

She laughed. "You have to do better than that! If you don't want to tell a person your name, you have to lie fast or you look retarded!"

Had she recognized him, too? "Ted," he said. "My name is Ted."

"Darla." She held out a hand, warm and soft.

"I know. Your brother told me."

"Brother!" She laughed again. "Is that what that little bastard said?"

"He's not your brother?"

"If he was my brother, I hope I wouldn't know how good he is at eating pussy." Justin choked on his beer. Darla smiled. "You want me to Heimlich you?"

"I'm okay," he gasped. "Went down the wrong way."

"Uh huh." Her eyes darted freely over him. He felt both turned on and turned off simultaneously. She was a man eater, anyone could see that in five seconds. "What about you? You got a sister?" He shook his head. She reached out and firmly took hold of his crotch. But the long-haired guy took that moment to walk into the kitchen.

"Hey, you got any more toilet paper around here?" he asked.

Darla let her hand slide off Justin's hardening dick. She smiled and walked out of the room. Justin wondered if he was supposed to follow. He stood, undecided, in the middle of the kitchen.

"She's got the clap, you know," the long-haired guy said, smiling a gap toothed grin.

"How would you know!" Justin said.

The guy didn't answer, but his grin grew wider. He went to the far end of the couch and began stuffing a pile of clothes into two dirty backpacks. One zipped, the other flapped open, exposing discolored briefs. The guy spat toward Justin, casually, so the glob landed on the floor halfway between them. One flicked booger later, he was out the door.

Darla returned to the living room, a roll of toilet paper in her hand, just as the door slammed. "Did that numb nuts leave without saying goodbye?" She let the TP fall on the couch. "Oh well." She smiled at Justin. "He's mean cause he has hepatitis or bipolar disorder or something. But he's not all bad. You staying for dinner?"

"Uh, yeah," Justin said, following her into the kitchen. The walls were a screaming yellow. She took three cans of generic tomato soup out of a cupboard.

"I'm starving," she said, finding a can opener and removing the tops of the cans. She licked soup off her finger. "Do you like extra salt? I like mine really salty."

"Uh, sure."

Justin's heart ached for Zoe, but his crotch argued that Darla would do. Especially since he didn't know if he'd ever see Zoe again. But this was Derrick's house, wasn't it, and maybe it wasn't cool to get together with Darla. But maybe it was Darla's house and Derrick really was her kid brother. Someone was lying, or maybe they both were. And while he yearned to see Darla's breasts freed of those useless coverings, shouldn't he be making more important plans? And wasn't Derrick smarter than Darla? Both seemed sex-obsessed, but Derrick definitely had something upstairs as well. So would Justin be squandering his chance at Derrick's helpful scheming if he got together with Darla? Or maybe she was just teasing him, so all this worrying was moot.

Justin still hadn't thought of the right thing to say, and then the soup was ready.

"The quiet type, eh? Is it true that still waters run deep?" she asked, placing two steaming bowls on a yellow fifties dinette table.

"Uh, I don't know," Justin said. Darla laughed uproariously. Justin sat down, feeling dumb. "That's my place," Darla said, adding, "Just kidding" when he began to rise. He was feeling less inclined to bed Darla. She seemed like the kind of girl to laugh at moments guaranteed to make you lose your hard on, and then laugh all the louder. A longing for Zoe flooded him.

"Mmm," Darla said, eating her first spoonful of soup.

Justin tried his. He had never tasted anything so salty. "It's good," he said. She laughed again. He didn't know why.

"So, Ted, where do you come from?" she asked in a way that let him know she expected an incredible line of bull. She rubbed her foot along his calf under the table.

"Nebraska," he said.

"Mmm. How do you like it here?" she asked, her foot moving up to his thigh.

"It's salty," he blurted out. She laughed so hard her foot fell back to earth. Who knows what further shenanigans and humiliations might have transpired if Derrick hadn't chosen that moment to return.

He burst into the kitchen, handsome and windblown, his cheeks pink. "Did you save me any soup?" he asked, then looked into the empty pot on the stove. "Jesus, sister, what's a hungry man to do?"

"Open a can, I suppose. There's still about a million in there."

"More like a dozen," Derrick corrected, peering into the cupboard and selecting two cans. "Operation Lima Bean in the morning," he said to Justin significantly, winking a dark eye.

"Huh?" Justin asked. He was starting to think he should leave tonight.

"Operation Lima Bean?" Darla repeated scornfully. "You are such a retard!"

"You'll find out in the morning," Derrick said to Justin, "and you'll never know," he told Darla.

"Like I care about your brainless fantasies," she said, frowning down at her bowl. "You'll get in trouble one day."

"At least one, I imagine." He kissed her on the top of the head, then fixed his own bowl of soup. Justin noticed that Derrick also added salt.

Justin was expected to sleep on the same couch, in the same unwashed sheets, of his gob-spitting, booger-flicking predecessor. He decided to make do with the one rough blanket, which seemed less intimate than the sheets. Derrick and Darla retired early to the off limits room, from which Justin was treated to the soundtrack of a sex marathon. The couch felt cold and lonely.

Typically, instead of planning or escaping, Justin fell asleep.

Operation Lima Bean started at sunrise. "Psst," Derrick whispered in Justin's ear.

Justin, stiff and disoriented, thinking he was still retarded, answered with his trademark, "Aaaaa!"

"Sssh! What the fuck? Be cool, man," Derrick whispered in disgust.

It all came back to Justin: the salty taste of the soup, Darla's thrusting bust, his own new hair and eyebrow look. Operation Lima Bean.

"What's Operation Lima Bean?" he mumbled, aware of his bad breath and lack of a toothbrush.

"Sssh. Are you dressed?"

"Of course."

"Well, get up then. Be quiet. Don't wake anyone."

When Justin came back from the bathroom, where he had rinsed his mouth out with someone's Aquafresh, Derrick was waiting for him by the front door. They slipped out into the cold March morning and climbed in Derrick's beat up car.

"So where are we going?" Justin asked as the engine warmed up.

"I found a good, wholesome place for you to disappear. Someone who needs your help. No ID required, no questions."

"Where's that?" Justin's heart sank. He just knew this was going to be bad.

"I don't know where. That's part of the beauty of Operation Lima Bean. I really can't say where you're going." The engine began to sound reasonable, like it could maybe do its job without blowing up.

Derrick put it in drive and they cruised down the street under the barely light sky. "I told him I don't want to know where you are."

"Who? Where are you taking me?" Justin's grogginess was making way for panic.

Derrick groaned. "Don't freak out. You're going to be a farmer. Say, how about an espresso?" He swerved across several empty lanes without checking his mirrors, and pulled into a drive-through espresso kiosk, just as the neon sign lit up "open."

"A farmer? I don't know how to farm."

"You don't know how to do anything. That's your problem."

"What! You don't know anything about me."

"Sure I do," Derrick said, fixing his intense, dark eyes on Justin. "You want double espresso? Latte? Cappuccino?"

"Double Americano," Justin said, digging into his wallet.

"It's on me," Derrick said. He ordered Justin's Americano and a triple espresso. When they were back on the road, Justin asked again, "What do you mean I don't know how to do anything?"

"If you did, you wouldn't need me to figure your life out. Don't bother arguing. Farming is useful. It's a skill. You'll thank me later."

Boy, it stung. This little punk, more than ten years Justin's junior. Justin burnt his tongue on the Americano. He had no defense, so he said nothing.

"It's okay. You have other qualities," Derrick said kindly.

Justin refrained from asking what they were, though he was curious. He suspected he'd regret it if he asked.

"So where are we going right now?"

"Hold your horses, sport. We're going to make the tradeoff."

"Tradeoff? You're trading me for something?"

Derrick sighed in mild disgust. "Just relax." He roared through a yellow light. The Americano splattered Justin's face as he saw the light turn red.

CHAPTER TWENTY-NINE

Sir Robert came for a second date with Zoe, then a third. Date two consisted of combing her hair, polishing her toenails and massaging her breasts. Date three featured shaving her legs, sucking her nipples and feeding her soup.

Zoe barely ate anymore, though Mother watched her intently at dinner and tried to ply her with the delicacies of the house. "Just try one," Mother would say in her attempt at coaxing, which sounded like barking, as she extended a platter of cream cheese-filled mini crepes. Zoe would try to nibble one, but the cream cheese congealed in her throat.

Nothing was the same since the dates. The other girls didn't understand, not even Deni, and Zoe had never been good with words. The depression that had swamped her after Justin's disappearance was seeping back.

Deni crept into Zoe's bed one night to comfort her. The girls slept, scrawny limbs entangled, giving off as little heat as two bodies possibly could. "I thought you'd be happy here," Deni whispered in Zoe's ear. "I'm sorry." Deni wasn't looking well. Her dark skin was grayish. "I haven't loved anybody so much since my foster sister. I'd do anything for you," she whispered. After a pause she added, "But I can't do anything." It sent chills down Zoe's spine, hearing Deni sound so fragile and powerless.

The next day, Mother called Deni and Zoe into her office and announced that a new fan wanted to see the two girls together. They were to kiss and fondle each other while the guy watched, and then lick his dick together until he came. "I would advise titillating him as much as possible with your performance," she said. "There's a good likelihood he will finish himself off, excusing you from further duty." Zoe saw the glee in Mother's eye, her delight in bringing Zoe to this. "And remember your manners. This individual seems less refined than your Sir Robert. But we need to welcome him and honor his wishes just the same."

The man was in his fifties, dressed in a business suit. Someone Zoe might have made a latte for and never thought about twice. "You look different in person," he said, peering doubtfully at Deni like she was a tray of ribs for sale in the supermarket. "How recent are the photos in your web gallery?"

"They're ongoing," said Deni, who looked scrawnier and grayer every day. She had no energy left for either friendliness or sass.

The trio entered Zoe's room, but Inanna, who sat on the bed, arched her back and hissed when she saw the man.

"Jesus!" the man said. "I hate cats. Get that ugly thing out of here."

The large, wrathful cat stood her ground and stared at them, yellow eyes narrowed into a dare. "We'll go in my room," Deni said.

The guy sat on a chair, the girls on Deni's bed. Deni slumped against Zoe's shoulder. They all waited for somebody to take the lead. Usually it would have been Deni, but not today.

The man cleared his throat. Nothing happened. "Clock's ticking, ladies," he said softly.

Zoe took Deni in her arms. The dark girl's eyes were huge and unfocused. Zoe kissed her tenderly. It was like kissing herself. She held the tiny, wasted body in her arms and gently rocked her. Zoe blinked back a tear.

"How about something a little hotter?" the guy prompted after a minute. "You know, take off some clothes. A tit or two wouldn't hurt."

Zoe glanced at the guy, who sat, unimpressed. He hadn't even bothered to unbuckle his belt. Deni was shivering. Zoe took off her own clothes. Her body wasn't much, but she still had more flesh left than Deni. She heard the guy unzipping his pants. "Deni," Zoe whispered, but the other girl didn't seem to know where she was. "There's something wrong with her," Zoe said to the man.

He sighed impatiently, pausing in mid-stroke, his cock squat and squarish. "I hate to break it to you, honey, but she's dying."

"I mean, I think we better get her some help." Zoe slapped Deni lightly on the cheek. "Deni, can you hear me?"

"Yeah, yeah," Deni said, eyes focusing. "Damn, I felt weird for a minute." Deni's eyes moved over to the guy with his cock out. "Oh, yeah," she said, as if it was all coming back to her. She raised her hands to pull her T-shirt off, but was too weak. "Help me, Zoe," she whispered. "Take my T-shirt off." Nobody had called her Zoe for weeks. Zoe took Deni's clothes off.

"This is more like it," said the man, reviving his erection.

"You just lie back," Zoe whispered. Deni gladly took the passive role. Zoe made love to her friend, kissing her lips and her breasts, then moving her face down between Deni's legs. Deni lay so still, Zoe wondered if she had fallen asleep. But suddenly the girl's whole body began to convulse, as in orgasm. She moaned and grunted.

"Yeah," the guy said, and from the corner of her eye, Zoe could see his hand moving furiously. "Yeah!" But something wasn't right. Zoe lifted her head away from Deni's pussy. "Jesus, don't stop now!" the guy said.

"Deni?" Zoe asked. "Deni?" The girl didn't respond. Zoe grabbed her wrist, thought she felt a faint pulse. "Call 911," Zoe said to the man. "Tell Mother. Call 911." The guy hesitated, erection drooping again. "Go, you asshole!" Zoe screamed. All the rage she felt – for the fans and Mother and George and the diseases that were wasting these beautiful girls – exploded. "Run, you asshole!" she screamed louder than she had ever screamed when she was well.

Footsteps on the stairs, then George flung open the door. "What is it? What's going on?" he asked.

"Call an ambulance!" Zoe cried. George took in the situation. He grabbed a robe, wrapped it around the shrunken girl, and bent to lift her. "Don't move her! Get the paramedics!" Zoe yelled. But George lifted Deni, who weighed practically nothing, and in no time they were down the stairs. Zoe heard the front door slam. Her anger burned anew. Of course George couldn't have an ambulance coming to the house. He would take his chances transporting Deni in his car.

"Shit!" said the man. "Well, I guess you could still give me a blowjob." Zoe picked up the nearest thing, a piece of amethyst from Deni's rock collection, and threw it at the asshole. It hit him on the left cheek, just below his eye. He screamed and went for her, but just then Mother appeared in the doorway.

"I'm terribly sorry," she said, her voice commanding enough to stop him before his hands reached Zoe's scrawny neck. Zoe could see a vicious bruise forming on the man's cheekbone. She was surprised by her strength. "Don't worry, Mr. Powell, you'll have a full refund and we'll have you back for a free visit with a girl more to your liking." She got rid of him in a few minutes, then came back to berate Zoe. "You handled yourself very badly," she said.

"Is Deni going to be okay?" Zoe asked, barely able to get the words out.

"Who knows?" Mother said. "This is a house of dying girls. We must expect episodes like this. We must keep our composure, especially in front of customers. They could get this place shut down! Where would you girls live then? Who would take care of you?" Zoe didn't answer. She drifted out of the room while Mother was still talking, a transgression nobody got away with, but what did Zoe care anymore?

She went to her room and lay on her bed, sick with powerlessness. She'd never been to a hospital since was born. She couldn't picture where Deni had gone, what they would do for her there, if she would ever come back. Life was a horrific series of partings. Soon Zoe, too, would go, and right now that was fine with her.

The closet door was open and Zoe could see the cat's yellow eyes peering down from a high shelf. They bored into her. "Is she coming back, Inanna?" Zoe asked. The cat blinked once, inscrutably. "What did you want to come back here for, anyway?" Zoe muttered. She lay on her back for hours, watching the light change outside the window.

Later, she was somewhere else. It didn't feel like a dream, but there was the sound of the beating wings, louder than ever before. She was on a river bank. On the other side, Deni sat cross legged and smiling, looking different than Zoe had seen her look. She must be twenty pounds heavier, normal thin now instead of dying thin. Her skin was bronze, and her shoulder-length dark hair looked real. Excited, Zoe stepped into the river to join her best friend.

But the water frothed and roared like a milk steamer. Zoe pulled her foot out, shocked. The water calmed. She tried again, and the water roiled, stinging her ankle like a million red ants were biting her. Deni stood now, waving excitedly. Zoe tried to yell to her that she would be right there, that she was grateful Deni had waited for her just like she had promised. But when Zoe opened her mouth, a wind kicked up and stole her words. The flapping was deafening now. Deni jumped up and down. Zoe put her foot in the water, frantic to cross the river. The water surged up around her thighs, but this time she was going to get to the other side even if she drowned.

She stepped forward, the water up to her waist. But just as suddenly as it had risen, the water fell back into a placid, welcoming stream. "I'll be right there!" she called, starting to run through the water. She glanced over, thinking she would see Deni return her smile. Instead, the other girl reached up and took hold of the hand of a black-haired Asian girl, who hung from the glistening talons of something enormous, the winged thing, a divine bird creature in a color Zoe had never seen and could never describe afterwards. It was Jasmine and the bird of death, come to take Deni away from her. "No!" Zoe screamed, kicking up water as she ran. "Wait! No! Wait! You promised!"

The wings got quieter and quieter as the creature and the dead girls flew away. Zoe reached the empty river bank and threw herself down on the spot where Deni had waited so happily just a minute before. She bawled like she hadn't since infancy. She screamed Deni's name, heartbroken, then cursed her for breaking their promise. Zoe had almost been there. And she was way past ready to leave. Suddenly she was two billion light years past ready to leave. She cried by the side of the river for what seemed like weeks, but the beating wings did not return for her.

Zoe became aware of a warm breeze after she had been breathing it for a while. She heard it blowing through the trees beside the river. It was a full-bodied breeze, more than just air. She thought she sensed wisdom in it, and an earthy smell, no, a bit fishy, like the ocean. The breeze was doing something to her mind and body. It felt as if this warm breeze carried nutrition both physical and spiritual, reviving her spirit while recharging her brain cells. She wasn't crying now, or yearning for Deni. Deni was okay somewhere else now. Zoe was curious to find out more about the breeze and about what would happen next. So she opened her eyes.

Bright yellow eyes flashed inches from her own. Inanna sat on her chest, breathing tuna cat food breath methodically into Zoe's nostrils.

Her first reaction was to shove Inanna away. But her mind and body felt so different, just like in the dream or vision or whatever it had been. Zoe would be convinced, forever, though she would never tell anyone, that the cat was doing this with some purpose. So she fought the impulse to move. Now that she knew that fish breeze was really cat breath, it wasn't easy to lie there. Inanna's eyes focused intensely on Zoe, who had the strangest sensation that the cat was breathing for her. This went on for maybe another half hour. Then the cat slowly retracted her face, sat on Zoe's chest and watched her carefully, turned her attention to cleaning her paws like a normal cat, arched her back, leapt off the bed and out the window, which Zoe did not remember being open.

Candi and Brenda cried in the hall, so Zoe knew they had heard about Deni. Any minute, the girls would come into Zoe's room with the news. But Zoe wasn't worried about Deni. She stretched her limbs. She was all new. The awareness seeped through her whole body and mind that she would not die for approximately another half century.

The house of dying girls seemed poisonous now, like a dangerous place for her to be. Later that night, after the crying and embracing,

Zoe crammed her clothes into a bag and followed Inanna out the window, down the tree limb and to the dark street below.

CHAPTER THIRTY

The first week on the farm, Justin hated being a farmhand. The mornings were too cold, his back ached, all the Mexican guys were obviously joking about him in Spanish. He found himself missing the group home. He had never lived anywhere so isolated, nor had to work so hard. The farm covered a few acres of an island in the middle of the Columbia River. Justin found it disconcerting that whole days would pass and there was nowhere except the small island grocery store to spend money.

Even worse than farming were his other duties, which involved the farmer's mother. The old lady must have been ninety. Confused by Alzheimer's, she was cranky as hell. The farmer wanted someone with good English to help his mother, and since Justin was the only non-Mexican, he got the job. In fact, he realized that this was why the boss had been trolling around for someone like him. That is, someone who spoke English but had reasons to take two difficult jobs – farmhand and caretaker – for less than the going wage of one. He was working for the same wages as the undocumented Mexicans, with double the duties. He was undocumented himself now.

The mother was named Desi, short for Desira. Justin had tried to call her Mrs. Salmon, but in her mind she had regressed to way before the point when she met Mr. Salmon. Desi had good days where she fed and dressed herself and listened appreciatively as Justin read to her from *Our Golden Treasury of American Poems*. These days were easier than farming, but they were in the minority. Other days, she threw whatever her feeble arms could throw. Though she was too weak to throw anything that would hurt from impact, she was ingenious about finding other ways to harm. Once she tipped an entire box of straight pins onto the bedroom carpet. Another day, she picked a turd out of the toilet and threw it square in Justin's chest. On the bad days, Justin would have infinitely preferred the cold and backaches of farming.

Justin and the Mexican guys all slept in a bunkhouse. They numbered twelve, exactly enough to fill the bunks. Some of the guys were friendly, once they got used to him. Mostly they called him Gringo, but sometimes Pablo, for his newest alias, Paul. Saturday nights they would buy beer and tequila, then they would stay up late listening to Tejano music or passing around the sorriest looking acoustic guitar Justin had ever seen. Justin learned the songs well enough to sing along with a few. He drank with the guys, but didn't match them shot for shot, for fear of spilling his secrets.

Once the guys grew accustomed to Justin, he was very useful. He helped them fill out forms in English, and explained letters and newspaper articles in simpler terms. Sometimes they enticed him to the pay phone at the island's one grocery store, where they would get him to communicate difficult English sentences into the receiver. He always liked to help out, because it made him feel like he belonged and had a purpose. Plus, they usually rewarded him with a beer.

Every week, the farming got easier. Justin developed muscles and stamina, learned about soil and compost, and became able to distinguish arugula from frisse. This time of year, the crop was mostly gourmet lettuces. The farm grew fourteen different kinds to sell to local restaurants.

Justin discovered that he enjoyed the growth of seeds, and the thriving of little plants. On the clear days of spring, he could see four snow-capped mountains in the distance. He discovered the joys of sunrise.

Within two months, Justin could have shown that pipsqueak Derrick a thing or two. Derrick had accused Justin of not knowing how to do anything. Now Justin could drive a stick shift or cultivate a field. He knew everything about caring for cranky old ladies. And, at old man Tucker's behest, had researched Alzheimer's treatments on the Internet to the extent that he could have held up his end of a long conversation on the topic with a doctor. He knew how to plant and harvest lettuce, how to teach English and befriend foreigners. And after two months, he realized he was happier than he had ever been, outside of those precious hours he had spent holding Zoe.

Most of the Mexican guys had girlfriends back home in some little village or other. Some of the guys were starry-eyed romantics, taking turns playing love songs on the guitar, dedicating them to their girls back home. Others felt entitled to go whoring in Portland now and then. But all of them would have sworn their allegiance, in their way, and killed any man who violated their sweethearts.

So when Justin admitted that he had lost track of his woman, his coworkers were astounded. "Amigo, what the hell?" they asked, shaking their heads. "No cojones!" They teased him, but with a real edge of scorn.

The Mexican guys were different than any people Justin had known before. None of them had much education, though some were obviously smart. But they had a tenacity no one in Justin's circle had ever demonstrated. These guys worked their asses off, saved money and sent it home to their parents and siblings and sweethearts. Some got pretty drunk on Saturday night, but everybody was careful to avoid trouble. They didn't complain about little things, and seldom belabored big things, either. They enjoyed the work and the land and had an optimism about the future that Justin never would have believed undocumented workers making shitty wages could have. Maybe this was an exceptional handful of workers, Justin didn't know.

Except for the pay, old man Tucker treated the workers well. Everybody had lots of good food to eat, and the low wages were paid on time. Nobody was verbally abused, except Justin by the old gal, which entertained the others. Justin never would have thought a bunch of illegal aliens would become his role models for being a man, but these guys became just that. They could do anything: plant, fix cars, play guitar, figure out how to get their paycheck to the most obscure villages in Mexico. It blew Justin's mind.

One day, Miguel and Ramon asked Justin to come to the store with them and help them make phone calls on their lunch break. Miguel was trying to find a Hello Kitty alarm clock for his six year-old daughter in Southern Mexico. Ramon needed an appointment at the county clinic because of a suspicious rash on his dick. After Justin had identified the Target on NE 122nd as a source of all things Hello Kitty, and set up an appointment for Ramon, the three men entered the store. There were only two people inside, the taciturn shop owner, a man in his sixties who often wore overalls, and a man with short hair and khakis, who was trying to engage the older man in conversation. He stopped talking and looked up as Justin, Miguel and Ramon entered. The man in khakis had an intent gaze but a friendly smile. Justin's months on the farm had relaxed him. He felt like such a different person on the inside, he figured his outside would have changed to match. In other words, he had become careless.

The Mexican guys usually took their time in the store, but today they marched straight to the beer cooler. "Hi, there," the stranger in khakis said, engaging his big friendly grin.

"Hey," Justin said. "What's up?"

"Nice day out," the man said.

"Yeah."

"How are the crops coming?"

"Good," Justin said. He was proud of his new muscles and knowledge, and thrilled that a stranger could recognize him as a farmhand.

"You from that nice patch of land right up the road?" the man asked.

"Lottery's up to nine million," the shop owner cut in. "Maybe you want to buy a ticket."

This interjection threw Justin, because he never heard the old man say unnecessary words. Maybe the lottery commission was offering some sort of extra kickbacks now. "No, that's okay," said Justin, then turned his attention back to the stranger. "Yeah, the Tucker place. You know it?"

"Been there before," the man said. "You got a good crew this year?"

"Yeah, a dozen of us." Justin felt something cold nudge his arm and jerked his head around to see Ramon thrusting two bottle of beer against him. "Hey, you guys done already?" Justin was stunned by the look on his amigos' faces. Ramon looked like he wanted to murder Justin, while Miguel's face was blank as a mask.

"Got you a couple of cervezas," Miguel said, hurriedly pulling a crumpled ten dollar bill from his Levis pocket.

"Oh, okay." Justin had been planning to get some Doritos, but since they were in a mysterious hurry all of a sudden, he decided to do without.

The storekeeper handed Miguel his change. As his eyes passed over Justin, he looked at him as though he were a cockroach on his clean counter. Justin figured the guy was pissed about the unsold lottery ticket. He didn't know what had gotten into his coworkers. Maybe Ramon's rash was acting up. It was a shame they were in such foul moods on the bluest, warmest spring day so far. "Nice talking to you," Justin said to the man in khakis, who lifted a hand in goodbye, no longer smiling.

Ramon and Miguel walked stiffly ahead of Justin and climbed into the pickup truck. Miguel started the motor before Justin was halfway in. They drove out of the parking lot at normal speed, but once they were a quarter mile down the road, Miguel began slapping the steering wheel, cursing, and picking up speed.

"Whoa! What's wrong with you?" Justin asked.

"Estupido! 'Nice talking to you,'" Ramon mimicked Justin. "'Nice talking to you!' Don't you know who the fuck was that man? The Migra! The fucking Migra!"

Justin had lived with a bunch of Mexican guys long enough not to have to ask Ramon to translate. "No," Justin said.

"Si!" Miguel yelled, crossing himself.

"But he wasn't wearing a uniform!" Justin insisted.

"Oh, we'll see uniforms when they come to the farm." Ramon spat. "Thanks a lot, Gringo!"

Miguel sped to the farm, tearing down the long dirt road to get to the bunkhouse. Everybody was heading toward the lettuce field when Miguel and Ramon ran into their midst and began spouting Spanish, much faster than Justin could follow. He picked out the words for "white guy," immigration police," twelve workers," and "let's go." Most of the guys joined in their panic. Only three remained calm and decided to stay. The other eight bolted, a couple of them not even stopping at the bunkhouse to gather their possessions. Old man Tucker was in the farmhouse with his mother. He didn't know his place had turned into a ghost town until an hour later, when the Migra came calling.

Justin took in every excruciating detail of that afternoon, though later he would tell himself it was a blur and try not to think about it. But he remembered his puzzlement about where these guys were going to hide on an island, his incredulous feeling when the white cars screamed into the drive. Because he hadn't fully believed it. He thought his comrades were being paranoid. If he had believed it, wouldn't he have run, too? What if the FBI and the INS shared information?

But there he was, his arms full of arugula, men in uniforms spilling out of white cars, old man Tucker running out the front door, panting like he would have a heart attack.

The men in uniforms rounded up Justin and his three remaining colleagues, all of whom looked equally terrified. Justin wondered if he was the only one praying to hold back diarrhea.

It turned out that two of the guys had the necessary papers, and the Migra couldn't touch them. The agents eyed Justin suspiciously, but his dye job had grown out and his hair was too blond for a Mexican, his eyes too blue.

"We heard there were twelve here," the man from the store said to Justin.

"Somebody must have miscounted," Justin said. His voice trembled and he couldn't look anybody in the eye, but his accent was flawlessly American, so they turned their attention to Pepino. Justin knew him less than he had known his other coworkers, because Pepino only spoke about three words of English. He was older than the others, close to forty, with a bum leg that could farm but not run. When the Migra's white minivan departed, Pepino's were the only haunted eyes to watch Justin from the back window.

Old man Tucker was another matter. The Migra remembered him from five years earlier, when he'd been fined heavily for twenty INS violations. Justin was excluded from this portion of the investigation, so he wasn't sure if it worked in the farmer's favor to be busted for only one illegal, or if the fact of a repeat offense was worse than the original twenty.

Justin and the two legal Mexicans were excused from the proceedings, so they returned to the bunkhouse. Justin lay on his back while the other two huddled, conversing in Spanish. He wanted to apologize, but he didn't know how. And weren't the Migra onto old man Tucker anyway? If Justin hadn't talked to the guy in the store, maybe the Migra would have come without warning and hauled away nine instead of just one. Justin's feelings of self-recrimination alternated with false persecution.

There wasn't any dinner that night, since the three men who shared cooking duties had fled. Instead of gathering around the big wooden table in the farmhouse dining room, Justin sat on his bunk, enduring mean looks. The silence grew heavy with hostility.

"Look, I'm sorry," he finally burst out. "I had no idea that guy was the Migra. I never would have said anything."

The younger man, Raul, looked at Justin disdainfully. "Anybody know la Migra."

"He wasn't wearing a uniform!"

"No matter. No need uniform to know la Migra."

"Your problem," said Leo, who had the round face and broad cheekbones of an Indian, "is you not man. You chicken." He pronounced it "cheeken."

"No sense," agreed Raul. "Estupido as chicken. A dog is smarter."

"Know nothing," said Leo. "Don't know la Migra when la Migra stand there talk to him."

"Don't know where his woman."

"Don't know who she lie with."

"Maybe he have child, he don't know!"

"Where his madre? He don't send her money."

"Don't have good gringo job," said Leo. "He gringo, but work Mexican job."

"Who is he?" asked Raul.

"He not man."

"He not even boy."

"He not even dog. He cheeken," Leo summed up, spitting lazily in Justin's direction. Raul spat, too, then the men trudged off to bed, the camaraderie of the bunkhouse shredded forever.

Justin lay on his bunk, hating himself and wishing he'd die in his sleep. Problem was, he couldn't escape being awake. Lives flashed through his brain, all the lives he had touched and loused up along the way. The disappointments he had layered upon his parents. Teachers who had taken time to write him recommendation letters, only to have him drop out of school. The college girlfriend he couldn't commit to because he wasn't sure who he was. All those people on the telephone who had answered his survey questions, not knowing their answers were being twisted to justify killing bunnies and chopping down the last tree in America. Look at all the jobs he had helped people lose! Pete had fled after trusting Justin not to fuck up at the group home. What about Surfer Dave and Rick and Marvin? They had certainly been canned for letting Jacob Arnold escape, never to be found. All these Mexican guys, he had lost them their jobs and housing. This moment, while Justin lay warm and comfortable in his bunk, eight Mexican guys hid somewhere on this island, hunkered down behind bushes, shivering in the moonlight. And Pepino was on his way back to Mexico. Old man Tucker might lose his farm. What would become of him and his batty old mother then?

And what of Zoe? How long had the other guys let her stay in Justin's room when she couldn't pay rent? They weren't rich. And why hadn't he forced her to go to the doctor? Because he was too scared she didn't like him enough, and would leave if his requests annoyed her.

The guys were right. He was a total fucking cheeken.

The next morning, old man Tucker called Justin out of the bunkhouse. The farmer looked twice as old as usual, his skin gray and his eyes puffy. "Son, why don't you come into the house for a minute?" he asked.

They sat at the big round table where all the guys used to eat. Old man Tucker poured coffee into a mug with the handle broken off. It said "Hawaii" in faded pink letters. Justin realized now that he had drank from this cup a dozen times, and never given it a thought. Had the farmer been to Hawaii? Had a friend brought it back as a gift? Had Justin ever given any thought at all to this man's life?

"One more slip and I'm in deep shit," the farmer said, stirring his own coffee.

"Yeah," Justin said. "Uh, what are you going to do?" He wondered if the farmer had heard about Justin talking to the Migra in the store. Justin stared at his coffee cup. He couldn't imagine old man Tucker laying on a beach, or attending a luau, plucking an apple from the mouth of a roasted pig.

"Son," old man Tucker said, fiddling with one of his white whiskers that grew unchecked in every direction, "I don't know what your story is, and I don't want to know. But I figure something ain't right or a bright young man like you wouldn't be holed up here on this farm, picking lettuce with the Mexicans and bathing my less than sainted mother."

"Uh…" Justin said, but the farmer held up a cracked and ruddy hand.

"I don't want to know, son. I hate to do this cause you're a good worker, and lord knows I don't want to take care of her alone," he said, nodding towards the upstairs to indicate his mother. "But I can't get caught with anything fishy around here again. They ain't giving me no more chances."

Justin had never before been called both cheeken and fishy within twelve hours. He could deny neither charge. He nodded feebly.

"I'm going to ask you something, but I don't want to hear an answer. Like I said, I don't want to hear your story. It's a question to answer inside your own head. Just think on whatever you're running from and ask yourself, 'Can I face the music?' You could do more than pick lettuce and tend a crazy old woman."

"I like picking lettuce," Justin said, his voice small and reedy.

"It's nice for a season or two when you're young," the farmer assented.

Justin tried to gauge if he was too sick to his stomach to drink his coffee. Would it help? Or make it worse? He picked up the mug but his hand shook so much he set it back down.

"I'm just saying think on it, son. Give it a long, good think."

All the wreckage of Justin's past loomed up in his mind, a towering rubbish pile of aborted plans, disappointed relatives, abandoned girlfriends and lost jobs. He had slunk away from courage and honesty at every turn, letting the axe fall on the next guy. Old man Tucker seemed to think Justin was worth something, but what if he found out Justin had brought the Migra down on his farm and lost him his whole crew of workers? Justin wanted to let things be, to keep whatever esteem the farmer might still have for him. But he was making himself sicker than ever, avoiding responsibilities, spurning the truth.

"Uh," Justin began, "uh, Mr. Tucker, I was at the store yesterday and one of the INS officers was there. I thought he was just a regular guy. He wasn't wearing his uniform. And I, uh, maybe talked too much. I definitely talked too much. I was trying to be neighborly. But I'm afraid this is my fault…" He stopped to breathe and opened his eyes wider, hoping the tears would dry instead of falling.

Old man Tucker smiled sadly. "Yes, so I heard. Folks out here can spot the INS from half a mile away. But you ain't been here so long."

Justin felt an unfamiliar sense of relief. "I'm sorry," he said simply.

"I know, son. And don't think I'm letting you go because you misjudged the Migra. They're tricky dogs."

"Okay," Justin said.

"Is there somewhere you can go?"

"Yeah," Justin said. "I'll think of something." His nerves and stomach had relaxed enough to drink his coffee. The farmer brought out some cold biscuits, butter and ham. The two men ate, not saying anything.

When they finished, old man Tucker carried the plates to the sink. He took his wallet from his back pocket and counted out a thick clump of bills. "I'm paying you for an extra week. A bonus for dealing with my mother. When I think about what I'm in for now, I realize I should have paid you double all along."

"Thanks," Justin said, folding the bills in half and shoving them in his front pocket.

"I'll tell the old girl you said goodbye."

"Yeah."

"You need a ride off the island?"

Justin shook his head. It was another gorgeous spring day. Portland was miles away, but he didn't know what he was doing so there was no reason to hurry.

Old man Tucker grasped Justin's hand. "Good luck, son," he said. "Go make something of yourself."

Half an hour later, Justin had his work clothes stuffed into a paper grocery sack, and was walking away from the farm.

CHAPTER THIRTY-ONE

After Zoe left the house of dying girls, her life was new. She had seen Deni, joyous and radiant, transported by an angel bird. A cat had restored her own life. What was there to be afraid of?

So starting over was okay, even without friends, family, a home, money or a plan.

That first night, Zoe walked in the dark, elated. She had barely walked for several months. After two miles, she had to admit to herself she had overdone it and needed to sit down. When she came to an all-night café, she went inside.

It was three AM on a Tuesday night, so the place was nearly empty, except for a few students hunched over textbooks. The cafe was a cross between a greasy diner and an espresso joint. Red vinyl booths lined the walls, but a few comfortable armchairs huddled around a fireplace, and Zoe heard the familiar roar of an espresso machine.

"You can sit anywhere!" a guy about her age called over the milk steamer. She sat in an armchair by the fire. A few minutes later, he appeared at her side. "What can I get you?" he asked.

Zoe's old self was fiercely proud, and would have sat on the curb outside rather than coming in here with no money. But now it seemed okay. "I'm in a transition," she said, "and I don't have any money. Could I just sit here by the fire for a while? I worked in a café for a year and would be happy to help you clean in exchange."

"You just want to sit here?" the guy asked. She nodded. "You don't have to do anything! I don't care. You can sit here all night if you want. The boss doesn't come in till noon tomorrow."

She smiled. "Thanks."

Zoe sat and looked at the fire, thinking of Deni and Inanna. They had given her something unspeakably precious, and she would not squander it.

Later, the worker brought over some day-old pastries and coffee. "I'm about to make a new pot, so I was going to throw it out. But it's still pretty fresh," he said. He was kind, obviously trying to save her pride. She remembered Justin's kindness, and for the thousandth time she hoped he was okay, wherever he was.

"Thanks. These look good," she said, accepting a raspberry Danish and a chocolate croissant along with the coffee. She recognized the croissant; it was from one of the bakeries that delivered to Jojo's. It tasted better than she remembered. After eating it she felt stronger, and it seemed natural to get up and sweep the floor of the café. "You'd be doing me a favor," she told the reluctant guy, trying to persuade him to hand her the broom. "I just got over a long illness, and haven't been able to do any useful work." And it was so true! She could hardly believe how good it felt to sweep crumbs and dirt into the dustpan and dump the whole mess in the trash. About a thousand times more satisfying for Zoe than assisting the wretched ejaculations of Sir Robert and his ilk.

The worker shook his head over Zoe's zest for cleaning. "You should come in and talk to the boss," he said. "We're a bunch of slackers here. Maybe she could give you a few hours. That is, if you're looking for work."

That's how Zoe began to get back on her feet. It started with a very part time cleaning job at the 24-hour café, and sleeping in a Christian-run homeless shelter for almost a week. She felt like she was listening for inspiration, so she kept her ears open in a way she never had before. Way back before she ever got sick, she didn't think much about the purpose of life or her individual gifts, what she might have to give the world. But now she had an eerie calm feeling, like life could unfold in a meaningful manner if she remained receptive and didn't get in the way.

One of the shelter workers told Zoe about a position in a downtown women's residence, a shabby weekly hotel called La Bahia. In exchange for twenty hours of work a week, she could have a room. It wasn't a good deal for most people, since at minimum wage that put the room's value at about six hundred dollars a month, and it wasn't worth half that. But for someone with no money for a deposit and references that were uncertain or worse, it was good enough for now. Zoe jumped at the chance. And the women residents appreciated her, because she got that dump cleaner than it had been for years.

Cleaning the La Bahia wasn't entirely fulfilling, but Zoe was content. She'd been there a month when she heard of the situation she knew she wanted.

A new La Bahia resident came down one afternoon to get towels, one of the few amenities that made it resemble a real hotel. She was the chatty sort that liked to find new ears in which to complain. Recently she had quit her job cooking in a home for sexually abused girls. "I couldn't take it," said the woman, shaking her tangled blond hair off her pitted face. "The tantrums those girls would throw! And always complaining about the food! Thinking they're so special. I mean, what woman wasn't abused as a girl?"

Zoe smiled and handed her a towel. "Where is this place?" she asked.

As soon as the woman trudged upstairs with her towel, Zoe grabbed the desk phone and tracked down the phone number of the abused girl house. It took several calls, since it wasn't a regular listing, but between her nights at the homeless shelter and her month amidst the down and out residents of La Bahia, Zoe had learned a lot about city, county and private non-profit agencies. On her fifth call, she got the director of the home for abused girls on the line. "I heard there's a position open," Zoe said. "I'd like to come in as soon as possible and talk to you about it." Later, the director would tell Zoe it was her voice that got her invited for an interview the following day. Zoe was short on qualifications and references, but the director thought the abused girls would benefit by hearing that calm, confident voice.

Zoe was more nervous the night before her interview than she had been since she left the house of dying girls. This was the first thing she had really wanted. But Deni was in her dream, tickling Zoe until they both laughed. And then Zoe dreamt that she slept in Deni's arms, just like she used to, but now both girls were healthy and free.

Zoe didn't know how much she would disclose to Ms. Barrett at the interview. Should she admit that she'd been dying but now she wasn't? That she had let her illness be exploited in exchange for room and board? That she knew about abused girls from living with a house full of them?

But when Ms. Barrett asked why Zoe wanted to work there, she answered simply. "I recently lost my best friend to leukemia," Zoe said. "She had been abused her whole life, and had this fatal illness, but she still loved the world and tried to take care of me." She blinked back a tear, but Ms. Barrett didn't seem to hold it against her. "She inspired me to make my life more useful. I don't have the education or experience to help girls directly by counseling or stuff like that. But if you're looking for someone to cook and clean for them, I know how to do that and I know I would feel useful here."

Ms. Barrett looked thoughtfully at Zoe for nearly a minute, the time it took her to realize that she was about to hire this young woman without the standard background check. They were protective of the abused girls, and closely guarded access to them. But Zoe would not pass a background check, Ms. Barrett was sure. Anyone who lived in that fleabag La Bahia Hotel in exchange for rent had something strange in her past. Yet she found Zoe oddly compelling. Ms. Barrett had never bent hiring rules in the three years she had directed the home. Then again, she was disillusioned with the background check procedure, which had failed to screen out three loony fuckups in a row, two in the kitchen and one on the counseling staff. She sighed. "I realize you are probably in a transitional period, if you're staying at the La Bahia Hotel. But it would help if you could provide me with a few references."

"Of course," Zoe said.

Ms. Barrett relaxed her shoulders. At least the paperwork would be on file, even if she didn't actually call the references. "Well," she said. "Welcome aboard."

The first two weeks were hard. On top of learning her new duties, Zoe still had to clean La Bahia until she collected a couple of paychecks. Plus, she had overstated her ability to cook. Zoe had often prepared meals for T-Bone, Rex and the twins, but that was mostly ramen, or macaroni and cheese. The abused girls were kids, and needed better nutrition. Luckily she was only in charge of breakfast and sack lunches for the girls to take to their day programs. Pancakes and bacon gave her enough trouble.

When Zoe got her third paycheck, she had enough money to find a better home than La Bahia. But what kind of place did she want to live in? Not a rave crash pad. She liked having her own room now. And what sort of roommates would be compatible? She hadn't thought much about what she wanted for a long time. For a while, she had no future. And when she regained her health, she'd been absorbed in pulling herself out of homelessness. But now she had enough money to choose between lifestyles.

Zoe called some roommate ads in the back of the Portland *Mercury*. After meeting one household of hippies, two condos full of Reed students, one meth freak, and an anarchist collective, Zoe opted to rent a room from a thirty-three year-old yoga teacher. The woman had a small two-bedroom house and four cats. Zoe's room was orange and came with a small gray and white cat named Daisy.

Clara was friendly but reserved. Zoe had never had a roommate like her. Clara didn't ask for loans, or keep Zoe awake whining about her love life. She didn't eat Zoe's food. She not only knew where the cleaning supplies were kept, she used them regularly. Clara had studied Chinese medicine. Often Zoe would find her in the kitchen, mixing up tinctures for the cats. Clara had a serious girlfriend, and was gone several nights a week, staying at the girlfriend's house. On these nights, Zoe liked to sit on the porch with the cats and ply them with catnip and other small treats.

Zoe couldn't remember a time that her home life was so relaxed. All she had to do was pay her rent and bills and do her share of the cleaning. She didn't have to hold anything together, stave off landlords, show her ass to cyber-strangers, or have any sex whatsoever with anyone. The absence of hassles was paradise.

Zoe hadn't thought she would see another May, but here it was. Some of the days were breathtaking, seventy degrees with blue skies, everything blooming. People in Portland showed skin: shorts and halter tops, tattoos and piercings everywhere. Zoe's hair was growing in thicker now, and she wasn't deathly skinny. She bought a green sundress and joined the skin parade.

CHAPTER THIRTY-TWO

So what happened to Justin? Did he finally become a man and start getting his shit together? Did he turn himself in to the feds? Did he hitchhike to Mexico? Did he slink off into another drifting situation– a farm, street life, perhaps a cave in a national park? Did he get more friends fired from jobs? More girlfriends reduced to the porn industry? Would he make his parents proud, or ashamed, like he usually did?

Justin did the courageous thing, though it's hard to say what he would have done without a kick in the pants and some inside information.

Life with the Mexicans had been the end for Justin. He couldn't be a wimp his whole life. Even before he had lost all their jobs and possibly got them deported – he'd never know if they were caught – they had shamed him about running out on his girl, leaving her with no livelihood and having no idea what had become of her. As Justin walked off Sauvie Island, he decided he would take the direct route to finding Zoe. He would go straight to Jojo's Fair Trade World Coffee Café and see if anyone knew where she was, whether the feds were waiting there for him or not.

It's a long walk from Sauvie Island to Southeast Clinton Street. Justin didn't get there until ten minutes before closing time. His feet were blistered and he looked and smelled pretty rough. He burst into Jojo's, heart pounding, then froze. Because who should be sitting there but Dale and Gillis. A different girl had her hand on Dale's knee, but it was unmistakably the radical, wiry fuck that had got them all in trouble.

Dale looked up and slowly smiled as he recognized Justin. One of his front teeth was chipped, giving him a snaggly grin. "Well," Dale said. "Look who's back at the scene of the fucking crime."

Gillis jumped up and hugged Justin. "Man, are you okay? Where you been?" He pulled out a chair for Justin and helped him into it, as though he expected Justin had been damaged in some way. "Did they get you, too?"

Justin shook his head, wondering if they'd be mad that they had suffered through detention and he hadn't. "No. Been underground." His voice came out quiet, unused since early morning. "You guys okay?"

"Fuck yeah," Dale said. "Those pussy ass bitches, they didn't get nothing out of me."

"There was nothing to get," Gillis said. "Yeah, man, we're okay. It was scary, but they fed us and everything."

"When did they let you go?"

"Oh, ages ago," Gillis said. "They kept us about two weeks."

"Those fuckers are gonna pay!" Dale said. "I have sixteen lawsuits in the works. This puss won't stand up to them with me. You in?"

"Uh," Justin said, swaying under Dale's rabid magnetism before righting himself. "No. Not me."

Dale ranted for eight more minutes before the girl who was running the café interrupted him. "Hey guys, I'm closing. You can hang out another ten minutes or so, but then I'm kicking you out."

Justin used the interruption to ask the one thing that was really on his mind. "Anyone know where Zoe is?"

Gillis looked at the table. The silence stretched out. "I heard she took off with a guy. Sorry, man. When you and I were gone, Pete and

Sam had to rent out our rooms. They let Zoe sleep on the couch, but she split one day."

Justin felt like Gillis had upended the table on him. His Zoe with another man? "What guy?"

"Nobody knows."

"What did he look like?

"I don't know. Pete said the guy was dressed like a professional."

"A professional what?" Dale scoffed.

"I don't know," Gillis said. "That's what I heard."

Justin felt like he might vomit. "Where did she meet this guy?"

Gillis shrugged. "No one knows. Pete said she hardly ever even left the house. He thinks they might have met over the Internet. I'm sorry to have to tell you, man."

The pain in Justin's gut got worse. "No one knows where she is?"

"No one's seen her," Gillis confirmed.

The café closed, so they went to Dale's revolutionary household. He lived in a ferociously filthy two-bedroom shack with four other anarchists. Justin thought he really should steer clear of this place, it screamed for surveillance. But he was hurting and had nowhere else to go at the moment, so he sat on a greasy couch and heard the rest of the story.

Dale's lawyer advised him to get out of Portland for a while once he was released from detention. So he and Gillis went to Alaska, where Dale had a brother they could stay with. "It fucking sucks ass up there in February and March," Dale summed up. They neglected to contact any Portland friends about their release, suffering from severe paranoia and questionable legal advice. So while they holed up with Dale's brother for the month it took them to way outstay their welcome, Justin had run away from the workshop and Pete had gone underground. Eventually Dale and Gillis blew back into town. Somehow Pete got word and resurfaced, but he had to remain semi-underground. The feds weren't after him, but a lot of local people wanted to question him about the Jacob Arnold fiasco.

Justin would later learn that Garth told his boss that he had discovered Jacob Arnold was a fraud just before he fled, thereby pre-empting the intensive search that would have been launched for a missing person like Jacob. Garth's disclosure saved the jobs of Dave and Rick.

Justin slept on the greasy revolutionary couch his first night back from the underground. The next day, he did the most courageous act of his life thus far: he turned himself in to the FBI.

It wasn't a big deal. The case had been dropped and they had moved on to juicier things. But still, Justin was terrified when he got off the bus downtown and entered the federal building. He wouldn't have done it, but he needed a new social security card and state ID to be employable.

The receptionist wouldn't let him past the desk. She was a pretty black woman in a blue dress. With one hand in her short afro, her eyebrows raised in exasperation, she said, "Sir, did I hear you right? You say you're wanted by the FBI for saying a golf ball could hit the president in the head?"

"Uh, yeah."

"Sir, the agents here are very busy working on real cases. Why don't you just write down your phone number and I'll let them know where to find you if they feel the need to pursue this."

"I'm not a crank," Justin said. "They thought I was part of a conspiracy. I've been underground. But I want to get an ID and a social security card again."

"Uh huh."

"Please."

She handed him a post-it and a pen. "Just leave your number."

"I don't have a number! I told you, I've been underground. I don't even have an ID! I had to burn it."

She looked pointedly at the post-it.

A man in a suit slipped out of nowhere. He was younger than Justin, with short, neat hair and a competent manner. "Is there a problem?" he asked.

"I'm trying to turn myself in," Justin said. "But she won't let me."

"What for?" the man asked, his face blank.

"Conspiracy to kill the president."

"With a golf ball, no less," the receptionist added.

"Oh, yes," the man said. "I heard about that."

"No kidding," the receptionist said, her face as surprised as the man's was unreadable.

Justin was invited past a metal detector to a more secure area, even though he'd already walked through a similar device downstairs. He sat on a black couch and read *Newsweek* for twenty minutes. He wished he could take a leak, but he wasn't about to ask anybody for directions to the restroom. These people were all immaculate in their suits. Justin wore his cleanest jeans and work shirt, neither of which was very clean.

Finally a woman in a navy suit invited Justin into her office. "I'm Agent Lloyd," she said. He was sure she could break his balls with one snap of her wrist. "You should have come forward and answered our questions," she said. "I could have you jailed for obstructing an investigation."

"Jailed?" Justin murmured.

"Of course. Don't you understand your actions were illegal?"

Justin nodded, not looking at her. "I never meant anything about the golf ball. It was a stupid comment."

"Yes," Agent Lloyd agreed.

"I got scared when Dale and Gillis disappeared. I'm sorry."

Agent Lloyd sighed. "Mr. Allen, sorry wouldn't cut it. But we have determined you posed no threat to anyone but yourself in the first place. So we are not going to waste America's resources housing and feeding you in jail."

"Will I be able to get an ID again? And a social security card?"

"Your name has been cleared." Agent Lloyd looked pointedly at a black clock on her wall. Justin had already wasted nearly three of her precious minutes.

"So I'm . . . free?"

She nodded. "Stay out of trouble. Don't say stupid things in public places to impress women," she said. "We're not impressed." She took a folder from a box marked "to do."

"Uh, okay. Thanks."

She didn't answer him. He stood up and left her office a free man. But it was strangely anticlimactic. He had been given the brush off by a federal agent after spending months of his life hiding like a worm underground. As he opened the front door of the federal building, instead of a wave of freedom rolling over him, his life came crashing back. What the fuck was he going to do with it? He walked across the street to pee in the McDonald's bathroom.

EPILOGUE

On a hot June day during the Rose Festival, Justin walked along the waterfront. Groups of sailors strode in sync, even off duty. Their ships clogged the river. Kids whizzed by on skateboards. Here and there, lovely women sat decoratively on grass, or leaned on posts, gazing at the river, or pointed at the carnival rides set up on the long strip of grass that ran along the waterfront. Justin especially noticed the girls, because he was lonely and in the last few months had managed nothing but a few majorly unsatisfying gropes with girls as sad and lonely as he.

Things were okay for Justin. He had a job photographing cars for *Auto Mart,* a free magazine based in Beaverton. His wage was low, but the company supplied an old Ford Escort to drive around in, and a nice digital camera. Every day, his boss gave him a list of addresses. He found the places and snapped photos of the cars. The owners were seldom home.

Like his job, Justin's new living situation was also mediocre. He had an attic room in a house where a young couple and their two kids lived. It was a nice house, but the family scene amplified his loneliness. Sometimes he played with the kids, and then he wondered if he would ever have any of his own. The problem was, that required a woman.

He missed Zoe. He missed the farm. Every day he thought about looking for another farming situation. It was funny, because he never would have thought the dirt and seeds and worms could hold such appeal. But he knew he wouldn't go anywhere unless he found out what had happened to Zoe. So far, he had hit only dead ends in his search for her. Once he ran into T-Bone and Rex, but they knew nothing. He was out of ideas. At this rate, he figured he might moon around Portland all his life, feeling low.

All this weighed on his mind, like it did every day, on this particular afternoon of the Rose Festival week.

Justin didn't recognize Zoe at first. She was walking toward him, talking to a tall, auburn-haired woman. Both carried yoga mats. "Zoe!" Justin called when she was almost past.

Zoe stopped dead, recognizing that she knew the voice in the crowd, but not identifying it. Then she saw him. "Justin!" she cried. She hugged him hard. Her arms were strong now. He held on until he felt her trying to break away.

Justin examined the woman he had longed for. Her face had good color, and her hair flowed down in two long ponytails. He could see the muscle definition of her arms. "You're not sick," he said. She wore a royal blue tank top with spaghetti straps. The top fit snugly over breasts that were twice the size he remembered, though still small. "You look great."

"I'm well," she said. "This is my roommate Clara. Clara, Justin."

Clara shook Justin's hand with a firm grip. "How do you do."

It was awkward to have a third person at their reunion. "Clara's a yoga teacher," Zoe said. "She lets me come to her classes."

"That's great," Justin said. He was strangely unsettled by Zoe's health. Seeing her aglow and muscled made him feel decidedly unnecessary. "Uh, you have a job?"

"Yeah. I cook for abused kids. In a shelter program."

"Wow."

"She'll be a counselor there before long," Clara said, her voice full of affection. "The kids love her. They already come to her with their problems."

"Oh, I don't know. Things are good the way they are." Zoe smiled.

Justin felt dizzy. All these months of hiding, this girl had been his beacon, the picture he held in his mind to get him through. Only the real girl didn't match the picture. In his mind, she was deathly pale, ribs sticking out, and he helped her walk to work, he helped her clean that café. She read rave fashion magazines and had skinny, druggy friends. These flaws had been endearing. But now? This creature before him was flawless. "Did you get muscles just from doing yoga?" Justin asked, an incredibly stupid question after months of missing the love of his life.

Zoe laughed. She told him all about some athletic form of yoga she was learning, but he couldn't concentrate. Panic crept up from his stomach to his throat. How could he get this woman back, and hold on? "Do you have a pen?" Zoe was asking Clara now. "I'll give you our number. We're on our way to class, and we're running late," she said apologetically. "But call me tonight. I can't wait to hear the whole story!" She handed him a yoga flyer with her number scrawled on the back, hugged him again and pecked his cheek. Then she and Clara were walking toward the Ferris wheel. Justin watched them go.

He didn't know what to make of it. Did she really want him to call? Who was this Clara, getting dewy eyed over how wonderful Zoe was? Since when did Zoe give a shit about abused kids? All this love for her had filled his heart for a year now, but in one encounter it had shifted. Now he felt edgy. She just didn't seem like his girl anymore.

Justin wandered past the kiddy rides and into the beer garden. He sat and drank a draft beer, watching the flashing lights of gyrating carnival rides. When he finished his beer he still didn't know what to do, so he bought another. It was getting late now, but the sun stayed high in the sky like it does in Portland during summer. The second beer relaxed him a bit. He sighed, his shoulders easing.

Just when he was feeling sorry for himself, he noticed a girl two tables away. Was she crying? Her eyes looked red, and were her shoulders heaving? Justin stood and walked casually by to get a close look. She was definitely crying.

"Hey," Justin said softly. "What's wrong?" She only looked up briefly, then shook her head. "You can tell me," he said, pulling out a chair. "Believe me, I'm harmless." She looked up at him again. She had a pretty little face, brown eyes and curly brown hair. She was a bit plump in a nice, soft way. Her eyes were still wet but she tried to smile.

"I'm just having kind of a bad time of it right now," she said.

"Yeah," Justin said sympathetically. "Would you like a beer?" She nodded. "Promise you won't go away while I get it?"

She smiled more authentically this time. "I promise."

Justin's heart lifted unexpectedly. "Don't go away." He raced to the keg, where a fat red-haired guy dispensed the overpriced beer. It was really strange, he thought, but suddenly he felt okay.

About the Author

Teresa Bergen has an MFA in fiction writing from Louisiana State University. Her work has appeared in many magazines and newspapers, including *Exquisite Corpse, River City* and *Ms.* She currently lives in Portland, Oregon. To learn more about her various creative endeavors, visit www.babylovecat.com.